LERMONTOV

SCHOOL NO. 64

CHISTOPRUDNYY BOULEVARD

Barkin's studio

Albert Schwartz's apartment

Site of attack on the KGB operatives

Oksana's and Viktor's escape from the demonstration

BOGDAN MELNITSKY STREET

KURSK RAILROAD STATION

MOSCOW SYNAGOGUE

Sakharov apartment

Yauza River

to Novo-Gireyevo →

Moskva River

TAGANKA THEATER

to The Birds Market →

to Malakhovka →

GARDEN RING

MOSCOW

◇ MONUMENTS

0 Miles	0.25	0.50

0 Kilometers	0.50	1

THE DISSIDENT

THE DISSIDENT

PAUL GOLDBERG

FARRAR, STRAUS AND GIROUX
NEW YORK

Farrar, Straus and Giroux
120 Broadway, New York 10271

Printed in the United States of America
First edition, 2023

Endpaper map copyright © 2023 by Jeffrey L. Ward

Library of Congress Cataloging-in-Publication Data
Names: Goldberg, Paul, 1959– author.
Title: The dissident / Paul Goldberg.
Description: First edition. | New York : Farrar, Straus and Giroux, 2023.
Identifiers: LCCN 2022060045 | ISBN 9781250208590 (hardcover)
Subjects: LCSH: Refuseniks—Fiction. | Jews—Soviet Union—Fiction. | Cold War—
    Fiction. | Murder—Investigation—Fiction. | Moscow (Russia)—History—
    20th century—Fiction. | LCGFT: Thrillers (Fiction) | Historical fiction. |
    Detective and mystery fiction. | Novels.
Classification: LCC PS3607.O4434 D57 2023 | DDC 813/.6—dc23/eng/20221213
LC record available at https://lccn.loc.gov/2022060045

Designed by Gretchen Achilles

Our books may be purchased in bulk for promotional,
educational, or business use. Please contact your local bookseller
or the Macmillan Corporate and Premium Sales Department
at 1-800-221-7945, extension 5442, or by email
at MacmillanSpecialMarkets@macmillan.com.

www.fsgbooks.com
www.twitter.com/fsgbooks • www.facebook.com/fsgbooks

10 9 8 7 6 5 4 3 2 1

In memory of Ludmilla Alexeyeva.
Her mentorship decades ago
renders this story visible.

Слышится отдаленный звук, точно с неба, звук
лопнувшей струны, замирающий, печальный.
Наступает тишина, и только слышно, как далеко
в саду топором стучат по дереву.

—АНТОН ЧЕХОВ, "ВИШНЁВЫЙ САД"

A distant sound is heard, as though from the sky,
the sound of a broken string, halting, full of sadness.
Silence descends, and from afar, from the cherry
orchard, the sound of an ax slamming into wood is
all that is heard.

—ANTON CHEKHOV, The Cherry Orchard

AUTHOR'S NOTE

dis·si·dent
disədənt
диссидент

Sometime in the early 1970s, translators at the Voice of America, BBC, Radio Liberty, and other enemy voices started to use the English word "dissident" in place of the Russian complex noun "инакомыслящий," pronounced *inakomyslyashchiy*, literally an "otherwise-thinker." No meetings were held before this linguistic projectile was lobbed into the heart of the Russian language. No one took aim, but the target was hit, and the act of naysaying renamed.

re·fuse·nik
rə'fyo͞oznik

"Refusenik" derives from the Russian word "отказник," pronounced *otkaznik*. *Otkaz* is a "refusal," the suffix *nik* signifies the subject of an *otkaz*. This fragmentary translation into English produced a robust hybrid. Few knew this to begin with, and those who knew have died or forgotten, but the term has an author, a coiner: Lou Rosenblum, a Soviet Jewry activist in Cleveland, Ohio, a pamphleteer of sorts, who started to refer to his Soviet brethren as "refusedniks," and the word caught on, first in Lou's version, then with the "d" shaven off.

CAST OF CHARACTERS

VIKTOR VENYAMINOVICH MOROZ, a young engineer, refusenik.

OKSANA YAKOVLEVNA MOSKVINA, his wife, an English teacher.

VENYAMIN ISAAKOVICH MOROZ, Viktor's father, a retired colonel, resident of Kiev.

YAKOV ARONOVICH MOSKVIN, Oksana's father, a cancer biologist.

LYDIA IVANOVNA, Viktor's KGB "curator."

ALBERT SCHWARTZ, a longtime dissident, nicknamed the King of Refuseniks.

ELRAD "ERIK" RUDOL'FOVICH BARKIN, a Moscow sculptor.

MARYA BARKINA, his wife.

FR. MIKHAIL SAULOVICH KISELENKO, a Russian Orthodox priest of Jewish descent.

VITALY ALEKSANDROVICH GOLDEN, a historian, refusenik, founder of the Seminar on Jewish Culture.

INA GOLDEN, his wife.

MADISON "MAD DOG" DYMSHITZ, a Moscow correspondent of an American newspaper.

NORMAN DYMSHITZ, Madison's father, a resident of Pittsburgh, Pennsylvania.

XII | CAST OF CHARACTERS

ALAN FOXMAN, an American diplomat.

MONICA WASHINGTON, a Russian history professor at Columbia University.

ELENA GEORGIEVNA BONNER, a dissident, wife of Nobel laureate Andrei Sakharov.

VLADIMIR LENSKY, an engineer, refusenik.

OLGA LENSKAYA, his wife.

ALLA MARKOVNA SHNEERSON, director of Moscow Special School No. 64.

YAKOV LEIBOVICH FISHMAN, chief rabbi of the Moscow Choral Synagogue.

HENRY A. KISSINGER, U.S. secretary of state.

PART I

1.

Here are the facts, dry, bare, like skeletons of rats that long ago took shelter in the filing cabinets on Lubyanka, in Langley, and at an undisclosed location in Tel Aviv—until now hidden, unseen.

Oksana Moskvina and Viktor Moroz met across the street from the Moscow Choral Synagogue, the scene of multiple demonstrations by individuals petitioning to leave the USSR.

They met on November 28, 1975. It is known that Oksana, then twenty-seven, kissed Viktor, twenty-nine, before she knew his name, and that on January 13, 1976, following a courtship that lasted six weeks and three days and that they believed to be unbearably long, Oksana stands beside Viktor, his bride.

The bride wears plaid. The groom is in American dungarees paired with a dark-blue sweater by Dale of Norway, with a red stripe and a band of large white snowflakes stretching across the chest. A Danish journalist gave him the sweater at a press conference at Sakharov's last winter. The dungarees are from a care package from American Jews.

Viktor is slight, shorter than Oksana by three centimeters. He looks like a man who forgets to eat. His oversized lower jaw, with a slight overbite on the right, balanced by an underbite on the left, is another distinguishing characteristic. It creates the false impression that this little man can be a source of grave physical danger.

Oksana is a woman of a difficult-to-place otherness. People notice her in a crowd of any size, seeing her and no one else—one Oksana Yakovlevna Moskvina and 183 others. It could be about the wild emanation of tightly curled hair that frames her pale, freckled face.

The dress is an interpretation of a cowboy shirt—a *kovboyka* in Russian—reaching three centimeters beneath the knee, a length known as midi. The fabric, a loosely woven polyester, combines brown hues. Voluminous, spongy, it begs to be rolled between the thumb and the index finger. The dress has snaps on the pockets, a bow to authentic Western shirts. Her boots are tall, shiny, deep purple, with gold zippers, Czech, like the dress. This ensemble and the fashion sense that assembled it would hold up well in Prague, but also in London, New York, Paris. In Moscow, where store shelves are bare, it stuns.

Dates matter. November 28 is the first night of the Jewish holiday of Chanukah. January 13 is the Old New Year, what New Year's Eve used to be before the Bolsheviks switched from the Julian calendar to the Gregorian. When you ring in the Old New Year, you negate history.

But how would you deny that January 13, 1976, comes fifty-eight years, two months, and one week after the Great October Socialist Revolution? None of the guests—and neither the bride nor the groom—know how Jewish weddings are performed, especially in the absence of a rabbi worthy of being allowed into a decent home.

■ ■ ■

Viktor has been unable to locate his copy of *The Laws of Jewish Life*,* a do-it-yourself guide to Judaism. The booklet is published in Russian in Montreal, smuggled in by tourists, and distributed by activists who risk prosecution under a distasteful provision of the Russian Republic's Criminal Code—Article 190-1, "Systematic dissemination by word of mouth of deliberate fabrications that defame the Soviet political and social system." Religious propaganda fits under this article with room to spare.

The Laws is small enough to fit into the back pocket of the uniform of a refusenik—Levi's, or as they are nicknamed, *Levisa*, with the accent on *a*. Does the booklet contain directives for conducting a wedding? Viktor doesn't know. It seems increasingly likely that his copy was confiscated at a KGB search a month and a half ago.

A booklet is a poor substitute for the living memory. Fortunately, one of the guests—Albert Schwartz—has promised to bring along three old men who remember how weddings were performed in their *shtetleh*. A Jewish wedding—*a khasene in shtetl*—creates its own context, even here, even in Moscow, even today, on January 13, 1976.

The old men—*alterkakers* is the Yiddish word, "old shitters"—will take the ritual through the paces, mumble the right blessings in Hebrew, sing something in Yiddish when it's over. There is a prescribed number of blessings—seven. Viktor has read that in a novel, Feuchtwanger probably.

---

* "Законы еврейской жизни," published by the Jewish Community Council of Montreal. Footnotes are denigrated as pedantic, Talmudic, German even. Their use here stems from the storyteller's belief that historical accuracy is inseparable from linguistic authenticity. While events documented here play out mainly in Russian, the storytelling is multilingual. Transliteration, translation, and the original Russian will be used as the storyteller sees fit.

Nothing to worry about—Albert Schwartz and the *alterkakers* will make it happen. Schwartz is what's known as a пузырь—pronounced *puzyr'*, a "bubble"—little, round, full of air, always on the surface.

In this volatile life, one thing is certain: the man can eat! If you set out the food and tell no one, just set it out, sit down, and wait, Albert Schwartz will show up. It's been tested.

Elrad "Erik" Rudol'fovich Barkin, an artist known for sculpting war amputees and archetypal Jungian beasts, hosts the wedding. (He and the groom have a business relationship.)

Like the majority of Muscovites, Barkin believes that the organs of state security rig telephones to serve as listening devices, obviating the need for bugs, but you can defend yourself by winding the dial halfway and inserting a pencil into one of the finger holes below the stopper—5 is a good number; it's in the middle—and freezing it in a partially wound position.

Tonight, a graphite pencil broken in half stands upright in the dial. Any pen or pencil, any thin sticklike object, will do. Barkin uses a reddish Khudozhnik* pencil, a splendid product of the Sacco and Vanzetti Pencil Factory here in Moscow. Some double down and cover the telephone with a pillow. Others place the pillow in a cooking pot and encase the telephone in a sarcophagus of feathers and aluminum. Barkin doesn't fear the KGB, but he doesn't believe in making their job easier. Make them earn their ruble.

Jellied meat—*kholodetz*—is on the table, next to homemade horseradish, two kinds, with beets and without. A bowl of "Pro-

---

* Artist.

vençale cabbage," which has no known relationship to Provence, but which achieves greatness by demonstrating that cranberries, plums, and a dash of oil have a legitimate place in the context of marinated cabbage, is positioned next to a larger bowl of *salat Olivier*, an inspired mixture of boiled potatoes and carrots, chopped hard-boiled eggs, peas from a can, morsels of ham, pickles, canned crabs, if you can get them, and Soviet mayonnaise. Vodka has never had a better friend than *salat Olivier*. Eggplant caviar, a delicacy that presents no threat to unborn sturgeon, is at the center of the table. Nobody can tell you why store-bought eggplant caviar tastes better than homemade. It's one of the great and enduring achievements of the Soviet culinary enterprise. Hungarian fatback, which owes its ethnic assignment to a thin coat of paprika, is present as well. No finer *zakuska* than Hungarian fatback reclining upon a bed of sour rye has ever existed or can exist. Ukrainian fatback, which owes its whiteness to a coat of coarse salt, should not be neglected, and is not. Cans of sprats in oil, sardines in brine, perch in tomato sauce, herring with a beet salad and sour cream on top, also known as "herring under a fur coat," and chopped herring, Jewish-style, represent the bounty of the sea. Also, mushrooms— *maslyata*, *Suillus luteus*, to be exact, which Latin allows us to be. Marinated, they are slippery, oysters of the forest. Drink a glass of chilled vodka, swallow a *Suillus luteus*, and emit a tear of joy!

Be it Solichnaya or be it Ekstra, vodka's functions in life include triggering blasts of emotion. Beloved, it has acquired a suffix, *vodochka*. If you don't love *vodochka*, if you are scandalized by the presence of two varieties of fatback, Hungarian and Ukrainian, and a hammed-up and crabby *salat Olivier* at a Jewish wedding, please address these questions in this precise order: One, how is this not a legitimate life-cycle observance? Two, who made you the judge? And, three, why don't you go mind your own business?

An hour has gone by, it's 9:15; still no Schwartz, still no *alter-kakers*. By 10:00, the glasses have been raised three times. First: "To the bride and groom." Second: "To all of us, and fuck them," a political toast. The third toast—the sacred one—has taken place, too: "To those who aren't with us." In this life you can make light of many things, but not the third toast, or why would you be here? To those who fought, to those who made the sacrifice, including but not limited to the ultimate, to their freedom and yours. To Yulik Daniel', to Andrei Sinyavsky, to Lara Bogoraz, to Tolya Marchenko, to Pasha Litvinov, to Andrei Amalrik, to Alik Ginzburg, to Yura Galanskov, to Seryozha Kovalyov, to writers, to poets, to citizen journalists who bang out *The Chronicle of Current Events*.

Where in the hell is Albert Schwartz? Should he not have been the first to arrive? And where are the *alterkakers*? Is there another way to know how Jewish weddings were done? There hasn't been one in nearly six decades, as far as anyone knows.

Calling is futile. Schwartz lives in a big communal flat on Chistoprudnyy Boulevard. He used to have a personal phone, in his room, but it was turned off two years ago. There is a shared phone in the water-stained hallway. That big, heavy-duty, wall-mounted apparatus hangs there unanswered, conjuring the aesthetic of a steam engine. It would bite a chunk off any pencil you might stick in its dial. No incoming calls are accepted. You use it only if you must, to call ambulances for the dying.

No Schwartz—no *alterkakers*. No *alterkakers*—no Jewish wedding.

"I'll go get him," volunteers Viktor.

Others around the table see the logic in the groom's offer to cab over to Schwartz's.

Would anyone insist on going in his stead?

Barkin, the sculptor, has been stepping away from the table to

take soulful swigs straight from the bottle, his supplemental forti-
fication, for in this city a mystic must stay drunk; a sculptor, too.
He doesn't volunteer to go get Schwartz.

Vitaly Aleksandrovich Golden, a Pushkinist who, owing to a
childhood bout of tuberculosis, is as pale and gaunt as a *politzek*,
doesn't volunteer.

Father Mikhail Saulovich Kiselenko, a leonine apostate famous for reeling godless members of the Moscow intelligentsia
into the Russian Orthodox Church, doesn't volunteer.

Professor Yakov Aronovich Moskvin, a cancer biologist, the
father of the bride, and an erstwhile paratrooper with a half-empty
right sleeve, doesn't volunteer.

Marya Barkina, drunk as a sculptor's wife should be, doesn't
volunteer. Oksana, the bride, wouldn't be expected to volunteer,
and does not.

Viktor will be the one to go get Schwartz and the *alterkakers*.

A cab ride to Schwartz's—at 17 Chistoprudnyy Boulevard—will
take ten minutes, maybe. It's nearly eleven. The groom will return
in forty minutes at the most. He will settle into his rickety chair and
this delightful bedlam will transform into a Jewish *khasene*, with
Schwartz, with the *alterkakers*, with the seven blessings.

2.

Viktor walks out of Bol'shoy Karetnyy, the winding side street where the Barkins live, and emerges onto the expanse of Sadovaya-Samotechnaya, on the Garden Ring. There is little traffic. Not a taxi in sight.

He turns right, heading in the direction of Tsvetnoy Boulevard, the "boulevard of flowers" in translation.

No taxis. It's late in the night; cold, too.

Viktor walks past the dark granite-faced monolith of a high-rise occupied by foreign journalists. Located on Sadovaya-Samotechnaya, the place was christened Sad-Sam, or Sad Sam, by English speakers. In the context of this story, Sad Sam will be the preferred version. In Russian, the word "sad" doesn't connote sadness. *Sad* is a garden—the gardening theme is big in this part of Moscow. Sam is not short for Samuel—it's short for a river's flow.

Sad Sam is a connection to the world outside, a vortex, and Viktor, because of his mastery of English, is the de facto chief communicator with the press corps. It's an important function, which he performs for the Jewish refuseniks and, increasingly, the not necessarily Jewish human rights activists.

If you are a dissident or a refusenik and your name is unknown in the West, you can be plucked from the street, and no one will notice. If the people at Sad Sam know about you, if they wrote about you, if you have been seen coming and going, and if your voice is captured on recordings made covertly at these apartments, the guardians of state security will think twice before ordering you gone, especially now, eight days before Kissinger comes to town to plan out the next phase of strategic arms talks.

People who live at Sad Sam buy Barkin's sculptures. Barkin treats this segment of the market as souvenir trade, selling only his rejects—derivative dreck, experiments gone awry.

Viktor does gigs at Sad Sam, too—sometimes a translation, sometimes acting as a Seeing Eye dog, guiding a reporter through complexity, geographic and otherwise. He has learned the English-Latin phrase describing such arrangements: "an unspoken quid pro quo." "Unspoken" is the key word; Viktor knows. You help a correspondent on a story, and, through this above-mentioned unspoken quid pro quo, he will look more favorably at a story you want to plant.

George Krimsky, an Associated Press reporter who speaks Russian almost like a Russian, smokes three packs a day, loves vodka, and is the greatest guy you'll ever meet, lives here. He is a friend of Viktor's, and Barkin's, and Golden's, and Father Kiselenko's. He was invited to the wedding, except he is on home leave, celebrating Christmas, skiing in the state of Vermont, town of Stowe, not too far from Solzhenitsyn's house, presumably. Bob Toth, from the *Los Angeles Times*, is a great guy, too. He turns to Viktor for leads and story ideas sometimes.

Madison Dymshitz, nicknamed Mad Dog, lives here as well. Mad Dog is not universally loved by either dissidents or refuseniks, but he has at least one redeeming characteristic: he uses translators, and he pays. If you have a story to plant, you go to Krimsky and Toth first, to Christopher Wren at *The New York Times* second. You go to Mad Dog only when everyone else is out of town, on leave for Christmas—like now. They will return in nine days, to stand ready like bayonets on January 22, when Kissinger arrives. Until then, Mad Dog is the only American correspondent in town.

Viktor likes these people, Mad Dog, too. Knowing them, helping them, being invited to their apartments, is an escape, a partial exodus.

Viktor turns right, walking alongside Tsvetnoy Boulevard, toward the Moscow Circus. You can find a cab there, even this late at night. He hasn't seen Paris, and unless something changes dramatically, never will. Should he get to the City of Lights, he will note the similarities between the boulevards, the green arteries that flow through Paris and Moscow. The boulevards of Paris are lovely indeed. Moscow's are lovely, too.

There is indeed a cab directly in front of the circus steps. Viktor knocks on the glass of the passenger door, and the driver beckons him in. It's warm inside, reeking of cigarettes. A small portrait of Stalin in generalissimo regalia is attached with sticky tape to the dashboard. You don't see this often. In Tbilisi—maybe. It's a Pride of Georgia thing, a shoemaker's son who made good. In Moscow, Stalin is Lucifer.

Seething under the generalissimo's contemptuous gaze, Viktor reaches into his coat pocket and begins to count change, adding coins as the numbers climb on the meter. Unlike your typical Moscow cabbies, this one drives in silence.

As he counts coins—a kopek, two, three, five, ten, fifteen, twenty—Viktor thinks of the dollop of *salat Olivier* that occupies the center of the plate awaiting him at the Barkins'. A half-eaten square of *kholodetz* smeared with red horseradish leans against Olivier's side. There is a pickle as well. And a morsel of Hungarian fatback, and black bread, buttered.

It's crass to ask why this wedding is taking place, but the question is fair and will be answered. First, let us consider what this marriage is not and what it will not accomplish. The Soviet government will not recognize this ceremony, this contract. As far as the authorities are concerned, this is a dinner party, a *sabantuychik*, *pirushka*. Residency papers that would entitle Viktor to live in Moscow legally will remain out of his reach. It's not an affirmation of Jewishness, either. The Orthodox Jews, who have declared themselves the final arbiters of such things, will not recognize Oksana as a Jewess.

This leaves one explanation for the wedding: Viktor and Oksana want to marry because they are in love, because they feel so complete in each other's arms, because this is a feeling neither of them has known before. Also, they don't give a rip about what the laws, Communist or Jewish, decree to be kosher and treif.

You may have noticed that the mother of the bride and the parents of the groom are absent from the celebration. Oksana knows her mother's address, but the two aren't in touch. This is because Oksana took her father's side, even though he isn't her biological father, even though he was technically the one at fault.

Before we lay out the reasons for the absence of the groom's family, a few words will need to be said about methodology that has rendered this story visible. What is memory if not an art form? If you like objective answers to go with your questions, if you like robust narratives, if you appreciate nuance, learn to like surveillance, annotation, and all the good practices of dossier-keeping. Does the word "record" not imply that someone has performed the act of recording of any variety, audio, photographic, videographic?

It is known that on December 19, 1975, at 21:48, a call was placed from a telephone booth at the Moscow Central Telegraph building on Gorky Street to the Kiev apartment of Colonel (retired) Venyamin Isaakovich Moroz.

The call was originated by his son, Viktor Venyaminovich.

A transcript follows:

VVM: *Allo, Papa?*

VIM: I am listening.

VVM: I am calling to invite you to a wedding—mine.

VIM: We will not come.

VVM: That's disappointing . . .

VIM: Fine. I must go now.

VVM: Where must you go?

VIM: To watch television. They are showing a concert. Kobzon is singing.

VVM: Fine.

Iosif Kobzon, a Jew by nationality, can be heard in the background. The singer often described as the Soviet Sinatra is performing "And Lenin Is Still So Young":

И вновь продолжается бой,
И сердцу тревожно в груди.
И Ленин—такой молодой,
И юный Октябрь впереди!*

The incompatibility between the father and son became apparent in Viktor's adolescence, when he failed to develop the heroic military posture Venyamin Isaakovich felt entitled to in a son. At Young Pioneer events, Viktor seemed unwilling to count steps as he marched. This signaled a lack of interest in military-patriotic activities.

Political incompatibility opened like a wound during the Six-Day War, in 1967, when the elder Moroz hung a portrait of the

---

* The battle is brewing again, / The heart beats alarmed in the chest. / And Lenin is still so young, / Revolution is still ahead!

Egyptian leader Gamal Abdel Nasser in his study and flew a Soviet flag on his balcony in solidarity with the Egyptian, Syrian, and Jordanian troops. Venyamin Isaakovich refrained from using the name of the state at war with the coalition of Arab states, referring to said country as "*a shtetl.*" He developed alternative names for the *shtetl's* leaders. Golda Meir was a "she-bandit in a skirt," Moshe Dayan a "one-eyed brigand."

Viktor spent those six days listening to the BBC, the Voice of America, and the Voice of Israel on a shortwave radio at the apartment of a friend who has since emigrated and is working toward a doctorate in econometrics at the University of Michigan.

A year later, in August 1968, in a letter to the editor of *Kievskaya pravda*, Venyamin Isaakovich voiced his wholehearted approval for the Soviet-led invasion of Czechoslovakia. "I support and approve the decision to render fraternal assistance," read the headline. In the letter, he was identified as "Col. (ret.), participant in the Great Patriotic War, 1941–1945." Does it matter that Venyamin Isaakovich spent the war years well out of reach of German bombers, in Sverdlovsk? Supply officers like him were essential in the war effort, and an abacus is as much a machine of war as a T-34 tank. Mercifully, Viktor, whose heart was with the Czechs, was at school in Moscow.

In late October of 1973, shortly after Venyamin Isaakovich took down the red flag he flew in solidarity with the Egyptian and Syrian forces during the Yom Kippur/Ramadan War, Viktor arrived from Moscow, where he was now working as an engineer, asking him to sign papers required for emigration to the country Venyamin Isaakovich referred to as the *shtetl*.

Did Viktor expect anything other than an unshakable no? The young man slammed the door and spent the night on a bench at the railroad station, awaiting the morning train back to Moscow.

It is known that on December 19, 1975, Venyamin Isaakovich was the first to hang up. It's known also that Viktor proceeded to vomit in the grand, walnut-paneled Stalin-era phone booth of the Moscow Central Telegraph. Was Viktor striving for approval, pity, reconsideration? All he got was a dose of secondhand Kobzon—a latter-day *Jüdische Ghetto-Polizei*—singing about youthful Lenin.

At the curb by Kirovskaya Metro station, across the tramway track from the Griboyedov monument and a few blocks from Schwartz's, Viktor counts out the coins, making sure that they add up to two rubles and ninety-eight kopeks. There is a three-ruble bill in Viktor's pocket, but that sum would provide a two-kopek tip, which is two kopeks more than this turd deserves.

"Two-ninety-eight," Viktor says, handing the cabbie a fistful of change. "Admirers of the biggest murderer of all time should accept the consequences of their affinities—no tip."

Viktor will walk the rest of the way to Schwartz's.

He is not followed, he knows. Perhaps his *toptun*, his "stomper," the flunky who follows him all day, got comp time. Also, no slow-moving Volga in sight. It's "his" car. It follows him sometimes. After a while, you stop having to turn around to steal a glance. You learn to sense their presence, you learn to feel with your back.

Nothing afoot on the boulevard—just Viktor.

A burst of light and a metal-on-metal hiss from the other side of the boulevard's cast-iron fence announces the passing tramway. It's the A—Annushka.

Seventeen Chistoprudnyy Boulevard is a two-story building, a palace sacked, still standing its ground in a new world—a relic, a slum. Greco-Roman cornices have dropped off the façade, and you can smell the rot of wood fused with the smell of cabbage boiling in the communal kitchen. Surely, on plans for reconstruction of Moscow, this place is slated to be demolished to make room for the USSR Ministry of Brutalism.

You would be forgiven for surmising that making the double door at 17 Chistoprudnyy budge is a job for a hefty doorman, but its height (three and a half meters) and weight (two hundred kilo at least) notwithstanding, on the night of January 13, 1976, the door obeys Viktor's hand, smoothly executing a movement practiced through two centuries.

Before stepping into the darkness of the entryway, Viktor looks out at the snow-covered pond behind the boulevard's fence. This is Chistyye Prudy, the Clear Ponds.

Seventeen Chistoprudnyy hasn't been carved up into smaller apartments. It remains what it was—a single place, a big communal flat, a *kommunalka*, with one kitchen—except now at least fifty people live in its rooms. Electricity was updated sometime in the twenties. Plumbing is as it was in 1917. The bathroom is down the hall. People line up to use it. There is no bathtub, no shower, no hot water.

Schwartz's room is massive—maybe thirty square meters, larger than many two-room apartments. The ceiling soars—more than four meters. It's the only room with a balcony, which serves as the overhang above the entryway. At some point, the balcony had a wrought-iron railing of breathtaking workmanship. It's gone now, replaced by something slapped together with rusted rebar. Two French doors and two tall windows—one on each side—lead to the balcony, which looks over the Clear Ponds. Before grime conquered these windows from the inside and out, this room was about light.

Over the past decade, Schwartz has been a *samizdat* poet, a human rights activist, a Zionist, a refusenik. Today, he is an exchange of goods and services, anything from anywhere. You turn to him when you need 5-FU, a cancer medicine, brought from America for your mother-in-law, or to get a story about your troubles fed to an American reporter, or when you have a manuscript to ship via the diplomatic pouch, bypassing postal censors. Schwartz gets it done—no one can tell you how.

Foreigners—Americans, Canadians, Brits—know how to find Schwartz, and they drop off their contributions. Redeeming dollars on the black market is tricky and dangerous, but demand is high, and the unofficial exchange rate holds steady. Officially, a dollar is stuck at .75 of a ruble. On the black market, a dollar is worth 12 rubles, give or take, but selling is risky. Sequelae include years in prison, all the way up to capital punishment.

It's safer to accept "certificate rubles," or "*cheki*." Americans can transfer money—dollars—to your account at a store called Beryozka, and you get certificates, which you can then redeem at the store, which sells clothing (Egyptian jeans, for example), as well as food you can't find in Soviet stores. Beryozka also sells Russian tchotchkes, carved wooden dreck that foreigners eat up.

Jeans—Lee and Levi's—are even better than certificates. They are worth about ninety rubles, roughly a teacher's monthly salary. A *Playboy* is worth fifty rubles, a *Penthouse* brings about the same. *Oui* is thirty or so. Many sex magazines in the West are specialized. Those are worth less. Schwartz once told Viktor that magazines that feature love between men are an exception—they can be redeemed for as much as a pair of Levi's.

Students from the outside world come to Schwartz to drop off their books on all things Jewish—leftovers from completed coursework. It's philosophy, religious thought: Martin Buber, Gershom Scholem, Franz Rosenzweig, Abraham Joshua Heschel. Some of these are anthologies with titles that include *Exclusiveness and Tolerance, Jewish Religious Thought, Four Jewish Philosophers, A Mai-*

monides Reader. Also, histories with titles like *Jews in American Politics*.

Viktor snatches up these books as soon as they are dropped off at Schwartz's. Golden, the Pushkinist, does, too. They read voraciously, they swap tomes, and they discuss. The stuff is worthless on the black market, so there is no rush to return it.

Six weeks ago, at the search, at his rented room off Arbat, Viktor lost his entire library—Judaica, plus Trotsky's *History of the Russian Revolution*, Eduard Bernstein's fascinating little book on Marxist revisionism, and an even thinner booklet containing Nikolai Berdyaev's ravings on the subject of national personalities.

Viktor hopes this material will make the *kagebeshniki* choke.

No one in the *kommunalka* kitchen. Stepping lightly, Viktor climbs up the narrow, squeaking back staircase.

He checks whether there is anyone in the long hallway; there is no one.

Reaching the center of the second floor, Viktor taps three times on Schwartz's door. It's unlocked.

In the dimly lit room, Viktor notices something that looks like a morsel of Marya Barkina's jellied meat beading on the surface of the dark-blue Kazak carpet Schwartz must have inherited from his grandparents. The morsel seems smothered in beet-colored horseradish.

Schwartz is a clean, careful man. That's why he is trusted with redeeming dollars. Since fiscal accountability is not feasible under these conditions (you don't keep books when you are a refusenik money launderer), integrity is important.

A streetlight catty-corner across Chistoprudnyy provides the little illumination there is in the room. Moving deeper in, toward the

French doors flanked by the windows, Viktor sees what looks like a tall pile of rags that has been dropped onto the bed. Cautiously approaching the pile, he slips on the carpet. Whatever substance made him slip has also moistened his right knee. There must be more of that slippery jellied meat, that *kholodetz*, or whatever it is. As his eyes adjust to the glow radiating from the streetlight and seeping through the lace curtains, Viktor sees more gelatinous material, some on the carpet, some on the walls.

The sound of knife-sharpening makes him look up. Twin steel bars gliding along the power lines release a stream of sparks outside the window. This is comforting: Annushka, the tramway, looking in.

Viktor is near the bed. He can see a man's foot beneath a blanket. He touches it, feeling its coldness. He should heed Annushka's warning and get the hell out; he would, of course, were he not drawn in by whatever is making him barely cognizant of the stickiness of the carpet and the abundance of slippery morsels that make movement treacherous. There are two feet here and two more above them, cold also.

All four are heels up, toes down.

He must get out, move fast, taking care not to slip and fall on this Kazak carpet, this treasure that has turned treacherous. If only his feet would agree to take commands from his brain, to move in any direction other than forward, toward the head of the bed.

Viktor's mind races through all manner of gushing nonsense, noise he is unable to process.

Kneeling by the pillow, no longer cognizant of the *kholodetz* on the floor, Viktor discerns a massive, rectangular gash at the back of a man's neck. The gash is about three centimeters by ten. The head above it seems to have nearly vanished, collapsed onto itself. What's left of it is semidetached, folded like a door on a hinge. Severed bones—the vertebrae—glisten, shooting back rays from the streetlight.

Gently, fighting back a wave of nausea, Viktor realizes that he must lift this man's head to see the face. This is Schwartz's room, yes, but is this Schwartz?

It is, alas, Schwartz, prostrate facedown upon another pile. Schwartz's closely trimmed beard is soaked in blood, eyes open, back of the head cratered, folded inward, half-gone; Viktor wants to say that his mouth is frozen in mid-scream, but he really doesn't know.

A scream would have alerted the neighbors, which would mean that Viktor would not be the one discovering the body, that he would not be slipping and sliding here, on whatever it is. It's not a body—it's bodies . . . The four downward pointed feet? He should identify the man beneath Schwartz, the one whose shoulder sticks out from beneath Schwartz's head as it tilts to the right in an unnatural angle.

Should Viktor call the militia? Should he dispense with this superfluous intermediate step and call the KGB directly, because this is Schwartz, the King of Refuseniks, after all? How does one go about calling the KGB? Never before had he considered that question. What does he tell Oksana, her father, Barkin, Marya, Golden, even that persistent, soul-fishing Father Mikhail Saulovich Kiselenko?

Before these questions can be addressed, Viktor must identify the pile of flesh beneath Schwartz.

This person's head is tilted in a contorted position, facing the wall.

Viktor grabs the hair beneath the bald spot and kneels down to look at the face. He has seen it before—several times. It's Alan

Foxman, an American. What is Foxman's exact title? Whatever it was, his job involved interaction with public groups. Foxman is in his midthirties, light-haired, tall.

Viktor has met Foxman once, at Golden's. That night, at a party, a farewell for someone leaving for Israel, Foxman wore a gray suit, a white shirt, and a wide reddish tie with a polka-dot pattern.

He looked like Golden's younger cousin might have looked: sour, dyspeptic, a guy with an ulcer, or maybe a runner. Even the shape of their noses was nearly identical. They could have been cousins; with Jews you never know.

Though an American, Foxman was a familiar type of human being. At the university, guys like him sat in the back of the classrooms at the obligatory courses, especially History of the Communist Party and Dialectic Materialism, ridiculing the professors and sketching group portraits of Marx, Engels, Lenin, Stalin, and Mickey Mouse.

Algebraic expressions of Marxian economics filled these back-row clowns with unconcealable mirth. Viktor agreed with their view of the material, but he steered away from their row, because some risks in life are unnecessary.

At Golden's, Foxman drank vodka, but didn't keep up with others. Schwartz was there, too. Does it mean anything? Probably not. Schwartz was always where there was food. He didn't seem to care much about vodka—just food and free-flowing speech.

They were light blue, both of them; no one knew, at least Viktor didn't. Schwartz's position on top of Foxman makes Schwartz an active homosexual. Those are more common, situational even. Some men you wouldn't think this of can, in some situations, such as in prison, turn into active homosexuals. Release them, and they go back to their wives as if nothing happened, at least some of them.

It follows that Foxman is a passive homosexual. Viktor doesn't know much about passive homosexuals, other than that in prisons they are known as Mashkas. Once you are a Mashka, you are at the bottom of the heap, socially.

Knowledge about the existence of two kinds of homosexual is racing through Viktor's mind as he runs out of that room. He slips on the carpet, falls once again. Now both his knees and his thighs feel wet. His entire overcoat must be wet, too. His hands are— definitely. He slams the door behind him, runs into the long hall- way, nearly knocks down an old crone Schwartz used to refer to as "the Rat." Bursting through the outside door, he sprints to the cor- ner of Chistoprudnyy, runs toward Makarenko Street, where, lean- ing against the corner of the building, he emits a torrent of vomit.

Why is he going in this direction? What does he do now? Head back to the wedding? Tell Oksana, her father, the Barkins, Golden, Father Kiselenko about this? He can't show up covered in blood, slippery substance, and vomit. He must run to his rented room, he must pray that no one sees him, change clothes, think about who should know about this and who should not.

Pushing away from the corner, Viktor leaps over the cast-iron fence of the boulevard and runs through the alleys, past bronze Griboyedov, toward his room in a flat at 3 Karmanitsky Pereulok. It's a side street off Arbat. It's a long run, but when your Levi's are smeared with blood and whatever else this is, you don't hop onto Annushka, or the B trolleybus, or the No. 10. Forget flagging down a taxi; run through dark streets and duck into courtyards when you see people coming.

Did Viktor expect this? Emigration should be a choice; mur- der is something from a different opera, rooted in suspension of disbelief. Being accused of having killed a Zionist stooge who is secretly involved in currency operations—as well as his light-blue lover? And what if Foxman is a CIA operative? He could be; he is American.

Should Viktor flag down a taxi, get to Lubyanka, bang on the massive gates till they open, and announce: "I've come to report a crime"? Maybe they will believe that he had nothing to do with it. Just as likely, it's a warped setup, a test they devised. Of course, they are the ones who did it. Ensnared Schwartz and Foxman, maybe together, maybe separately, butchered them, stripped the corpses, threw one on top of the other, dumped out a bucketful of blood, guts, and brains—some human, some porcine, some bovine—on the Kazak carpet. Who would possibly believe it's not so? Under these circumstances who other than the perpetrators would have the capacity to investigate? Can Viktor substantiate this hypothesis? Does he have proof? What proof can there exist in this country?

What has he done other than walk in, discover the bodies, and run? In what universe is that a crime? Ipso facto, nothing to report. Let them find him if they must, if they can. No point in making their job easier. Let them earn their ruble.

Was Schwartz light blue all along, or did the magazines the Jews sent from America cause his transformation? Viktor has leafed through them occasionally. He looked at pictures of women only, never men. The photos were interesting from the technical standpoint, but the women they featured didn't look enticing to him. Oksana is enticing; more than enticing. His Oksana, Oksana whom he is marrying, if it's still possible, without Schwartz, the dead secretly light-blue friend who knew the *alterkakers* who knew the blessings that should be said to make a Jewish wedding Jewish.

Viktor never stopped to think that there may be homosexuals among people he knows; there have to be some, statistically, though some are just suspected unfairly. Viktor's father doesn't know any homosexuals but has an expression for them nonetheless: "Gone mad from fat!" It's an exclamation, always: "С жиру бесятся!" Pronounced: "*S zhiru besyatsya!*" For greater emphasis, Venyamin Isaakovich spits on the ground.

The good-life madness occurs in people who have it easy. Bored, ungrateful for what they have, they seek novel forms of entertainment. In the estimation of Col. (ret.) Moroz, participant of World War II, member of the Communist Party of the USSR since 1942, this affliction passes over people who have work to do, like digging ditches and fighting wars. The good-life madness figures in his condemnation of anyone who seeks to emigrate, people like his son, people like Schwartz. Schwartz, a homosexual seeking to emigrate, is twice stricken by the good-life madness, a man who warrants a double spit on the ground.

In charitable moments, Viktor surmises that Venyamin Isaakovich fears losing his military pension should it become known that he allowed his only son to leave the Motherland. Or perhaps it really is a matter of principle. Either way, thanks to Venyamin Isaakovich, Viktor is stuck here, in Moscow, between two worlds.

The war Viktor is forced to fight has rules of engagement. To the best of Viktor's knowledge, there have been no killings on either side. There was one misguided effort to hijack an airplane,*

---

* In 1970, a group of refuseniks in Leningrad attempted to hijack an airplane and fly it to Sweden. Originally, the plan was to gather two hundred escapees, but in the end, only sixteen were brave enough to show up at the airfield. No greater gift could have been made to the KGB: clear evidence that the Jewish movement was not peaceful after all. One of these would-be hijackers had a pistol. How were these crazy Jews different from the Arab terrorists of Black September? Was this a provocation by the KGB or the Leningrad Communist Party? Or was this genuine idiocy on the part of Jewish hijackers? Inexplicably, the West came to regard these people as heroes, or at least martyrs. Working on their behalf, one noted American jurist—Harvard professor in Leningrad, five and a half years ago, but that was done by would-be émigrés. It was a close call, but no one died either in that misadventure or in the aftermath. There were two death sentences, but both were commuted. Have the rules changed since the Leningrad hijacking caper?

Schwartz's head was bashed in, almost completely detached. Foxman's was tilted at an unnatural angle toward the wall. Viktor must vomit, right now, at this moment; either that or he will suffocate. Is it physiologically possible for a man to vomit while continuing to run? He must try, must, must.

These months ago, at that gathering at Golden's, Viktor asked Foxman about anti-Semitism in America. Is there any?

"It's complicated," Foxman said, but Viktor's curiosity was so intense that he couldn't relent.

Finally, Foxman mentioned something about universities. Harvard and Yale deny that they have quotas, yet Jews make up only 10 to 15 percent of every class, every year, Foxman said. Some of their conversation was in English, some in Russian. Foxman had an accent, but his grammar was unfailing. You could imagine that he could write well, too.

"To us, a ten percent quota is like no quota at all. Were you kept out of Harvard? Do you feel yourself* deprivated?"

"Deprived? No; not at all. I don't give a fuck. I went to the University of Chicago. They don't play those games."

Viktor decided not to try to unpack that reference. Instead, he

---

Alan Dershowitz—floated a theory that under Soviet law the Leningraders were not hijackers but "joy riders."

* In Russian, the verb "feel" is reflexive. For inexperienced students of English this causes awkward moments.

asked a follow-up question: "How can America have anti-Semitism when your secretary of state, Henry A. Kissinger, is Jew?"

This subject was important to Viktor. He had to press on. His central question revolved around Kissinger's Judaism. Does it not make sense that Kissinger is trying to help his Soviet brethren? He can't let this be known too widely, or he will lose effectiveness. Surely, he had to disclose this to Nixon, but Nixon would be sympathetic, too. Richard M. Nixon couldn't possibly be an anti-Semite. Nixon is no longer president, true; Gerald R. Ford is. Ford, too, is not an anti-Semite. And Kissinger is still the architect of America's foreign policy. Imagine the USSR with a minister of foreign affairs who is a Jew. Actually, Viktor recalled, there was Maxim Litvinov, under Stalin, but he lost out, and we got the Molotov-Ribbentrop Pact as a result, and you know the rest.

Foxman didn't wish to join Viktor in hypothesizing about the role Kissinger's religious and ethnic identity and his immigrant past played in shaping his worldview.

"Kissinger is a narcissistic prick," Foxman said.

After making this pronouncement, Foxman told a joke about German Jews, their affinity for rules. German Jews, he said, were called "Yekkes," which doesn't sound like a compliment. Viktor remembers Foxman straining to contain his own giggles, but the joke didn't seem funny at all.

That night, Viktor jotted the words "Yekke" and "narcissistic prick" on a scrap of paper, with the goal of looking them up at home.

Viktor has had no formal instruction in English. He began the learning process by reading Communist newspapers from England and America—the *Morning Star* and the *Daily Worker*—and listening to the BBC. He had an English grammar book, too, but that was secondary. He thought he would leave pronunciation for later, but hours of listening to the BBC left a mark, creating a Slavic/Beeb brew.

At home later that night, Viktor sat down with the *English-Russian Polytechnical Dictionary*, the thick, purple-tinted tome, the only dictionary in his possession. The word "narcissistic" could not be found. However, Viktor surmised that the word is Greek-rooted, vaguely connoting self-importance, pride. In the absence of the nonextant *English-Russian Mythological Dictionary*, he assumed as much and moved forward.

The word "prick" was in the dictionary. One of its possible meanings is "укол," *ukol*, an "injection." Was Foxman saying that Kissinger makes some people—especially his co-tribalists—feel more important, literally injecting them with pride?

"Prick" might also be translated as "прокол," *prokol*, a "puncture," as in a flat tire. In Russian, "прокол" also means an "error," a "faux pas." Does this meaning carry over? Is it translingual?

So, a "narcissistic prick" might be something that (or someone who) punctures the bubble of self-importance, a gadfly, a hole-punching instrument. An *ukol* injects or inflates the sense of importance. A *prokol*, by contrast, deflates it. Admittedly, these are two opposite meanings. The expression "narcissistic prick" must be specifically American, with roots that span both culture and language. You either know the meaning of such expressions or you do not.

Viktor will stop running now. He will vomit. When the mind races, as it's doing now, it tires out, inevitably. Viktor will get home, to the rented room in a flat off Arbat. He will do nothing until this carousel stops, until images flash no more. He must change, he must get back to the Barkins', to complete the wedding—his.

The mind doesn't stop, the mind cannot stop, not at this altitude; you must wait, wait for it to slip to a lower orbit—no, that would make it move faster, burn up on reentry. He must stop. He

must get back to the wedding. He must wake up from this night-
mare . . . Oksana. Oksanka. Oksanochka.

Reaching his rented room in a flat on Karmanitsky, off Arbat,
Viktor recognizes that even after the slog through the snow, red
specks are clearly visible on the suede of his moccasins. Looking in the mirror, he sees that his Levi's are darkened with blood,
brains, and vomit. This mixture has similarly stained his scratchy
gabardine overcoat and Dale sweater.

He takes off the Levi's and the sweater. His turtleneck is stained
as well. He places these clothes in a plastic bag from Beryozka. The
bag is big enough for Viktor's jeans, his sweater, and the turtleneck.
Alas, it's not big enough for the jeans, the sweater, the turtleneck, and the overcoat. Fortunately, he has another Beryozka
plastic bag.

Viktor owns another pair of jeans, also Levi's. They were going to be passed on to Schwartz, who would sell them, but Viktor
needs them now. He has no other turtleneck, but he does have a
T-shirt that reads "Don't blame me! I voted for McGovern." It has
to do with the Watergate case, of course. His suede moccasins—a
gift from Monica Washington, a professor at Columbia University,
in New York, a black woman who speaks Russian like a Russian—
don't look especially bloodstained. She gave Viktor the shoes
during her last visit. Her next visit is coming up in a few days.

Viktor has worn his Danish sweater so much that it has become
an organ of his physical being, but he has one other sweater. It's
soft, brownish, from the Andes. The design on the front, opposing
llamas, echoes the opposing lions you often see in heraldry and
Jewish ritual objects.

He has a spare jacket, too, made in the USA, the state of Maine, by a company called L.L.Bean. The jacket is blue, the same color as Schwartz's Kazak carpet. The jacket is puffy, uglier than anything they make even in the USSR, but it has value, because it's American, and because it's warm.

All this clothing was going to pass through Viktor's hands and get sold by Schwartz—Viktor didn't expect to have to use it.

There is a bottle of Jack Daniel's whiskey here, American, hidden deep in the breakfront, in one of its crystal caverns. It's intended to be sold on the black market and converted into money for refuseniks. But Viktor is the one who needs it now. He opens the bottle and takes a swig. Jack Daniel's is not sweet; it has an intense, unfamiliar taste, like an exotic sauce. Viktor lets the taste fill his mouth, gargles, then opens the window and spits it out onto the snowbank below. He takes another gulp. He can comprehend how some people might like Jack Daniel's, but it will never replace Stolichnaya.

On the way out, Viktor stops in the bathroom and washes his face. It's a good thing he shaved off his beard almost two months ago, a week before he met Oksana.

Before flagging down a taxi, Viktor stomps around in a snowbank. This may get rid of whatever blood, brains, and vomit still linger on his moccasins.

3.

Oksana opens the door of the Barkins' apartment, and for some time she and Viktor smooch in the entryway.

"I thought you ran off," she says, pulling away for a moment.

"That wouldn't be me."

"Wouldn't. No."

She is right. Viktor Venyaminovich Moroz is not of the ilk that runs off. Oksana isn't what one might call sloshed. She is what one might call stumbling along on the happy side. Thank God she hasn't noticed Viktor's change of costume.

Oksana's back is against the wall, next to a bronze sculpture known as *Uncle Grisha*, the sculpture that made Barkin a Moscow legend. *Uncle Grisha* is a double amputee. His legs were blown off in the war.

Barkin floats in, presumably on the way to take a supplementary swig, stammers something about "ваше дело молодое, а наше дело старое,"* or some other nonsense, and floats back to the table.

Sometime after the turn of the millennium, Moscow will open a museum dedicated solely to the work of Elrad Barkin. His

---

* Rough translation: "Young people have their agendas while old people have theirs."

bronzes will be included in permanent collections at MoMA, the Pompidou, and the Tretyakov Gallery. Russian art historians will note with pride that the renegade sculptor oft accused of hooliganism in bronze stands shoulder to shoulder with Henry Moore. But that will come in due course. It's not helpful to consider posthumous recognition preposthumously.

The absence of the groom was barely noticed, but now, as Viktor and Oksana walk back in, someone shouts "*Gor'ko*," and they comply with the wishes of the guests and smooch some more.

The following is a segment of the conversation that takes place upon Viktor's return:

GOLDEN: Where is Schwartz?

VIKTOR: He wasn't at his place. I don't know.

GOLDEN: You must have just missed each other. Perhaps he was getting his *alterkakers*.

BARKIN: What if Schwartz has run away with a new mistress, say, to Crimea? What do we do if Schwartz doesn't come? Can we find the eight blessings?

FR. MIKHAIL: Seven. I would be happy to officiate a real wedding.

GOLDEN: Father Mikhail, my dearest, I love you like a brother, but please get it into your gentile head that you can't perform our kind of wedding. You are they and we are us.

FR. MIKHAIL: We are all God's children. Our savior was a Jew. And I am listed as a Jew, in the passport.

GOLDEN: Not that again . . .

OKSANA: Can we just count to eight?

FR. MIKHAIL: Seven.

BARKIN: Seven, eight . . . What if we drink eight shots of vodka to the health of the bride and groom, shouting "*Gor'ko*" each time? Then say whatever prayer we happen to know. Viktor, do you know any prayers?

VIKTOR: I know *Shema*. It's in Feuchtwanger.

GOLDEN: *Jud Süß*.

FR. MIKHAIL: I get it from the same source.

BARKIN: My name really is Bar Kahan. It means "priest" in Hebrew, they tell me.

FR. MIKHAIL: People accuse me of being a Jew. And they are right.

GOLDEN: Please, Father Mikhail, you wear a cross. Whatever your lineage, whatever your documents say, you are not a Jew.

FR. MIKHAIL: We think . . .

GOLDEN: And we disagree . . .

MARYA BARKINA: Oh, stop it! Who can object to co-priests— Bar Kahan and Father Mikhail? Yes?

GOLDEN: Yes, as long as the name of a certain individual— real or fictional, dead or resurrected—doesn't get mentioned, with said limitation also extending to his parentage, real, purported, or imagined. And if anyone asks us, we will say that a religious marriage ceremony was performed, and that we consider Oksana and Viktor man and wife. How would anyone dispute that? Can the KGB convene a rabbinic court? So . . . First blessing . . .

ALL: *Gor'ko!*

FR. MIKHAIL: The couple shall comply, and we drink the first shot of vodka.

(And so forth, till seventh cup—one cup per blessing.)

BARKIN: I say we add the eighth: blessed be those who aren't with us.

ALL: За тех кто не с нами!

FR. MIKHAIL: Now the only prayer some of us may know.

VIKTOR, GOLDEN, AND FR. MIKHAIL: *Shema Israel Adonoy elo-heynu Adonoy ehod.*

ALL: Bitter!

BARKIN: And if any person or persons here or elsewhere still thinks that these kids aren't married in the eyes of their community and their God, if such exists, they can go fuck themselves.

It's exactly 3:25 a.m., January 14, 1976. The bride—the wife now—reaches for her husband's hand on top of the table. He has been mostly silent since his unsuccessful effort to locate Schwartz and the *alterkakers* who remember the blessings.

Funny how that works, *alterkaker*, an epithet, lives, and the blessings die.

Perhaps Viktor feels responsible for failure to make their Jewish wedding more Jewish, but it's really okay. If it's indeed a void, it's not Oksana's. Sitting around that table are people she has known for years and people she has just met, people who walk the same Moscow cobblestones, people who breathe the same air, read the same *samizdat*, and listen to the same radio stations on their shortwave radios. Also, poetry, don't forget the poetry, both the sort you read and the sort you sing. Galich. Okudzhava. Vysotsky. Kim.

Her father is here, too, obvious in his joy, obvious in his approval, holding forth on subjects that matter to him: politics, Moscow intelligentsia, science, art. Here he is, a man who has passed through the toughest trials of the twentieth century and emerged joyful, triumphant, missing half of his arm, but whole in spirit.

The goodbyes, the hugs, the good wishes take up forty-seven minutes—abbreviated by the standards of a Moscow night that doesn't want to end.

As the wedding party heads to Sadovaya to wave down the taxis that would take them their separate ways, Yakov Aronovich, the father of the bride, points his index finger at Viktor.

"Viktor Venyaminovich, we have a separate conversation," he says in a tone that's less hushed than he seems to believe.

As Yakov Aronovich reaches into his pocket, Viktor fears that he is reaching for a stack of one-hundred-ruble bills. This would be uncharacteristic of the man Viktor believes Yakov Aronovich to be.

As Viktor prepares to whisper a polite "No thank you," the item passed from Yakov Aronovich's left hand to Viktor's right turns out to be an envelope rather than the wad of hundreds.

"It's two tickets. To Taganka."

"Taganka? *The Cherry Orchard*?"

"*The Cherry Orchard*. With Vysotsky."

Vysotsky is none other than Volodya Vysotsky, a revered actor, bard, and enfant terrible. The pair of tickets printed on rough paper is the most sought-after commodity in all of Moscow.

The dream of obtaining two tickets entitling Viktor and Oksana to watch Volodya himself play Lopakhin onstage at the Theater of Drama and Comedy on Taganka is so unfathomable that Viktor wouldn't have dared to dream it.

The time is now 4:14 a.m., and Viktor and Oksana are in a taxi, heading toward his place on Karmanitsky. For a moment, Viktor has set aside the images of busted skulls and gelatinous *kholodetz* beading on Schwartz's Kazak carpet.

"I saw you talking alone with my father, in the end. Was he threatening you to be a gentleman—or else?"

"He was fumbling in his pocket to give us a wedding present."

"Not money, I hope. He is not gauche."

"He gave us tickets to *The Cherry Orchard*."

"How did he get them? Through the academy, of course . . . Thank God for the academy. To see Volodya Vysotsky as Lopakhin—now that's a present worth getting married for!"

"She married me for Chekhov. She tells me now—when it's too late."

"Of course, I did! Let me see the tickets!"

Tickets to Taganka are printed on paper so rough, it will give you goose bumps. There is a red, rectangular stamp, just short of a square, on the top left corner. The words "Moscow Theater of Drama and Comedy on Taganka" run along the boundaries of the rectangle.

For the first time, Viktor looks at the tickets, seeing the word "Партер," "orchestra," in boldface. Row 1. Seats 11 and 12.

"Front row! In the center! Three meters from the edge of the stage. Please, Vitya, give me your absolute assurance that we will not be thrown out of the country before the evening of January sixteenth!"

"That's three days from now. You are reasonably safe, I think. I will try not to provoke them excessively."

"Don't even jaywalk! For the next two days, I will be thinking of nothing but white petals." She pauses. "And what's that final line, in the staging directions: 'A distant sound is heard, as though from the sky, the sound of a broken string, halting, full of sadness. Silence descends, and from afar, from the cherry orchard, the sound of an ax slamming into wood is all that is heard.'"

Her eyes now closed, Oksana continues: "White petals, set aloft . . . Gnarly tree trunks . . . The sound of an ax. You may find this difficult to believe, but I am drunk. I better shut up."

Please, please, Oksana, don't talk about anything that involves an ax, not even an unseen, Chekhovian, behind-the-curtain ax, a sound-effect ax, the variety of ax that chops no wood and cracks no skulls.

Viktor takes a deep breath. It's a futile attempt to expel thoughts pneumatically. He is an engineer by training, so you can't fault him for trying. Now he will try to think of something else, anything but blunt instruments of any sort, anywhere, onstage, behind the curtain, in the orchestra.

Looking out the taxi's window, with Oksana seeming to be taking a series of brief naps, Viktor welcomes any thoughts other than the ones that are crawling into his head . . .

"Vitya, I love this city, I love our friends."

"I do, too."

The Young Pioneer who wouldn't march, the engineer who loathed his slide rule, has found his place, his people. He is not an oddity among this crowd, in Moscow. It's probably for the best that Viktor's parents sat out his wedding. His father's presence would be hard to imagine at that table, among people Venyamin Isaakovich would surely deride in a manner worthy of Comrade Stalin: *intelligentiki*, intellectuals, effete, little, here, in this bedlam of the good-life madness.

Is it possible that lovers read each other's thoughts, sometimes?

"Imagine that you are a fictional character, and someone says to you, 'Viktor Venyaminovich, if you love this place, why do you yearn to leave?' What would you say? Why?"

"Because it's a tragedy?"

Was it so tragic that Viktor's application to leave the USSR was denied two years ago? Had his departure been obstacle-free, would he have met Golden, the Barkins, Father Kiselenko, Lyuda Alexeyeva, Yura Orlov, Alik Ginzburg, the Sakharovs, George Krimsky,

Bob Toth, Mad Dog Dymshitz? Would he have met his Oksana? Out there, in Israel, would he have slipped into the anonymous life of an émigré, returning to engineering, mortifying the mind to put food on the table? Yes, he yearns to get out, but has he ever known the happiness he feels with every breath of Moscow air? Is this how freedom feels? Is this brand of freedom too fragile to last? Does it come with a price tag attached? Has Schwartz paid the price? Has Foxman? Is Viktor next?

Viktor's memory drills into a book Schwartz gave him—*Major Trends in Jewish Mysticism*. That book presents the Kabbalistic view of the world as the union of male and female principles. This union is re-created time and again through sexual union.

Reading Scholem, Viktor learned that after God created the world, it broke into shards. He learned also that every shard of the macrocosm is a perfect miniature of the whole—the broken whole.

If you accept this relationship between big and small, you might also accept the possibility that manipulation of the microcosm leads to harmonization of the macrocosm. The American student who owned that book originally appeared to have purchased it from a place called Book Exchange, in Durham, North Carolina.

Her name, recorded on the inside page, was Sandy Daugherty.

Sandy was an enthusiastic practitioner of underlining.

"Why did this student underline everything with this thick yellow pen?" Viktor wondered as he pondered Scholem's insights into the cosmic spheres. But in the sea of acrid yellow underlining and the tightly written notes on the margins, America's Sandy Daugherty saw something that has stuck with Viktor, something he could apply:

"Microcosm and macrocosm interact. More than that: one

determines the other. You can effect change in the universe by changing your corner of the universe. Wow . . . WOW . . . Triple WOW!"

Viktor-the-Soviet-engineer will be Viktor-the-mystic tonight.

On their wedding night, or, if you wish, call it their post-wedding morning, Viktor and Oksana will toil to repair the world.

And so it will be. By tending to his vessel of the universe, the microcosm, Viktor will force God's hand to make right all that is wrong in the macrocosm: clean up the *kholodetz*, unsplit the skulls, mend the vertebrae, fuse the arteries, make Schwartz not dead, raise Foxman, erase all traces of Viktor's presence in that room, untrack the tracks, unvomit the vomit, fuse the gnarly tree trunks, and let my people go.

Viktor will "effect"—he likes this word—this mystical inter-vention without informing Oksana—mysticism and secrecy walk hand in hand. They will unbreak the world, and if the world is whole at sunrise, Viktor will be the man to thank. Oksana, too, of course.

It's 4:39. The lovers are on a mattress in Viktor's room.

The lion-clawed breakfront stands at their side, a beast spun loose from a mad prophet's vision. As Viktor manipulates the spheres above, beneath, and behind her, Oksana believes that she and Viktor are making love, and on the terrestrial level, this is, of course, correct.

PART II

4.

I n September 1964, during the first week of his freshman year at Harvard, Madison A. Dymshitz was christened "Mad Dog." Though his initials happen to be M. A. D., he aimed to impress others with his brilliance and achievements, as opposed to liver-defying feats and sexual antics that genuine freshman Mad Dogs commit in order to live up to this venerable name.

The moniker Mad Dog was more respectful than young Dymshitz's middle school nickname. No prize will be offered to any English speaker who reads the name Dymshitz slowly and guesses what that previous nickname might have been.

Had he not stumbled into journalism early, Mad Dog would have made a fine career in law. Given enough alcohol, journalists will tell you that the mission of their profession is to comfort the afflicted and afflict the comfortable. This is, of course, bullshit. Every profession has its version of the founding myth. To Mad Dog, power is journalism's main attraction. Reporting doesn't ennoble the soul; maybe it has that effect for some people, but Mad Dog is not among them.

At Harvard, Mad Dog declared his major as Russian. Choices made by college freshmen defy interpretation. It's plausible that the decision had something to do with his family history; more on that later. Mad Dog stuck with the major, realizing that with his smarts and academic pedigree he would stand poised to become a Moscow correspondent for *The New York Times*, or maybe *The Washington Post*, or at the very least the *Los Angeles Times*.

If you study Russian at Harvard and are good at it, by year three, expect to get contacted by the Coney Island Amusement Co. It's the Harvard Russian department equivalent of being named a National Merit Scholar. They don't try to set you up with a spy camera and a license to kill. A relationship is what they want, letting you know that lines of communication are open, that if you have questions, you can get answers, that leads can come your way, that favors—big, small—can be traded.

At Harvard, Mad Dog was able to read and translate poetry— Pushkin, Lermontov, Akhmatova, Mayakovsky. It would follow that his spoken Russian would be good enough to understand street conversation. Alas, seven years after graduation, when Mad Dog hit Moscow's streets, he realized that he was able to understand about half of what he was hearing. Try to block out half of what you hear. What you get is enough to give you the lie and leave you in a fog in this cold, dark, inelegant city that his brethren in the press corps have nicknamed the Big Potato.

Might it have mattered that so many of Mad Dog's professors at Harvard were not native Russian speakers, but rather WASPs with OSS language training? Did they teach him speech that should be, or has been, as opposed to speech that is? It could be analogous to the chasm between Shakespearean English and the banter of Liverpool pubs, or biblical Hebrew versus the language of the streets in today's Tel Aviv.

After less than a year in Moscow, his wife, Melissa, left for Connecticut. Her flight was completely unexpected. Mad Dog got home after meeting with an embassy source, a guy named Alan Foxman, and found a note banged out on his typewriter—just one enigmatic, make that nonsensical, sentence, retyped twelve times, single-spaced:

Was she happy? Not for a moment!
Was she happy? Not for a moment!
Was she happy? Not for a moment!
Was she happy? Not for a moment!
Was she happy? Not for a moment!
Was she happy? Not for a moment!
Was she happy? Not for a moment!
Was she happy? Not for a moment!
Was she happy? Not for a moment!
Was she happy? Not for a moment!
Was she happy? Not for a moment!
Was she happy? Not for a moment!

It's the morning of January 14, 1976. Mad Dog puts on his Soviet overcoat. To blend in, he has acquired something cheap, vicious, and scratchy. Looking at himself in the mirror, he slips a muskrat *ushanka* on top of his head. The hat looks like a puppet, its fur glistening with shades of brown, red, and gray that deepen to maroon and charcoal. The reporter Mad Dog succeeded left it behind. The *ushanka* belongs to the bureau.

It should be established here that: (1) the bureau has a staff of one, and (2) the bureau and the apartment of the bureau chief are one and the same. As we maintain our focus on the muskrat *ushanka*, we will expend no effort on validating the hypothesis that this unity of residential and work space had deprived Melissa of even a moment of happiness.

A tattered, yellowed label inside the aforementioned hat

indicates that it was made in 1962 and cost twenty-eight rubles and zero-zero kopeks. When you move to London, Paris, or Washington, you leave that hat at Sad Sam, in the pantry, next to the telex.

Having taken on a vaguely Russian appearance, Mad Dog locates his navy blue Zhiguli on one of the side streets around Sad Sam. He hates that thing. It's afflicted with a chronic tremor commonly observed in Soviet Fiats. His parents in Pittsburgh drive Cadillacs. "Fuck you, Hitler," his father muttered when he brought the first one home two decades ago. Hitler was dead, Norman Dymshitz alive, the score is one to nothing—the Jews win.

At Harvard, Mad Dog had to sit through a lot of 3-Ms—Marx, Mao, Marcuse. One tidbit, in an essay called "On the Jewish Question," by Marx, resonated:

> The monotheism of the Jew, therefore, is in reality the polytheism of the many needs, a polytheism which makes even the lavatory an object of divine law. *Practical need, egoism*, is the principle of *civil society*, and as such appears in pure form as soon as civil society has fully given birth to the political state. The god of *practical need and self-interest* is *money*.
>
> Money is the jealous god of Israel, in face of which no other god may exist. Money degrades all the gods of man— and turns them into commodities. Money is the universal self-established value of all things. It has, therefore, robbed the whole world—both the world of men and nature—of its specific value. Money is the estranged essence of man's work and man's existence, and this alien essence dominates him, and he worships it.

It's bullshit, sure, but some of it seems consistent with Mad Dog's experience among the Jews of Pittsburgh. What's wrong with practical need, "egoism," and civil society? Nothing whatsoever. The lavatory bit, though fun, goes too far. Cadillacs—yes, clearly—are the object of divine law to a Jew like his father. But the lavatory—not!

Norm, Mad Dog's father, is still kicking. He escaped from Sobibor, taking out some Nazis along the way. Then he fought in guerrilla detachments, in the forests of Belorussia and Ukraine. Someday Mad Dog will write a memoir, but he'll spare the reader the bits about his father.

The fathers of Mad Dog's friends played catch with their sons, took them to football games—all that Little League, tennis, golf nonsense. Norm was as reclusive with the family as he was gregarious with friends. There was always a punching bag in the basement. Dull thumping sounds, something akin to a truck hitting a tree, could be heard throughout the house.

There was no way to know why Norm went to the office at 5:00 a.m. every day or why on weekends he spent hours in his study, with the door double-locked. Once, Mad Dog broke into that verboten zone and fiddled with the desk drawer, finally getting it to open. Perhaps he was looking for something that might explain the geezer's volatility. He found a set of drawing charcoals, a small stack of sketch pads, and a brass folding knife with engravings on the blade: a swastika, "Waffen-SS," and some other writing.

The charcoals were clearly well used, many sheets of paper were ripped out of the sketch pads, but there were no drawings.

Small Soviet cars that emulate small Italian cars get the shakes, like neurotic Chihuahuas. Mad Dog weighs this notion as his Zhiguli experiences tremors and convulsions, going into St. Vitus' dance on Sadovaya-Samotechnaya.

Mad Dog's most reliable translator, a glum guy named Viktor Somethingberg, is waiting on the corner, across the street from the Ministry of Foreign Affairs, the hideous Stalin-era skyscraper that desecrates the flow of Arbat.

Viktor is dull but useful. His English isn't especially bad, but his pronunciation is insidious, nasal. His "s" sound in "yes" starts with a "z" and dissolves into a hiss. Articles, definite and indefinite, confuse him. He employs roughly a quarter of the number required, sprinkling them in places where they are unwanted.

This morning, Somethingberg, whose real last name is Moroz, seems especially glum. His people are glum even on bright summer days, which this is not. They look like death—and they want, want, want. If it were money, that would be easy, but it's attention they are after.

They want you to write about them. Every Russian naysayer wants to be the subject of a news story. The gadflies here believe that the better known they are in the West, the less likely it is that they will be arrested here. This could be true, probably is. But how can you write all those stories? Who will publish them? To make sure you get coverage, you need to get prosecuted for something big, like an airplane hijacking. Some crazies in Leningrad famously tried just that a few years back.

Glum Viktor mutters "Hello" and settles into Mad Dog's Chihuahuamobile.

Before sunrise, after trying to right the world through microcosmic manipulation of the macrocosm, he drifted into a state akin to sleep. It wasn't the enveloping, full sleep; it had no depth and couldn't have lasted long, an hour at the most. Bobbing upon sleep's surface, Viktor imagined flight. No map, no cityscape, just slow, vertical liftoff, and flight for its own sake—tranquility.

Sometimes your thoughts escape, a centrifuge unhinged. Was the scene he stumbled into last night a real, corporeal murder scene? Schwartz, Foxman, light blue, skull-cracked. Maybe it, too, was a dream. Should he return to check? What if Schwartz opens the door and there is no sign of bloody *kholodetz* that makes you slip and fall upon the Kazak carpet?

"Where will we go?" Viktor asks.

"Dog story, remember?"

The Birds Market is far, maybe forty minutes away by car. If ever Viktor needed advice, that time is now. Would Viktor feel less jittery, more focused, if he could get guidance from someone from the outside, someone who might have a different perspective— like Mad Dog? He feels the urge to confide, but can he tell this story in a coherent manner? Can Mad Dog be trusted? Would he get scared and throw Viktor out of the car? Maybe that would be wise. Should Viktor disclose what happened? But what has he done wrong, and what if all of this blows over?

"Yes, Birds Market, *Ptichiy rynok* it's called, turn on right."

"Turn on right what?"

"Did I say it wrong? Turn *to* right?"

"Do you perchance mean turn right?"

"Yez-s-s. Firstly, we must go in other direction on Garden Ring."

No, Viktor will talk about something else—anything else—to fill the forty-minute void.

First, he must get his thoughts in order. He will focus on something concrete: 20 certificate rubles is a mind-boggling sum if you trust someone to exchange it at black-market rates—240 rubles, 100 more than his former monthly salary.

You need money to run around Moscow, meeting with out-of-town refuseniks who come to town to seek attention from Western press, taking visiting foreigners from refusenik to refusenik, dashing off to the Sakharovs to translate, then off to Golden's to help a refusenik from the provinces write an appeal that stays on point, then to Central Telegraph to order a call to Michael Sherbourne, an activist in London. Just then, you learn that a professor from Columbia has arrived with a dozen students, all of them carrying money, jeans, *Playboys*, letters. If this were a dance, it would be a romp.

Mad Dog is cursing loudly in English, something about his car being an underpowered piece of Chihuahua shit, something else about a truck cutting him off.

"Viktor, Viktor! Earth to Viktor! This is mission control . . . Viktor? Viktor? Viktor?"

Has Viktor once again dropped into the abyss where conscience taps out a jumbled SOS? He should say something—anything. Let it be the first thing that comes to mind.

"Your newspaper should know about some very important conversations about Helsinki agreements," Viktor blurts out.

It's too early to mention this to anyone in the press, and an argument can be made that this will never be Viktor's story to tell. Alas, there are at least thirty minutes to burn, and talking about the Helsinki agreements is a safer bet than speaking of the double murder in which he, Viktor, a clueless, failed engineer, could become a suspect of convenience.

"Excuse me? Viktor, it's a bit jarring, what you just said, coming from another planet—Neptune, I would say."

"You don't know Helsinki agreements?"

"You are talking about the shindig in Helsinki last year? The thing that was the treaty that ended World War II? A lot of noise about nothing?"

"You have read it?"

"Viktor, Viktor, I have news for you. In the free world, people don't read international treaties for the joy of it. My job is to get on page one, not 17A. So—no, I have not read the Helsinki fucking agreement, and I feel no shame over not having read it."

"You don't need to read everything in Helsinki agreement. You must read section called Third Basket—it's about human rights. Everyone read it here. All dissidents. Do you want to know what is being said?"

"Enlighten me."

Enlightened is the last thing Mad Dog wants to be, but if you want these people to shut up, you let them drone on until their fuel runs out.

The worst of them is a guy named Albert Schwartz. (Alan Foxman, an embassy source, introduced them.) This Albert Schwartz takes you by the button and lectures, lectures, lectures as you plot your escape. He, too, asked whether Mad Dog has read that fucking treaty. If you love America, if you love Israel, you want guys like Schwartz to stay in refusal here, as secret weapons. His kind will bore you to death. Keep them here, and they will obliterate Communism from within. Some of these people are basic losers, people who will not fit into any system. Some are agents provocateurs, pretending to be your best friend and writing reports to the KGB. Glum Viktor is not trying to be your best friend, which makes him almost credible, somewhat, maybe.

Mad Dog hasn't seen Viktor drone on like this before, but now it seems that he and Schwartz are more similar than he suspected.

"Helsinki agreement makes good promises, but we need to tell our authorities that we, representatives of society, want to help them implementate."

"Implement?"

"Yez-s-s. Implement, then. I can tell you more if you promise to not talk about it until it's time?"

"Believe me when I say this: that would be no problem for me."

"Then, okay, it has been proposed that if all otherwise-thinking groups form umbrella organization and write letters to all signatory states about implementization. You see: if we say Helsinki agreement is serious agreement with serious promises, it will give opportunity for members of society to chronicle how government implements its promises. We will not have to address to governments, except in beginning. We can address reports to all freedom-loving people of goodwill everywhere."

Viktor is showing his true face: a bore to end all bores. Is he done? Is it over?

"Let's see if I understand you correctly, Viktor. You are talking about the usual suspects here in Moscow organizing under a different name and monitoring what you might refer to as 'implementization' of the Helsinki agreements Dumpster Three."

"Not Dumpster Three—Basket Three. And it will be different people in group—representatives of Moscow human rights defense organizations, Jews, Christians, separationists."

"What, pray tell, are separationists? Is it the same as divorce lawyers?"

"Separationists are representatives of peoples in republics and other provinces who want to separate from USSR. This could start international movement. You can do this in other countries where they don't have rights."

"Viktor, listen to me, that movement of yours will last for three minutes—maybe. It may not even get off the ground, if the KGB is watching, which I assure you is the case. Members of this organization will get arrested, one by one. What you are describing is not just equivalent to walking the tightrope. It's like using high-voltage wires for tightrope, Viktor. I am telling you this as someone who has studied Russian history, in great detail, at Harvard."

"But this idea has solid foundation, on theoretical level. Unless USSR is afraid of ruining relationship with West, especially now."

"This is arising in the Jewish movement, your friends the refuseniks?"

"Mostly no. Not Jews, so what is going to be especially interesting is how Israel will react."

"How *Israel* would react? Why would they give a rat's ass?"

"They will give very much rat's ass. They already warn Jewish refuseniks to avoid dissidents. I have been told to stop translating at Sakharov's press conferences. They want refuseniks to be separate. They don't want to worry about what happens to the people here. They don't care about rights of believers, the sects like Baptists, Seventh-day Adventists, Pentecostalists, separationists at republics."

"Viktor, this is crazy. I can tell you as your friend, when you see people who are devising this Helsinki idea, dive under the table. Hide from them, don't take their phone calls."

Alas, Viktor has more.

"Here, for first time in the history of this country, you can see people act as though they are free. This is important change. The Americans should know about this."

"Look, Viktor, I love you like a brother, but my hands are tied. It's possible that the Foreign Desk will go for it on an extra-slow day, but, as I said, the story will end up on page A19, with travel agency ads. To get to page one, you need color, you need real life, you need real people, not dissidents who protest. Fuck . . .

"So feed it to AP when the time comes. George Krimsky has a soft spot for dissident shit and Jewey shit. He will take anything that has 'dissident' or 'refusenik' on the forearm, plus he has a Jew hiding somewhere in his pedigree. You don't need me; you already have him in your pocket. And if Krimsky doesn't take it, there's Bob Toth—the *LA Times* is an okay second-rate paper. His wife is Jewish."

"And you?"

"My wife is not Jewish."

"Turn to right next . . ."

"Now, can we focus on the issue at hand, the reason we are here, the shit that I am paying you for?"

"Yez-s-s. Can you tell me what is main theme of this story?"

"Viktor, let's make sure we understand each other: I am paying you to help me get around; I am *not* paying you to guilt me, or lecture me on the meaning of dissent, or ask me about what Jew shit means in my life. I don't need an external conscience, least of all while you are on my dime. Capisce?"

"I literally need to understand theme of story you are pursuing if you want me to help you gather information. I know it's about dogs, that's all."

"Okay, here is the thrust: in a state built on Marxist ideology, your people are taught egalitarianism. Everybody's equal, everything's-the-same kind of shit. But what can be more bourgeois than a fucking dog with a pedigree? Get it? It's a contradiction!"

"Yez-s-s, I see logic. Maybe . . . But you are very, very noticeable here, even in Soviet coat and old hat. It will be better if I will walk around, talk with people, conspectize mentally, and tell you what I get."

"Conspectize? What the fuck is that, Viktor?"

"Make conspects."

"What are *conspects*?"

"'Conspects' is not right word?"

"Are conspects anything like notes, taking notes, jotting shit down to help you remember?"

"Notes—yes, thank you."

"I will hang back behind you, but I will give you hand signals and questions to ask. Clear?"

The Birds Market is a group of steel hangars, some filled with vendors of aquaria, some filled with terraria, and some with all manner of cages. Living things that can be incarcerated in said enclosures are being offered for sale. Birds, dogs, cats, fish, rodents, snakes, and, for some reason, hunting trophies—dead wolves, dead bears, heads of boars and deer.

They get out of the car silently. Viktor will walk slowly, keeping an eye on Mad Dog, waiting for gestures.

This is a color story. Mad Dog has been at this long enough to learn to turn off his judgment, drink in the atmosphere, the smells, the sights, the sounds—impressionistic shit.

You can't get on the cover with parakeets—boring. And the fish fail to establish a visceral connection. Ditto hamsters, gerbils, et al. Cats are way too difficult; you have to be damned good to do cats. Dogs, however, are straightforward. People get dogs.

As they get to the dog section of the market, Mad Dog points at a docile St. Bernard bitch prostrate next to a cardboard box filled with puppies. A piece of cardboard with some scribbling tells a story of some sort, presumably something about shots, pedigree, etc. A lot of acronyms Mad Dog has no use for or interest in: МКСС, ОКД-1, ЗКС-2.

With an index finger, Mad Dog directs Viktor to go there, ask questions, "conspectize."

When all the information is in, Mad Dog will come up to take a swig of color, take it in with gusto, much like you chug vodka straight from a bottle, not that he ever would. Mad Dog is trying to keep his mouth shut and is costumed in a Soviet overcoat and a native hat, but you can still tell he is a foreigner. The whole thing will be subverted if he becomes the center of attention—from that point on, it would be about him, about America, about Russian patriotism, about God knows what.

You can rely on a surrogate to do the bulk of your reporting. Your job as a writer is to rise above the fact, to make the story your own. He'll use Viktor's conspectization shit and spice it up with erudite discourse on the strictures of collectivism, which appear to be in contradiction with what he will describe as an obsession with pedigreed dogs. Said obsession, he will continue, represents an irreconcilable contradiction with pure Marxian ideology, not that anyone ever gave a flying fuck about pure Marxian ideology or even determined what it is.

The Foreign Desk will squeal with delight, or, to use a Russian expression Mad Dog has learned recently, will piss boiling water— кипятком ссать будут—even though some folks on the Foreign Desk are not his friends. (For the most part, they didn't go to shit-hole schools like Duke or UChicago, so it's not a class thing. They are Yalies mostly, which makes it even worse.)

There is no way to fact-check this thing. The comrade selling these blue-blooded St. Bernard puppies will end up getting a fictitious first name and no last name. This is kosher—when you are reporting from Moscow, you are allowed to change names. The Foreign Desk will not ask whether Mad Dog used a surrogate to do his reporting. This is both kosher and none of their business.

Viktor is deep in conversation with the St. Bernard–selling comrade—good work, Viktor, $20 well earned!

Mad Dog tries to listen, but gets nothing—too much peripheral noise. This thing's a beauty—a St. Bernard takes a wrong turn in the Alps, loses his brandy cask, only to find his grandchildren sold out of a cardboard box at the Birds Market in the Big Potato. Page one!

As Glum Viktor moves away from the similarly glum St. Bernard–selling comrade, Mad Dog moves in to touch that phlegmatic prostrate lard bucket of a bitch and, if not stopped by the dogmonger, touch the puppies.

He doesn't really care about that dog, or any dog, but the rules of feature-writing demand . . .

Mad Dog kneels to feel the dog's massive head. He stretches out his hand to touch the lower jaw, the place where a St. Bernard's slobber gathers into gooey icicle-like structures.

Does he realize that he has made a mistake?

Probably not.

Touched under the chin, the sleeping bitch springs to life, grabbing Mad Dog by mid-arm. It's a silent motion, not a shallow, grazing bite of surprise, but a resolute chomp and hold.

The puppy-selling comrade's repeated command "*Otpustit'!*" goes unheeded.

So does "*Fu!*" and so does the comrade's threatening exclamation that would be literally translated as "Kill, bitch, slut, mother, yours."*

The dog stays on his right arm, holding, thinking. What comes

---

* "Убью, сука, блядь, мать твою."

out of the reporter's mouth next will be in English—what other tongue does he have to express shock and pain?

"Fucking hell, asshole, get your fucking dog off my fucking arm! Goddammit! I will fucking sue your fucking Commie ass!" This is an abridged version. Mad Dog keeps it gushing even after the bitch relaxes her massive jaws and blood begins to trickle through the right sleeve of his Old Bolshevik overcoat.

As a crowd gathers, Viktor grabs Mad Dog by the good arm, the left one, and proceeds to rush him toward the Chihuahuamobile.

The crowd follows.

"Are you Americans?" asks a young man carrying a plastic bag containing what Viktor nostalgically recognizes as an axolotl, a wondrous creature that is erroneously described as a "walking fish" and is, in fact, a distant relative of a salamander.

"No," says Viktor in English. "We are from Belgia."

"What the fuck's just happened?"

Sitting behind the wheel, with the car doors closed, Mad Dog considers his wounds: four deep punctures, red dots, connected by thin blue bruises.

"Nobody gets bit by a fucking St. Bernard . . . Do they beat their St. Bernards in this fucking country until they turn into secret weapons? Do they have throat-ripping goldens, blood-drinking poodles?"

As Viktor's head begins to spin, he closes his eyes and breathes in deeply. The feeling of flight returns, and for a moment he is tranquil. It's the sight of blood, it's making his head spin, and he might throw up—it's better not to think about throwing up, or else you will. Blood never bothered him before; that's something new . . . He'll look away.

"Hey, Viktor, are you all right? You've turned a little pale there."

"I'm fine. What were you saying?"

"I was saying that nobody gets bit by St. Bernards . . . Was this a fucking secret weapon?"

"Yes . . . Actually, yes. This is not St. Bernard. It is Moskovskaya Storozhevaya, Moscow Watchdog. It's partially St. Bernard, partially Caucasus Sheepdog, with some other dogs also in hybrid."

"What the fuck is a Caucasus Sheepdog?"

"It's most angry dog on the earth. If you see it—you must run. I will write it in my conspects as you drive. Can you drive? Is your arm broken?"

"Bleeding like motherfuck, but okay . . . Not much pain yet."

"Do you want to see doctor? I know *refusenitsa*. She was physician-in-chief in biggest hospital in Moscow. Now rides in ambulance. You will not need to pay her."

"Fuck no. I don't need a fucking doctor, especially not a *refusenitsa*."

"Okay. I have English question. If man is called 'refusenik,' is woman called 'refuseness'? I used Russian suffix, but it can't be right in English—scratches my ear, so to say."

"You know, Viktor, it's really up to you."

"Do you have notebook and pen for conspectizing?"

"Look in the back seat, Viktor. There should be a few of them, used and unused. You can write on back pages of a used one."

"Can I look at newspaper? There's one there."

"Be my guest."

"This one is one month old. Page nineteen is where refuseniks are most of time?"

"Yes. Interspersed with travel agency ads. It's better in Jamaica—only three hundred fifty-nine dollars. It is better than this fucking place, for sure, no Moscow Fucking Watchdogs that look like St. Bernards but are actually spotted white bears."

Indeed, page A19 that day—December 1, 1975—provides a decent burial for an AP story, presumably by George Krimsky, about a demonstration in front of the Moscow Choral Synagogue that occurred three days earlier—on November 28—resulting in a request from the chief rabbi of Moscow—Fishman—that Moscow militia restore order in the street.

Chanukah in Moscow. Holy Man Fishman asking the KGB to rough up his brothers and sisters: don't let my people go! Let them get beat up instead.

The photo is what grabs Viktor's attention: a young woman breaks through boxy shoulders of the KGB goons, launching into a leap across Arkhipov Street. Her hair is wild, free, illuminated by a spotlight, her plaid scarf translucent, unraveling, a halo.

It's Oksana, his Oksana, his wife, locked into an instant that will never cease, an instant that captures history, embodying, epitomizing it.

You can't see a boxed *tort Arakhis*, a peanut cake, in her hand, but it's there, it's there, Viktor knows.

"Did you see photograph on page A19?"

"I did. Some refusenik must have given it to Krimsky. It had to have come from inside the demonstration. The roll must have gone out by pouch. And, you see, even with this picture, it ended up way deep inside the paper. I hear Jewish groups in New York are using it everywhere now. It is a beautiful image, I'll give you that. You know her?"

"Yes. I do. May I take newspaper?"

"Be my guest. Take the rest of the garbage back there while you're at it."

5.

The time has come to develop an understanding of events of November 28, 1975, and the significance of the photograph Viktor sees in a newspaper on the back seat of Mad Dog's Zhiguli.

Those who saw it believe they remember it still. Those who couldn't have seen it believe that they saw it as well, and thanks to the latter contingent, this story has acquired detail, clarity, resolution.

We reshuffle the dossiers and turn back the clock.

After a full day of training children to pronounce the soft English "t" and weirdly rolled English "r," Oksana places a cardboard box containing a partially eaten cake into a mesh bag, passes through the doors of the Moscow Special School No. 64 with Instruction in Multiple Subjects in Foreign Languages, turns left on Ulansky Pereulok, and heads in the direction of the Moscow Choral Synagogue.

A loosely knitted mohair scarf covers her head. It's scratchy, it's plaid, it obstructs vision, but it will enable her to observe without being observed. Her overcoat is mohair, too, with black tiger stripes on a muted yellow background. It's Czech.

Oksana carries a white mesh bag—much like a fishing net—in her left hand. You don't need to look too carefully to recognize a cardboard box containing a cake—*tort Arakhis*. "*Arakhis*" is "peanut" in Russian. The cake is an overgrown wafer, milky, light-chocolaty, with a thin layer of cream, wavy, like ripples on a kilometer-wide, calm river, with clusters of peanuts on top, arranged symmetrically, in the corners and in the middle.

It's a gift from the school director. Alla Markovna Shneerson remembered that November 29, tomorrow, is Oksana's birthday. At lunch, in Alla Markovna's office, they cut off two small squares, consumed them with tea, and spent a half hour talking about nothing important.

By law, regulation, or tradition—probably all three—a portrait of Lenin must hang in Alla Markovna's office, over her desk. While some school directors, including her predecessor, an old drunk known as Comrade Malakhov, procured the largest Lenin available, Alla Markovna hunted down the smallest black-and-white Lenin she could get away with. Hers is a Lenin with Children. It's a stretch to call it tasteful, but it is minimal.

"Look, Oksanka, a small *tort Arakhis*—so simple, yet so tasty!" Alla Markovna exclaimed in a smoker's voice. It's hoarse yet booming; it sets off asthmatic halts within itself.

Alla Markovna, who until last year was an ebullient teacher of Russian literature, owes her survival to her ability to feel silly, unrestrained joy. Her parents, "enemies of the people," were executed in 1939, the state stepped in to complete the task of her upbringing, and she spent her adolescence in orphanages.

Alla Markovna is well read in nineteenth-century Russian literature, obsessed with Saltykov-Schedrin's *History of One City*, and anxious that at times her speech betrays her orphanage upbringing, making her sound like a radish trader at a collective farm market. Alla Markovna's complex root structure pushes her toward chain-smoking Belomorkanal, the cigarette of simple folk, named after Comrade Stalin's most murderous construction project.

In moments of anxiety, Alla Markovna peppers her speech with the word "говорю," "*govoryu*," or "I say." Blurted out fast, Alla Markovna's "*govoryu*" becomes "*ghryu*," which can be inserted anywhere in a sentence. It's a Siberian thing. She knows that teachers have nicknamed her Ghryu, as in, "Ghryu called me in for a talking-to."

It's customary for people in positions of authority to address their young subordinates formally, using the first name and a patronymic. Ghryu likes Oksana enough to address her in an ultrafamiliar manner—Oksanka. And if Alla Markovna likes you, she tells you repeatedly that surviving extreme hardship makes simple things in life so much more precious.

"Listen, *ghryu*, Oksanka, nobody can appreciate vodka and herring more than a former *politzek*,"* she whispered to Oksana at a New Year's celebration for children a few days ago. This pronouncement seemed abstract at the time. There was no vodka, no herring, and no *politzek* in the room—just piles and boxes of excellent Soviet candy, a group of apathetic adolescents, and a rednosed old drunk playing an accordion in a Father Frost getup.

Arkhipov is a perfect little street: it slopes down as gently as it curves to the left.

Oksana's face and her hair obscured, she will be a casual passerby. It will be akin to running your hand rapidly through candle flame.

To get to Arkhipov Street from Moscow Special School No. 64, you go to the end of Ulansky, turn left on the oh-so-Paris-y Boulevard Ring, walk past the frozen-over Clear Ponds, slow down to take in the sight of ice skaters, fight your own impulse to put on a

---

* Political prisoner.

pair of skates, cross the tramway tracks, and turn right on Pokrovka, a street with a name that connotes a shroud or divine intercession.

With no warning, Pokrovka changes its name, becoming Maroseyka. Moscow being a city of changing street names, Maroseyka in 1975 was formally christened Bogdan Khmelnitsky Street. Why would you name a street after a seventeenth-century warlord who led a Cossack rebellion against Poles, killing at least a hundred thousand Jews along the way? Adolf Hitler Way would send a similar message as a street named after Khmelnitsky.

Arkhipov is on your left. Turn.

The slope of Arkhipov makes descent treacherous. You must pay attention.

The sidewalk is slippery, and Oksana's suede boots—also Czech, also chic, also a gift from Professor Moskvin, her father— almost completely lack tread.

High heels can look better than low, concurred, but they are suboptimal on black ice that lurks beneath fresh snow. Prague may be different, but here in Moscow in the winter, women should avoid high heels and opt for footwear with hefty tread, one might suggest, though it's clearly too late for this bit of sober advice to reach the target population.

Wearing her boots with the grace of a lifelong skier, Oksana is walking behind two middle-aged men, the auxiliary police, *druzhinniki*.

You don't want a busload of uniforms to get provoked into a street fight, militia vs. refuseniks. Foreign press, should one of them be in the neighborhood and should they manage to get the photos, will make it look like the Kishinev pogrom of 1903.

Druzhinniki are civilians called up to help the militia, genuine police. These people are amateurs who embrace the challenge of fighting disorder in the streets. Since they are volunteers, many of them regard the license to bust a nose in the name of the Mother-land as a reward in its own right.

You identify *druzhinniki* by thin red bands worn on their street clothes, above the elbow. They may be workers from a ball-bearing plant, a place with a name like Lenin's Path, or they may be KGB operatives costumed as Everymen for a political masquerade.

In Moscow of 1975, shoes unfailingly reveal the identity of their wearer.

In the winter, young workers, the bona fide *druzhinniki*, wear black felt boots on rubber soles, with a zipper on the arch—normal boots worn by most men of ordinary means, basic footwear you see on the nearly bare shelves of shoe stores.

False *druzhinniki*, those who pose as auxiliary police, wear black shoes on thick rubber soles. These lace up on the front. Shaped vaguely like oversized eggplants, they are the sort of objects that must, by design, cost the wearer nothing. Not bought, not sold, they are issued; law enforcement equipment, armored personnel carriers. And they are the same for uniforms and plainclothes.

If you are a plainclothes KGB operative and your feet are en-cased in these, you have to suspend disbelief to think that you are undercover. And while you are at it, you might also convince yourself that you have uttered the right incantations—invoking God's name, if you happen to know it—to make yourself invisible.

The two men who walk slowly in front of Oksana are plain-clothes militia or KGB, false *druzhinniki*, gone undercover to make whatever is about to go down by the Moscow Choral Syna-gogue seem less sinister.

Oksana considers turning around and heading back uphill, out of this shimmering little street, to the safety of Bogdan Khmelnitsky, but she keeps on, drawn by whatever is happening down Arkhipov, sensing that it, whatever it is, must be seen.

She picks up the pace, getting close enough to the *druzhinniki* to hear them talk:*

FIRST DRUZHINNIK: Here, Sasha, I have a simple question: In our country, those shits avoided the war. They sat it out, in Uzbekistan, while we were spilling our blood. But as soon as they ran off to their Israel, they transform into big warriors, whipping our Arab brothers on the ass. Why is that? A simple question, Sasha, yes?

SECOND DRUZHINNIK: It's simple, all right. Don't tell me you don't know the answer. They've never given a shit about us. They've lived here for hundreds of years, but they still don't give a shit, the bastards.

FIRST DRUZHINNIK: If that's so, what the fuck are we keeping them here for? Let them go to their Israel. Fuck them.

SECOND DRUZHINNIK: That's hard to argue with, but it wouldn't feel right. Make them pay us back first. Aren't they all engineers, economists, fucking professors?

FIRST DRUZHINNIK: You mean pay back with money?

SECOND DRUZHINNIK: Maybe with money; maybe with blood, as is customary here in Russia.†

---

* It's a fool's errand to separate a story from its language. The words Oksana hears are so important to this narrative that for the purpose of creating historical record, they will appear in Russian and, for the appeasement of non–Russian speakers, in translation. There is an added bonus: the presence of the Russian text may give Russian-speaking readers the pleasure of watching this translator fight for breath and ultimately accept defeat.

† ПЕРВЫЙ ДРУЖИННИК: Вот, Саш, такой простой вопрос, у нас они ни хера не воевали, в Узбекистане суки отсиживались пока мы кровь, блядь, проливали. А как в Израиль ихний уехали—сразу вояки большие, арабов наших по жопе лупят. Почему вот так? Простой вопрос, ну Саш, да?

ВТОРОЙ ДРУЖИННИК: Простой то простой. Сам же ответ знаешь. Насрать им на нас всегда было. Сотни лет у нас, блядь, жили, а все равно—насрать. С большой буквы "Н" насрать—Насрать, блядь, понял?

ПЕРВЫЙ ДРУЖИННИК: Если так, то на хера мы их здесь держим? Пусть себе в этот Израиль их катятся. Хуй с ними.

. . .

Oksana's father has a big, proud beak, as big as on any Yid in a caricature in any anti-Semitic pamphlet. This should not be denied. But it would be incorrect to suggest that he sat out the war in Uzbekistan.

Hearing the false *druzhinniki*, Oksana imagines her father in the belly of a plane, cradling his PPSh, preparing for a nighttime jump. Professor Moskvin spent the war the way a teacher should—imparting wisdom, leading. And in the context of that war, a lead-spraying PPSh was a teaching tool, a pointer.

His stories never leave her. Getting dropped in the forests, joining the guerrillas. He was an explosives expert, among other things. On one raid, he joined a group of Yiddish-speaking madmen as they blew up a German ammo dump. Then, defying orders, they derailed a passing train. And while the fighters slaughtered the SS, the prisoners, Jews also, escaped into the forest. It's possible that some survived till liberation.

Only two fighters lived to tell that story: her father and another man, a student from Krakow.

After that mission, her father went off to find his Red Army unit, and his comrade disappeared into the forest.

"Did he survive the war?" Oksana asked her father years ago.

"By accident, maybe, but statistically unlikely. People like him are programmed to die. His ability to exercise caution was deactivated. It's a disease with no name. The man was pure valor."

"And you?"

ВТОРОЙ ДРУЖИННИК: Это ты прав, но обидно как то. Пусть сначала долги выплатят. Они же все инженеры, экономисты, профессора ебучие.

ПЕРВЫЙ ДРУЖИННИК: Деньгами, что ли?

ВТОРОЙ ДРУЖИННИК: Может деньгами, а может и кровью; такой у нас на Руси обычай.

"Me too; must you ask?"

When she was a child learning to draw, Oksana thought she could see her father and his comrades as Robin Hood's outlaws in Sherwood Forest. Would these *druzhinniki*, these Shakespearean clowns, these bureaucrats sans desks, have the valor to eliminate an ammo dump, and then derail a train, slaughtering the SS as prisoners run?

Credit or blame Professor Moskvin for Oksana's cautious descent to the Moscow Choral Synagogue. Parents are always the first to be credited or blamed for such things, because, in addition to storytelling, they curate their children's reading.

The Master and Margarita was on Oksana's bedside table from adolescence on. It was still there this morning—she has read it and reread it continuously from the beat-up light-blue copies of the journal *Moskva*, where that novel appeared after its return from oblivion. If you were in Moscow in November 1966, nine years ago, you remember the shock waves that emanated from those pages. Oksana has since read it in unabridged versions, too; carefully, slowly, questioning, drawing connecting lines to Moscow's map, to history, to Goethe's *Faust*, to all of Gogol, to Marlowe, to the Gospels.

The Master and Margarita is three stories woven into one. First, there is Satan, who comes to Moscow in 1930 or so, most likely to check on the progress in the making of the New Socialist Man. Then there is a love story: an unhappily married Moscow woman, Margarita, and her lover, a writer, the Master, obsessed with the story of Jesus and Pontius Pilate. The Master is writing a novel, an interpretation of the Passion of Christ. It's the Gospel according to Bulgakov.

Bulgakov made Oksana see Moscow as Jerusalem's cold, dark

half, a part of a continuum, spiritual and geographic whole. Perhaps one sunny day Oksana will follow the Boulevard Ring to the mound where the temple stood. She will not pray—she doesn't know how and feels no need to learn—but she will place her hand on a stone.

She will close her eyes, she will see the faces of her ancestors, those who lived outside photography's reach, those enslaved, those whipped, those chained to the oars, those kicked in the gut, those humiliated, those slandered, those spat upon, those dispatched to foreign lands, those shot by firing squad, those raped, those gassed, those buried alive. Also, those who rose against the pharaohs: her father, his Merry Men, all legendary, some martyred, and her grandfather, the American Negro, one of the fallen fighters of the Abraham Lincoln Brigade. His photographs may exist in Detroit, but not here.

Should she be fated to walk the ramparts of Jerusalem's Old City, Oksana will, as though from a past life, recognize the sweeping vistas.

Oksana has heard about protests that with some regularity break out across the street from the Moscow Choral Synagogue. She learned about that the way everyone has, by listening to the enemy voices: the Voice of Israel, the Voice of America, Radio Liberty, Deutsche Welle, and—best of all—BBC. The Beeb's Russian broadcasts are as good as their regular English offerings, which she loves also.

If you ask her as she carefully negotiates Arkhipov Street, Oksana will tell you that her quest is sociological and historical. Observational even.

She is heading to the synagogue to see how some brave

people—Jews in this instance—are starting to conduct themselves in our country.

It's not just about Jews, of course. There are others who are standing up to the state: democrats, i.e., defenders of human rights, sundry Christians. Also, Muslims. Separatists, too. But Jewish protests are easiest to spot—they have a parade ground, the spot across from the synagogue.

A dozen years ago, Oksana's father signed a letter of support of two imprisoned writers, Sinyavsky and Daniel'. The letter demanded their immediate release. Nothing came of it, and it cost Professor Moskvin dearly—he was declared politically unreliable, was expelled from the Communist Party, and hasn't been allowed to travel abroad since. He has no regrets. Yulik Daniel' is a friend, and Professor Moskvin is nothing if not loyal.

Thanks to him, from childhood, Oksana has had access to the freshest of *samizdat*, "self-published" literature, clandestinely typed and retyped.

The mechanics of *samizdat* are simple: To make *samizdat* you need onionskin paper, the thinnest, plus carbon paper. For every page, you arrange a pack, collating your sheets of onionskin and carbon; this way, you can produce one original page and maybe a dozen carbon copies. The word for that pack is "закладка," pronounced *zakladka*.

If you manage to procure a prerevolutionary typewriter, an Underwood, for example, you are in luck. It's a beast of a machine.* Its keys strike hard; you can make an original and a dozen copies. Use a new East German piece of junk, an Erika, and you'll get a half dozen pages at the most. On an Erika, the seventh on-

---

* Зверь-машина.

ionskin of your *zakladka* will be illegible, plus the "E" key will bend and start to stick permanently after your third manuscript.

Oksana once helped prepare the manuscript of Tolya Marchenko's *Moi Pokazaniya*, a prison memoir. *My Testimony* is the English title; look it up, read it. The lead typist—Lyuda Alexeyeva—was ferociously fast, maybe one hundred words per minute, maybe more. Her fingers could break the sound barrier, or so a joke went. Oksana was in ninth grade, too young to type. Her job was to prepare the onionskins and carbons, to make *zakladki* for Lyuda.

She and Lyuda later collated the final manuscript. There were twelve copies; thank you, Underwood!

Oksana imagined these copies making their way to Paris, London, New York, via diplomatic pouch, presumably. Literature will find a way, literature will make mockery of its oppressors; ban it, and it will go underground, finding its Tolya Marchenko, its Lyuda Alexeyeva, its Oksana Moskvina.

Oksana was able to read *Animal Farm* and *1984*—both banned—in the original English. The books were a gift to Professor Moskvin from a foreign colleague.

Oksana hasn't rooted for the USSR in any sporting event in eight years—since Czechoslovakia. That was 1968, August, when our tanks rolled in.

She knows of two street protests that took place in Moscow—the 1965 demonstration on Pushkin Square and the 1968 demonstration on Red Square. The former was about prosecution of Sinyavsky and Daniel' for publishing their work pseudonymously in France. The latter was about the invasion of Czechoslovakia. Oksana has heard a lot of free speech, but it was muffled, repeated among people you trust. A protest is a different thing altogether—it's in the open, brazen, unveiled, intended to be seen.

Is it permissible to let history roar by without stealing a glimpse? How do protests begin in our country? How do they end? Does everyone get arrested? This was the case in 1965 and 1968; does this still hold true? Is it possible to just say no, to state publicly, openly, that you are a free man among slaves?

Oksana is no visionary. She sees what everyone can see:

Before her is a country at a halfway point. If those fat faces* want control, they should take total control—now. If they allow some liberty, to some people, in some cases, they better realize that liberty begets more liberty. Speaking of which, Oksana wouldn't mind seeing the world: Paris, London, Rome, Jerusalem, New York, Los Angeles. Freedom is not about speech alone. It's about seeing, too.

Hers are elegant questions, formulated by a scientist's step-daughter. Make it daughter, for what is blood?

A crucial distinction must be made: Oksana is walking *toward* the Moscow Choral Synagogue, not *to* the Moscow Choral Synagogue.

There is never a reason to step inside that place; the rabbi—Fishman—is an ass-licker to the Bolsheviks, an Orthodox Bolshevik, the worst of both worlds. Maybe he has a first name, maybe he has a patronymic, but nobody cares enough to use either, and it's possible that no one knows, or needs to.

Fishman is Fishman. It is said, unfairly, that Fishman lives up to his name, that his blood runs cold, that he has developed fins and scales. It's been said, unkindly, that he has been dry-rubbed and smoked at various points in his life, and that a herring's tail grows between his buttocks. This is neither slander nor magical realism—such things happen to some rabbis.

---

* Толстомордые.

There is a technical term for this kind of person: a walrus prick,* which allows us to stay faithful to the metaphor of bounty of the sea, albeit jumping species, from herring tail to walrus penis. A man must be free to switch his sea metaphors, especially when dealing with Fishman and his ilk,† if such exists. Did you know that he once worked at the Likhachev Automobile Plant, probably bolting cages into Black Marias for the goons to use in arrests of his brothers and sisters?

What would you do at Comrade Rabbi Fishman's Choral House of Bore? Pray? Should you choose to, and should you find yourself wanting for words to mutter to cover up your liturgical bald spot,‡ you will find a prayer for the government of the USSR, in Russian and in Hebrew, displayed on a bas relief above the bimah, about even with the women's balcony:

A PRAYER FOR THE WELL-BEING
OF THE GOVERNMENT:

May He who blessed our fathers Abraham, Isaac and Jacob,
who laid the path across the sea and a road through the
mighty waters, bless and preserve, and defend, and protect,
and glorify, and aid, and trumpet, and exalt
THE GOVERNMENT OF THE USSR.
May the Holy One, blessed be He, breathe life into it, and
protect it from all the troubles, hardships, sadness and

---

* Хуй моржовый.

† "Eelk" might be a good neologism, stemming as it does from an eel, a delicious, fatty fish that, sadly, lacks scales and is therefore unfit to be consumed by those Jews who care about such things.

‡ Литургическая плешь.

harms, and save it, and smite all the foes before it, and may
all the tasks it sets forth be crowned with success.
*Amen.**

Oksana went to the Moscow Choral Synagogue once, as a child, as a sightseer, taken there by her father, who also took her to many a church, to acquaint her with iconography. For analogous reasons, those two rarely missed a museum. On that visit, Oksana noted that there was no prayer for the Soviet government on the wall of any church she has ever seen.

It's possible that to those who come to the Moscow Choral Synagogue to pray—old men, leaning on canes, ambulating as rapidly as congestive heart failure permits—the shameful prayer on the wall is something akin to paying rent, taxes, protection money, kickbacks—something off the top for the caesar.

It's possible that they don't notice this overarching blasphemy as they mutter the prayers that really matter to them—millennia-old material that takes a different view of prostration before despots.

A younger crowd congregates outside the Moscow Choral, milling around across the street, smoking American cigarettes, stomping their feet, trying to keep warm, dreaming of another life, life in Jerusalem, maybe, or maybe in Rehovot, or in the Negev, with a

---

* Молитва за благополучие правительства: Тот, кто благословил наших отцов Авраама, Ицхака и Яакова, продолжил путь через море и дорогу через могучие воды, да благословит и сохранит, и охранит, и поможет, и возвеличит, и прославит, и вознесет вверх Правительство СССР.

Святой, благословен он, да вдохнет в него жизнь и охранит его от всех бед и несчастий, горестей и вреда, и спасет его, и свергнет его ненавистников перед ним, и пусть во всем, к чему оно обратится, его ждет успех.

И скажем амен.

machine gun dangling across the chest, or in New York, or Los Angeles, or Miami, perhaps even.

These young people regard the prayer on the synagogue's wall with a proper mix of shame, embarrassment, and disgust.

Hey, god—yes, you, god, you don't get an uppercase "G" or a skipped "o" here—should you exist, the holy, the exalted one, the one who has never listened to Fishman and his cadre of arthritic old shitters—don't you start now!

Note this, god: If you are contemplating turning your back on your people by helping the government of the USSR pursue its fat-faced, mighty-fisted goals or, worse still, should you indeed smite its enemies (America? Israel?), a blessing will be the last thing you'll get on this trampled spot across the street from the Moscow Choral Synagogue! Holy, my foot!

It's November 1975. You are in refusal. If you are able to pray and if you believe that such endeavors serve a purpose, you pray for drought, you pray for locusts to decimate Soviet harvests, you pray for hunger so black that it reaches deep into the Kremlin.

So, god, should you (a) exist, (b) have a listening organ, and (c) have the inclination to listen, make the masters of our fate beg for American wheat! And what if American wheat has a price that's not measured in dollars alone? What if our freedom is part of the price? Enough nonsense from you, god—just make it so.

Oksana may muster the courage to file an application to emigrate—someday, in due course. Perhaps her father could be convinced to leave as well. The gates of great universities in Europe, America, and Israel would swing open before the brilliant, fearless Professor Moskvin.

Today, Oksana needs to be careful. Schoolteachers who are found to be ideologically unreliable get fired immediately.

. . .

Beneath, down Arkhipov, someone starts a song Oksana recognizes from the Voice of Israel—"*Hatikvah*," Israel's anthem.

Kol od balevav penimah
Nefesh Yehudi homiyah,
Ulfa'ate mizrach kadimah,
Ayin leTziyon tzofiyah.

The anthem of an enemy state resounds on a Moscow street. Not a small thing. Oksana is by the synagogue's steps now, gazing across Arkhipov at the group of maybe two dozen men and five or six women, holding up homemade signs, painted on pieces of bedsheets.

"VISAS—NOT PRISONS," reads one, all caps, in English.

"Отпустите нас в Израиль,"* reads another. Not all caps, in Russian.

And so forth, along the same lines. Everyone seems to have a sign.

Oksana pulls the scarf lower on her forehead. This will make her less recognizable. If her fiction that she is just a passerby is to remain convincing, Oksana will be able to walk past this disturbance, this public demonstration, only once.

She slows down, her gaze focused on the protesters across the street, catty-corner, maybe fifty meters ahead.

A flash makes her stop.

Is it a gunshot?

A young man in blue jeans and a puffy dark-green nylon jacket,

---

* "Let us leave for Israel."

who seems to have been walking in front of Oksana's goons, takes off running. There is a camera in his hand.

He has snapped a photo, presumably, for them, for the outside world. He might be American—a student perhaps? Who else would wear those puffy nylon jackets, especially in a brazen color like green?

There are quite a few Americans here in Moscow now, dozens at any given time, more than ever before, some of them students, some just people passing through, gawking at our workers' paradise.

Oksana's thoughts: "Run fast, boy, run, get that roll of film to their AP, or their UPI, or their *New York Times*! Run across borders, run across time! Get out into the world!"

The goons Oksana had followed down Arkhipov take off after the young man, but their sort is not known for bursts of speed, even when not held back by icebreakers on their feet. One of them slips on the ice beneath the fresh snow and slams into the back of a sky-blue Volga, the very old kind, the one with a chrome deer taking a leap off the hood.

The second *druzhinnik* steps over his prostrate comrade and continues frontward ambulation, but in the absence of the fighting spirit, it's never any use. How can you be expected to catch up with a much younger man fit to run a one-hundred-meter dash while you are trying to avoid stumbling over a prostrate, bleeding colleague? Someone else will have to finish this little task.

The boy doesn't get far. Another false *druzhinnik*, who is posted down the street, slams into him from the side, sending the boy and his camera flying into the path of a green military truck that seems to harbor bulky machinery on its flatbed.

Squealing godlessly, the truck stops with maybe a meter to spare.

A crowd of uniforms and *druzhinniki* gathers, laughing at the spectacular trajectory of the young man's fall. They lean over the boy, who is trying to hold on to his camera. It's futile, of course. One of them gets down on one knee and twists the boy's left arm until his right hand lets go. Let the Spaniards have the Running of the Bulls. We have the Twisting of the Arms. All Soviet citizens learn this maneuver early in life.

Oksana can't see definitively whether anyone is kicking the boy, but she is fairly certain that swift kicks are being dispensed. This, too, is fundamental.

One of the goons leaves the scene, carrying the camera. It's a good camera, professional: a Nikomat FTN. There can't be many of these in Moscow; you can only obtain one if you have friends abroad. Oksana's father has one. A cancer biologist in Boston, an American who had spent a few months at Moskvin's lab, had one sent to him by way of one of their famous American historians, Richard Pipes, a Harvard professor who was recently allowed to pass through Moscow.

The boy who tried to snap this photo might be a foreigner, of course, which would probably mean the goons will show some restraint in roughing him up and turn him over to the appropriate embassy tomorrow morning.

Two goons lift up the boy, grab him under the arms, and drag him off like a drunken third comrade.

Oksana hears the boy speak Russian—not a foreigner, yet clearly not afraid. Blood drips from his chin and onto the front of his green jacket.

Oksana's plan is to keep moving, but she is walking so slowly that she has almost stopped, staring at the gathering across the street.

The military truck that had come so close to crushing the young photographer is a pug-nosed sort; its motor sits beneath the cab. It looks like something used to pull intercontinental ballistic missiles on Red Square at the November 7 parades.

A highly technical Russian word for a mysterious machine of war is a "железяка," pronounced *zhelezyaka*, a "metal thing," a "gizmo." Alternatively, you might call it a хуёвина, pronounced *khuyovina*, a *fucking* gizmo.

"They've dragged in a fucking Katyusha—our heroes! Here's your Soviet military doctrine on display! Behold and fucking rejoice!"* shouts one of the demonstrators, setting off laughter on the refusenik side of the street and smirks among the militia and the KGB across Arkhipov.

Note One: "*Pripizdyukhali*," the Russian slang word for "dragged in," sort of, is wholly beyond a translation's reach. A definitive translation will not be attempted. It is noted here for (a) the amusement of native Russian speakers, and (b) creating a complete and reliable historical record.

Note Two: Explanations of humor should be confined to settings where one's duty as a historian creates an obligation to unpack the hidden meaning. The suggestion that the guardians of state security are so heavy-handed that they would prepare to deploy a World War II–era rocket launcher against a street protest in the center of Moscow is good comedy, regardless of which side of Arkhipov you are on. Hence, the laughs on one side of the street and smirks on the other. The idea of using a rocket launcher against a street protest occurring a few meters away addresses the classically Soviet inability to deliver a measured response. Shoot a

---

* "Катюшу, блядь, припиздюхали, герои! Вот она, советская, блядь, военная доктрина! Любуйтесь, бля!"

rocket across Arkhipov and you will make a crater in the center of Moscow.

Now, "the Soviet military doctrine" bit. The Soviet military doctrine is not complex: throw all your *zhelezyaki*, all your *khuyoviny*, into the field and think later, if absolutely necessary, if you still can.

Note Three: Here we focus on the extreme juiciness of Russian speech coming from the "*Hatikvah*"-singing Zionists. Well—"*Hatikvah*"-*schmatikvah*—we are all people of Russian culture here, fuck your mother! Our speech happens to be juicier than the KGB's, because we are free men and women.

We feel no fear. Does this mean that there is nothing to fear? Does this mean that we actually are free? Does dispensing with fear beget freedom? Was the fear that we have discarded illusory to begin with? Isn't all fear illusory by definition? Isn't freedom? Go ask someone else; we don't know, we don't care right now, and it's possible that we never will.

The truck spews black smoke, not just at demonstrators, but all around. This is neither an act of aggression nor a threat; the thing is working exactly in accordance with its design. The gizmo on the truck bed is not a cluster of Katyusha rockets, as the joker on the refusenik side of the street has suggested.

When two soldiers jump out of the cab and pull off the tarp, the *zhelezyaka/khuyovina* is revealed to be a spotlight. It has the look of an object that can turn night into day and singe your nose hair if you face it as you sing your songs of protest.

An explosion of laughter and applause from the refusenik side greets a third soldier, the driver, as he hops out of the truck.

The soldier smiles, bows. Yes, bows! Can't help himself. What is he, an actor? They draft those, too. Actors of burned-down theaters especially . . . After the curtain falls, he will get so fucked for pandering to this crowd.

With the bravado of a performer of the Red Army Choir, the driver walks around the truck and, as his comrades stand back, opens a large green metal box, pushes a button, and pulls a lever, making the street turn bright. As though on cue, the choir of refuseniks restarts "*Hatikvah*," now shoehorned painfully into Russian:

Пока внутри сердца всё ещё
Тоскует душа еврея,
И в края Востока, вперёд,
На Сион устремлён взгляд.*

The choir is loud, easily projecting over the truck engine and the generator. Is this a homespun translation by an anonymous refusenik poet? It's a warning: you are up against a deceptively mighty foe—quake in your Red Army boots and KGB-issue lace-ups.

Oksana is having difficulty with adherence to her original plan to saunter by slowly, to witness and move on, and move on she would have had she not recognized the chasm glaring before her.

It's here, unmistakable, a seismic fault running down the center of Arkhipov.

Oksana sees the chasm clearly. Will she stay on this side, in its safety, or will she leap to its other side? Ours or theirs? Safety or peril? Allegiances jumble. Is she with them, or has she become one of us, and which one is which? Where will you go, Oksana?

---

* As long as in the heart, within, / A Jewish soul still yearns, / And onward, toward the ends of the east, / An eye still gazes toward Zion.

Will you be able to walk by, following your self-inflicted protocol, or will your experiment break out of its glass container, taking the in-vitro-to-in-vivo leap?

What's the value of the nights you spent by the shortwave radio, feeling intense shame for your country's crimes stemming from idiocy, committed in malice? What is the value of all the *samizdat* you have read, all those *zakladki* you have made of onionskin and carbon paper, twelve for Underwood, seven for Erika? What is the point of all of this if you are able to walk by, failing to sing along? Imagine how good it would feel to hum along with those words, to lip-synch, to join.

Set "*Hatikvah*" aside for a moment. Galich, our Galich, has a song about the Decembrists, "The St. Petersburg Romance"—you know it, you heard Aleksandr Arkadievich Galich himself sing it at your father's apartment not so long ago!

Можешь выйти на площадь,
Смеешь выйти на площадь,
Можешь выйти на площадь,
Смеешь выйти на площадь
В тот назначенный час?!*

Can you walk by, Oksana? Dare you walk by? Can you? Choose your side of Arkhipov, choose your side, choose, Oksana, choose!

Oksana didn't come here to toss the gauntlet, and had she paused to think, there would be no image to capture, no story to tell. Ex-

---

* Can you come to the square, / Dare you come to the square, / Can you come to the square, / Dare you come to the square, / When that hour strikes?!

cept Arkhipov is no ordinary street. It follows the curves of its own logic, poses its own challenges.

With the power she didn't know she had, Oksana slams into the cordon of goons. Are they uniforms? Are they plainclothes? Are they *druzhinniki*? She has no idea, and what does it matter in a masquerade?

Passing easily between the shoulders of goons, she slams into the group of "*Hatikvah*"-singing refuseniks. As their lines open, she continues the trajectory deep into their midst. Someone breaks her fall. What does he know about her? Is it a friend? Is it a he, a she? It's a friend, surely a friend, a new friend.

Her thought at that moment: "*Tort Arakhis!*" It's still here, in its white mesh bag, though the cardboard box seems smashed a bit from contact with friends and foes.

She doesn't know that one of the refuseniks in the group has a little Soviet MIR camera, a knockoff Leica. He sees a young woman break through the KGB cordon and leap across Arkhipov, her figure illuminated by the spotlight, her plaid scarf translucent, unraveling: an instant captured, an instant that will never cease.

Oksana does not hear the shutter.

The photographer, forever anonymous, does not yet know what he has.

Uniformed militia are shouting for the demonstrators to move on, the goons in plainclothes stand watching, but the demonstrators do not budge.

They sing. "*Hatikvah*," in Hebrew, in Russian, in English, again, and again, and again, a Zionist carousel of eternal return. It's one of the faces of war: you show them who you are, you show them that they aren't as fearsome as they believe themselves to be. If you convince them that you have no fear, it's the same as spitting deep into the darkness of their souls. You stand your ground, you defend your little patch of Jerusalem. They can try to push you off, they can rough you up if they wish, they can insult you, but you fire back, and if it gets too physical, they cart you off for fifteen days and fifteen nights in the slammer for hooliganism; hooliganism is rarely hooliganism, loitering is never loitering.

"Let my people go, assholes!" someone shouts in Russian amid the shoving.

"Sure, we'll let you go. To the militia precinct," someone responds from the other side.

"To the polar bears," shouts someone else from their side.*

Such nonsense would not have gone far in the old days, when the Old Man ruled. But in the Year of Our Lord 1975, fifty-eight years and change after the revolution, people are losing compunction, falling prey to the good-life madness, demanding to relinquish the dream, to escape from it.

You let them go, then republics will go off in their own directions, Japan will lop off Sakhalin, the Chechens will get armed. Then what? Capitalism?

If this thing falls, the world's biggest free-for-all will ensue. The crooks will end up with everything, the bigger the crook, the greater the pile of loot. A nationwide kleptocracy? Worldwide? Is "kleptocracy" even a word yet?

Now across the street, Oksana looks back into the KGB spotlight, toward the synagogue, which has acquired a rainbow halo around its steps.

---

* "Отпустите народ мой, мудаки!"

"Отпустить то отпустим—в отделение."

"К белым медведям вас, бля, сейчас же отпустим. Непременно. Без промедления."

. . .

The singing stops briefly, but it begins anew, slowly, in Russian:

Ещё не погибла наша надежда,
Надежда, которой две тысячи лет:
Быть свободным народом на своей земле,
Земле Сиона и Иерусалима.*

Oksana takes a spot on the group's edge, but the place she thought was the *arrière-garde* is rapidly becoming the avant-garde.

She is getting into the KGB photos. She will be identified, and later, at the school, she will be called in to the director's office and dealt with accordingly. She thinks of Moscow Special School No. 64, she thinks of Alla Markovna Shneerson, known as Alla Markovna Ghryu to those who love her. Ghryu will hate to have to fire her Oksanka.

This thought goes away quickly. Oksana is too deeply shaken by the realization that, far from fearing the KGB spotlight, she craves it. Bathed in light, she shakes loose the mane of black hair, staring brazenly into the light, the cameras, too. Let your shutters click! I am here! Photograph! Identify!

Since it has been established previously by many others that Moscow is not a part of the world of real things, this work need not be replicated.

More than brick, more than mortar, more even than cobble-

---

* Our hope is not yet lost, / The hope two thousand years old: / To be a free nation in our land, / The land of Zion and Jerusalem.

stone, Moscow is a distillation of literature, literatures, really, also art. Caught in the spirit of distillation, Oksana imagines herself on the barricades of Paris, as per Eugène Delacroix's *Liberty Leading the People*, a unity of the allegorical and the corporeal. Her breasts are covered, yes, but not her hair, not her face.

For the next few minutes, she will be unaware of Viktor. How would she know that he beholds her through the light filter of—of all people—Sir Walter Scott? Moscow or not, Oksana or not, Viktor sees Rebecca, the fair daughter of Isaac of York, a moneylender in *Ivanhoe*, taking a wrong turn out of twelfth-century England. Any young man or woman of their age and education knows every page of *Ivanhoe*. Also, pretty much all of Alexandre Dumas, and Mark Twain, and Hemingway, and Fitzgerald, and Salinger, and Pushkin, and Shakespeare, and Lermontov, and Il'f and Petrov—and Bulgakov; never forget Bulgakov! And Gogol. And the Germans . . . Feuchtwanger, Heine, Goethe, Remarque, Brecht—all that. And don't forget *samizdat*. Sinyavsky, Daniel', Solzhenitsyn, Marchenko, Orwell, and, weirdly, Leon Uris, the author of that Soviet-style American novel called *Exodus*, which has gained so much in translation into Russian.

Pushing ensues. Oksana stands poised to resist, to lead even, and God knows what would have happened were it not for Viktor, who a minute ago was taunting the militia from the front of the group, demanding that they identify the officer commanding this operation, an insane request from an improbable leader. What would he propose to do with this information? Pass it on to *The Washington Post*?

Viktor's right hand grasps Oksana above the elbow of her *tort Arakhis*–bearing left arm, and as someone returns to belting out "*Hatikvah*" for what must be the twentieth time, and as pushing and shoving intensifies, the young man pulls Oksana back from the edge, into the human cluster in the center, then, kneeling down, they slip deeper in, moving toward the noxious steely blue rays of the spotlight—then out.

They break into a sprint up Arkhipov, Viktor slightly ahead, Oksana's right hand in his, finding a sacred form of motion that lies between ski and skate, in the middle, her Czech-booted movement homage to the glory of Prague of not quite eight years ago, the place and time of gravity's near defeat.

They turn off into the darkness of a gateway to a courtyard off Maroseyka, which is the real name of this street, fuck Bogdan Khmelnitsky and his marauding, pogroming Cossacks, down with the tanks, down with truck-borne lights that rape the night. Some battles run uninterrupted, sheltered from the tyranny of chronology, freed from fact, falling into a sacred cadence of their own. It doesn't matter what came first. Polarity is what matters, not the order of things, not time, not place. Us. Them. "*Hatikvah's*" Russian verse will not be silenced on Arkhipov Street, East German Erikas with sticking "E" keys will tap out *1984*, symphonically, seven copies at a time. The Panzers will be stopped, stand firm, Decembrists, the fighters of the ghetto will not surrender, fly high, Tuskegee Airmen, *no pasaran*, and on Wenceslas Square the crowd will not disperse.

Can you come to the square,
Dare you come to the square,
Can you come to the square,
Dare you come to the square,
When that hour strikes?!

In the gateway, they stop long enough to look around. There is no pursuit.

In the safety of the archway of 9/2 Maroseyka, Oksana takes both Viktor's hands in hers, and standing with her back against the crumbling stucco of a deep passageway too narrow for a horse and buggy, she kisses him.

She kisses him because her heart is beating exactly as rapidly as his, because she is breathing deeper than ever before, because snowflakes glisten amid her tight, stiff, black curls, because she belongs, because of her longing to belong more—because of the rapturous nobility of it all.

Even photographing the execution and progression of a kiss captures only its outward manifestations, and the experience of the initiator of a kiss can differ from that of its object.

In analyzing this kiss, we will rise above the subjective. Does Oksana expect to extract temporal advantage from kissing Viktor? Is she cognizant of the sequelae her actions have already triggered, a cascade that can no longer be halted? How is it possible to seek union with a man who has made himself into a pariah, eliminating any prospects for advancement he might have had in a country that barely allows emigration and may never let him leave?

A mesh bag hangs down from Oksana's left wrist.

"What is it, in your bag?"

"*Tort Arakhis.*"

On November 29, 1975, the morning sun plays a joyful game in Oksana's unruly hair next to Viktor's prematurely receding hairline. Rebecca of robust black hair is in Viktor's arms.

She looks at him, and he is as she remembers. His oversized lower jaw with a slight overbite on the right is balanced by an underbite on the left.

They are on a mattress on the floor. The room is large and mostly empty.

Two clock faces, side by side, look down from a yellow poster above the mattress.

One clock is painted the colors of the Italian flag, the other French.

"FLY TO ISRAEL.

"Fly EL AL Israel Airlines.

"5 hours from Rome.

"8 hours from Paris."

On the floor, within a step or two from the mattress, atop Oksana's plaid Czech mohair scarf, her Czech tiger-striped mohair overcoat, her Prague suede boots, her dark-blue dress, etc., rests a white mesh bag with a battered cardboard box that still contains an almost intact *tort Arakhis*.

It is their first meal, a sacrament.

6.

They spend Saturday, November 29, Oksana's twenty-seventh birthday, in bed.

Schools are open on Saturdays, but Oksana's class is going on a field trip to the Lenin Museum, and since she isn't the one leading this "cultural excursion," she has a day off.

Midmorning, snow begins to fall. Oksana draws open the gauzy brown polyester curtains, and for the rest of the day, when she and Viktor aren't busy with each other, from the mattress they watch snowflakes descend onto the roof of the building across the courtyard.

It's a steep roof—copper, green with patina, an artifact of another time, before the mansions were carved up into communal flats, a survivor of a century of frosts and wars. Oksana loves snow more than she loves flowers.

As night falls, the lovers take a walk through the winding streets that branch off Arbat, meandering through the courtyards, those secret passages you know because you do, because of all that makes Moscow Moscow and you you.

Oksana feels a new certainty. No, strike that, not certainty. "Certain" is not the word for what she is. She feels obedience; not to Viktor, of course, but to something bigger, a feeling that she is being led by a force that she is not quite able to identify. Is it inside her or out? Do such distinctions matter? You can't dissect a force. You get nothing if you try.

Viktor is not a native Muscovite, but he has learned, and Oksana—a native whose Moscowness gets close to the boundary of snobbery and stops—approvingly follows through the maze of courtyards, snowdrifts, and doorways. Yes, Viktor knows these magical, winding streets.

It's snowing lightly, a dusting. Somewhere in their meanderings, Oksana quotes a line from an Okudzhava song about Arbat, half singing it: "*Peshekhody tvoi lyudi nevelikiye*" (Your pedestrians are people unremarkable), and he responds with the next line, "*Kablukami stuchat, po tebe speshat*" (Their heels clang on you as they rush along). There is no Moscow without Arbat, no Arbat without Okudzhava. Oksana will try more Okudzhava on Viktor later, but he will pass, she knows. Surely, he knows Galich, too.

"If I were to leave tomorrow, you know what I'd miss?" she asks.

He looks at her in silence.

"Sometimes, overnight so much snow falls that they cannot clear it, and it keeps falling. This happens once a year, maybe. Have you seen that?"

Viktor nods.

"On those mornings, I call in sick, put on my skis, and go out onto the streets, Arbat, the Garden Ring, the embankments. Especially the embankments. I would miss that."

They drift toward Red Square, wordlessly, purposelessly, and if you happened to be walking behind them, you saw with a surprising degree of certainty that their love is new and that they had spent the day making love and watching snow deflect from a copper roof.

"Will you come with me, to Israel?"

"Maybe. Probably. Yes."

"Next time I apply, we will apply together."

"How?"

"With you as my wife."

"But we've just met—last night."

"Time is that which we are given. We don't make time."

"Ah, time, space. Hyphenated? You are a philosopher, a physicist?"

"An engineer, not much of one . . . was, sort of."

"What if we don't like each other next week?"

"We will like each other next week."

"What about next month?"

"Don't you just know—instantly, for the whole life?"

"Maybe. My parents have been divorced, multiple times, both of them. What if we like each other for exactly one year, and that's it—no more?"

"Israel has divorce. It's a civilized country, a liberal country, European, sort of."

"I guess that could be done."

She takes his hand in hers as they walk toward Lobnoye Mesto, a white, round elevated platform near St. Basil's Cathedral and the Spasskaya Tower of the Kremlin. Any schoolchild—especially the boys—will tell you that this was the place of public beheadings. It was not. From this white platform the czar's *ukazy* were read to the people. It was a podium, that's all.

The Old Man, had the devil not taken him when he did, was getting ready to start using this spot for public executions—of Jewish doctors—in March 1953, not quite twenty-three years ago.

For Oksana this is a monument of another sort. This is where in August 1968 Larissa Bogoraz and her valorous comrades unfurled a banner in protest of the invasion of Czechoslovakia. Theirs was one of the protests that filled Oksana's heart with pride. Yesterday, this pride had led her down Arkhipov Street to the Moscow Choral Synagogue.

On Sunday, November 30, they wake up with an unfamiliar feeling of calm—an absence of all urgency. Let's leave them alone in bed for another hour—another half hour to keep doing what they've just started, then a nap.

It's 11:09.

"I want to understand something about who you are. What was it like for you in Kiev?"

"The city or my place in it?"

"Either. What did your family talk about?"

"Acquisitions."

"Big things? Cars? Dachas? Cooperative apartments?"

"No. East German wall systems with glass shelves and the whatnots to put in them."

"I am afraid to ask."

"Lomonosov china—the kind with the blue netlike pattern."

"It bespeaks prosperity—yes."

"There were figurines on sundry Russian themes. Soviet bourgeoisie collects figurines. There was a full set of characters from *The Inspector General*. My mother started that collection, and after she died, my stepmother completed it. Those figurines in the breakfront have ruined *The Inspector General* for me."

"We'll have to address that. I'll look for tickets. I have a friend at the Gogol Theater. You can't have Bulgakov without Gogol. You haven't told me what kind of an engineer you are."

"Mediocre—on good days."

"Mechanical? Civil? Electrical?"

"Boring. I was a young specialist at the Department of Turbo-drills, Core Sampling and Special Tools of the All-Union Scientific Research Institute of Boring Technology. Until the morning of October twenty-ninth, 1973, when I was thrown out of the job after asking for verification of employment for my exit visa application. I wanted them to certify that I had no access to state secrets."

"Were you sad when you were fired?"

"It was the happiest day of my life. I ran to the Moskva River, next to the Kremlin—the place where they blew up the Cathedral of Christ the Saviour."

"You made a pilgrimage? You prostrated yourself?"

"Not quite. I went there to cast my slide rule onto the moving ice."

"And?"

"I watched that cursed instrument bobble on the surface, worrying that it might open up squid-like, suck in icy water, expel it rapidly, and use the energy of recoil to leap back into my pocket."

"Did it?"

"No. It was subsumed by a twenty-meter chunk of ice, and I performed a dance, stomping primally, until I attempted a kick that caused pain."

"I wish I could have danced with you."

"Now—my turn to ask questions."

"What do you want to know?"

"What you ate as a child, a girl turned loose on the big city with a handful of kopeks in your pocket."

"What age?"

"Nine, maybe. What was there to eat?"

"If you know that, you will know something important. It hasn't changed since I was nine. But you'll be sworn to secrecy. You swear?"

"I swear."

"Then let's put on clothes, and let's be off to the Metro! Outside Kirovskaya, there is a pirozhki seller with the best meat pies in this city! I call them pies with meat filling, they say it's cat meat.* They are deep-fried, in motor oil, they say. The onions are what gives them the flavor—ten kopeks for a *pirozhok* with cat meat, five kopeks for a *pirozhok* with jam. The ones with jam aren't worse. Let's go!"

Oksana jumps out of bed—or, to be exact, jumps up from the mattress—quickly putting on the blue dress.

"They sell out!"

By noon, the lovers are seen on a marble bench by the Gri-boyedov statue, devouring both kinds of pies—with meat and with jam.

"They really are deep-fried in high-viscosity motor oil," says Viktor. "You are right."

"That's what makes them so good."

"It's not just high-viscosity motor oil; it's high-viscosity *used* motor oil. That's what gives it this deep, smoky taste. I know this because I am a boring engineer, which is kind of like mechanical, but with a dash of civil."

"Whatever it is, I love this deep, smoky taste! This one, mine, with jam, is a chef d'oeuvre, by the way."

"What do we eat next?"

"We go to the ice-cream lady at that kiosk—operating next to the pie lady with a pushcart—and procure two portions of ice cream. I prefer a cup of fruit-flavored ice—there is no fruit in-volved in generating its flavor. Citrus is tolerable, too, if you must. It's seven kopeks either way! They give you a cup and a wooden tongue depressor. Did you have anything like this in Kiev?"

---

* Котятина.

"It's not about me, and we aren't in Kiev. And no—eating street food wasn't traditional in my household or my school. One could get whipped for less. I certainly could. My father loved using his belt to uphold discipline."

"Oh . . . We are permissive here in Moscow. Which ice cream will you have?"

"Fruit."

"We are eating them on the hoof. We must get *ponchiki*.* Kiosk on Lermontovskaya—across from the skyscraper—before they make all the doughnuts and they get cold. You want hot!"

"Indeed—doughnuts!"

They cover the distance from Griboyedov to Lermontov in less than ten minutes, a feat, considering that they finish the fruit ice cream soon after passing by the crumbling Le Corbusier structure of the Central Statistical Bureau.

"My classroom windows overlook the back of this. It's even more stunning from the back. I love it so much that sometimes I can't concentrate on teaching."

"We should go to Lyon. That's where Le Corbusier did most of his work."

"I didn't know this about you . . . You know Le Corbusier, his buildings?"

"I've learned a little about a lot."

The doughnut kiosk, located at the edge of a small park in front of the exit from Lermontovskaya Metro station, is open only when they have the dough and the doughnut-maker feels like working.

At 12:37, the doughnuts are not just available, but piping hot.

---

* Doughnuts.

"Here you ask for four doughnuts, and they sell them to you by weight, not by the piece. Two doughnuts could cost you as little as seventeen kopeks or as much as twenty-one kopeks. You must always have extra coins. But they are generous with powdered sugar."

They get four doughnuts and quickly consume them at a stand at the side of the kiosk.

"What did I tell you?"

They get eight more.

"What do we eat next?"

"*Chebureki*, what else?"

"Where?"

"On Tsvetnoy Boulevard. Café Kavkaz, in front of *Literaturka*.* Need to catch the B or the 10 across the street. Let's go! Long live gluttony!"

"Long live gluttony!"

Readers familiar with such tours of Moscow would not be surprised to see Oksana and Viktor at Café Cosmos, on Gorky Street, two hours later. Viktor orders crème brûlée ice cream with cherry sauce. Oksana orders vanilla with chocolate sauce and a sprinkling of peanuts—*arakhis*.

Viktor votes nay on Oksana's suggestion to stop for "milk cocktails" and eclairs at Gastronom No. 40. He doesn't like the view, he says, referring to the ominous gates of the KGB headquarters.

They walk down Kirovskaya roughly to the spot where the gluttony tour began, and on Griboyedovskaya past the Palace of Marriages, a place that was once and remains a palace. It's

---

* *The Literary Gazette.*

painted a shade of malachite, the intricate trim around its windows white.

Oksana steps away from Viktor and pulls the door. Is this not a reasonable joke in the context of a couple that has been in bed for thirty-six of the past forty-four hours? Also, it's a Sunday, for God's sake. How can a Soviet building be open on a Sunday?

Unbeknownst to Oksana and Viktor, the Palace of Marriages is open from 3:00 to 6:00 p.m. on the last Sunday (and Monday) of every month, and in November 1975, the last Sunday falls on November 30.

The door opens.

Viktor follows Oksana as they walk past a stooped cleaning woman mopping the white marble steps, through the hallway. At the top of the stairs, Oksana's steps suddenly turn into a dance. The dance starts on a whim, another in a series of half-hearted jokes brought on by lovemaking, if not love itself; the dance is unmistakably a waltz, Viennese to a fault, with Oksana leading and Viktor, the Young Pioneer who wouldn't march, following woodenly, at the outer bound of his minimal ability, across the mansion's parquet. Natasha Rostova does something like that in a very similar setting, if you recall the book or at least the movie.

They stop the waltz at a doorway to what looks like an office, where they encounter a Soviet madame* who doesn't seem to be doing anything in particular, which is just fine, because in the context in which she operates the act of sitting constitutes a tangible output subject to being measured in man-hours.

SOVIET MADAME: We are open, but we are not holding office hours. Take the application for marriage and leave.

---

* Советская тётя.

VIKTOR: What if, let's say, we fill out the marriage application and return tomorrow, what happens next?

SOV. MME: You will wait.

VIKTOR: For what?

SOV. MME: For the application to be reviewed and acted upon.

VIKTOR: How long does that take?

SOV. MME: One to three months.

VIKTOR: Who gets one month? Who gets three?

SOV. MME: If you were born the same year, you get priority.

VIKTOR: Why? What does being born the same year signify to you?

SOV. MME: We don't write the regulations. They are written for us, and we implement them.

VIKTOR: Were we born the same year, Oksanochka?

OKSANA: I don't know. I was born in 1949.

SOV. MME: Month?

OKSANA: November.

SOV. MME: And you?

VIKTOR: 1947.

SOV. MME: Month?

VIKTOR: June.

SOV. MME: Not same year. No priority. Three months.

VIKTOR: This is an illogical rule—unscientific. Have people born the same year been shown to produce more battle-worthy sons and daughters with wider hips? Why do you have such stultifying, incomprehensible rules?

SOV. MME: Please don't waste my time. Our office implements instructions. Take an application, fill it out, and come back—if you wish. The state is not the one telling you to get married. The state doesn't care what you do.

VIKTOR: If only that last thing you said were true! But let us suppose for a moment that we were not born the same year, but that we have extenuating circumstances?

SOV. MME: Pregnancy doesn't concern us, unless you are currently married to other citizens, which would make this attempt at marriage polygamy, which would be a criminal matter.

OKSANA: That's not the case. None of it is.

SOV. MME: Then what is?

VIKTOR: If you really must know, we want to emigrate to Israel. We want to file an application together, as a married couple, you see, as is our right.

SOV. MME: Hmm . . . This is a first . . .

VIKTOR: Do you have a rule that precludes people seeking to emigrate to Israel from getting married prior to departure from the USSR?

SOV. MME: We don't take such situations into consideration. Only year of birth and concurrent marriages.

VIKTOR: I see. Oksanochka, maybe we should consider a religious ceremony.

OKSANA: How do you do that?

SOV. MME: A church wedding?

VIKTOR: Jewish. Synagogue. Not church.

SOV. MME: Synagogue?

VIKTOR: No, that's not an option, you are right. The rabbi is a pig, but you don't need a rabbi for a Jewish wedding, I don't think.

OKSANA: How do you know that?

VIKTOR: Read it somewhere, probably Feuchtwanger.

SOV. MME: Not church? Not even synagogue? I've never heard of synagogue weddings in my thirty years here, by the way.

OKSANA: Jewish wedding? Is that possible? *Are* there Jewish weddings?

VIKTOR: Must be, somewhere. Why not here? Why not us?

SOV. MME: Because they are not recognized by the state?

VIKTOR: I am a citizen of the state of Israel.

SOV. MME: You can do anything you wish. Church. Synagogue. You can even dance naked around a bonfire and pronounce yourselves man and wife—it's your business. But listen to me, comrades, if you wish to enter into a marriage recognized by the Soviet state, you must fill out one of those forms you see in the reception room; fill it out, present all the information required, and wait.

VIKTOR: Until when?

SOV. MME: Until you hear.

OKSANA: For a month?

SOV. MME: Three. Minimum.

"Do you want to pick up an application and put our names on the waiting list, just in case?" Oksana asks as the door of the Palace of Marriages closes.

"Oksan, why do we need their louse-infested registration of marriages to validate our love? The Soviet Union has been in place for just fifty-eight years—historically, it's not even day before yesterday. We, Jews, have been around for . . ."

Pointing at the Moscow sky, Viktor slowly completes the sentence: "Three . . . thousand . . . years! When was Abraham? Three thousand? Four? Do we even know what happened here, on this spot, four thousand years ago?

"Hunter-gatherers, in skins, sat in trees like this one. Waiting for saber-toothed tigers. They weren't even the sort of barbarians who took up arms and sacked Rome. Rome was too far and not yet worth sacking. No telephone, no telegraph—they didn't know how to grow crops. They lived in ice caves and clobbered each other with sticks. They still do."

Oksana thinks he might be done, but he has more:

"What right do these snot-nosed Bolsheviks have to slow us down? On what basis? Me, a citizen of Israel."

"What is that about? Is that even true?"

"Technically, yes. Israel has a law called the Law of Return. You are a citizen the minute you get there."

"So you just have to get there?"

"Yes."

They walk in silence along the Boulevard Ring, near Sretenskiy Boulevard.

"Would you know how to have a Jewish wedding?" she asks. "Because I don't."

"I should still have a little red brochure from Montreal, Canada, in my room somewhere, unless they took it at the search two weeks ago. Let them argue that a Jewish wedding is not a valid wedding. The Jewish organizations, and therefore the American Congress, will not be amused. We could ask someone to appeal to Kissinger himself."

They spend Sunday night at Oksana's apartment in Zamoskvorechye, not far from Gorky Park.

It's a one-room apartment at a building originally occupied by the academy members, obtained through a series of complex exchanges that tracked a series of parental divorces. These divorces and their real estate sequelae can be enumerated in mind-numbing detail, but neither the teller nor the listener would become a better human being as a result of this transfer of data.

The place, 17 Bol'shaya Polyanka, overlooks a small park with the recently dedicated statue of Bulgarian Communist leader Georgi Dimitrov. In bronze, Comrade Dimitrov holds up his right arm at an awkward forty-five-degree angle. This position and, more importantly, the clenched fist, while intended to symbolize the Bulgarian Communist's preparedness for heroic struggle, is widely interpreted as a bragging allusion to penis size.

Extrapolating from the dimensions of the statue vs. human proportions, it would compare favorably with the largest of stallions. Some observers extend this interpretation further, seeing a reference to an activity in which Comrade Dimitrov may have engaged moments earlier. The statue is thus referred to as "Медный онанист" (the Bronze Onanist), or "Болгарский дрочитель" (the Bulgarian Wanker). The alignment of the hips and the sculptor's decision to insert the subject's left hand deep into the pocket of baggy pants further lend credibility to this interpretation.

A story is told about pranksters, students all, who were arrested for placing a bar of soap or another foam-generating substance into Comrade Dimitrov's fist. The students were said to have been convicted of hooliganism, even though, technically, anti-Soviet propaganda—Article 190–1—could have been invoked.

On Monday, December 1, Oksana expects to be called into Ghryu's office and summarily fired.

By the end of the day, she is pleasantly surprised to remain employed. When the exact same thing happens—or doesn't happen—on Tuesday, December 2, Oksana starts to wonder whether someone at the KGB has screwed up the processing of photographs and subsequent identification of individuals.

Viktor is away on Monday and Tuesday, taking a trip to meet with refuseniks in the provinces.

When Ghryu calls her in on Wednesday afternoon—this is December 3—she doesn't offer tea and *tort Arakhis*. Instead, she launches into a torrent of obscenities:

"I thought you were one of us, *ghryu*, and you are, *ghryu*, a Zionist bitch. Slut. Have you decided to go off to their Israel, *ghryu*, after everything that, *ghryu*, our Motherland has done for you, *ghryu*."*

If you were to count the number of times Ghryu says "*ghryu*," or "I say," the unfortunate expression to which she owes her nickname, you might conclude that she is teetering on the verge of physically harming her young soon-to-be-former subordinate.

You would have no way of knowing that Ghryu begins this oration by pointing at the grate in the ceiling or that in front of her she is holding a piece of paper on which she has written, "Good going, Oksanka, get out of this fucking country!"†

On the same piece of paper—while keeping up the torrent of insults that would have made a *politzek* cringe—Ghryu offers to connect her with a friend who could get her a job as a Negro. (The word "Negro" in Moscow describes people who toil without getting credit—doing translations, writing dissertations, getting paid under the table. There is hardly a dissident who hasn't toiled as a Negro.)

"Negro! Ha! You can honor your historical roots," Ghryu jots down with an impish smile while continuing her audible torrent of insults. Oksana returns the smile. Yes, Ghryu knows about the genuine Negro in Oksana's past—there is one. Nothing like a trace of Africa to make a girl look so perfectly Ashkenazi.

---

* Я думала ты наша, а ты говно, грю—сучка ты их сионистская. Блядь. Что-ж, ты, в их Израиль собралась, грю, после всего, что тебе, грю, наша, грю, родина сделала—грю . . .

† "Молодец, Оксанка—беги из этой мудацкой страны!"

Ghryu takes another drag of Belomorkanal, emits another complex torrent of insults and dry, asthmatic hacking and wheezing, and jots down: "Пришли мне вызов как-нибудь. Я-ж тоже еврейка по батюшке."*

"Выходи из моего кабинета в слезах, дура,"† she writes finally, setting a match to the piece of paper while continuing her verbal onslaught.

"Thank you, Ghryu."

Oksana has never called her mentor Ghryu before. Now that their professional relationship is over, she can.

---

* "Send me an invitation someday. I am also Jewish, on my father's side."
† "Be in tears as you leave my office, you fool."

PART III

7.

The U.S. Embassy and Sad Sam are a few blocks apart. If you don't know about the trolleybuses—routes B and 10—you walk it, even when the weather sucks.

It's late afternoon, January 15, 1976. Mad Dog has wasted a couple of hours at a going-away party for the press attaché, who is returning to Foggy Bottom or, more likely, Langley. The place was in a state of anxiety verging on panic. Kissinger, known as HAK around here, will pop into town in one week to the day. No one talks shit about HAK better than Alan Foxman, a curmudgeonly Foreign Service Officer who has something to do with public groups. Yes, HAK is famously abusive to the *untermenschen*, but he is a fact of life, like stroke, cancer, and diabetes—deal with it. And—don't forget—HAK is a Harvard man. He made the cut, quotas notwithstanding—unlike Foxman.

The press attaché is a recovering alcoholic, and the bon voyage was an early-afternoon tea-and-cookies affair. Mercifully, the guests included a Marine lieutenant who had a flask. The United States Marines are generous with their hooch. Mad Dog guesses it was Jack Daniel's. No Foxman, though. It's just as well. He has been trying to give Mad Dog a briefing on the Helsinki agreement and its newly discovered potential—probably the same nonsense he heard from Glum Viktor and Tedious Schwartz. Foxman's job is to keep track of what giants of their ilk are thinking.

Getting soused in midafternoon is one of the perks of being a foreign correspondent and administering a bustling bureau of one. If you glance at Mad Dog walking merrily past Mayakovsky Square, you might mistake him for a young Soviet engineer in a cheap, scratchy but warm overcoat. On closer look, you might notice that his scarf is Burberry, plaid, green, red, etc., the sort that shouts, "Merry Christmas, goyim." His boots are Willis & Geiger, purchased by his mother, Miriam "Mary" Dymshitz, at Abercrombie & Fitch. W&Gs are indestructible, but their soles are white rubber. They look sharp, but for the love of God, who but a foreigner wears white-soled boots in Moscow in January 1976?

Mayakovsky Square is intended to make you forget that there was ever such a thing as subtlety. It bangs on your skull like Maya-kovskyan staccato, but beyond that its relationship with the Poet of the Revolution is a fraught one. The colossal statue of Mayakovsky sticks out amid the frigid waves of asphalt, his bronze hairdo eter-nally billowing in the winds that sweep this vastness. His gaze is resolute, the jacket of his baggy suit—frigid metal channel-ing gabardine—is open. If the future looks so grand, so heroic, Comrade Mayakovsky, why did you put a bullet in your heart at age thirty-seven? They said it was love, or lack thereof. Is a bullet through the heart from your own revolver in 1930 preferable to a bullet through the back of the head from someone else's in 1937? One good thing about Mayakovsky: he is translatable. Staccato in Russian is staccato in any language, probably, a ladder is a ladder. Even a sophomore at Harvard can translate Mayakovsky and feel good about his conquest of the Russian language.

So, Mayakovsky is a good poet, significant, great even, maybe— and that's the thing: complexity, subtlety. Shit . . .

Imagine all the ghosts of the Big Potato staging a convocation, rising out of mass graves, open pits, the NKVD basements. Would they choose this square, to creak silently beneath Comrade Mayakovsky, to thank him for the revolution he is the poet of? Uppercase "the" and "poet." The Poet. As Mad Dog sees it, the shadow of Mayakovsky himself would probably wish to pass beneath his own pedestal, a revolver in hand.

Since we are on the subject of Mayakovsky-the-person, being a modernist, he'd probably want to set up a howitzer and blow the clock tower and the statues off the top of that Stalin-era monstrosity over there, across the way. Mercifully, the statue is sited to shield The Poet from ever facing that thing.

That thing there is as far from futurism, or modernism, or anything Mayakovskian as you can imagine: the clock tower, heroic statues, hanging colonnades, balconies, sundry whatnots that threaten to crack and crumble onto the skulls of pedestrians below. You'd think totalitarian architecture bespeaks permanence. No. It makes shit fall on your head.

There is the Peking restaurant on this square, in that very building. This Peking is nothing like the hole-in-the-wall Chinese eateries we love. It's a place massive enough to bellow, "Avoid me!" from the depth of its irritable bowels, and living in the Big Potato you learn to recognize places that will get you bogged down, make you listen to a moronic band, and send you home to nurse gastritis and breed salmonella.

Melissa wanted to go there on her birthday, except she hightailed it back to Connecticut a full month before that could happen.

Bulgakov's flat was somewhere near here, they say, as are the Patriarch's Ponds, the setting of the opening of the novel Mad Dog once started to read, and will, if he senses a story in it—a feature perhaps, a human-interest number. He used to be a hard-news guy, a steaming factory of news-gathering and analysis—now he has to file an occasional feature, which he does quite well.

Bulgakov didn't come up in any of the classes he and Melissa took at Harvard, but on the first leg of their journey to Moscow, the flight to Frankfurt, Melissa started to read *The Master and Margarita*. Once they got to Sad Sam, she tried to figure out where the story was set—the address of the apartment where, per Bulgakov, Satan and his retinue set up residence sometime in the 1930s. The street existed and was easily found, but the building didn't seem to exist. And she did locate Patriarch's Ponds, the place where someone's head gets cut off by a tramway as the story begins. Except the tramway tracks were gone; Melissa kept telling him all this, and he pretended to care.

You can keep yourself quite busy in Moscow. At one point, they talked about buying up unofficial art—she had a degree in art history, so it fit. You can make a fine business of picking art old and new and shipping it via pouch, through Foxman et al. But Melissa didn't get around to that. She just kept rereading the same fucking novel, again, and again, and again. Mad Dog will try to implement this business idea now, as a sideline—without her. He has identified a piece he wants to acquire, actually.

After Melissa's flight, Mad Dog looked at her copy of that novel of hers. It was dog-eared and underlined. One section was underlined in red pen:

"Was she happy? Not for a moment!"

Of course, Mad Dog immediately recognized the farewell note she had banged out on his typewriter. You don't forget such things. Was Melissa referring to Mad Dog or the Big Potato? She was losing her equilibrium, no question. Like when they stopped having sex because Melissa feared that their bedroom was bugged. Maybe it was, maybe it wasn't, who knows, who cares. And why did she leave that novel behind? Maybe because she didn't need it anymore?

When your wife leaves, maybe for a brief period, maybe not, how do you deal with the aftermath? Let's say, for the sake of argument, that you are on the Western side of the Iron Curtain. You circle back to old girlfriends and old would-be girlfriends, maybe put a personal ad in *The New York Review of Books*.

Now, suppose you are here in the Big Potato. The U.S. Embassy is full of angry, semi-abandoned wives and strung out female Foreign Service Officers who are precluded from "fraternizing" with local men. It's a high-maintenance cohort, especially the pissed-off wives, and if Melissa returns, as he'd like her to, all sorts of details would come out, and things would get ugly.

You can set aside clapophobia and pay for sex. What can you catch that American antibiotics can't cure? Alas, nothing looks less enticing to Mad Dog than a Russian woman who has beautified herself for sex: hair chemically teased, blouse strategically unbuttoned, legs crossed.

The Committee for State Security has entire departments that care passionately about sexual satisfaction of foreigners. Many of the women at the National, Metropol, and Intourist hotels are probably bona fide freelance, but they have deals to operate in prime locations, turn one trick to feed the children, then turn two for the Motherland. That sort of thing can blow up in your face, too.

Mad Dog is not interested in the cheap and vulgar. Melissa has strings of pearls, Melissa has cashmere sweater ensembles in pastels, Melissa has practical turtlenecks with calico designs. Melissa is in Connecticut. He could curse Melissa for her selfishness, but would that make a difference? What do you do when—here Mad Dog makes an absolutely dead-on use of an expression he learned in a Harvard course on Russian vulgarisms—у тебя с конца капает—when it drips off your end?

You might be having a similar cascade of thoughts as you am-bulate toward Sad Sam after chugging a therapeutic dose of Jack Daniel's out of a flask—semper fidelis.

Mayakovsky Square—Mayakovka—is as crowded as Times Square. There is a theater here, Sovremennik, a place Mad Dog might have to write about, if the right news peg comes up.

In the midst of a rapid 4:30 crowd, Mad Dog feels a hand on his shoulder. He knows that it's a woman's hand, because no woman has touched him in the past three months, and even three months prior to Melissa's flight, sex was perfunctory. This is a tap on the shoulder, as far from sex as you can get, but the mind is a jumpy contraption.

Looking at the woman, Mad Dog quickly recognizes that his projections of steamy encounters were misplaced. She, whoever she is and whatever she wants, is the opposite of a KGB sexpot at the National, Metropol, and Intourist. Short, stout in a black kara-kul coat with a thin blue mink collar and a matching soft blob of a hat, she looks like somebody's mother standing on the precipice of becoming somebody's grandmother.

Her getup might have screamed prosperity a generation ago. It looks absurd now, a furry inheritance.

"You are journalist. American?" she says in Russian.

"How were you able to determine this?"

"By your walk. It's more decisive than ours."

"How can I be helpful?"

It's a stupid expression, not modern Russian, more reminis-cent of Chekhov than that bronze guy over on his left, he knows, but the OSS dicks at Harvard knew what they knew.

She motions to Mad Dog to bend down closer to her level.

"Does name Yezhov mean something to you?" she asks in article-*frei* English.

He nods.

Nikolai Yezhov . . . Yep . . . Stalin's executioner, head of the NKVD, or whatever the name was at the time, nicknamed the Bloody Dwarf, lasted a short time, but made the most of it—bad years, 1937, etc., a drunk, fucked everything he didn't kill, the girls, the boys, then turned around and killed everything he fucked—the man swam in booze, blood, and semen.

"I have something I want to discuss with you. He left diary with writings and drawings," she whispers.

"This is a dangerous place to talk. Meet me at exactly six in the crowd in front of Obraztsov Puppet Theater," Mad Dog suggests.

She nods.

The place is catty-corner from his apartment. It makes sense to meet there. There is a clock with puppets on the façade. Crowds gather there on the hour to watch the puppets come out. Not his thing, but crowds are safety, less of a chance of being seen.

The woman dives back into the crowd. Mad Dog stands still, frozen in place, mouth agape.

Mad Dog was not a snob about coffee. There was coffee in all the cafeterias he has known. In the newsroom canteens there are machines that spit out cardboard cups and fill them with a brown, warm substance. Melissa made coffee, even when things were bad, and since her flight, Mad Dog has been buying instant at the embassy commissary and dissolving three tablespoons per cup every morning to produce a passable swill. This time, four tablespoons are indicated to counteract the elixir he had chugged from the Marine lieutenant's flask.

At the bureau apartment complex, there is a copy of Robert Conquest's classic history, *The Great Terror*. It's been here for a decade, precisely in anticipation—make that the hope—of encountering opportunities like this one.

Mad Dog has just thirty minutes to thumb through the book before the rendezvous in that anonymous crowd in front of the puppet theater. It's a precaution, better than nothing, but, ultimately, you wonder whether the KGB has posted extra goons at that spot, considering its location across Sadovaya-Samotechnaya from Sad Sam.

Imagine obtaining Yezhov's memoir, or better yet, his diary! Did she say it was a diary? The Great Terror, a day-by-day account, in the perpetrator's own words. Some fine careers grew out of turning up lost memoirs of sundry murderers here in the Big Potato. Start with Khrushchev's memoirs, volumes of it, by the kilo. Yezhov is more interesting . . . Yezhov knew many writers, he killed many writers. But was the Bloody Dwarf himself . . . a writer? And, better yet, a doodler? A secret manuscript, a memoir of a murderer, with drawings by his own bloody hand. The Great Terror! The Inside Story! Illustrated by the Bloody Dwarf!

Is this middle-aged woman resplendent in black karakul and blue mink Yezhov's daughter? He had a stepdaughter, Mad Dog sees per Conquest.

Granddaughter maybe?

Every hour on the hour, the clock at the Obraztsov Puppet Theater attracts a crowd, people from out of town, mostly.

They think the figures that come out of the enclosures of a clock that occupies much of the theater's white marble façade are, for lack of a better word, endearing. Clocks are good that way: predictably, every sixty minutes you get a dose of reassurance. In a country that pounds ideological messages at every step, Obraztsov's puppets don't. They tango. They sing. They tell jokes about the lives of humans they purport to be. And—don't forget—the absence of politics is politics, too. Is it possible that they are lying in wait? Will they, too, rise some day? Whatever you do, don't trust a puppet.

Deep thoughts pass through Mad Dog's head as, Jack-Daniel's-ed and caffeinated, he watches the figures come out of their enclosures to spin and dance to a carousel tune.

The woman is next to him now. She is five feet tall at the most—same height as Yezhov.

"Here, put this in your pocket," she says, placing what looks like a rolled-up photograph in his hand.

The pockets of Mad Dog's Soviet coat are deep enough. He realizes suddenly that he should have done something about the bloodstains on the right sleeve. His ears are red now, burning, possibly frostbite-bound. In a rush, he forgot to crown his head with the bureau's pet dead muskrat.

"This is Yezhov's drawing, plan for execution chamber, in cellar."

"He was killed in one of those, yes?" Mad Dog says, lowering his ear to her level.

"Same one. In NKVD building in Varsonofyevskiy Pereulok, very near to here. There is drain in middle. You can wash blood and brain with rubber hose or bucket of water."

"Do you think you are followed?" he asks.

"I can't tell. Are you?"

"Not seeing my usual detail. Meet me over there, in that street, in five minutes," he says, pointing in the direction of a quiet street, where he often leaves the Chihuahuamobile. "I will be waiting in the third courtyard on the left."

"You mean meet on Bol'shoy Karetnyy?"

"No, that doesn't sound right."

"It was called Bol'shoy Karetnyy Pereulok till soon after Revolution. Now it's renamed after Yermolova, who was respected actress. Names change a lot here, except with this place more than name changed. Bol'shoy Karetnyy was '*pereulok*,' which means 'lane.' But when it was renamed after Yermolova it became '*ulitsa*,' which means 'street.' I can't always understand difference between *pereulok* and *ulitsa*, so I can't explain."

"That's okay. It's over there, whatever you call it. Third courtyard on the left. See you there."

"Who are you? Why do you have this material?" he asks as they meet in the courtyard off Yermolova (formerly Bol'shoy Karetnyy).

"My aunt was nanny of Yezhov's daughter. Natasha. Before he was repressed, Yezhov told her to take files, one at a time, when he was expecting the arrest."

"What do you have?"

"Diary, drawings, plans."

"What kind of drawings?"

"*Gomoerotika*, mostly. Naked male figures, their, excuse me, penises."

"What else?"

"Official, stamped, transcription of Yezhov's wife having sex with Sholokhov, author of *And Quiet Flows the Don*. You know about him?"

"I've read the book, saw the movie. It was assigned at Harvard."

"Yezhov had their hotel listened to and their sex meeting was transcripted. Not conspectized, but transcripted, word to word, including notations like, 'He leads her up to bed.' Then Yezhov confronted her, she denied it, but he showed her transcript and beat her cruelly. Is that right word? Cruelly?"

"Seems to be."

"My aunt saw that."

"Is your aunt living?"

"No. She was repressed, too, but survived and was rehabilitated in 1956. I spoke with her and can fill in details."

"Why are you doing this? Taking a risk, meeting with me?"

"My daughter is going to apply to leave to Israel, and I want her to benefit financially from these documents."

"Why do you speak English so well?"

"I am translator at the Central Statistical Bureau. English is my specialty. Written English, though. Economics texts, journal articles, indexing also."

"What do you want me to do?"

"I want you to get publisher in America, and to propagandize it."

"How will I contact you?"

"You will not. I will contact with you. Give me your telephone."

Mad Dog pulls the reporter's notebook out of his back pocket to jot down the bureau's phone number.

"Okay, you know the plus-one/minus-one code?"

"No."

"If I say two o'clock Tuesday, it means three o'clock Monday."

To make certain, Mad Dog writes down: "2 pm Tues = 3 pm Mon."

Also, his telephone number: "Bureau: 297–8656."

He rips the page out of his notebook and hands it to her.

"Call only from pay phones, of course," he says.

At the bureau-apartment, Mad Dog returns to thumbing through *The Great Terror*. Some of the stuff this woman gave him checks out. Most of it doesn't—including the juicy bit about Mrs. Yezhov's tryst with Mikhail Sholokhov, the guy who won the Nobel Prize for literature sometime in the sixties. Sholokhov was banging Mrs. Yezhov! How about that! These are new details, shit, even Conquest didn't know! Maybe he would write a foreword.

The xerox copy of a photograph this woman had given him is rolled up, held together with a rubber band, crumpled in places now. He would, of course, insist on getting the original. It's a sketch of a simple room with two doors and an aggressively sloped floor with a street-sized drain in the middle. It might have been a bath-house cabin, except instead of a showerhead there is a thick fire hose, specified unambiguously as "пожарный шланг." Who would have thought Yezhov's handwriting was so neat, so meticulous?

The same handwriting on top of the sketch identifies the room as "камера для экзекуции." Execution chamber.

If the NKVD shield—two crossed rifles—is an indication, this was an official document, a design concept rather than just a doodle.

So, there you have it: A would-be émigré trying to cash in on blood-soaked family lore. Make that family gore. You don't take material like that through customs. Access to the diplomatic pouch is what you need. Mad Dog can make that happen. He will just have to say yes to the source now and finagle the details later.

Mad Dog goes to the freezer and pours a steady stream of Stolichnaya into the bureau-owned martini glass. Can a guy be faulted for feeling giddy when things are going so well?

. . .

On January 16, Mad Dog's story about the Birds Market makes the paper:

RUSSIA, THE MOTHERLAND OF ST. BERNARDS

By Madison A. Dymshitz

MOSCOW—One might think that purebred dogs would be condemned as a form of bourgeois excess in this country of victorious revolution.

Not so.

When Ivan wants to buy a dog, he goes to the Birds Market, a set of hangars on the outskirts of Moscow. There, he enthusiastically plunks down 90 rubles, an equivalent of a teacher's one-month salary, to buy a six-week-old *Moskovskaya Storozhevaya* puppy.

At a glance, a *Moskovskaya Storozhevaya*—the breed's name means Moscow Watchdog—looks like a benign, slobbering St. Bernard, but don't stake your arm on it, the way this reporter did on a recent visit.

"They say our country's symbol is a bear," a man who identified himself as Arkady said as he stood beside a cardboard box of white-and-red puppies. "It's not. *Moskovskaya Storozhevaya* is a better symbol. It lies and it sleeps all day, but when it feels a threat, it will bite you—and bite hard."

Drawing on Viktor's "conspects," but not mentioning either Viktor or his role in the reportage, Mad Dog goes on to describe the day's events, including his injury.

Mad Dog and the gentleman identified as "Arkady" never

spoke directly. First, the guy spoke with Viktor, then he screamed at the bitch as she sank her fangs into Mad Dog's arm and refused to let go. It is therefore possible that Mad Dog made up the breezy quote in the third paragraph, just like he made up the name Arkady.

Mad Dog half expects to receive a call from Melissa, who would express concern about his sufferings and inform him that she has had enough Connecticut and would return to the Big Potato forthwith.

Mad Dog's phone doesn't ring the day the story appears, but records show that it does ring at 3:21 a.m. The incoming call is from Pittsburgh, Pennsylvania, from Mad Dog's father, Norman Dymshitz.

"I was bit by a dog, too; the last mistake that dog ever made. Have I told you about it?"

"Yes."

"It was in the forest, not far from Lvov, the Germans sent dogs ahead of them—idiots. All you do is let the dog have a bite, then hit it through the ribs with a bayonet, or what have you."

"My bite happened days ago. The wound has stopped bleeding and is healing fine, thank you, if that's what you are asking."

"What you need to treat your dog bite is very simple . . . The Russian word is 'перекись водорода.' I'll say it slowly: *perekis' vodoroda*."

It's been like this for as long as Mad Dog can remember: Mad Dog does something big, spectacular even, like beat the quotas and get into Harvard, and the old man diminishes it, tries to one-up. And what has the old bastard accomplished in his life? What is he other than a white-shoes-and-white-belt-wearing, Florida-going scrap metal dealer? A garbage man with a Cadillac is all he is. Mad Dog will not prostrate himself before the tyrant.

"I know how to say hydrogen peroxide in Russian, thank you."

This is not true. Mad Dog has just learned the words from his father seconds ago. In any case, the therapeutic window for hydrogen peroxide is as closed as the wound itself.

"You know, *boychik*, at first, I didn't think I wanted to visit you in Moscow, but now I think I will; *farvos nisht*?* Your mother is in remission again, she doesn't need me for a few months. Also, Lou Rosenblum, the guy who coined the word 'refusenik'—ever heard of him? He'd make a good story for you . . . But that's not the point . . . Lou says I must go there and maybe give some advice. You have room in your big, empty apartment for me, yes?"

"How do you know about it being empty?"

"I know, I know."

"Do I get a say in this?"

"You always get a say in everything, but I will do as I say. *Zay gezund*."†

With a resounding "Shit! Piss! Fuck!" Mad Dog slams down the receiver of his massive Soviet phone.

You can't escape from that old one-upping bastard! Not even to the Soviet Fucking Union! Half a fucking world away!

Just then, the telex awakens with an urgent communication, a note from the executive editor complimenting him on a "solid story painfully reported."

The story is, by the way, on page one, above the fold.

_____

* "Why not?"
† "Be well."

8.

S oon after Viktor became a refusenik, a group of visiting American lawyers showed up across the street from the Moscow Choral Synagogue. After striking up a conversation with Viktor, they asked him to take them around Moscow. They had already suffered through a stiff, official tour, which left them hungry to see something meaningful.

Viktor is not a tour guide, and he could have said no. Instead, he accepted the challenge. The next day, with no preparation, he improvised a tour of places that had meaning to him.

The tour begins on Red Square, near Lobnoye Mesto, the white stone platform, the spot where on August 25, 1968, Larissa Bogoraz and Pavel Litvinov led a demonstration protesting the Soviet invasion of Czechoslovakia. This is where the demonstrators unfurled their banners: "Long live free and independent Czechoslovakia" and "For your freedom and ours."

Then comes a walk down Gorky Street, to Pushkin Square, the site of the December 5, 1965, "glasnost meeting" protesting prosecution of the writers Sinyavsky and Daniel'. "Respect the Soviet Constitution," the protest signs read.

Viktor has organized his tour thematically and dramatically rather than geographically and chronologically. Hopping on a trolleybus, the tour circles back to Lubyanka, the massive complex of buildings housing the KGB. There, from the trolleybus, Viktor points at the colossal statue of Dzerzhinsky out front and tells a joke of one sort or another. Here is one possibility:

"How is Lubyanka the tallest building in Moscow?

"Because you can see Siberia from cellar."

It's an absurdist joke, which makes it resistant to translation. Not everyone gets it, even with a detailed explanation, but it's okay, everyone chuckles.*

Foreigners in Moscow are conspicuous and rarely observed on city buses, the Metro, tramways, and trolleybuses. People stare, especially if they understand what's being said.

The tour pops off the trolleybus and meanders through streets and courtyards in the direction of Arkhipov Street, to the Moscow Choral Synagogue. Before stepping inside, Viktor urges everyone to check out the prayer for the government of the USSR, in Russian and in Hebrew, displayed on a bas relief above the bimah, about even with the women's balcony:

"May He who blessed our fathers Abraham, Isaac and Jacob, who laid the path across the sea and a road through the mighty waters bless and preserve, and defend, and protect, and glorify, and aid, and trumpet, and exalt the Government of the USSR. May the Holy One, blessed be He, breathe life into it, and protect it from all the troubles, hardships, sadness and harms, and save it, and smite all the foes before it, and may all the tasks it sets forth be crowned with success. Amen."

Since talking is not allowed at the synagogue, the tour resumes across the street, at the spot where refuseniks gather. A chat ensues

---

* It's like this: The Lubyanka prison is in the cellar—and from there a prison camp in Siberia is a likely next destination. You can almost see it. Hence, the joke—the building is so tall that *even from its basement* you can see Siberia. It's complex, it doesn't translate, but it's presented as a joke, and they like Viktor, so they laugh. There are better KGB jokes around, but Viktor likes this one. Enough said.

in English and Russian. Viktor loves this portion, because it's direct, people to people.

From the synagogue, the tour catches a city bus to Albert Schwartz's. It's close, and it's a cue for everyone to drop off their stuff: books, magazines, money, Levi's. (What's happening in that apartment today? Is it under seal? Has another family moved in?)

Next stop is Chkalov Street, Andrei Dmitrievich Sakharov's. It's the last building before the Yauza River bridge, on the inner ring of the Garden Ring, catty-corner from the Kursk Railroad Station. They don't go in—Sakharov, a physicist and laureate of the Nobel Peace Prize, gets entirely too many visitors.

However, if Alik Ginzburg, now employed as Sakharov's personal secretary, has a moment and if he isn't too hungover, he might come out and talk with the group. If you are fortunate enough to get on Viktor's tour, there is a good chance that you know who Alik is, and that you admire him immensely, by reputation. How the hell can you not? Alik is, after all, one of the pioneers of dissent, a citizen journalist who has done time for compiling the White Book, a document that brings together the materials from the trial of Sinyavsky and Daniel', the writers convicted for having published their books in France.

Alik's other gig—besides being Sakharov's personal secretary, which is largely bullshit—is running a fund of assistance to political prisoners, an endeavor founded by Aleksandr Solzhenitsyn, a Nobel laureate for literature, who now lives in a village called Cavendish, in the state of Vermont.

A walk past a prison is an important part of the tour, too. The KGB Lefortovo Prison is especially relevant, though Butyrka, the place where Solzhenitsyn was once famously held, is quite good, too.

Sometimes, the tour concludes at the apartment of Larissa

Bogoraz, in Cheremushki. She is no longer married to Yuli Daniel', but her husband now—Tolya Marchenko—is a writer as well. Sometimes, rarely, he is in Moscow. (The authorities are using residency requirements creatively to keep him out.)

You can descend on Lyuda Alexeyeva, too, if she is able to clear an hour on her insane schedule. If her husband, Nikolai Williams, is in the right mood, he might start reciting poetry, his own, with Gumilyov, Brodsky, Korzhavin, and Esenin-Volpin thrown in for good measure. You might get him to recite his poem "Communists Caught a Young Lad."*

On the inaugural tour, the American lawyers asked Viktor for an overview of the articles in the RSFSR Criminal Code used to prosecute dissent. He loved the question and made it a standard part of the tour. Usually at a courtyard or a playground, with *toptuny* watching from the doorways or lurking behind trees, Viktor describes the practical difference between Article 190–1,† Article 70,‡ and Article 64.§

Article 190–1 is primarily a *samizdat* article. Its purpose is to punish those who produce copies of forbidden books, like Orwell, Leon Uris's *Exodus*, or almost anything by Solzhenitsyn. It's

---

* "Коммунисты поймали парнишку."

† "The systematic dissemination by word of mouth of deliberate fabrications that defame the Soviet political and social system, or the manufacture or dissemination in written, printed or other form of works of the same content." Punishable by up to three years of deprivation of freedom or corrective labor for a term not exceeding one year.

‡ "Agitation or propaganda carried on for the purpose of subverting or weakening the Soviet regime or of committing particular especially dangerous crimes against the state, or the [verbal] spreading for the same purpose of slanderous fabrications that defame the Soviet political and social system, or the circulation or preparation or keeping, for the same purpose, of literature of such content." Punishable by deprivation of freedom for up to seven years followed by up to five years of internal exile.

§ "Betrayal of the Motherland, i.e., actions deliberately committed by a citizen of the USSR to the detriment of its national independence, territorial integrity and military might." Penalties include execution.

political libel and slander. "Joke I told you on bus, in front of the KGB building, formally fits under Article 190–1," Viktor explains.

Article 70 is aimed at efforts to weaken the Soviet regime—it's used to prosecute dissent that goes beyond production of literature; Article 64 is treason. It was used to prosecute the band of Leningrad Jews who tried to hijack a plane. The authorities often bypass legal prosecution by declaring you insane. One frequently used diagnosis—"mild schizophrenia"—is used specifically to medicalize dissent.

One of the lawyers on the inaugural tour, a judge from California, called it "Democratic Moscow." Very few people have taken this tour—just visiting lawyers, academics, students, people associated with the American Jewish organizations called the Union of Councils for Soviet Jews and the Student Struggle for Soviet Jews.

Viktor has been leading roughly one tour per month. There is just one rule—money never changes hands.

On January 15, 1976, Viktor shepherds a group of students from Columbia University. Their professor, Monica Washington, has done the Democratic Moscow tour before—last year.

"Do you care if they don't let you into USSR ever again—until it falls apart?" Viktor asks the group as they meet at the appointed place, the white stone platform in front of St. Basil's Cathedral on Red Square—Larissa's spot.

"It may not be very long, historically speaking," he adds.

His English vocabulary is becoming so impressive that you can forgive him for skipping over the articles.

Of course, the goons who follow Viktor know that the tour begins here. But what can they do? Arrest a Jewish activist in front of a group of Americans? Arrest the group of Americans, too?

Maybe someday, but not now. You have to consider détente, you have to consider American wheat. Don't forget, Kissinger is coming to town on January 22, which is a week away.

"If you don't care, I don't—as a matter of solidarity," responds Professor Washington. "We aren't risking a tenth of what you are."

"A millionth," one of the students cuts in.

The student is long-haired, bearded, wearing one of those American puffy jackets. In fact, all the students and their professor are wearing very similar jackets, only in different colors. Viktor is wearing one as well. This kind of jacket is apparently called a "parka." A parka is a strange fashion statement. It looks like our *vatnik*, a quilted cloth jacket that laborers wear. If you see a *vatnik*, you are looking at a worker or a peasant. If you see a parka, the nylon-and-goose-down version of the same thing, you are most likely looking at a visitor from a capitalist country.

"Fuck yeah!" says another student.

"I like your enthusiasm," says Viktor.

"Okay, let's do it, whatever it is!"

"I've been meaning to try this for months now, and since Professor Washington is a recidivist on this tour, I would like to try it . . . Do you see that gentleman over there? The one between here and Lenin Mausoleum. He is looking down, diligently studying cobblestone. And there is another. He looks like he is looking for mushrooms. Except it's January. No mushrooms. And it's cobblestones, where mushrooms don't grow. Does everyone see them?"

Nods all around.

"Have you, in Columbia University Russian Department, learned Russian word 'топтун'?"

"'*Toptun*' translates as a 'stomper.' A goon, someone who follows you."

"Indeed, Professor Washington. As you can see, I have two *toptuny*, stompers, today. Sometimes I have three. Where I go, they go. I never look at them directly. I feel them with my back. Let us, as they say in America, fuck them up!"

"You are a sick motherfucker . . . You know this expression in English, Mr. Moroz?"

"I did not, until now, when I figured it out from context, Professor . . . But now it's important that we follow exactly same plan. Exactly—okay? Remember, we do this for sake of friendship between our peoples?"

"Right, Viktor, in the name of détente, long live Henry Kissinger!" answers Professor Washington. "Lunatic."

The following description of the ensuing events is based on documents generated by appropriate authorities:

The Subject meets a group of American students near Lobnoye Mesto. They confer briefly, after which the Subject leaves the group of Americans, heading toward GUM.

The Americans begin to move toward the Lenin Mausoleum, unceremoniously pass through the line, and view the burial site of I. V. Stalin and John Reed, etc. Following that, they take a left turn to Alexander's Garden.

The Subject is being monitored by a surveillance detail of two Operatives. A Mobile Unit is not deployed.

The Operatives make the decision to stay with the Subject, as it appears that Americans are now heading in the opposite direction, and their plans to conduct a tour have been suddenly terminated.

The Subject pursues a meandering path through GUM, dropping a coin in the fountain. Operative 1 follows at the protocol-specified optimal distance of fifty meters as the Subject steps into a cleaning supplies and housewares department, where he asks to examine a mop. Based on subsequent interviews with the sales staff, the Subject comments: "Какая у вас роскошная швабра."*

He leaves the cleaning supplies and housewares department without purchasing said mop.

The Subject exits GUM, returning to Red Square and proceeding to cross next to the State Historical Museum, with Operative 1 and Operative 2 following at protocol-prescribed distances.

The Subject accelerates his pace, then enters the complex of obelisks of the Grave of the Unknown Soldier, passing through it, with Operative 1 now following at a distance of twenty-five meters and Operative 2 at a distance of fifty meters (approx.).

At this point, a group of eight American students from Columbia University in New York City, state of New York, as well as the group leader, an American Negress, congregate in a circle in the proximity of the gate to the garden.

The Subject passes through the gate, followed by Operative 1.

At this moment, the group of Americans proceeds to surround Operative 1, photographing him from multiple cameras, some of which are equipped with flashing devices, which would have ordinarily been not needed in daylight. Operative 2 takes an evasive maneuver.

While Operative 1 is being photographed, the students and the professor in unison proceed to shout pro-détente slogans: "Long live Soviet-American friendship!" and "Long live Kissinger!" in English, and "Русский и янки братья навек!"†

The Subject—who had passed through that spot prior to Operative 1 being ensnared by Americans—returns briefly to join

---

* "What a luxurious mop you have."

† "The Russian and the Yankee are brothers for eternity."

the group of Americans and mockingly salutes Operative 1 and Operative 2, who is observing this incident from a safe distance.

After saluting, the Subject continues to walk away rapidly, taking a right turn to Manezh Square.

A detachment of regular militia arrives on the site of the disturbance and Americans are instructed to surrender their cameras. The task of exposing all film is completed without altercation and all photographic images of Operative 1 are expunged.

Surveillance of the Subject will resume following his return to established patterns.

Going down the escalator to the Moscow Metro, one of the young women in the Columbia group, apparently a gymnast, places her hands on one strip of the moving rubber railings and her feet on another, rising bridge-like over the rapidly moving escalator steps. Muscovites look glumly at this irresponsible and irreverent effort by an American to use urban transportation as mobile parallel bars.

"Thank you for teaching us lesson in democracy," says Viktor, stepping out from behind a massive white marble column.

"We didn't teach you anything. You taught us, Mr. Moroz," says Monica Washington.

"Okay, I say we change the order of things and go to Lefortovo, KGB prison. It's where quests for freedom end in our country."

"Do you ever worry about getting arrested?"

"Why be afraid? My friend Lyuda Alexeyeva says, 'If your friends go to Paris, you see nothing unusual about going to Paris. If your friends go to prison, you see nothing unusual about going to prison.'"

Was Viktor venerating his Inner Poseur, or did he feel indifferent toward events he lacked capacity to control? Though this question is beyond the scope of conventional information-gathering, dossiers provide a foundation for enhancing our hypotheses and channeling them into informed guesses.

Tours are Viktor's window onto the outside world, a reminder that he, a product of Soviet upbringing and education, is a man who can be understood, even respected, by outsiders. He is able to communicate with Americans and the British, anyone who speaks English or Russian, as one human being to another. His Democratic Moscow tour has grown into a profound act of friendship.

Professor Washington would never forget the question Viktor asked her that day, in the Metro, on the way to Lefortovo: "What is your opinion of Henry Kissinger?"

"He is a formidable adversary," she answered in Russian.

"Your adversary?"

"Everyone's adversary. Everyone but himself. It's a long discussion. The kind that takes half a liter of vodka to sort out, as your people say."*

"Do you understand him? As person? That's what's most important."

"Kissinger? As a person? I try not to, Viktor. Don't want to explore those labyrinths."

"Someone I know called him 'narcissistic prick.'"

"Sounds about right."

Viktor has more questions. Alas, it's time to get off the Metro.

---

* "Без пол-литра не разберёшься."

9.

D emocratic Moscow tours never fail to put Viktor in an uproariously good mood. After bidding adieu to the Columbia crew, he is walking along the snowy Arbat, toward his courtyard on Karmanitsky. He is here to pick up more of his things—surviving books mostly—and take them to Oksana's; the plan is, he will give up the rented room in a couple of weeks.

Viktor is wearing new L.L.Bean boots, another gift from Professor Washington. These boots were made for duck hunters in the state of Maine, she said. Designed for marshes, on Moscow sidewalks the boots emit squeaks of delight. So, at one instant, Viktor is listening to the music of his boots, and at another he finds himself in the back seat of a car he never saw approach, squeezed in between two men he doesn't recognize. Two more men, whom he also doesn't recognize, are in the front. Benign reasons for four men in heavy coats and big hats to travel in the same car do not exist.

Viktor looks at the dashboard and recognizes a Volga. A well-conducted operation of this sort—grabbing a man in the street at night—is intended to go quickly, so mission accomplished. Inside the car, the stench of cigarettes smoked long ago blends with the stench of cigarettes being smoked right now by these four guardians of state security, who are apparently so overwhelmed by desire to render good service to the Fatherland that they haven't slowed down to shower or launder their clothes in quite some time.

"I believe I was kidnapped by brigands," Viktor says to the man to his left. "Are you perchance a brigand, good sir?"*

Getting no response, Viktor turns to the man on his right.

"Yes, brigands, I am certain. Had I been detained by law enforcement authorities, they would have identified themselves and provided a document authorizing my detention."

Again, no answer. It's a good thing Viktor doesn't accept money for the Democratic Moscow tour. It would have been unpleasant to have been detained on Arbat with a pocketful of dollars.

Prostrating yourself before executioners is a flawed strategy. Licking their boots is imprudent. Projecting a nonchalant attitude about being plucked from the street, searched, arrested, interrogated, tried, imprisoned, etc., is more sensible, but the best way to mask fear is to have none to hide.

Viktor thinks of his search six weeks ago. He was on the telephone with Golden when the goons came. "I have uninvited guests," he announced to Golden, who proceeded to trumpet this urgent news bulletin across all of Moscow.

In a matter of minutes, friends started to show up, ringing the doorbell, trying to get in, then settling down on the stairs, playing chess, drinking coffee from thermoses. It's a tradition—show your solidarity, demonstrate your lack of fear. Schwartz showed up, the Sakharovs stopped by, Lyuda Alexeyeva brought candy, cookies, and a large pink thermos filled with hot tea. Everyone who showed up rang the bell once, and everyone shouted something—

---

* "Вы случайно не разбойник, добрый сэр?"

jokey words of support, mostly. Viktor sat in an armchair, watching the goons dig through his papers and stuff his belongings into canvas bags. Of course, there was enough for prosecution on some Article of the RSFSR Criminal Code, or, more likely, several.

At 3:00 a.m., as the goons opened the door and started to cart out the bags, Golden abandoned his chess game; he wasn't much of a player; Schwartz was murdering him.

Waiting for the chief of the search crew, Golden stood up from the stair, delivered a courtly bow, and uttered an invitation:

"Next time, you should come to search my apartment. I have superior taste."*

As the KGB Volga speeds through nighttime Moscow, Viktor continues the soliloquy:

"It seems that over the past fifty-eight years, the authorities in our country have evolved a curious doctrine, believing that while some laws apply to some citizens some of the time, the authorities charged with enforcing said laws are bound by no limitations whatsoever. Having read the Soviet Constitution deeply, seriously, more than once, I would have to conclude that it's not altogether a bad document. But having just been kidnapped by brigands in the center of Moscow, I have to conclude also that our constitution has limited practical relevance."

---

* His exact words, in Russian: "В следующий раз приходите ко мне. У меня вальяжный вкус." The word grudgingly translated above as "superior" doesn't do justice to this invitation. A Pushkinist, Golden used the largely antiquated word "вальяжный," pronounced *val'yazhnyy*, which stands for "solid," "monolithic," "significant," "great"—a vast range of meaning. His message—equating a KGB search with a social visit akin to a house tour—demonstrated utter lack of fear. Come to my place, bring your goons, bring your bags, and I'll show you my collection and offer you some tea. For reasons probably unrelated to this invitation, the same crew indeed showed up at Golden's later that week.

Viktor observes a smirk on the face of the driver. He continues:

"Brigands are bound by no laws. Woe is me; woe is me. Don't look for me, my dear mother. I will be robbed and hanged from a tree branch . . ."

The car drives through the gates of a darkened three-story building. The gates close.

Getting out, Viktor raises his hands, signaling surrender, but, clearly, these men are instructed not to react to being ridiculed.

"I see that the brigands have brought me to their lair," Viktor keeps on, looking at the square of starry sky framed by the buildings surrounding the courtyard. There are no bars on the windows. These buildings are not as tall as Lubyanka. Clearly, he is at one of the KGB satellite offices.

"Follow me," the man who was traveling in the front passenger seat instructs him.

Years ago, when they came to take the poet and law scholar Aleksandr Sergeyevich "Alik" Esenin-Volpin to an insane asylum, he refused to go.

"Не пойду,"* Alik said to them famously. It was slogan-worthy: "*Ne poydu.*"

Much of Viktor's improvisation in the back of the KGB car is owed to the teachings of Esenin-Volpin: The state must respect existing limitations on its power. Not cooperating with incursions upon individual freedoms is a moral imperative of a citizen. You do not cooperate with illegal detention when you are being illegally detained.

Viktor doesn't say "*Ne poydu.*"

He has already made his point.

---

* "I will not go."

. . .

Viktor has been through an interrogation, a year and a half ago. It was about someone else's case that had to do with production of *The Chronicle of Current Events*.

In that case, Viktor wasn't nabbed in the street. He received a notice in the mail, showed up at the specified address, met with a man in plainclothes, said that he couldn't recall a thing, and that was that. What could they do? Trepan his skull and see that he could, in fact, recall?

Alik Esenin-Volpin believed that lies are never acceptable, in any setting. Others believe that lies spun in dealings with Gestapo, the KGB, etc., to help your comrades are sacred.

At the previous interrogation, Viktor still had Moscow residency papers. Now he has no job, no official status. They could have him picked up for violation of "passport regime" at any time.

Perhaps this is it—time to perish. This morning, as he held Oksana, a flash of fear struck. He felt it reach deep into his soul. He held Oksana as she slept, then he left to conduct the Democratic Moscow tour.

Viktor would have felt less jittery if more people knew his name in the West. If he is arrested, there might be some stories in the press—by Krimsky, by Toth. Mad Dog would see no news value in Viktor's disappearance. He will find himself another guide dog and soldier on. Will the Union of Councils for Soviet Jews raise hell? Will the Student Struggle for Soviet Jews? They will try. Monica Washington, too, will spring into action as soon as she gets back to New York and gets the news, if she gets the news. Someone will need to pester U.S. congressmen, U.S. senators— and let's not forget Henry Kissinger. Maybe starting at that visit— seven days from now.

Viktor is led up a marble staircase, down a hallway, and into a room with a massive tall window, a prerevolutionary sort. It looks like someone had carved up a music room. Opening a heavy, ornate door, the plainclothes vanish.

The room is dominated by a mahogany desk that may be as old as this repurposed palace. The woman who stands up to greet him might be forty-five, perhaps a bit older. She is round-faced, shorter than Viktor even. There is a soft fold beneath her chin. Her blue velour dress is bell-shaped, topped off with a white lace collar. A large ivory cameo brooch holds the collar in place.

"Viktor Venyaminovich, I am happy to see you in person at last. I am Lydia Ivanovna, your curator."*

"I didn't know I am such a treasure that I warrant a curator."

He will try to keep his tone neutral, short of gruff.

There is no sacred imagery in the room—no Lenin, no Dzerzhinsky. The walls are freshly painted a shade of muted green, the color of Soviet official premises. This vaguely green surface rises to Viktor's entire height, which is to say to the shoulder level of an average male. Above it, the wall is vaguely white and very, very dirty. Above the palatial window, Viktor notices a water leak that has been devouring plaster on the ceiling for a decade or six.

"Please sit down. Would you care for tea?"

"Would I care for tea? Let me make certain I understand this, Lydia Ivanovna; you sent your falcons to nab me in the street to take me to a tea party? If I knew, I would have dressed for the occasion."

His tone has slipped into mockery, he knows.

"We don't have the luxury of establishing a dress code. Our

---

* "Виктор Веньяминович, рада вас наконец увидеть своими глазами. Я Лидия Ивановна, ваш куратор."

visitors show up dressed as they are at the time when our falcons, as you say, locate them."

"I am under arrest, I presume?"

"No, you are not, Viktor Venyaminovich. May I call you Viktor?"

"Please don't."

This woman doesn't look like someone who would kick you in the solar plexus—she is able to smile. Maybe their higher ranks are allowed to smile.

For whatever reason, they didn't give him to a hard-ass officer in KGB uniform, a Yezhov heir who gets his jollies from watching his victim squirm. That might have been simpler. When they press you hard, resistance is automatic, preprogrammed, Newtonian. Why did they choose a softer approach? In a blue velour dress with a lace collar and a large ivory cameo brooch, this curator of Viktor's seems to be attired for the funeral of somebody's grandmother.

"Viktor Venyaminovich, I am not certain that you appreciate that we have been charitable toward you. We have tolerated your chronic violation of residency laws. You could live in Moscow lawfully when you were employed—but that has ended. We have exercised restraint as we observed your dealings with the American correspondents. We have been lenient as we observed your infractions of currency laws—which occur every time you are paid for translating."

"Let the record show that Viktor Venyaminovich Moroz ignored this prompt to express gratitude toward the apparatus of state security for exercising prosecutorial lenience."

"Viktor Venyaminovich, you remind me of my children. This is why sometimes I fight the urge to call you Viktor or even Vitya."

"I feel no urge to call you Lida or even Lidochka."

"Let's be formal, then. I am worried about you, Viktor Venyaminovich. It seems likely that if we take your fingerprints, we will learn that you were on the scene of a gruesome murder, something very much like Dostoyevsky, except in Moscow—and men. I don't believe you are capable of committing this crime—so I am acting as your advocate in this matter."

"I did not request an advocate here at the organs of state security. Please let the record show this."

"You have made no such request, true, but you have an advocate nonetheless—a curator can serve as an advocate in some situations, unofficially, of course. No record is being made of this conversation. I want us to be able to speak freely—both of us. I am going to share sensitive internal information with you."

"Let the record show that I have not asked to be made privy to information of any sort, sensitive or not, internal or not, and that I have not agreed to any limitations on disclosure of any information, sensitive or not, that may or may not be shared with me."

"That was well phrased; I say this as an attorney."

"How would you know that I would not come out of here, call a press conference, and publicize whatever it is you are about to say?"

"You would not, because it will reflect badly on you—and would end badly."

"For me?"

"For you. You would be arrested and charged with killing two men."

"I have committed no crime. I wouldn't know how it's done—a single murder, let alone double."

"On January thirteenth, at a communal flat at 17 Chistoprudnyy Boulevard, two men were murdered with repeated blows of an ax. One was a currency operator, Albert Schwartz, known as the King of Refuseniks, and the other was a U.S. diplomat whose function was to interact with so-called public groups—Alan Foxman.

"Neighbors saw you entering that apartment, and we have

several excellent-quality fingerprints that we believe will confirm that you were at the scene. Would you like us to take your finger-prints now, for comparison?"

"You will do what you will do."

"What we will do—what I want to do—is prevent your arrest here, right now, by securing your help in investigating this crime."

"Aren't you an investigative agency?"

"This is a common misconception. Here at the Fifth Direc-torate of the Committee for State Security, we see ourselves as something akin to epidemiologists, a public health service. We control the spread of pathogens. Unfortunately, when we need in-formation like this, we get sloppy. Most of the time, we are dead-brained, self-important bureaucrats unable to get out of our office chairs. Viktor Venyaminovich, may I tell you a joke?"

Viktor nods.

"In 1967, for the fiftieth anniversary of the Great October So-cialist Revolution, the Party organs in Odessa open a whorehouse that serves foreigners and accepts only hard currency . . . Stop me if you know it . . ."

Viktor knows this joke, of course, but doesn't stop her. It's a good one.

"On the first day, the crowd of foreign sailors stretches around the block. On the second day, the crowd gets a little smaller. On the third day, only three sailors show up. On day four—no sailors.

"Comrades in Moscow see the financials and place a long-distance call to Odessa. 'What do you think is the problem, comrades?'

"'We don't know, we are looking for what could have gone wrong, but finding nothing.'

"'Perhaps it's the cadres?' one of the comrades in Moscow hypothesizes.

"'Cadres? No, we have the best! All of them Party members since 1902!'

"And that's the conundrum here, Viktor Venyaminovich. Your most reliable cadres are rarely your best cadres. There is a whole floor full of women here at the Fifth Directorate—mostly former teachers—whom we pay three hundred rubles a month to tape-record and transcribe telephone conversations. And what do we do with these transcripts?

"We file them!

"Have you heard the rumor that our surveillance teams go home after midnight, even at such high-value sites as the embassies? That's true—actually. They go home at midnight, and we don't have the budget to add an extra shift.

"We hire some less-than-stellar operatives—the falcons—who might as well be the husbands of the former teachers. Look at what you and your Americans did to them today, in Alexander's Garden of all places! Our simpletons* stomp around this city, following people like you, and, at every day's end, writing undecipherable reports, which also go into our filing cabinets.

"These files aren't useful. They contain no operational information. Whose interests do these people serve? Their own interests: the interests of the former teachers and their husbands, who together earn six hundred rubles a month for generating piles of dross. It's called 'intelligence,' but is the opposite of. Welcome to the Fifth Directorate!

"Don't feign surprise. This is well known, well documented. Let's be genuine. This is what enabled you and those American children from Columbia University to lead our operatives by the nose this morning."

---

* Дундуки.

She pauses, waiting for Viktor to respond.

"Thank you for sharing, Lydia Ivanovna. I feel your frustration as acutely as if it were my own. But forgive me, this murder you are telling me about really does sound like the work of the KGB, possibly not your Fifth Directorate, but the KGB nonetheless.

"Perhaps another directorate, down the hall, or maybe the curator next door? I can accept the notion that you weren't consulted a priori, or informed post hoc. But I will wager a ruble that the answer will be found here."

"It was not us. I have looked into it. I can make arrangements for you to receive assurances from the highest level."

"The highest level? Yuri Vladimirovich? Your esteemed chairman? Assure *me*—a refusenik?"

"False modesty is a form of self-adoration."

"Your Yuri Vladimirovich Andropov is probably the one who ordered something of the sort you describe. I've been reticent to suggest this—understandably."

"Yes, and he assures me he did not. And I believe that you did not kill these men, either. Unfortunately for you, an appearance of having this crime solved would satisfy our needs. We can arrest you right here. But that would mean the real murderer will be left freely wandering the streets."

"I am a simple engineer. What do I know about cases like the one you've just described?"

"You are a logical thinker, resourceful, strategic, not without connections. And your reputation is quite good among your like-thinkers. But enough—this is our first interaction. For now, as an advance, you will learn, perhaps as early as tomorrow, that your wife—who isn't your wife under either Soviet or Jewish law—is being called back to work. It seems a mistake was made in handling her case. I am so, so sorry."

"What if I warn her about the price of this largesse? She would not accept it."

"You would do no such thing because that would require you to reveal our, shall we say, nascent collaboration. Our nascent secret collaboration."*

"'Collaboration' is an ominous word in the context of your organization. Let's say the murderer is found and punished. Let's assume charitably for a moment that it's neither you nor your Yuri Vladimirovich. Let's say it's someone else, and let's imagine that I will lead you to that someone else. Then would it be correct to assume that I would be allowed to leave the country?"

"That would be correct."

"And this is a solemn promise on your part?"

"It's a solemn promise on my part."

"On behalf of your organization?"

"On behalf of my organization."

"You are giving me the word of a Communist?"

"I am giving you the word of a Communist."

"And the word of honor of a KGB officer?"

"And the word of honor of a KGB officer."

"How would you know that after I leave this country I would not call a press conference in, say, Tel Aviv, or Washington, and tell this story?"

"You would not."

"No?"

"Would you really wish to let it be known that you were once our secret collaborator? I propose that we interrupt these negotiations. You need to do some reflecting. And when you tell us of the choice you have made, you will either submit to being finger-

---

* Сотрудничество.

printed and charged with the double murder that I don't believe you committed, or you will help us solve said heinous crime in a compressed time frame."

"Compressed time frame? Compressed by what?"

"On January twenty-second, seven days from today, Henry Kissinger will be arriving for talks in Moscow."

"I would have seven days?"

"Less."

"Let's say this remains unsolved. What would Kissinger do? What are you afraid of?"

"It's unclear, and we don't want to find out. The embassy has sent a request for information about the disappearance of this Foxman gentleman to the Ministry of Foreign Affairs, and they looped us in through the Supreme Soviet. High-voltage circuitry all around—we are obligated to be prepared to provide Mr. Kissinger with an answer. This can't remain unsolved, so we have no choice but to identify the responsible party."

"Even if it's an innocent man. Or woman."

"Yes. Even if. Innocence or guilt are matters of secondary importance in politically charged situations like this one—you know that."

"Assuming a miracle, hypothetically, let us imagine a miracle: In six short days, I have found you the guilty party. What happens to him—or to her?"

"That, Viktor Venyaminovich, would likely be nonjudicial, and you will be spared the knowledge."

Viktor asks the driver to let him out in a darkened courtyard. He will make his way back by trolleybus, like a normal person. Having

Oksana see him get out of a Volga would be a bad thing. It's just him and the driver; no other operatives. Are they sending him the message that they now trust him, that he is one of them, a secret collaborator?

As he looks out of the iced-up window, Viktor assesses the magnitude of the calamity that has befallen him. Should it be allowed to ripen, this affair will acquire all the elements of the Beilis Trial, the Dreyfus Affair, the Moscow Trials even: espionage, dollars, Levi's, *Playboy*s, homosexuals, swinging axes, blood, brains, dissidents, détente, Kissinger, Ford, the international community (make that conspiracy) of Jews. This has to be a partial list.

Perhaps a clear conscience is a luxury meant for those not in the vise grip of the KGB. Read Goethe; it doesn't work out for Faust. Read Bulgakov; things don't go well for the Master. Is it possible to make a limited deal with Satan? Limited in scope and duration and still consider your own image in the mirror without feeling disgust? Is it possible to rent out the soul instead of selling it outright? Make a deal for a defined period of time and for limited applications?

What if the truth is not obvious? What would be lost if Viktor is to believe Lydia Ivanovna in her assertions that the falcons of state security were not the murderers of Schwartz and Foxman? Let's say they didn't wield the ax, and someone else did; how would Viktor find that someone else, and what would he do should he find him, or her, or them? What if that person or persons, upon being discovered, does to Viktor something similar to what was done to Schwartz and Foxman?

And if Viktor survives all that, he would need to trust that the KGB will: (1) let him live, and (2) let him out, and that (3) upon letting him out, would refrain from using the leverage of this episode of limited collaboration as a means for blackmailing him into slavery. Set free by the USSR, he will become its slave. A limited collaboration would go unlimited, global.

At Zemlyanoy Val, Viktor catches a trolleybus, a No. 10.

A vs. B—a Faustian bargain vs. an anti-Semitic trial. Bad Choice A vs. Bad Choice B is still a choice. What could prevent them from changing the ground rules? They could still make it extrajudicial, a bullet in the back of the head; maybe it will be a full-blown trial, with newspaper coverage. Dreyfus . . . Beilis . . . the Leningrad airplane-*niks* . . . and now me . . . Viktor Venyaminovich Moroz! What has he done to deserve being cast into this deepest, noxious pool of sludge?

It's undeniable, real. There will be no mystical intervention. The *kholodetz*-like substance that activates this international conspiracy. Compared to this gathering tidal wave, the Leningrad hijacking case is a picnic of Young Pioneers. Were the Leningrad hijackers anything other than a band of amateurs and naifs? Plus, nobody died. Here, people have died, two of them.

Would his trial be more deserving of his father's attendance than was his wedding? Will the old horseradish conduct himself like the family members of the defendants at the Moscow Trials? Will he shout, "Shoot him! Shoot him like a mad dog!"? "Firing squad is too humane!"? "Long live Stalin!"?

Shout away, but will he be able to look at himself in the mirror without feeling disgust? Actually, yes. He will do just fine. He will find justification in the history of such things, recognizing that Ivan the Terrible, Peter the Great, Taras Bul'ba, and your Iosif Vissarionovich Stalin had killed their sons, some directly, some indirectly, but with the same outcome.

Maybe they should talk in person, one-on-one, man-to-horseradish, and do it sooner rather than later. And that's the checkmate: living on different cosmic planes, they cannot speak, never could.

Looking out at nighttime Moscow, Viktor wonders whether he should have an urgent conversation with Toth, Krimsky, or even Mad Dog. But wouldn't this exposure in American newspapers present us—Soviet Jews—in less-than-complimentary light? It's best to keep this quiet, to close all doors and seal all windows, lest it spin out of control and become public.

On the way to Oksana's—the final couple of blocks from the trolleybus stop—Viktor pauses in front of the bronze likeness of Comrade Dimitrov. Tonight, a coat of ice obscures the pervy expression on the Bulgarian Wanker's face, a comical brushstroke, a fleeting edit that makes tyranny easier to stomach.

PART IV

10.

t's 2:37 a.m., January 16. He has returned.

In street clothes still, Viktor settles on the bed next to his wife, as she lies stretched diagonally across the disarray of bunched-up covers, asleep.

He lifts the bottom corner of the feather duvet. Oksana stirs. She understands the struggle he wages. How is he not akin to fighters trudging through the forest? Unarmed, but a fighter still, for your freedom, for ours. She knows that his every day is a small triumph.

As his lips meet her knee, he knows that she is from a place that lies beyond his dreams. What in his past could have prepared Viktor to dream such dreams? How could an offspring of Kiev zhlobs have dreams of this pale skin? How could he have known the certainty, and calm, and comfort that radiates from her and spreads to shield him from the turmoil?

Her paleness, the power of her limbs, the crescendo of the hair splayed upon this pillow, a glorious echo of Africa's distant drums, a compañero's hearty greeting from Spain, from the brave men and women of the Abraham Lincoln Brigade. Wholly a Negress, wholly a Jewess, exuding Moscowness that struck him when he first saw the luminescence of her flight across Arkhipov Street— into his arms. Those who saw it remember it still. Viktor, the man who caught her in mid-flight, will not forget.

She feels his lips above her knee, she moves it slightly, outward, toward the world. There is tightness in her breasts, a surge of pleasure. She touches them beneath the gown's silk and thinks of all the pages that have passed through her typewriter. She sent them off into the world, but they are circling back, to her, their maker, projecting upon the dark side of her eyelids, and leaving her no choice but to watch their antics. Onionskin paper is soft, gauzy. Assembled into stacks, the pages are passed on, they travel down the invisible line, as fragments upon fragments, images upon images: Akhmatova outside Kresty Prison, honesty that dooms Mandelstam, Bulgakov's censored pages, snapshots of *zek*-filled cattle cars crawling eastward, to Port Nakhodka, and *zek*-filled barges trudging through the ice—to Magadan. These pages she has typed, they alter souls, they uproot lives.

A gentle breeze sets them aloft, and forming a white funnel, the pages blend into the sky.

She is in his arms, and for a long time, they are silent.

"Oksan, have you ever had dreams of flying?"

"Everyone has, from time to time, I think."

"Almost every night since we met, I dream of flying."

"I haven't had any dreams, Vit'. I guess I am just content."

"A month ago, Schwartz gave me a book on mysticism. And it got me thinking about what it would be like not to read about mysticism, not to study it, but to *do* mysticism, to force God's hand to intervene when we need Him."

"In despair?"

"No—not despair—an illusion. Great things begin with an illusion."

"Or remain such. As you are talking, I keep thinking about

Margarita, from *The Master and—*. Her flight over Arbat, your building, actually. It's a beautiful scene—two witches, naked and invisible, learning to fly, negotiating the curves above Arbat."

"It's a fine scene . . . What if we take it further? Make ourselves invisible and catch an Aeroflot flight to Rome."

"I am in."

"And then, invisible still, catch a connecting flight to Tel Aviv."

"And become visible once we get there?"

"I haven't worked out the details."

"Do you think they would be prepared for travelers like us? For the invisibles? Do they keep robes on hand at Ben Gurion Airport?"

"Flowing, white, biblical—robes?"

"Yes, those."

"If anyone does, they do."

They drift off to sleep.

In the morning, Oksana places her hand on Viktor's shoulder, waits for him to wake up and turn to her.

"Vit', Vitya . . ."

It's a whisper, it's insistent.

"Vitya, I am unable to just sit. I want to be a part of it, whatever it is."

"What are you saying?"

"I am saying that I want you to give me something to do."

At 6:39 a.m., a call from a pay phone at the Novogireyevo exchange is placed to the apartment of Oksana Moskvina. Pinpointing the origin of the call beyond identifying the Automatic Telephone Station (ATS) is beyond technical capabilities.

A transcript follows:

"Hello," the caller—obviously, an acquaintance of Viktor Moroz—begins.

"So, did they come through?"

"Yes, they came through."

"Did they get them through?"

"They got them through."

"How many?"

"Many."

"Around thirty?"

"More, more."

"A hundred?"

"A hundred."

"Do we now distribute them?"

"We now distribute them."*

The inhabitants of the apartment—Oksana Moskvina and Viktor Moroz—proceed to wind the telephone dial halfway, in an effort to disable surveillance.

The transcript continues:

"Who was that?"

"You heard the conversation?"

"Just the beginning."

"That, Oksana, was a Hóng Wèibīng."

---

* "Привет . . ."
  "Ну, как—были?"
  "Были."
  "Провезли?"
  "Провезли."
  "Сколько?"
  "Много."
  "Штук тридцать?"
  "Больше, больше."
  "Сто?"
  "Сто."
  "Распределяем?"
  "Распределяем."

"A Chinese Red Guard? Calling *you*? What does that have to do with us?"

"We, Jews, invented Zealots, the whole concept of zealotry. Remember Masada? Josephus Flavius description? How is that not equivalent to Chairman Mao's Cultural Revolution? It's about the spirit. Why shouldn't there be a Jewish Hóng Wèibīng? Or Jewish Komsomol, or Jewish anything?"

"I do remember Masada. And there was that hooligan Bar Kokhba—definitely not a Chinaman. And the Leningrad hijackers—ours, too. What's this Jewish Hóng Wèibīng's name?"

"Lensky."

"Please . . . It can't be . . ."

"Yes. Lensky. You know him?"

"No. Seriously! Like *Evgeny Onegin* sort of Lensky?"

"One and the same. It might have been shortened from something more ethnically indicative at some point. I don't know."

"And his first name? Please tell me it's not Vladimir."

"Actually, it is Vladimir—Vovka Lensky. Engineer. Like me. A better engineer than me, I hope, for his sake. Very enthusiastic about all things Israel, devilishly religious,* or at least devilishly observant, all the way up to wearing hats indoors, which I think is rude, forgive me."

"Is it demonstrative or is it from the soul?"

"Am I capable of trepanning his soul, looking in and making a determination of authenticity of his religious zeal?"

"Forensic certification of authenticity would be helpful in matters of faith."

"All I know is Lensky is a piece of work. Golden is the guy who christened him a Hóng Wèibīng. Our Jewish Hóng Wèibīng."

---

* "До чёртиков правоверный."

. . .

A reader familiar with Pushkin should feel justified to demand a time-out.

Lensky? Vladimir Lensky at that? From *Evgeny Onegin*? The young gentleman Onegin kills so nonchalantly in a duel? How can a nonfictional twentieth-century Jewish refusenik share his name with a fictional nineteenth-century Russian nobleman?

In this case, documents show that the name Lensky is a Russified form of the authentically Jewish name Vilensky, as in the town of Vilna.

Vladimir Lensky's mother, Ada Isaakovna Vilenskaya, now senior economist at Moszhirtrest, a sprawling enterprise that produces milk products, shortened her name from Vilenskaya to Lenskaya in 1944. While some Jewish writers and sundry other intellectuals have adopted pseudonyms that they use in their publications and appearances only, Ada Isaakovna changed her actual last name without changing either her very Jewish first name or her equally Jewish patronymic. Her appearance, too, remained constant.

Also, the nationality entry—Item Five—on internal passports cannot be changed, so on Item Five of said document she remained a Jewess, choosing partial assimilation over extreme, unbroken Jewness that had been dealt to her at birth.

A half-liter of vodka would be required to begin to understand what possessed Ada Isaakovna Lenskaya to name her son Vladimir. It was said that the naming decision was entirely up to Ada Isaakovna. The boy's father was a lieutenant who died during the final months of the war. His name, too, was Vladimir. Hence, the son's name was recorded as Vladimir Vladimirovich.

As a young single woman with a child on the way, Ada Isaakovna would have been too preoccupied with other considerations to be thinking about Pushkin and his novel in verse. Should she be held responsible for failure to predict that snarky observers, who aren't in deficit in this town, would note that naming the boy Evgeny would have made more sense since Onegin presumably shot more accurately than Lensky?

"You have to be making this up, Vitya. I am afraid to ask what your business with Hóng Wèibīng Lensky might be."

"Books. What else?"

"Of course. Sometimes I forget what country we live in. Americans have their drugs. We have our books. And their books."

"A group of Americans from the city of Indianapolis, state of Indiana, near Chicago, brought them here, to us. At least one hundred copies of *The Laws of Jewish Life*, those red books from Montreal. Now we have to give them away."

"In *samizdat*, we don't deal with one hundred copies of anything. You get what your typewriter can handle, eight copies here, twelve copies there."

"It's the same process. You break up the shipment into batches and send them down the line, hoping not to get arrested."

"How many copies do we have to distribute?"

"We?"

"Yes, we, you and I. I thought you agreed to give me something to do. I have been a Zionist, or something like it, for more than a month, and I haven't done anything yet. Plus, I'd like to see a real-life Revolutionary Guard named Vladimir Lensky and pick up the little red books from Montreal, before that thug Onegin whacks him."*

---

* "Пока его этот бандит Онегин не пришьет."

"*The Laws of Jewish Life* is a little red book, except not by the chairman—point taken. Are you volunteering to pick them up?"

"I am."

"That would be very helpful today, actually. Except you will not see Vovka Lensky. His wife will be bringing the books."

"His wife? Just a reminder, in *Onegin*, the real Lensky, by which I mean fictional Lensky, was killed before he could marry, which he surely would have. What's the name of our Hóng Wèibīng's actual wife? It's not perchance Olga, is it?"

"Actually, it is. Olga Lenskaya."

"No! Please . . . Olga *Lenskaya*?"

"Yes, Pushkin has Onegin kill Lensky before he marries Olga, but here, in Moscow, today, young lovers get another chance!"

"Such things can happen only in the land of victorious revolution. Please tell me Olga's maiden name. Is it, perchance, Larina, like the real Olga, by which I mean the fictional Olga, of course?"

"No, it had to have been something like Rabinovich. Very religious, wears a wig. I think she and her Hóng Wèibīng are learning religion straight from that little red book."

"So, where do I meet this Jewish Hóng Wèibīng Zealot Olga Lenskaya?"

"To obtain your thirty copies of *The Laws*? Like Moses?"

"You are confusing Moses with someone else. Moses didn't receive thirty pieces of anything. He received only one copy of the Laws. It was called the Law. Singular. We are receiving thirty copies of the Laws. Plural. And please, please don't tell me I will need to meet Olga Lenskaya at the Pushkin monument."

"Actually, yes. At the Pushkin monument . . . It's a convenient place."

"Can't wait to meet this Olga Lenskaya. When?"

"Tomorrow. Lensky said that today they have an all-day Hebrew seminar."

"Just to recap . . . Olga Lenskaya can't meet me at the Pushkin monument today because she and Vladimir Lensky have an all-day Hebrew seminar."

"Precisely."

"You'd think a simple sense of humor would have precluded such an avalanche of absurdity?"

"I think the Lenskys' sense of humor may have atrophied; either that or they may not have been allotted such at birth. Have you ever seen Hóng Wèibīng with a sense of humor?"

The phone rings again at 7:28 a.m. Oksana picks up. It's Ghryu. She sounds formal, officious, bewildered perhaps. It seems a mistake has been made—hers, she says. Oksana is asked to appear at Ghryu's office at noon to discuss the matter. It's urgent.

What matter? What mistake?

"Can this so-called 'urgent matter' be handled over the telephone?"

"I am afraid not. It requires an in-person conversation," said Ghryu in her most officious tone. "At your earliest convenience."

"Today is inconvenient. I am too busy learning Hebrew," said Oksana, blurting out the first bit of nonsense that came to mind and ending with a "Maybe tomorrow—shalom."

Viktor expresses puzzlement, too. He hasn't asked for this. He hasn't accepted any deals with the KGB. This is not payment for collaboration. Lydia Ivanovna seems to have thrown it in, an advance payment, a gesture of goodwill.

If only he could tell Oksana what's happening, how and why.

11.

At 9:45 a.m. the same morning, January 16, Viktor Moroz, using the telephone at Oksana Moskvina's apartment, calls Elrad Barkin.

"Listen, old man, I know a reporter, a turd, but American," says Viktor.[*]

What does he want?

The answer is difficult to interpret. According to Viktor, Mad Dog might be interested in buying art, or he might want to profile a semiofficial or unofficial artist for his newspaper. It is clear, however, that he wants to meet Barkin.

For Barkin, this is an important distinction. He keeps only a few pieces at the apartment, and none of them are for sale. A profile in a major American newspaper wouldn't hurt him. It would infuriate the USSR Union of Artists, but when has Elrad Barkin exhibited concern about infuriating the USSR Union of Artists?

Likely, it will not run afoul of his deal. (Everyone has a deal.) He has been told, unofficially, that he can do whatever he wants as long as he doesn't venture into politics. As long as there are no unofficial groups, no political statements, no declarations, he can

---

[*] "Слушай, старик, тут у меня корреспондент, мудак, но американец."

sell his art to foreigners, even accept dollars, as long as he doesn't get too conspicuous.

"He speaks Russian, more or less, but he gave me a directive: 'Make it look like I don't speak it.'"

"What the fuck?"

"Fuck if I know. Thinks that it's more impressive to show up with a translator."

"What's his name?"

"His nickname is Mad Dog."

"So, bring your rabid dog to the apartment."*

A flurry of phone calls follows. First, Viktor calls Vitaly Golden, and the two agree to meet "at the same place."

Then Viktor receives a call from Father Mikhail Saulovich Kiselenko. The call is placed from a pay phone, and pinpointing location of pay phones beyond the region covered by an ATS is not feasible for technical reasons.

"Thank you for calling me back, Father Mikhail."

"Please give my regards to your bride. She is quite a Bulgakov-ist. A very attentive reader. Has very original ideas. How can I be of help?"

"I need some guidance."

"What about the rabbi?"

---

* "Он по-русски более не менее, но мне, блин, прямое указание дал: Мол, делай вид, что не говорю."
"А на хуя?"
"Да вот так, блин. Думает, что с переводчиком более впечатлительно."
"А зовут его как?"
"Кличка у него Мад Дог. Бешеный Пёс."
"Ну приводи твоего бешеного пса на квартиру, блин."

"You know the answer."

"I do know the answer. Is it a spiritual matter?"

"It's a theoretical matter."

"Theoretical we can do on the telephone. Spiritual—you would have to come see me. Theoretically, what is it?"

"You might call it a temptation."

"A temptation to kill? To commit adultery? To enrich yourself at the expense of others?"

"Temptation to avoid some unpleasant events the nature of which I am unable to discuss."

"Can you help me a little more, without necessarily giving away the specifics?"

"Theoretically, is it possible to make a limited deal with Satan?"

"The scripture is quite specific on this point—no. Are you familiar with the last temptation of Christ?"

"In very general terms—yes."

"Christ said no. Resolutely, absolutely—no wavering. That's the right answer."

"Even to save your life?"

"That was Christ's dilemma precisely—it's the whole point."

"Hasn't Satan become more nuanced, smarter, more capable of modulating his actions, able to go a little softer here, a little harsher there?"

"No. Satan is stupid. He never changes. That's why we always defeat him."

"I envy you, Father Mikhail."

"Me? Why?"

"Your moral clarity. I wish I had that."

"I can't take credit for that. It's what I've been taught; it's what I teach."

. . .

Whoever said that confidential conversations should be held in out-of-the-way places? Photographic evidence shows Viktor Moroz and Vitaly Golden repeatedly meeting beneath the statue of Mikhail Lermontov.

A Russian Scotsman whose early poems show intimate familiarity with gay sex, he stands atop a black marble pedestal in the center of a small park that, alongside the statue, also includes a modernist take on one of his most enduring characters, a despondent demon.

Young Lermontov—he was killed in a duel at twenty-six, so there is no other kind—looks away from you, away from the Garden Ring, away from the Stalin-era skyscraper that dwarfs him. Compare him to Pushkin, who stands, preposterously, in the proximity of the street named after Maxim Gorky. You will note that the curvature of Lermontov's neck is more noncommittal, less engaged, vacant, nihilistic, compared to his senior peer in bronze. Lermontov is cloaked in a billowing military-style overcoat and planted in the shadow of an architectural monstrosity in a style best described as Hitler Gothic, but he is nobody's doorman. If it's a doorman you want, go see Mayakovsky—he opens the door into the future from his pedestal a few trolleybus stops away. Or Gorky. He is in the park.

The morning is particularly cold, the small park surrounding Lermontov is empty.

"Vitaly, I'm sorry to be so direct. Could I ask you for a historian's perspective on anti-Semitic trials?"

"Common themes in anti-Semitic prosecutions? I am, actually, exactly the right person to ask. I've thought about this a lot. Could be an interesting subject for a seminar."

"Could we focus on the outcomes, just between us, for now?"

"If you limit yourself to the big, famous ones, the outcomes aren't too bad."

"For the defendants?"

"Yes, the defendants. Dreyfus was convicted of treason—with us it would be equivalent of our Article 64—but exonerated after twelve years and reinstated in the French Army."

"What about Beilis?"

"Beilis was accused of ritual murder in Kiev, but was acquitted and left for Palestine, then popped up in America. He wrote a memoir, then Bernard Malamud wrote a book about that book. *The Fixer.* I've just read it. Not bad."

"Anything more recent?"

"The Doctors' Plot—here. They were arrested, yes, but most of them were released from prisons and delivered to their apartments by the same people who arrested them. In a matter of months—an excellent outcome, except for the two or so who died during interrogation. It was a close call, but nearly all of them ended up in the 'survived' column."

"What about the Leningrad airplane case?"

"Two death sentences, both commuted—even though they did undeniably try to hijack a plane and were stopped at the airfield. Also, there was a matter of a pistol. They had one, unfortunately. It's a safe guess that they will be exchanged for spies sooner rather than later. So it's still in progress, but prognostic indicators are strongly in their favor.

"I think the Leningrad case is about something else. It's a reminder that every one of our crazies is a gift to the KGB. Great movements are measured by their ability to control their crazies. We should be careful; I just don't know how to be more careful. The Jewish movement is so panoramically visible to the KGB that sometimes I wonder why democrats allow us Zionists into their apartments."

"So, to summarize, over the past eight decades, defendants in anti-Semitic trials have done reasonably well—worldwide?"

"Only a few have died. There's Leo Frank, in America—but that was extrajudicial—murder by a mob."

"Could you run a calculation to determine the risk?"

"Now, that's taking it too far. We don't know the risk group. By which I mean we think we have the numerator—the number of people wrongly accused, if we exclude the Leningrad case, because they really did try. But what's in the denominator? All Jews? We will need to exclude fascism from our analysis, too. Fascism is wholesale extermination—no trial. A completely different setting."

"So, in theory, if you are threatened with prosecution in an anti-Semitic case, historical record shows that you will eventually prevail?"

"That's my analysis—if we are limiting ourselves to non-fascist anti-Semitism. Not to change the subject, but I have to pick something up at a friend's on Sretenka. Do you want to walk a few blocks before I catch a trolleybus?"

The two are observed walking along the Garden Ring.

"This isn't really important, but I have been trying to remember the joke Foxman told at your apartment about a year ago. I remember you were laughing. I must have been distracted."

"The Yekke joke?"

"Yes. Yekke . . . Strange word."

"Nobody really knows where it comes from."

"Do you remember the joke?"

"I am a historian. We don't forget jokes. So, at an American university, a just-arrived German-born luminary invites a colleague for a glass of sherry at his apartment.

"Let's say it's Columbia, in New York. So the American, let's say he is a gentile and a sociologist, asks how German Jews are so different from all the other Jews. The German luminary tries to explain it this way and that, but the result is unsatisfying, he is unable to get at it. So instead, he decides to conduct a demonstration.

"'Heinz!' he calls out, and his college student son appears in the study.

"'Heinz, I want you to go to the Viennese coffeehouse on Broadway, see whether I am there, and report back to me within thirty minutes.'

"Heinz turns around on his heels with military precision and marches out of the study. Exactly thirty minutes later, he returns with a report: 'No, Father, you are not there.'

"Two weeks later, the American sociologist runs into Heinz on the quad.

"'Heinz, did you really take your father's orders and run to the Viennese café to find out whether your father was there, when it was clear that he could not possibly be there? He was, as we both know, in his study.'"

"'What kind of a Yekke do you think I am? Of course, I didn't run to the café. I picked up the phone, called them, and asked whether he was there.'"

Viktor walks in silence, giving the joke space to roll around in his mind.

"I don't hear you laughing," says Golden.

Viktor takes a moment to respond. "It's more profound than it is funny. The more you fight being a Yekke, the bigger Yekke you become."

"Foxman told it as a joke about Kissinger. What does it actually have to do with Kissinger?"

"He follows orders?" asks Viktor. "Is that bad?"

"Could be very bad. Speaking of which, have you seen Foxman lately?"

"No," says Viktor.

"What about Schwartz?"

"Haven't seen either of them."

"Well, maybe Schwartz has a girlfriend. Maybe they left town."

"They could be in Yalta."

Now, thanks to this quick consult with a historian, Viktor's choices are clear. Lydia Ivanovna is giving him an ultimatum:

A—face prosecution, or
B—become a secret collaborator.

QUESTION 1: In which part of the bargain do I get to keep my self-esteem?
ANSWER: A, clearly.

QUESTION 2: Where do I get the highest probability of survival?
ANSWER: A again, hands down . . .

A—for you, Oksana! Oksanochka . . . A—for me! A—for us! Until they snap on the handcuffs, and, of course, after that, I will keep fighting, because, statistically, ceteris paribus, the probability of our victory is higher than if I choose B.

Viktor catches the B trolleybus and heads to Barkin's.

12.

Uncle Grisha, the sculpture that made Barkin a Moscow legend, greets visitors in the vestibule of his apartment. Technically, *Uncle Grisha* fits into the genre of Socialist Realism. Yet he is not a shock worker, not a buff athlete, not a heroic soldier. *Uncle Grisha* is a double amputee. His legs were blown off in the war.

After being discharged from military hospitals, invalids like *Uncle Grisha* acquired small squares of plywood mounted on ball bearings. Mechanics use similar contraptions to get under jacked-up cars. Cut off at mid-thigh, they live low to the ground, viewing the world from the height of medium-sized dogs. To propel themselves, they use wood blocks vaguely reminiscent of door handles. Some wear army hats. If you beg for a living, you need a hat to illustrate your ask: "I suffered for you, brother. How about helping me out with a few kopeks toward a glass of vodka?" Ball bearings rattle as these men approach, their wooden blocks banging on the pavement, and if you've heard them sing, their hoarse voices will haunt you.

Uncle Grisha might be classified as a sculpture, mixed media, an installation, and a float. It's a piece of performance art as well, and a piece of literature.

Barkin utilizes an actual plywood cart and wood blocks that had served a real-life war veteran, a neighbor. His name was Grigoriy Semyonovich Korolyov, Grisha for short, the real Uncle Grisha.

One day in 1963, Uncle Grisha's wheeled plywood board, complete with leather straps for attaching stumps to the deck, appeared near the building's dumpster. Uncle Grisha's push-off blocks lay amid the garbage. Barkin fought the urge to check whether Uncle Grisha was similarly disposed of in the trash. Eighteen years after the war, the man's suffering was over.

A few months later, a bronze likeness of Uncle Grisha rattled into immortality, set up on the invalid's real-life ball-bearing-wheeled cart. Here he stands, if "stands" is the right word, in Barkin's anteroom, cast in bronze, Barkin's neighbor once again, a fighter maimed by the Nazis, cast off by the country he served.

The simple pine box Barkin nailed together is a crucial part of the installation. Barkin calls it a pedestal-coffin-cart.* It can serve as a pedestal, making *Uncle Grisha* into a formal statue, vaguely evocative of busts of Marx, Lenin, and Stalin. Alternatively, *Uncle Grisha*'s bronze stumps can be unstrapped from the cart so he can be laid to rest inside the box, thus making it function as a coffin. You can strap the cart to the bottom of the box and hang the wood blocks off the hooks on its sides. This enables you to wheel the coffin.

Barkin's typed directions, which are a part of the piece, stipulate (in verse) that *Uncle Grisha* is to be rolled out, in or out of the coffin, every May 9, at Victory Day parades. This is to be done "so as to give purpose to Uncle Grisha's existence and meaning to his sacrifice," Barkin's directions read.

This was never done, because not even Barkin had the guts to show up on Red Square with *Uncle Grisha* in tow.

---

* Пьедестал-гроб-коляска.

Uncle Grisha places Socialist Realism on its head, making it function as surrealism, a fuck-you from the inside.

In 1964, at a special meeting of the party organization of the USSR Union of Artists, some goat accused Barkin of making light of our country's sacrifices in the Great Patriotic War.

"I am sorry, Comrade Whatsyournameagain,* but I didn't happen to notice you in Stalingrad when I was there," Barkin, a member of CPSU since 1942, famously replied to his accuser. "I don't know whether you've heard about this while you were keeping your smooth, pale ass safe in Kazakhstan, but in Stalingrad we experienced events called 'shelling.' Had someone in the German artillery taken a slightly different aim, yours truly would have been turned into a tenderized cutlet—or would have ended up on a little board on wheels, like my friend Uncle Grisha.

"Also, in Stalingrad, we encountered devices called 'land mines.' Had I taken an unfortunate step, my intestines would have been scattered on the branches of nearby trees, not that there were many still standing—or, again, I could have ended up on a board, like my friend Uncle Grisha."

Since nobody had either the balls to interrupt this lecture on the art of war or a hook to pull Barkin off the podium, the sculptor intensified his counterattack:

"More than that, we had small objects called 'bullets.' The Germans, too, had these"—here Barkin paused to make sure his message was sinking in—"'bullets,' and while we tried to embed *our* bullets in *their* bodies, they reciprocated with efforts to embed *their* bullets in *ours*. Sometimes this was done rapidly, with what

---

* An undertaking rooted in art and culture, translation will never be fully entrusted to engineers. In the absence of footnotes, a Russian speaker wouldn't know that the salutation "Comrade Whatsyournameagain" was uttered as "тов. Какбишьвасзовут," transliterated as "*tov. Kakbish'vaszovut.*"

we called '*machine-gun* fire.' I know this is getting complicated, but machine-gun fire came from *both* sides. Both . . . It's a lot like an equation with two variables, an *x* and a *y*.

"Now, Comrade Whatsyournameagain, do you know why I have this long, thick beard? It's lush, it's beautiful, of course, I know, and women find it irresistible, but I sport it mostly because one of *their*—that would be German—bullets ended up in *my* jaw, where it had the audacity to explode. My face is partially nonexistent, sculpted from hair, fuck your mother, and *you* are lecturing *me* about sacrifices on the battlefield?"

Barkin's concluding stanza became a Moscow classic:

"Why don't you go fuck yourselves; how's this for a slogan?"*

As a consequence of creating *Uncle Grisha* and delivering this forceful apologia, Barkin was mostly left alone. He was able to keep his underground atelier at Zemlyanoy Val, the cellar of 1/4 Chkalov Street, but commissions and exhibits went to sculptors who—unlike Barkin—didn't stand shoulder to shoulder with Henry Moore and whose pious dreck would never find a place at MoMA, the Pompidou, or the Tretyakov.

There is no reason to pity Barkin. He makes a stellar income selling sculptures to foreign diplomats and reporters, relying on dissidents and refuseniks like Viktor Moroz to place his works.

As Mad Dog and Viktor knock on Barkin's door later that morning, Mad Dog has yet to tell Viktor whether he is here to report a story or to acquire a work of art for his private collection.

Marya is at work, and Barkin, who is proud of never getting hangovers, nonetheless looks mistreated by life. He offers the

---

* "Да пошли вы все в жопу; хороший я лозунг придумал?"

visitors tea, which Viktor accepts and Mad Dog declines. If Viktor could advise Mad Dog, he would have told him to accept the tea, and the cookies, and the candy—always.

"I understand you've been an unofficial artist longer than anyone," Mad Dog says in English, and Viktor translates.

"You have, apparently, received erroneous information,"* Barkin counters.

Viktor has seen good interviews and he has seen bad interviews. This opening seems to be going badly.

Having corrected Mad Dog's opening question, Barkin proceeds to explain that while many of his friends are so-called unofficial artists, he is, officially speaking, "official," by which he means that he is a member of the USSR Union of Artists, and while his work doesn't get applause from the authorities, he does get to have an atelier. Having an atelier is one of the benefits of being a part of the club. Special pricing of works—and the flow of official orders—is another. By being in good graces with the Union of Artists, you get big orders, such as, for example, a contract to build a monument to heroic fighters, or heroic workers, or heroic leaders, especially after said leaders die. Being official but unloved, Barkin doesn't get offered prime commissions—only lousy ones, but over the years, when the money was tight, he has taken a few.

Barkin doesn't mention selling works to foreigners, provided the pieces aren't significant and the prices not insulting; Mad Dog surely knows that, or why would he be here? Speaking of which, why *is* he here? Barkin notices that Mad Dog hasn't reached for his notebook. Viktor notices this, too.

"How many artists, would you say, are in opposition to the regime?" Mad Dog asks, and Viktor dutifully translates.

---

* "Вам вероятно дали неправильную информацию."

This is a jewel of a question, and Barkin's genuine answer to it would be worth hearing, except you will not get his true answer unless you sit at his table and drink not just tea, but the elixir of truth—you know what that is. To get there, Barkin would need to trust you enough to invite you. Also, as a precondition, he would have to determine whether God has given you the capacity to understand what's being said. And if you are there, the vodka-in-hand rule will apply—anything said would be surrounded by omertà, code of silence.

Heeding his self-preservation instinct, Barkin replies that he has no idea how many artists are in opposition to the regime. How the hell would he know? At official gatherings of artists, which Barkin hasn't attended in decades, the mood is presumably very pro-regime, except in whispers, which Barkin, had he attended, would have paid no attention to. Would Mad Dog wish to speak with the secretary of the Party Organization of the USSR Union of Artists? Barkin has no idea who that might be, even though he—being a Party member since 1942 (he joined at the front)—is technically still listed among members of the Party Organization there. It's like being registered for follow-up at a psychiatric hospital; once you get on the list, you are on the list. Mad Dog would be welcome to use Barkin's name to get the name of the secretary of the Party Organization, though it's unclear what good it would do him.

"Can we talk about your famous encounter with Khrushchev?"

That would be a fine subject of discussion, Barkin acknowledges, except he doesn't recall having had any encounters with Nikita Khrushchev, famous or otherwise.

"Didn't you have a run-in with him?"

No, says Barkin, that wasn't me. Surely, Mad Dog is referring to the famous incident in 1962, at the Moscow Manege, when Khrushchev derided Ernst Neizvestnyy's work as "degenerate," etc. You might be confusing me with Ernst Neizvestnyy, a great sculptor, and a good friend. I am Elrad Barkin. It's easy for a foreigner to confuse the names, granted. My first name is Elrad, which is short for "Electricity-Radio," a relatively common name in the twenties. I go by Erik, understandably, because who wants to be named Electricity-Radio? Would you? And Neizvestnyy goes by Ernst. His parents were less crazy and gave him a human name. So, Erik/Ernst; you can see how confusion might set in. They are about to drive Ernst out of the country, by the way, but Erik is staying put. So in the foreseeable future, this distinction might help you separate me from Ernst. You will soon be able to look at these sculptors' relationship to national borders to be able to distinguish them. One will be here, the other there. Erik here, Ernst there. The one here will be me.

My work might have been degenerate, too, but my famous run-in wasn't with Khrushchev, Barkin continues. My run-in occurred at the meeting of the Party Organization of the Union of Artists. It was about ideological unreliability, as demonstrated by the sculpture of Uncle Grisha, an actual war invalid I had brought back, if not quite resurrected, super-realistically in heroic bronze. At that meeting, I told them where they could go, and that was the beginning of my personal Cold War with the USSR Union of Artists. So with this and a sort of similar first name, it's understandable how an uninformed foreigner, by which I mean an outsider not steeped in these matters, might get mixed up, of course.

"I am sorry, my mistake," Mad Dog acknowledges after hearing Viktor's heroic translation of this drivel.

Is Mad Dog in the midst of a moment of self-doubt? Perhaps he realizes that talking with ordinary people, and for that matter, artists, isn't his greatest strength. Mad Dog doesn't want their tea, doesn't want to have to warm them up with small talk. He hates absurdism, especially Russian absurdism, which is akin to speaking in tongues. Why do these people regard idiocy as entertainment? Why can't they just be direct?

Maybe Mad Dog's strength lies in talking with government officials, people who are vying to use him and his newspaper to advance their agendas. He is getting sick of being used like that. There's no place like the Big Potato to make you feel underappreciated. He should be stationed in Washington, doing in-depth interviews with the likes of Henry Kissinger. Henry Kissinger will be here, in the Big Potato, on January 22—in six days. There will be a press conference, where—maybe—news will be committed.

Henry Kissinger is an easy guy to cover—he understands that everything in life is transactional, it's all about the deals you make, so make the deals, for God's sake!

With sculptors, there can be a transaction in the end, but a lot of talk gets flushed down the toilet of time before a handshake can occur.

"You mentioned Uncle Grisha. I'd be very interested to see that piece."

To understand Barkin's work, you must begin with *Uncle Grisha*, and there is no better way to see that sculpture than with Barkin as a guide.

Barkin begins by explaining the uses for the pine box, the versatile *pyedestal-grob-kolyaska*, pedestal-coffin-cart. Place the statue atop, and it's a pedestal. Unstrap *Uncle Grisha*'s stumps from the cart, and you can lay him to rest inside the box, making it a coffin. Attach the bottom of the box to the cart, hang the wood blocks off the hooks, and you have a float. You can display him inside the box or out—giving you two kinds of floats. The best part of the demonstration is having Barkin read his directions, which require that *Uncle Grisha* be aired out at Victory Day parades, every May 9. Of course, Barkin points out that this has never been done, because not even he . . .

Mad Dog exhibits no emotion during the showing, then waits to make certain that Barkin is done.

"I am excited to tell you why I am here. I have been working with several key people in the art world in the United States, major collectors—plus some major gallerists. And, working with them, I have been trying to put together a collection of the most important Soviet artists, on both sides of the official/unofficial divide."

He waits for the translator to catch up, which Viktor does, causing Barkin to begin stroking his vast beard, concentrating his efforts on the area beneath his chin.

"This is a very major opportunity, because for the first time in history, key artists in Moscow will be linked with key tastemakers in New York. My wife, of course, has a degree in art history from Radcliffe, which is actually Harvard, and I want her to spearhead this initiative."

Then, as an aside to Viktor: "Does he understand?"

Barkin's hand grabs on to a thick clump of hair beneath his chin, but his gaze remains impenetrable.

"This works best when I own the pieces outright, you see? This gives us the most freedom to work on your behalf, building a market for other pieces."

Barkin waits for Viktor to catch up with the translation.

"Fridom-m," echoes Barkin, apparently recognizing the word. "Yes. Yes."

"*Da*," Mad Dog echoes. "So, I'd like to make you an offer for your *Uncle Sasha*."

"*Grisha*," Viktor corrects.

"How much does this shitass wish to offer me for this, my most important fucking sculpture?"* Barkin asks in Russian.

"How much do you wish to offer to acquire my most important work of art?" Viktor translates.

MAD DOG: That's where I am somewhat limited. I am financing this entire enterprise on my salary—my *reporter's* salary. And they don't pay reporters much, as you might imagine.

VIKTOR: If I may offer advice, Mr. Dymshitz, you need to give him a number, or he will throw both of us down the stairs.

MAD DOG: Okay. How about $185?

BARKIN: Давай я тебе картинку нарисую.

VIKTOR: He wants to draw picture for you.

Barkin takes a piece of paper and the broken *Khudozhnik* pencil he uses to disable the telephone's listening capacity and proceeds to draw a cucumber-like shape, and, beneath it, two smallish apples.

Silently pointing at Mad Dog and nodding, he starts drawing another picture, which looks like two large melons, side by side.

"*Khuy*," he pronounces slowly, pointing at the cucumber-and-apples arrangement, and in big letters writes out the word "хуй." Pointing at the side-by-side melons, he pronounces slowly, "*Zhopa*," and, in small letters, writes out "жопа."

Then, drawing an arrow emanating from the cucumber and ending between the melons, he declares, "Хуй тебе в жопу."

Seeing that Viktor is reluctant to translate, Barkin urges him on: "Переведи, переведи ему."

VIKTOR: Не буду.†

BARKIN: Well, then I will say it in English. *Khuy tebe v zhopu*—usually pronounced rapidly as *khuytevzhopu*—is translated

---

* "А сколько этот засранец мне предложит, за эту мою самую важную, блядь, скульптуру?"

† "I will not."

literally as "a dick up your ass," but it really means "no." It's an expression we have, always emphatic—and always final.

VIKTOR: I didn't know you speak English.

BARKIN: You didn't ask.*

Viktor and Mad Dog are silent as the elevator crawls down to the first floor. Downstairs, a mouse-gray Volga is parked behind Mad Dog's Chihuahuamobile.

They are waiting. Are they playing with their kill? Are meetings with the curator becoming a daily occurrence? Or is this it—the arrest? Having had a chance to think through it, Viktor knows what to do.

As Mad Dog opens the door on the driver's side, Viktor, looking away from the Volga, pulls on the opposite door and gets into the passenger seat.

"What the fuck?"

"I need you to get me out of here."

"What am I now, a taxi driver?"

"That Volga behind us. They've come for me. I want you to take me away."

"Where can I take you that's any better? We are in the middle of fucking Moscow. Nothing is safe. Besides, you screwed me with that artist asshole. You will forgive me if I am inclined to say fuck you."

"I didn't know he speaks English. He didn't know you speak

---

* *Uncle Grisha* was sold in 2001—for just under $1 million—in order to pay for Barkin's treatment at Memorial Sloan Kettering Cancer Center. Since then, *Uncle Grisha* has bounced from oligarch to oligarch, selling most recently for $18.3 million in 2015. The current owner, who wishes to remain anonymous, has generously allowed the Tretyakov Gallery in Moscow to display the sculpture.

Russian. I was not needed. All I did was arrange meeting. Will you really throw me out of car?"

"I guess not, now that you are in and comfortable, though I have no idea what we would be accomplishing."

"I am aware of your concerns. Which way will you turn?"

"Left, I guess. I need to get to Sheremetyevo. My fucking father is landing in an hour, speaking of *khuytevzhopu*. A heroic Polish Jew partisan is the last thing I need on my ass right now."

"I am sorry you have problem. Will you please help me?"

"Look, I love you like a brother, Viktor, but I am not the fucking Holy Catholic Church. I'm not set up to offer sanctuary. I am on a journalist's visa, for Christ's sake."

"Go. Please."

"Fine, I guess."

Traffic on the Garden Ring moves rapidly—too rapidly for Viktor's mind to keep up.

"Volga is fifty meters behind us. Please come to quick stop exactly when I ask, just a few more meters on Sadovaya-Kudrinskaya."

"Sure, sure, it's your funeral, you write the instructions."

"When I jump, you will take off, like nothing happened."

"This is the fucking Garden Ring, the busiest thoroughfare in Moscow. Don't you realize where we are?"

"We are on Sadovaya-Kudrinskaya."

"I can't fucking pronounce it."

"Just say Garden Ring."

"Just for the record, Viktor, people on Garden Fucking Ring are required to use underground crossings . . . And I am nowhere near the curb . . ."

"Now!" shouts Viktor, opening the passenger door and taking off into traffic on Sadovaya-Kudrinskaya.

To avoid slamming into Mad Dog's Chihuahuamobile, the mouse-gray Volga shifts into an inside lane, emitting a loud screech of the brakes as it tries to avoid slamming into Viktor.

Viktor hears the dull heaviness of a crash. Someone has rear-ended the KGB Volga. One more lane . . . he will take it like a bullfighter, avoid the rapidly moving hulk, then move in, fast, heeding his body's commands.

Now the other side . . . Two lanes are clear, a trolleybus—good old No. 10, probably—run! If I have to die here in Moscow, may I be harvested by the No. 10. The B trolleybus is good, too. I love the B also.

He is at the entrance to the parklike alley, at the end of which stands the dome of the Moscow Planetarium. Viktor has been there more often than anyone will ever understand. Why? Because of the sky, its enormity reproduced and projected on the inside of this dome. He loves looking at the machine at the heart of it all, a mechanical circus master of the universe. He runs in. No one seems to notice. A small inner chamber is unmanned; a showing is in progress, the belt of the Milky Way is moving hazily above. Then comes the music of dawn—*Swan Lake*, wouldn't you know? But what is this? A Sputnik is dragging the red banner of the Revolution? Who but the Bolsheviks would dare plant a banner upon the rising sun? This ideological appendage to dawn is cheesy, yes, agitprop, yes, but even the Bolsheviks can't succeed at befouling the sky. Viktor likes being here—a lot. Who but a fallen engineer would see so much wonder in a planetarium, this piece of nineteenth-century technology, this gizmorama of light?

It will take the goons a while to regroup, to organize a search. They may look alongside the Garden Ring, but not here, in this darkness, beneath this slowly rising sun. As light intensifies, dawn-like, Viktor sees that attendance here isn't huge, even by the planetarium's standards. There is just him and a group of school-children from one of the stans.

As the machine is turned off, Viktor heads toward the projectionist's booth and, with no one there to stop him, leaves through the side door. He finds another side door that takes him toward the garden that features pieces of interplanetary kitsch, schematic representations of distances between celestial bodies, and—inexplicably—an observatory that has been rendered useless by the proximity of multiple buildings, including one skyscraper.

Anyone who has had a Moscow childhood, anyone who, like Viktor, wishes his childhood to have been in Moscow, knows that if you scale the two-meter fence behind the Moscow Planetarium, you will jump down in the New Territory of the Moscow Zoo.

The New Territory isn't new. It was added sometime in the 1920s, but even after half a century of adaptation, it feels like a badly planned afterthought.

It's a bit after 3:00 p.m., schools haven't let out, and, with the day being especially cold, the animals are mostly in hiding, some sleeping, some freezing to death. Viktor watches a lioness pace in her enclosure in the grotto. Grottos are curious structures—a relic of nineteenth-century zoo design, stone outcroppings in which animals are displayed in faux, operatic wild.

The lioness's movements are fluid, her eyes detached. Is she aware of the absurdity of her situation, far from the savanna, next door to a polar bear? Has she seen the savanna, or was she born in captivity, fantasizing it into existence?

In the terrarium, located inside the grotto, Viktor contemplates the motionless alligator. Why does this place, while seeking to project the freedom of the wild, instead re-create the look and smell of a public bathroom? In which way is a zoo like a prison? None, actually. A zoo is about displaying. A prison—about putting away. It's healthier to stop parsing through the metaphors of the zoo. A zoo is a zoo, it is its own thing—love it. Projection gets us into trouble.

Viktor devotes an hour to looking inside every enclosure, empathizing with the sadness of some animals and admiring the playfulness of others. The zoo is one of Viktor's favorite places in Moscow, perhaps more so than the planetarium. He loves the fence around the Old Territory. Someone—clearly a good sculptor—designed Communist five-pointed stars into that fence. It's a reminder of less cynical days, a time when artists silenced their better judgment and believed in the bright future of mankind.

If there is an opportunity, he will invite Oksana to join him here. She will be amused by his passion for watching big felines pace. It's a dream, of course. Viktor knows he will be arrested today, in a matter of hours. Viktor has made his choice: based on historical record, becoming a target of an anti-Semitic trial provides more favorable outcomes than collaboration with the KGB. Golden supported his point of view, even without knowing the facts of the case. Golden is still waiting for Schwartz to come back, isn't he? Some nonsense about Schwartz's girlfriend, about Crimea. Of course, Oksana is better off not knowing about any of this; still, Viktor wishes he could have told her. *Zeki*—Alik Ginzburg, notably—have a saying: "The sooner you go in, the sooner you'll get out."* Not every *zek* comes back, but the saying is reassuring. It would be preferable to be arrested tomorrow, after *The*

---

* "Раньше сядешь—раньше выйдешь."

Cherry Orchard. Didn't he give Oksana his absolute assurance on their wedding night that they would not be thrown out of the country before the evening of January 16, tonight, when they would see *The Cherry Orchard*—with Vysotsky as Lopakhin? You don't have any more control over being thrown out of the country than you do over your arrest.

The pond at the New Territory is vast, and some exhibits here aren't exhibits at all. Migratory birds drop down for a free meal. Moscow pigeons, too, are among the regulars, as are predators—raccoons and such—who come here to procure fresh fowl.

"Ah, Viktor Venyaminovich, as I expected!"*

Lydia Ivanovna greets him as he reaches the pond.

"I worry about you sometimes, Viktor Venyaminovich."

"I was just heading home, actually."†

"We can talk in my office, if you prefer, but this is so much more pleasant. I brought us sausages and Pepsi. I do like Pepsi. It's going to become a habit."

"I am neither hungry nor thirsty, but I thank you for the thought."

"It's the mother in me. You look like you habitually forget to eat."

"Am I under arrest?"

"Why such terminology? No, Viktor Venyaminovich, you are not under arrest. At the moment, at least, you are not useful under arrest."

"Then if I am free to go, I will not be joining you for a meal."

"You win, we will forgo the meal. Will you indulge me by listening for a few minutes? We can stand by the railing and look at

---

* "Ах, Виктор Веньяминович, я так и знала!"

† "Я вообще-то домой направлялся."

this frozen pond. In the summer, they keep baboons there, on that island."

"I am aware. I have five minutes. After that, I will bid adieu—with all due courtesy."

"Then I will tell you a story. On April twenty-second, 1948, I was walking back from the Young Pioneers palace, the one near Kirovskaya—very close to Chistoprudnyy Boulevard, actually—returning from something related to Lenin's birthday, when an NKVD car swept me up. I was a very pretty fifteen-year-old girl. They took me straight to Beria, of course. You know how much he liked young girls—and, without getting too much into details, Beria raped me. The following morning, I was in a prison train. My parents looked for me, but I would not be found for the ensuing six years."

"Why are you telling me this, Lydia Ivanovna?"

"Because I am sometimes envious of people like you, people who think they can pick up and go and everything will fall in place elsewhere. I am the exact opposite. I stay in place, I return, I try to make repairs. I joined the same organization that Beria once headed; I did it so I could drive away his ghost, to make certain that lawlessness would be purged from its ranks."

"Since we are making light conversation here, how is it going, your crusade to reform the KGB? Also, we are down to four and a half minutes."

"Our cars aren't picking up girls off the streets, taking them to places where they get raped, and making them disappear, if that's what you are asking. Today, people don't disappear, except under exceptional circumstances. And laws get observed, to a great extent. Personally, I am happiest when we observe the laws. I am a lawyer by training."

"Thank you for sharing, Lydia Ivanovna. We are down to four

minutes. I am thinking of cutting our conversation short and leaving you here to enjoy this view in solitude."

"Legally, you can do that at this point in our collaboration. But as a courtesy, you might want to indulge me for a few moments more."

"Collaboration? I don't recall consenting to a collaboration. But I will give you three more minutes, as a courtesy."

"You know, on my most optimistic days, I think we will eventually learn to understand each other."

"Does everyone in your organization share your hopeful, bright-eyed attitude?"

"I understand how you would say this, but it was unnecessarily cynical and uncalled for."

"Forgive me, but surely you understand that history hasn't conditioned me to believe that your organization is bursting with compassion and the joy of living."

"It's not just about my organization. It's also about your so-called movement. About our interaction. It's nuanced, and the nuance is getting lost."

"Nuance? You kidnap me in the street, drag me to your den of brigands, and try to blackmail me into behaving indecently. And the main issue is an ax murder. Forgive me, but what role does nuance play in an ax murder? Especially one that looks like the work of your organization?"

"I am seeing this conversation as introducing you to the world as it is, and—as a consequence—convincing you to do your country a good deed, repay your debt, and go. We have been very kind to you. Your wife has been offered her job back, and I objected when my heavy-handed colleagues proposed reeling you in, to use their language. You have tickets tonight, to *The Cherry Orchard*."

"Do I?"

"I am envious. Since you are in a rush—we seem to have lost a minute there—I should just tell you directly that I worry about your fundamental approach to what you do. You, my dear friend, idealize the West."

"And you say this based on what?"

"Conversations."

"I don't recall us having discussed my attitude toward the West."

"We have not. But it's evident in your other conversations."

"Other conversations? Informants? Eavesdropping?"

"Some of each. Here is what makes me worry: clearly, you have a keen understanding of our domestic varieties of lowlife,* but I am not at all certain that you understand their kind of lowlife. Just because people pretend that they want to help you doesn't mean that they have your interests at heart."

Why is she lecturing? Is that what the KGB always does before they put you in handcuffs? How could she have not abandoned the idea of convincing Viktor to help in the investigation of Schwartz's and Foxman's murders?

"Please don't worry, Lydia Ivanovna, I am an adult capable of navigating life's challenges."

"You are one of those people who have illusions about Kissinger."

"I respect his achievements."

"A poor Jewish immigrant boy who will now discharge his duty to help his people?"

"I do not exclude that possibility."

"Exclude it. Kissinger is not a fighter of the ghetto. Kissinger is *Jüdische Ghetto-Polizei*. Kissinger is about Kissinger. Kissinger

---

* Сволочь.

would not have stood in the way of the Nazis throwing Jews in concentration camps, his own grandparents included."

"Thank you for this invaluable lecture on history and geopolitics. You have just slandered a high-level American official."

"Please don't tell me you expect to be rescued by Kissinger . . ."

"I expect that he will hold you accountable. As an American diplomat—the highest-level American diplomat—he would not be indifferent to the fate of his colleague, a Mr. Foxman, whom I believe your people have murdered."

"We did not."

"Then who did? Pushkin? Was it a duel?"

"Pushkin has an alibi."

"I would happily stand here and argue with you all day, Lydia Ivanovna. And I would, were my watch not ticking. As you said, I have tickets."

"Well, before you storm off, hear this . . . Have you heard of a gentleman named Jamie Jameson? He was running the USSR field operations for the CIA."

"Never heard of him. How does this relate to me?"

"Mr. Jameson believed that the CIA should draw a clear line between our public groups, our social movements, and intelligence-gathering. In practical terms, if they got a walk-in who was also a member of a public group or had some standing with the public, he or she would get a polite no-thank-you. By contrast, if they got a money-hungry fiend or someone deep in our defense complex, they would greet him with open arms. The idea is public groups, as well as writers and intellectuals and such, should not be allowed to meddle in filthy Cold War shenanigans—even if they yearn to."

"And you know this because you've spoken with this Mr. Jameson, Lydia Ivanovna?"

"Hardly. I know this because we have tested this policy around the edges over the years, sending over potential double agents, that sort of thing."

"And?"

"And nothing. It was real—for many years. It made some of us admire their principles. A smart policy, conservative, consistent, well executed. A protocol adhered to—a system."

"Well, it sounds like we have a shared admiration for the West. Except, of course, unlike you, I have no feelings whatsoever—positive or negative—toward the CIA."

"We are here, having this conversation, because there is a problem."

"There could well be a problem, but what does it have to do with me? I have tickets to *The Cherry Orchard*, as you know. Do you want me to say, 'Thank you for delaying my arrest and I am honored to have you as my curator?' Well, I will not say this, because I have committed no crime and I don't want to have a curator. Nobody in the world requires a curator, good or bad."

"The problem is, the Jameson Doctrine, if you will, is showing signs of fraying around the edges. Trust me, I know of what I speak when I tell you that they aren't turning down assets who are connected with public groups. You follow me? They've betrayed you—when rewards got high enough. Even Israel—their Mossad—has warned the CIA against using refuseniks as assets. I think many of you are naïve, unprotected, ripe for exploitation, and I know I am wasting my breath trying to warn you. This will blow up in their face and yours, because who do you think makes refuseniks? We do! We can make double agents all day long, each with his own compelling story."

Viktor knows this to be true—everyone does. The KGB can find our names on the applications for exit visas, which they get to decide on. If they want to place a spy in our midst or squeeze one of us until he cracks, they can. We are wide open—completely aboveground. How can you have an exclusive emigration movement? We don't get to choose participants. Moses, too, had to accept all comers.

Democrats have an easier life. Democrats are a self-selected group, mostly selfless; take Andrei Dmitrievich or Lyuda Alexeyeva. They know who comes through the door. Sometimes it's surprising that they let us in. But thank God they do.

"I see no point in this rehashing of the obvious, Lydia Ivanovna. Plus, I am distracting you from the important task of making double agents. I don't wish to be a part of that endeavor. I will not offer my services to your organization, or to the CIA, or to Mossad."

"Don't you understand? This departure from the Jameson Doctrine played a role in what happened with your friend Schwartz and his friend Foxman. This is what got them into bed together, figuratively speaking. The more you fall prey to delusions about the West, the deeper your wounds will be."

"Lydia Ivanovna, I believe I've soaked up enough wisdom for one meeting."

13.

Viktor's hungry look prompts fellow refuseniks—and even his KGB curator—to want to give him food. Often, people insist on stuffing containers of food into his briefcase.

Since the vast majority of people Viktor knows these days have been unemployed for years, they aren't lacking for time to revive the dishes that their mothers and grandmothers once prepared in their *shtetleh*. Abandoning the pork-rich diet, today's refuseniks grate carrots for *tzimmes*, grind carp for gefilte fish, and chop eggs and onions for *gehakte eier*.

On the evening of January 16, dinner includes the dishes people insisted Viktor take with him this week: *helzel*, also known as false kishke, a chicken neck stuffed with dense dough and fried onions, acquiring the appearance of an amputated body part; *kaikeleh*, or sweet-and-sour meatballs; and *kreplach*, a variety of dumpling known to Russians as *vareniki* and Poles as *pierogi*.

Next door, neighbors are blasting Vysotsky, songs about Moscow street characters, his early stuff. The quality of recording is borderline undecipherable—it's taped through the air again and again—but most words still make their way through the hiss, and you know the rest.

You can be born a Jew, a Georgian, or a Chukcha and still be a person of Russian culture, and cultural Russianness in 1976 is measured objectively by the degree of familiarity with Vysotsky. On a summer day, Volodya's raspy voice can be heard screaming from open windows not just in Moscow and Leningrad but in Karaganda, Magadan, Brooklyn, and Syktyvkar. People know Volodya's songs, but very few among the hundreds of millions of his admirers have seen him from the front-row seats at Taganka, where that little man will make you laugh until you cry, without letting you forget for an instant that you are in the presence of a great tragedian.

It's said that when Volodya runs red lights, due to inebriation, nonchalance, or panache, the militia stretch out and salute. Viktor thinks he might have seen Volodya's gray Mercedes speed by some months ago, but he isn't sure.

"Oksan, I have literature questions, but go slow on me, I am a simple Soviet lad."

"You used to say, 'I am a simple Soviet engineer . . .'"

"I am a person with no formal grounding in humanities and a literal mind more suitable for working a slide rule than sitting through twelve-volume sets of anything."

"There is an English word you may be familiar with: 'bullshit.' Look it up. What's your question?"

"Can you enlighten me on Chekhov and the Bolsheviks?"

"I don't know that he ever met a Bolshevik, at least knowingly."

"But they love him!"

"Not his problem."

"So it's a good thing Chekhov died before our Great October Socialist Revolution?"

"You mean before Bolsheviks could do something disgusting with his corpse, like stuff him into a mausoleum or bury him in the Kremlin wall, next to John Reed?"

"Something like that."

"To be fair, the most egregious crime against Chekhov was committed during his lifetime. Stanislavsky turned *The Cherry Orchard* into a tragedy, and a bloody bore at that.* This was fifteen years before the storming of the Winter Palace. It's that rare occasion when the Bolsheviks are innocent."

"You think Stanislavsky failed to notice the word 'КОМЕДИЯ' on the title page, or did he deliberately overlook it?"

"It was deliberate desecration."

"Did Chekhov object?"

"He did, but how do you stop a director from fucking up your play? Chekhov was still alive but coughing up blood. He complained bitterly to a young director named Vsevolod Meyerhold,† who did a fine job of staging *The Cherry Orchard*, by the way. But the Stanislavsky interpretation endures. It's usually what gets performed."

"Don't tell me this performance, tonight, will be a bore . . ."

"The opposite. The Taganka interpretation is consistent with Meyerhold, not Stanislavsky. It's something Anton Pavlovich would have tolerated, perhaps even liked."

Taganka is small, devoid of grandeur, a movie theater repurposed. A modernist appendage of an entrance is slapped onto its Art Nouveau façade. From the outside, that entrance looks incongruous, a riding saddle upon a cow's back. This imbalance is symbolic,

---

* "Скукотища."

† Not quite four decades later, Meyerhold would be whipped with rubber straps by NKVD torturers. Some say his limbs were broken, some say he was urinated upon as he flailed on the floor. It's not clear whether he was in any condition to stand up straight during his appointment with a firing squad in February 1940.

you might argue. Here in Moscow, Taganka is "other," a taste of freedom, a hint of treif amid the tyranny of Red imperial kashrut.

At Taganka, *The Cherry Orchard* begins with a simple song, a Russian romance alluded to in the play. It's sung by the actors, accompanied by guitar, played softly, like a mandolin. The costumes are white, the set minimal.

This understated, delicate backdrop makes Vysotsky seem like a giant. You've heard his voice, of course, but here, onstage, he is a ball of flexed muscles. Yermolai Lopakhin, Vysotsky's character, is the only clear thinker in the play. He is a merchant, with enough money to buy the estate where his father, an illiterate, violent drunk, had been a serf. The owners of the estate are thinking magically about ways the manor house and the adjacent cherry orchard would remain in their hands.

Cherries are beautiful, granted, but they aren't the most lucrative of cash crops. You get a harvest every two years, and you have to be there, cultivating buyers, arranging transportation, watching the books, staving off strangulation by debt. Alas, the owners of the estate haven't been there much, and management is not among their strengths. They have no observable strengths, in fact.

Lyubov Andreyevna, the principal female character, and, in this interpretation, Lopakhin's love interest, has been mostly living in Paris, first with a husband who "produced nothing but debts" and died "of champagne," then with a lover, an equally uninspiring man. Lopakhin makes repeated sober warnings. His proposal to chop down the cherry trees and build a development of dachas for people living in the nearby city fails to get so much as an acknowledgment. Ignored, he buys the estate at an auction.

Act III is the stretch that Stanislavsky, to Chekhov's horror, turned into a protracted slobberfest. Today, as the players at

Taganka do what Chekhov envisioned, Act III moves fast, to the sounds of the "famous Jewish orchestra."

In that scene, Vysotsky draws energy from the above-mentioned orchestra—klezmer, of course. Act III of the Taganka production of *The Cherry Orchard* hinges on the finest klezmer concert heard in Moscow in exactly twenty-eight years—since the closing of the Moscow State Jewish Theater in 1948:

LYUBOV ANDREYEVNA: Who bought it?

LOPAKHIN: I bought it . . .

Lopakhin is subdued in his response. "I bought it." Then, in an aside that is also the play's crescendo, he tells the audience how he really feels:

"I bought it! Wait, gentlemen, indulge me for a moment. My mind has dimmed, I am unable to speak."

He laughs maniacally—a Vysotsky strength.

"Oh, my Lord, the cherry orchard is now mine! Mine! Please, assure me that I am drunk, that I am imagining things."

He stomps his feet.

"Don't laugh at me. Had my father or grandfather risen from their coffins and considered what is happening, how their Yermolai, their beaten-down, semi-literate Yermolai, who ran barefoot in the winter, how that very Yermolai has acquired an estate that is more beautiful than any estate in the world!

"I bought the estate where my father and grandfather were slaves, where they weren't even allowed to enter the kitchen. I am asleep, this must be a dream. This is a fruit of your imagination concealed by darkness of the unknown . . .

"Hey, musicians, play, I want to hear you! Come, one and all, come and watch Yermolai Lopakhin raise an ax and take a whack at the cherry orchard, watch the trees fall to the ground! Here we will build dachas, and our children and grandchildren will see a new life here . . .

"Play, musicians, play!"

As *klezmorim* heed Lopakhin's orders, can Viktor be forgiven for closing his eyes to surrender to the vision of Schwartz and Foxman dancing wildly onstage, not as he last saw them, but as living, breathing men yearning for joy?

They walk in silence along the Moskva River embankment.

"Oksan, do you think Chekhov would have understood us?"

"He would—yes."

"Explain."

"In *The Cherry Orchard*, you hear the sound of a string breaking. Stage directions call for it. You don't know what that string is, you don't see all that happens as a result."

"What does it have to do with us, Oksan?"

"Can't you see? You and I, we inhabit that sound. It's our transient state, in-betweenness, neither-here-nor-thereness—fleeting, fragile. We know that we are leaving, yet we are here—living, happily, fully. Vit', this, now, is the best moment of our lives. Anton Pavlovich understood this."

PART V

14.

January 16 is day two and leg three of Norm's schlep: Pittsburgh to Kennedy, Kennedy to Frankfurt, and now this final stretch. He has been avoiding Germany for three decades, but he is done with that, probably, prepared to forgive, but not forget.

The layover in Frankfurt is a test. How will he feel if he hears words like "*schnell*," to pick just one of the words that surely have less ominous meaning today than they did when Norm (then Nuchim) wore a striped uniform, trudging in a column of prisoners?

Norm does get a "*Schnell*" from some asshole businessman when he dillydallies to look out the window. Norm is looking for signs of remorse in the heart of Germany, but a cold, wet tarmac is all he gets. *Schnell*, my ass! Norm's hand, by reflex, searches for something that stabs, slashes, spits bullets, or detonates.

This is Frankfurt, an airport, not Sobibor, where they put a number on his forearm and from where he escaped; it's not the forest, where killing men with knives, bullets, explosives, and, yes, bare hands healed Norm better than any "therapy" or "analysis," forms of torture that Miriam and the boy have subjected themselves to in Pittsburgh.

Outside the home, Miriam goes by Mary. Mary? *Vos* is Mary? Miriam—yes; Mary—no! In the DP camp, after the war, he married a *Miriam*, not a Mary, like the Blessed Virgin, *Matka Boska*, as Poles say; *Yoshke un Matke Bozhke*, as we Jews say, mockingly, or used to, when we still had our language. Mary-*schmary* ate a berry . . . And what the fuck is a Madison? *Moyshe* Norm can understand, but *Madison*? To Harvard he sent that boy, to learn to be a *goy*.

Baruch HaShem, by God's grace, Norm passes through Frankfurt without killing anyone.

There is no first class on Aeroflot, at least not on this flight. Norm ends up sitting next to a round-faced gentleman who was lured away from Atlanta and the Coca-Cola Company to operate a Pepsi bottling plant in Novorossiysk, "way the fuck out by the Black Sea," as he puts it.

People who give a rip about Soviet Jews abhor Pepsi, and Norm never drank that swill to begin with. Pepsi has a deal with the Sovs: an in-kind exchange—Pepsi-Cola for Stolichnaya vodka. The drink is bottled in Novorossiysk, and the vodka is shipped to the United States.

To Norm, this is exactly the wrong thing. Why aid the enemy? It's like the English with Peace in Our Time, and the Swiss with storing the gold the Nazis pilfered from the Jews. If you want them to behave like human beings, boycott them, set off stink bombs at their ballet performances, should they come to New York or Pittsburgh or what have you. Let their *Swan Lake* silt up, or even better—drain the thing! If you fill their bellies with Kansas wheat and their bladders with Pepsi-Cola, what incentive will they have to let out everyone who wants to break free from their workers' paradise? It's common sense, should be obvious to everyone, but apparently not to that fancy Heinz A. Kissinger. Doctor. Henry. A.

Kissinger. Does the "A" stand for Alfred or Adolf? *Schmendrick.*
Yekke.

The jovial Atlantan says he has developed "a system."

"Before boarding an Aeroflot flight, I go to the bar and have
them make me three vodkas, each in a martini glass, chilled, three
full martini glasses. Mark my words, back in the USSR, they will
never learn to chill vodka and pour it into a proper martini. I have
them line up the glasses, like soldiers, here in Frankfurt. It's my
farewell to civilization. It has to be pepper-flavored or it doesn't
work; can't use our Stoly, too clean.

"Then I drink them like this: One! Two! Three! You can hit me
with anything you got after that—I am ready!"

The Atlantan likes his posting, but can't imagine bringing the
family to Novorossiysk, or even to Moscow. Maybe for a short visit
next year, when the kids are older. After learning that Norm's son
is a reporter in Moscow, he exhibits impressive familiarity with
Madison's work—particularly the False St. Bernard Bites Journalist story.

Norm wears a military-style wool overcoat he bought from an
outfitter purporting to dress hunters and prospectors in the Pa-
cific Northwest. A young scientist who now works with Bernie
Fisher's brother Edwin, in the pathology shop at the University of
Pittsburgh, lent Norm the hat he emigrated in. (Bernie is Norm's
friend and Miriam's doctor.) The young scientist's name is Alex;
it's always Alex with Soviet Jews.

Alex said the hat was made of wolf fur, and it has that look.

Norm has two suitcases: a new Halliburton filled with his own
dreck, and a yellow, hard-sided American Tourister that has to be
delivered to an Albert Schwartz, in the center of town, and if this

Albert Schwartz happens to be away for some reason, Norm has another address.

Stacks of one-hundred-ruble bills—five hundred of them— are sewn in beneath the American Tourister's lining, a thick layer. Anna Kaplan, a tattooed alumna of Bergen-Belsen, did this job for him. A seamstress, she is the only one who knows. Norm didn't tell Miriam, of course.

With fifty thousand, you can buy twenty one-room apartments in Moscow, or you can pay the salaries of five hundred experienced teachers or three hundred young engineers for a month, or fully cover exit-visa filing fees for more than fifty-five Soviet Jews, or pay for taxis, legal bills—anything that involves the emigration movement—for a very, very long time.

There are other ways to send money. You can bring in dollars. Black-market exchange rates are wildly good for the dollar, but penalties for breaking currency laws are bad. People get executed. You can buy "certificate rubles" legally and send them to refuseniks, say to Vladimir Slepak or to Ida Nudel. This lets Slepak and Nudel buy better sausage at special stores. You can fatten them up, but does this advance the movement? Selling certificate rubles on the black market is as illegal as selling dollars.

Jeans, on the other hand, are good. You get one hundred rubles for a pair that cost you $8 at the mall. But someone has to sell them on the black market. *Playboy* brings in money, *Penthouse*, too, but they, too, must be sold, and if they catch you, they can get you for distributing smut.

That's why Soviet rubles are your best bet. You can buy rubles at official rates, which are stacked in favor of the USSR State Bank. On top of that, as you transfer the money, you pay a tax, which brings the cost of a ruble up to $1.60; who wants that? So here is a secret: You go to Deutsche Bank (any international bank will do) and buy rubles that have, for whatever reason, ended up outside the USSR. No way to know how and why. They might have been brought in by Pepsi employees returning to America, or maybe dumped by Czechs, Poles, Hungarians, or Bulgarians to make up for losses on transactions with the USSR—does it matter? What matters is these stray rubles are dirt cheap: fifteen cents for a ruble.

Do the math: $7,500, a trivial sum for Norm, less than a clean three-year-old Coupe DeVille on trade-in, buys fifty thousand rubles! Then, after the low-risk feat of transporting the suitcase across the border, you've financed an international movement! This American Tourister on this luggage cart in Sheremetyevo is the Norm Dymshitz Aid Program, the Norm Dymshitz Airlift, the Norm Dymshitz Lend-Lease!

It's a piddly law he is breaking: failure to make proper customs declaration. And there is some risk: the amount is likely to lead to suspicions of financing espionage. But what are the odds of getting caught? They look for weapons, drugs, dissident tracts—not rubles. Under occupation, killing Nazis was a crime, but did that stop Norm?

A young border guard, a *pisher*, glances over the photos on Norm's American passport and his Soviet visa, and with fluid motion of the neck looks into Norm's face, repeating the motion slowly. Photo, face; face, photo.

The most dangerous part of the job is done—Norm got the cash through customs.

He has never been to Moscow; his parents were Russophiles in Krakow, so his Russian is native, almost unaccented, no Yiddish lilt, but if your ear is sharp, you will catch traces of Polish, a softness. It was offset partially in the war, when Norm, upon escaping from Sobibor, got a lot of practice in what might be termed "forest Russian," in the partisan detachment.

Norm has the address of an old friend he believed to have been long dead. He couldn't have imagined the man even made it back to rejoin the Red Army after that exhilarating, blood-soaked day of blasts and gunfire in 1943. That day, Nuchim thought he, too, was dead twelve times over. First, the ammo dump, then the train. There were eight of them at dawn: four parachutists, four partisans. By noon, four remained; after nightfall, two.

A few of the prisoners they freed that day survived in the forest long enough to see Soviet tanks roll in. Some left Europe immediately after the war, and in those families, in Israel, New York, and Montreal, firstborn boys get named after the partisan and the paratrooper who saved the lives of their ancestors.

Talking with this Alex, in Pittsburgh, Norm learned, completely by happenstance, that his Red Army friend is not dead.

A comrade in the genuine sense of the word, not Marxist gibberish—alive! Call it what you will: life after death, life defying death. That electric current surging through Norm's jaw, down his spine, and into the right arm a little, that cold shudder, these dry tears, is all that matters, the meaning of meaning. Some say poetry helps in such situations, but Norm must not have found the right poetry. Some poetry, in Yiddish, speaks to him, because of the loss aspect; he sort of likes Mordechai Gebirtig, and there is a particular song by a ghetto fighter named Hirsch Glick, but we'll have more to say on this matter later, probably.

This is a lot to keep track of, but the truth is the truth. To summarize, all of this prompted Norm to leave Miriam in Pittsburgh, in the care of the Great Bernie Fisher. If anyone can save her life, Bernie can.

None of it involves Norm's son, and the boy can't know anything about any of it. Norm will be back in Pittsburgh soon enough to face the music, as they say, surely before Miriam's disease comes back, which, whom are we kidding, it will. He will be gone just two weeks, maybe three, four at the most.

Looking at Madison, who awaits him outside customs, Norm wonders how they can possibly be related.

They look different. Madison is tall, thin, in a fashionably rumpled Burberry trench coat and those ridiculous white-soled boots Miriam bought him, an aristocrat in the slums. A hat on Madison's head seems to be made of a muskrat. It's the same kind of hat as Norm's—an *ushanka*, with floppy ears, except Norm's is wolf, not rat.

They are the same height—about six feet—except Norm is broad-shouldered, peasantlike, a man with the roly-poly movements of a wrestler. Years ago, at home, Norm made Madison angry by wearing what the boy called the Full Cleveland, white shoes and a white belt. The boy once asked Miriam to tell him how embarrassed he was by this wardrobe choice. Norm responded by buying a wider white belt and a coral-colored shirt, short sleeve. Short sleeves show off the tattoo he got—at no cost, he likes to point out—in another life, before escaping into the forest, before the DP camp, before Miriam, before Pittsburgh, before scrap metal, before Madison, before the class divide with his own son—in Sobibor.

What do you do at an airport when you see a son you would have surely disliked had he not been your son, whom you probably love, because you have to, and whom you know to be unable to hide the fact that he doesn't like you very much, either?

You shake hands—firmly.

Later that evening, Madison suggests grabbing burgers at the commissary at the U.S. Embassy.

However, after setting down his bags at the boy's apartment

at a building called Sad Sam, Norm notices a kitchen and gets a better idea.

"Do you have rubles?" Norm has many rubles, but they aren't exactly accessible. So maybe the boy has some.

"I can look. Why?"

"I want to go get some food, look around, get the lay of the land."

"Aren't you tired? How about a Scotch? I have Red Label, nothing great."

"I'm feeling strangely energized. A glass of vodka would be better for my soul than Red Label."

Rifling through a kitchen drawer, Madison locates a modest-sized wad of what looks like Monopoly money: taupe ones, greenish threes, bluish fives, reddish tens, purplish twenties. Melissa must have used rubles for taxi rides. She left a handful of coins, too.

Norm is fascinated by the massive Soviet-looking overcoat on the hook in the anteroom. He asks Madison whether he can borrow it.

"Help yourself," the boy says.

Slipping on the overcoat, Norm notes four small holes on the right sleeve. The holes are outlined by what looks like a dried bloodstain. The dog bite, of course. He turns up the fur collar, noting its generous proportions.

Norm briefly considers getting on an elevator but takes the stairs instead.

Sad Sam faces Sadovaya-Samotechnaya, which makes up a stretch of the Garden Ring, but the original doorways were closed off so long ago that no one seems to recall them being open. To get in and out, you use the back doors that lead to the courtyard and pass by the guard's shelter reminiscent of the cigarette kiosks a few meters away.

In this world, many buildings are taller, but few exhibit the geological might of Sad Sam. Sided in granite, Sad Sam is a rock outcropping dropped into this city's flatness. On its block, Sad Sam is the generalissimo, mustachioed, fearsome, commanding a parade.

Sadovaya-Samotechnaya is as wide as I-70, except you have no reason to cross I-70, unless you are a deer and want to die.

Norm notes that piles of snow here have the color and texture of Pennsylvania coal. A substance that had been snow at some point in its existence lies in chunks big and small, thawed, frozen, again and again, saturated with debris and runoff, broken up, plowed, pushed into rocky piles.

"Want to be the third?"* asks a man outside a Gastronom, a food store, on the corner of Sadovaya-Samotechnaya and Tsvetnoy Boulevard. The third? The third what?

Norm responds affirmatively. He likes being mistaken for a Russian; it's the hat and the coat, of course. This is his first contact with today's Russian culture. How bad can being the third be?

The man is probably a good five years older than Norm; maybe sixty-five, but a beat-up-by-life sixty-five. He looks vaguely like Lenin; same height, carrying a leather briefcase. He may be a bureaucrat, perhaps at an agency like Gosplan, perhaps an economist whose mission is to plot out the functioning of the Soviet system. Norm can imagine him bending over tables of inputs and outputs, checking entries against the long garland of tape from an adding machine.

A younger man stands quietly next to the man from Gosplan.

---

* "Третьим будешь?"

He may be thirty—he looks like he could be the older man's son, but the clothing suggests that the two come from different strata. The younger man wears a dark-blue cloth jacket filled with cotton, a low-tech equivalent of the ugly, shapeless coat kids back home now call a "parka." This jacket is called a "*vatnik*," Norm recalls. If you wear a *vatnik*, chances are you spend your days standing behind a lathe, making the norm.

"A ruble and thirty-seven," says the younger man in a *vatnik*.

Norm reaches into the pocket of his son's bloodstained overcoat and counts out a paper ruble and four ten-kopek coins.

The young man grabs the money and heads toward the doors of the Gastronom.

"I hear an accent. What's your nationality? A Pole?" asks the man from Gosplan.

"Yes, a Pole."

Norm did, after all, begin his life as a citizen of Poland.

"Is your life like ours? A bordello? Sitting deep in the ass?" Gosplan follows up.

In Russian, "бардак," *bardak*, has a dual meaning: a bordello and systemic dysfunction.

"A bordello; we are sitting."* Yes and yes.

The younger man emerges from the Gastronom, a half-liter bottle sticking out of the pocket of his *vatnik*. In Pittsburgh, you get used to what a fifth looks like—that's 750 milliliters, a good 50 percent larger.

"Let's split it on the bench over there, in a cultured manner,"† the older man proposes, pointing at a bench in what looks like a park.

---

* "Бардак, сидим."

† "А ну разопьем на скамеечке, как подобает людям интеллигентным."

This is starting to make sense: Three men who don't know each other are about to split a bottle, in the street, with no bartender presiding. It's analogous to a pickup volleyball game at the YMCA. The objective must be to split the bottle that none of the three can afford on his own. Norm is the third. Hence, his cut is a ruble and thirty-seven. The label on the bottle reads "Ekstra." It's a good word. What can possibly go wrong?

After the trio crosses the road and settles onto a park bench, the man from Gosplan reaches into his briefcase and pulls out a glass.

The bench frame is cast iron, rounded, ornate, its wooden planks chunky, covered in thick paint. Looking across, beyond the alley and another line of benches, Norm spots a gray building that looks like something from this century rather than last.

"*Literaturnaya Gazeta,*" he reads. *The Literary Gazette.* The newspaper of the intelligentsia. Started by none other than Pushkin. The building, actually a gem, makes him think of the asymmetrical Bauhaus structures in Tel Aviv.

GOSPLAN: Across from *Literaturka*, like people of refinement. What do you think, Pole?

VATNIK: Are you a real Pole, or one of their Jews? You do have Jewish eyes—shifty, fuck your . . .

GOSPLAN: If a man says he is a Pole, he is a Pole. A Jew wouldn't waste time with our brotherhood—the alkies.

VATNIK: That's true, brother—pour!*

Gosplan sets the glass on the bench, fills it a hair above the

---

* ГОСПЛАН: Напротив Литературки, как люди благородные. Ничего себе, поляк?
    ВАТНИК: А ты на самом деле поляк аль еврей ихний? Глаза у тебя еврейские, бегают.
    ГОСПЛАН: Говорит человек поляк, значит поляк. Чего еврею с нашим братом алкашом делать то?
    ВАТНИК: Ну да, братишка—наливай!

three-quarter level, exhales, tilts his head back, and downs the contents in a single gulp.

GOSPLAN: Went down well . . .

VATNIK: Good—except for the cost. Four rubles and twelve kopeks, fuck your . . . *

It's Vatnik's turn with the glass. His style is different. No apocalyptic exhale, no devil-may-care tilting back of the head. He takes one sip, as cautious as dipping a toe into a cold stream, then a series of determined gulps: one, two, three.

In the forest, whenever they captured spirits from the Germans or—more likely—taken *samogon* from the peasants, Norm liked watching his comrades flaunt their drinking styles. He doesn't remember what his drinking style was then—the exhale, the tilting of the head, the number of gulps per glass, etc.

At the Green Oaks Country Club, in the lounge, Norm has been known to sip a martini or three, always Tanqueray, always shaken, one-third vermouth, two-thirds gin, with an olive. Vermouth is about herbs, the forest floor, etc., but it's also the least forestlike substance Norm can think of.

VATNIK: Hey, Pole, drink for friendship between our peoples, fuck your . . . †

Norm's share of the bottle is about the size of a martini—hardly a Herculean feat of alcohol intake. Norm takes a sip, drains the glass in one gulp, and emits a hearty grunt.

With approximately 166.667 grams of Ekstra making a home within his innards, he bids adieu to his acquaintances.

---

* ГОСПЛАН: Хорошо пошла—курва . . .

ВАТНИК: Хорошо то хорошо, только цена то какая—четыре-бля-двенадцать, ёб твою . . .

† ГОСПЛАН: Эй, поляк, давай дерябнем за дружбу, блядь, народов, мать твою родину душу за ногу . . .

■ ■ ■

Across from the park, Norm notices a building that looks like it might be the circus. He hasn't been to a circus since 1936. He recalls the feeling of the circus—pure, screaming delight. Has this pure, screaming delight been placed out of Norm's reach?

He turns into what looks like a farmers' market, recognizing it by the smell of garlic and dill emitted by vats of marinating pickles. At a dry goods store, to the left of the entrance, Norm notices a Jewish-looking old man at the register.

"*Tsi hot ir an avoske?*" he asks in Yiddish.

"*Avade,*" the old man answers. "*Vifl avoskes vilt ir koyfn?*"

"*Ikh mayn az tsvey is genig.*"*

Americans, especially wealthy Americans, don't always have the best attitude when they travel abroad. It's plausible that Norm was less likable in Rome, Paris, or Tokyo. But here in Moscow, on January 16, 1976, Norm's attitude is respectful and culturally sensitive. In less than an hour, he has split a bottle with anonymous alcoholics and done business in Yiddish.

Madison is on the phone when Norm lets himself into the apartment. By the time the Foreign Desk gets done with Madison's story, everything is on the table: a bottle of Ekstra, Orlovsky sour rye, a jar of horseradish, two hundred grams of sliced bologna-like† sausage, two hundred grams of mortadella-like sausage,‡ a

---

* "Do you have a mesh bag?"
  "Of course. How many mesh bags do you want?"
  "I think two would be sufficient."

† Докторская.

‡ Любительская.

similar amount of Ukrainian fatback, cut up in chunks, radishes sharing an oval plate with a modest pile of green onions. Also on the table are three bowls, the first of which contains pickles, the second marinated mushrooms, and the third Provençale cabbage.

"What is all this?" asks Madison, looking tiredly at the table.

"What does it look like to you, Madison?"

"I fixed myself a peanut butter sandwich while getting reamed out by the Foreign Desk. I'll need to turn in early—you suit yourself."

15.

At 6:17 a.m., January 17, 1976, a tall man wearing a checkered overcoat and a gray hat that looks like it might be made of wolf fur walks past the guard's booth at Sad Sam.

After a light snowfall, the road crews have cleared the streets, but the broad alley of Tsvetnoy Boulevard is pristine.

As his leather boots break up the powder on Tsvetnoy Boulevard, past *Literaturnaya Gazeta*, past the circus he longs to attend, Norm's left hand rests atop the keychain in his pocket. His Cadillac key is the biggest of the bunch. This morning, he positions it between the index and middle finger, letting it stick out, like a bayonet atop a rifle.

At school, in Poland, a left-handed child was forced to shift the pen from the left hand to the right. Even recalcitrant children ultimately learned that holding a pen in your left hand brought on being struck with a ruler on your right. Most children were rendered normal as a result of this treatment. For others, normalcy wasn't complete. Consider Norm. He squeezes the trigger with his right hand, he writes with his right hand, he sketches with his right hand, but when death is less than a meter away and a knife is all he has, he trusts only his left.

Norm passes by the tall brown granite column. Atop the column, in a duel that never ends, a bronze St. George slays a dragon.

Stopping to admire the structure long enough to force his thoughts back into the real world, Norm turns left, toward Chistyye Prudy, the Clear Ponds, setting the course toward the residence of Albert Schwartz, a man nicknamed the King of Refuseniks.

Norm didn't call ahead. It's both futile and compromising to the mission. Of course, Schwartz's phone is monitored.

One thing to remember: You don't want to be stopped while carrying this suitcase. The consequences of carrying fifty thousand rubles, even sort of legally procured fifty thousand rubles, can't be good. But why would anyone want to detain him as he trudges through predawn Moscow, disguised in his son's Soviet coat and a wolf hat?

Seventeen Chistoprudnyy Boulevard is on the left.

Through a missing section of the ornate cast-iron fence that separates the boulevard from the tramway tracks, Norm crosses Chistoprudnyy and circles the building. It's Greco-Roman in style, Russian in execution, two stories in height.

The balcony that overhangs the entryway has a view of the pond across the street. Schwartz lives here, in this room with this balcony, in this former palace that long ago became a cold-water communal flat.

It's best to come in through the former tradesmen's entrance in the back of the building. Norm walks through the courtyard archway on the side. The back door to the building opens without a creak, and quietly letting himself in, Norm enters what seems to be the kitchen.

Bedsheets are drying in the middle of the room. The oven is on, its door open. In this maze of damp bedsheets, Norm's cheek rubs against the linen. The cloth feels harsh, a bit like plywood.

Has Norm forgotten that poverty is moist, moldy, smelling of cabbage, with bedsheets drying in the heat of an open oven beneath the bubbling plaster, punctuated by the wheezing sounds of asthma? A "chest toad,"* it's called in Russian. The chest toad is not a toad at all. A toad projects satisfaction with the swamp; asthma is about incompleteness, unsatisfied urgency to finish a breath, respiratory disappointment. Norm moves toward the spot where a staircase might be, and it's here indeed, as dark and creaky as he had imagined.

From behind the door of one of the rooms facing the courtyard, Norm hears the sounds of the start of morning exercises. It must be seven o'clock—the radio is on:

"*Prepare for conducting gymnastic exercises . . .*" a sugary voice commands in Russian.

"Go fuck yourself," Norm mutters as the voice instructs the physical culturalist behind the door to "*straighten up, hold your head higher, shoulders back slightly, breathe in, and—in place—march!*"

A blast of piano music douses Norm like a splash from a piss bucket. That voice again:

"*And a-one, two, three, four! Straighten up!*"

That's what Lenin would have sounded like when drunk. In the free world, a voice like that would get you beat up.

Somebody is actually behind that door, marching in place, taking commands from the radio. It's equally likely that this isn't about exercise at all. Someone is playing this thing loudly to piss off the neighbors.

A woman's voice from behind another door, on the boulevard side, seems to support the latter hypothesis.

---

* "Трудная жаба."

"Turn it down, torturer. People are sleeping!"*

"Shut your trap, old cunt. You should drink less!"† retorts the physical culturalist whose voice suggests that he, too, should consider cutting down on short-sighted pursuit of pleasure, starting with smoking.

"*Straighten up . . .*" the voice on the radio blasts louder. "*Cease marching. Now it's time to stretch and breathe deeply.*"

Norm taps lightly, then tugs on the door handle. It's brass, it's Polish. He recognizes the shape from his childhood in Krakow. Privacy is a foreign concept here, in this big communal flat, where lives of others constitute a form of free entertainment. Any second, a door might swing open, and a neighbor would emerge, perhaps in pajamas or a night coat, asking who, what, and why. What if Schwartz is a sound sleeper? Norm can't stay here, in this dark hallway, for more than a minute or two. He can't bang louder, he can't shout.

What if a neighbor calls the militia? What if they show up before Norm gets away, what if they order him to open his bag? What if they decide to monkey with the lining? What would he say? That he is a millionaire from Pittsburgh, Pennsylvania, bringing Schwartz a shipment of *Playboy*s, *Penthouse*s, Levi's—and fifty thousand rubles?

Norm got this far; there is no way back. He will need to leave this bag at Schwartz's even if it means breaking into this room and shaking the bastard awake.

"*Bend forward, straighten up, exhale, inhale, exhale, inhale,*" the radio commands.

---

* "Выключи, изверг. Люди ещё спят!"
† "Заткнись, пизда старая, пить меньше надо было."

Exhale-inhale is a good idea. What if Schwartz isn't alone?

Fuck it . . . Norm reaches for his keys—he has a dozen, each unlocking a part of his life in America. He tries three keys that look like they might work, but none of them fits into the keyhole. He could break the door, but that would be heard, even with gymnastics of doom chasing away the morning cockroaches.

"Three . . . four . . . straighten your back, softly lower yourself on one knee."

A thought flashes: "What about a credit card?" Norm pulls out an American Express, sticks it into the doorjamb, running it gently next to the frame to find the bolt. He tilts the card toward the doorknob, then bends it the opposite way. It's up against the lock's mechanism. He leans on the door, wiggling the card.

"One, two . . . And now lie down on your back on a mat. Put your legs together and position your arms along the core, with palms down."

The streetlight is the first thing Norm sees as the door opens and he straightens up to walk in.

The metal-on-metal sound he hears is a tramway. He sees sparks sent flying from the power lines. The streetlight puts out enough light to tell Norm that the curtains aren't just left ajar. They are gone, together with the curtain rods. The glass of these splendid windows has been cleaned, meticulously, industrially, as has everything else beneath this soaring ceiling. There is no one in bed. There is no bed, no table, no chairs, no carpet, no armoire. Nothing but the stench of ammonia lingers in this room once inhabited by Albert Schwartz.

"The exercises are complete. Move on to water procedures," is

220 | PAUL GOLDBERG

the last thing Norm hears as, his suitcase in hand, he runs down the stairs toward the tradesmen's entrance of that stinking, big *kommunalka*.

Where is this Schwartz? Arrested? Disappeared? Killed? They haven't killed anyone yet, as far as Norm knows. Two of the airplane crazies were sentenced to die, but the Sovs got cold feet. This war has been so much less treacherous than Norm's last one, when people vanished by tens of millions, but in war things change.

As Norm considers retracing his path back to Sad Sam, he hears a car door slam shut.

A flash startles Norm amid the morning's darkness.

It seems to come from a car parked directly in front of the entrance to 17 Chistoprudnyy. Norm must have walked right past it, not realizing that someone was inside. Norm pivots 180 degrees, turning left, walking rapidly.

A half a block away, Norm turns left onto Makarenko Street, glancing back as he makes the turn. There are two men behind him. Norm's suitcase . . . The jeans aren't a problem, the porno magazines are a bit of a problem, but the fifty thousand rubles— definitely a problem.

This is not Norm's first mission, not his first time realizing that he must not be captured. Come to think of it, Norm has never been on a mission of the sort where getting captured alive was acceptable, in a forest or out. What does anyone know about Schwartz? Is Schwartz indeed a refusenik? Is Schwartz Schwartz? What does anyone know about anyone? Was this a trap all along?

Questions about Norm breaking into the communal flat, forcing open the door to the room of an internationally known Jewish activist or, potentially, a KGB double agent would be dangerous enough, but there is more. The manner in which he came to the USSR—to visit his son, a U.S. journalist—is the biggest problem of all. Madison would be accused of currency crimes, assistance to seditious elements, and, for good measure—espionage.

His mind racing through scenarios, Norm looks back quickly, to see whether the two men are gaining on him, which they are.

Where were they when Norm walked into this apartment? Were they snoozing in their car? Were they drunk? Wasting time watching the front door when anyone with a semifunctional brain would go in through the back?

The two men are gaining, Norm feels it. They are, maybe, fifty meters away.

Norm's thoughts turn to his Waffen-SS butterfly knife, a marvel of engineering, with a brass handle that folds around a double-edged blade. He wishes he had it now, because no better fighting knife has ever existed. He took it off a corpse. Is there another way for someone like Norm to obtain something like a Waffen-SS butterfly knife? You make a Waffen-SS corpse, then you take a Waffen-SS butterfly knife off said Waffen-SS corpse.

The thing is covered with swastikas, but make no mistake, it's ours, rehabilitated in the service of Red partisans. Having used it to cut at least four German throats, Norm has kept it through DP camps and immigration. It's his only wartime memento. He keeps it in his desk drawer, not because he is afraid of anyone, but because it reminds him of who he once was. Madison will never want his Waffen-SS knife. Maybe his children—should he have any—will understand. It can take generations for big things to be understood.

Sometimes Norm opens the desk drawer and unfolds that knife—it's neither a jackknife, which opens like a doorframe, nor a stiletto, which flies out with the pressing of a button. When you don't use it, your butterfly knife's handle acts as its cage. You open this brass cage, freeing the steel blade, and the cage transforms itself into a handle. The knife makes Norm think of Krakow, of his parents, of his grandparents, of Sobibor, of the comrades in the forest, of that particular mad day of killing. Could the man who stamped the swastikas on that knife's brass and steel have foreseen that it would turn against the Nazis and come to rest in a Jew's desk in Pittsburgh, Pennsylvania?

The tide must be turned, right here, in this archway—5 Maka-renko Street. Norm's left hand is in the coat pocket, grasping the Cadillac key. Norm, as noted, is not fully right-handed: he shoots, writes, and sketches with his right hand, but he wields a fighting knife in his left.

Norm turns sharply into the archway. His right hand grasps the handle of the American Tourister. Much will depend on its sturdi-ness. His left hand is in the pocket, the Cadillac key between the middle and index finger.

He walks slower, waiting for them to catch up.

One, two, three, four . . . The physical culture idiot was right about breathing. It must be done, even when it interrupts concentration.

Right shoulder will come close to the stucco wall of the arch-way, here, by this graffiti, this word "ХУЙ" painted in big cursive letters on the wall. Do not stop, not fully. Now, open up—hard, sharp. They are two meters away when his right shoulder touches the wall and with this light tap, he opens into a pivot, sending the suitcase-bearing arm toward them.

The bag feels heavy at first, but it lightens as it finds centrifugal force, becomes weightless, or close enough, and, with a thud, finds the target—perfect, slamming into someone's head. It will knock him unconscious, maybe kill him. As the man falters, Norm lets go of the handle, and with his left hand Cadillac-keys the second pursuer in the solar plexus. Who knows what that will do; Norm is not an anatomist, and not having done anything of this sort in thirty-one years, he is out of practice.

The bag has opened, the Levi's, *Playboys*, and *Penthouses* have spilled out. He will need to tidy up, but first he will recover the camera. One of the men is bent over after taking a hit in the solar plexus.

A simple boxing jab under the chin brings him down. As he tumbles, Norm gives his comrade a kick on the ear. This might kill, too, but you can't let such considerations stop you. They have cameras, both of them. Here, in the overcoats. This is it, stomp on the cameras, expose the film, fast. One of the men stirs again, the other moans. A kick on the ear ends that.

Now, clean up. The jeans are here, folded as books, throw them in, then throw in the three *Penthouses*, two *Playboys*. Something like that. The bag doesn't close, its lock broken. Get their belts, one is enough, wrap it around the bag, tighten it—done . . .

A man less savvy than Norm might have run back out onto Makarenko Street and taken a left. Norm knows that if returning alive is among your objectives, you must stay as close to the site as your nerves allow. A fighter must drill inward, which in this case means running into the courtyard, opening the first entryway door in sight, then up the stairs, to the attic, or, better, the rooftop. There, you can wait for hours as search parties are dispatched to all corners of the city to hunt down God knows what.

At the top of the stairs of building 1A of 5 Makarenko—on the fifth floor—Norm spots a steel ladder to the attic and, presumably, the roof. The latch atop the ladder is locked, but with a sharp pull, both the latch and the padlock tumble to the floor.

The crawl space to the roof is right here. Norm opens the window.

A half-meter-deep snowbank has formed on the roof's southern incline. The northern is a solid sheet of ice. As a gust of wind covers his face with dry snow, Norm takes off his wolf hat, unties the laces on top, drops down the earflaps. Staying on the snowy side of the roof, with his gloved hands (good thing he didn't forget his gloves) he digs out a seat at the roof's crest. It's best to stay at the very top. The snowbank can begin to move at any moment and the ice isn't exactly your friend as you sit atop a steep roof.

It's 7:46 a.m. Perched silently above, Norm is unable to see activity below. He can, however, hear the sirens and the footsteps of many men.

Norm watches the mighty city begin to stir.

Tramways negotiate the fluid curve at Chistyye Prudy. Snowplows trudge through the Garden Ring, ambulances and other vehicles—some white, some black, some green, some without sirens, some with—rush toward the archway of 5 Makarenko, the place where two KGB operatives are found unconscious or, possibly, dead.

While they tend to the wounded or the dead, in dawn's red light, Norm studies the confluence of the Moskva and Yauza rivers, the golden cupola within the walls of the Kremlin. Soon, the disk of the sun will start to rise beyond the Kursk Railroad Station, beyond Yauza, and, from a safe distance, nudge the golden domes behind the Kremlin walls to begin a new day.

. . .

They've fanned out, looking for the perpetrator. They are enthusiastic at first, but their commitment will wane after an hour. Who would look for him here, on top of this iced-up roof of 5 Makarenko, reclining in the white Adirondack chair he has carved out of a snowbank?

Watching the sun rise above this city, Norm recognizes that the long-forgotten feeling of absolute calm has returned. It's a feeling that comes from knowing who you are. Norm is a partisan, Norm is a Jew, or a Jew and a partisan, the hunted, the hunter. People shouldn't be allowed to walk out into the street without demonstrating that they know what they mean when they say "I."

This roof is a fine place to think. In Sobibor, Russian prisoners taught Norm the word "доходяга," pronounced *dokhodyaga*, someone who has reached the edge. A *dokhodyaga* has lost identity, dignity, humanity. In a demented daze, he'll put everything in his mouth: leaves, weeds, blades of grass, leaflets, dead rodents, pieces of rotting flesh of any provenance, human included. A *dokhodyaga* will throw himself on a fence, invite a volley of bullets from a guard on the tower.

You need to understand the essence of a *dokhodyaga* to do the exact opposite; you push harder, past the edge, you hold on to the things that were given to you, you define who you are and go from there, to push through, to bend the world. This strategy has guided Norm through the cataclysms of the twentieth century, and here he is, now, in Moscow, on a rooftop, with a bent Cadillac key in his pocket.

An American Tourister, held together with a KGB operative's belt, sits in the snowdrift next to Norm. There is only one thing to be done with it—dump it, carefully, with the brain fully engaged.

Norm's contact is gone, his room cleaned out, devoid of curtains, reeking of death and ammonia.

Perhaps Norm can stash the money in the attic here till he finds another contact. But how would he know that he isn't walking into a trap? Returning to the stash is asking for trouble—always. Just leaving the bag here and forgetting about it is risky, too. What if they return with dogs? He opens the bag, and, using the bent Cadillac key, cuts into the lining. One stack of hundreds is all he takes. The rest must go.

Miriam would plotz. Miriam, who has come to savor all things American, Miriam who doesn't have a number tattooed on her forearm, Miriam who was taken in by the nuns in Krakow, Sisters of Our Lady of Something or Other. She gets furious when Norm calls them *dem Shvester der Yoshke un Matke Bozhke. Yoshke un Matke Bozhke* is a Yiddish saying that mocks Jesus (calling him Yoshke), his mother (Mother of God in proper Polish is *Matka Boska*, not Yiddishized *Matke Bozhke*).

Perhaps he should stop.

Avalanches begin with a sound reminiscent of cracking. When you sit straddling the top of a tin roof and a meter-deep layer of snow begins to move, you get a sharp, shallow sound of icy tin, deepened by vibration of century-old dry oak timbers beneath it. The result is something akin to the sound of a church bell, deep, bronze.

A crack forms within a foot of Norm's perch and snow begins to move, slowly at first, then speeding up. He must have weakened it when he was carving out his seat atop the roof. The rest is reflex, something his body can pull off only if he allows his mind to disengage. Shift slightly to the left, toward the ice as the snow on your right begins to move, trying to pull you into the abyss of the courtyard. Not too much to the left, just enough to counteract the snow's movement, but not so much that the ice will funnel you off the roof and onto the asphalt five stories below. If you do it right, keeping one foot on the southern incline and the other on the northern, while remembering to hold on to the handle of the American Tourister containing nearly fifty thousand rubles, you will settle gently onto the roof's crest.

Once again, Norm keeps his wits about him, and once again Norm survives.

By 9:30, the noise below subsides. They must have gotten cold, given up on their semblance of an investigation, gone back to the office to drink tea. Norm waits for another half hour, just to make sure, and at 10:00, give or take, he slips down into the dark attic below.

On the third floor, he walks past an old woman with a cane. Their chat, if you can call it that, consists of Norm confirming that he is staying with the Birulins on the fifth floor, that he is an uncle visiting from Kiev, now going back (hence the suitcase).

Then Norm does his best to feign outrage about thugs who have beat up two middle-aged men in the archway earlier this morning.

"They've lost all manner of restraint," says the old woman, resolutely tapping her cane on the gray terrazzo floor.

"Indeed, they have."

On Chaplygin Street, less than a block away, Norm catches up with a snowplow.

Moscow has developed a magnificent piece of equipment for snow removal, a machine called Golden Hands. Looking like a truck-sized Machine Age puppet, it's a moving plow that grabs snow with handlike shovels, places it on a conveyor, and jauntily, as though over its shoulder, drops it onto the bed of a truck that travels directly behind it.

If you want to lose something—like, for example, a busted American Tourister containing five new pairs of Levi's, copies of *Playboy* and *Penthouse*, and fifty thousand rubles—and have it go away forever, just throw it in the truck that follows Golden Hands.

Come April, it will be making its way to the bottom of the Moskva River. By that time, Norm will be sipping martinis at the Green Oaks Country Club. Tanqueray. The usual proportion of vermouth. Shaken. Olive.

16.

Moscow is shaking off the night's sprinkling of snow, making a morning adjustment, Oksana-like, rubbing her eyes.

Flash-forward a year or two. Would Viktor, in private moments, long for dry, cold Moscow mornings, when you wake up and quietly soak in the sound the street sweeper's shovel makes clearing a narrow path through the darkened courtyard?

Medical books make no mention of *nostalgiya*, but belles lettres overflow with accounts of its deadly toll. It's a disease that makes the sufferer long for snow, birch trees, mushrooms, the Russian language spoken in the streets. Yes, language above all else.

This variety of longing has been known to result in the blowing out of the brains, or, in slow-flowing manifestations, cirrhosis of the liver. Folk wisdom teaches that it is best to suffer through *nostalgiya* early, to let it take its bite while you are still here, to manufacture a vaccine and start to weep as you behold this iced-up river or the boulevards' white curves, long benches turned to snowdrifts, and puffs of white that perch atop St. George's column—upon his sword, upon the dragon's jaws—and, as you reach Gorky Street, weep as you behold the powdery turban on Pushkin's bowed head and thick, white epaulets on the poet's shoulders.

Viktor leaves early, before Oksana wakes up.

Walking out of the building, he sees two Volgas idling across the street: the mouse-gray one and the black one. The left fender of the mouse-gray Volga is banged up, the headlight smashed, after the Garden Ring episode.

It's dark. Their headlights are on. They aren't hiding.

Viktor remembers a century-old joke he heard from an old man in Odessa a month and a half ago:

"I can already tell this is going to be a bad day," says a Jew facing a firing squad.

That's it—the whole joke. One line; you get it or you don't. Does it not connect with Viktor's situation right now? No need to laugh when a smile of recognition will suffice. Perhaps today his turn will come.

Two men step out of the mouse-gray Volga; two more step out of the black one. They will follow him on foot, conspicuously, keeping close, as the cars crawl behind.

It's up to Viktor to lead this procession of dunces. He could take them for a march around the Bulgarian Wanker, then inside a courtyard, pick up a broomstick maybe, playing the part of a priest with an oversized crucifix, or a goofy majorette. He could march them around the dumpster, tie up the morning traffic, walk them into the Moskva River, where all of them would freeze and drown, but what would be the point? Besides, the river is iced up.

Someone in the apparatus of state security, perhaps Lydia Ivanovna, perhaps someone above her, wants to roll him in for another soulful talk or, perhaps, a protracted stay.

Viktor turns around, facing his marchers.

"Now what?" he asks, moving his arms quizzically apart.

Flash-forward a moment, and he is in the back seat of the

banged-up Volga driven by a man now wearing a neck brace that rises high above the collar.

Viktor's gaze follows the contours of the river. What if this time they plucked him off the street to let him leave the country—right now? As a logical exercise, a thought experiment, imagine this: they let us go, Viktor and Oksana—this very afternoon.

The KGB building's massive façade, on Dzerzhinsky Square, is dead, a curtain that obscures the play.

It's plausible that the grand entrance in the building's center was nailed shut years ago. Would any bearer of the cloak and dagger wish to be seen passing through the double-high front doors of that block-long edifice? Anyone in KGB uniform and, arguably, Andropov, the chairman himself, wouldn't be harmed by the demonstrative act of using the front door, but that's about it. If you are in plainclothes, you enter through the amalgamation of buildings in the back, where the committee's real work is done.

Muscovites observe this parade of state security from behind the windows of Gastronom No. 40, on Lubyansky Proyezd, on the corner, where you can avail yourself of a better-than-usual selection of sausages, meats, and pastries, as well as a splendid "milk cocktail," a milkshake. You can stand at a marble-topped table and, savoring the crispness of the outer shell and the inner softness of an eclair, watch the Volgas and anemia-green prison Gaziks enter the castle-like gates as you, in twain homage to Dante and Solzhenitsyn, repeat within your skull: "*Lasciate ogne rofesso voi ch'intrate*" and offer praise to the Divine Providence for sparing your body and your soul.

Contemplating the KGB gates off Lubyansky Proyezd, Viktor

has often played out fantasies of how his arrest might transpire. It's a ubiquitous fantasy. It involves spitting in the faces of leather-jacketed, jackbooted thugs. This archetypal rehearsal is why the KGB favors single-shot-to-the-back-of-the-head executions. Such positioning makes it impossible to spit into your killer's face.

At 7:43 a.m., the mouse-gray Volga comes to a full stop in front of the KGB gates off Lubyansky Proyezd. The driver steps out, leaving the car idling as he shouts into a grate in the wall, then rushes back into his seat, awaiting disposition. Viktor's inner engineer notes the dull hum of an electric motor as it engages the pneumatic arms that make these tons of metal budge and slide toward a long, tunnellike archway illuminated with a single line of lights.

It's not quite 8:00 a.m., and Viktor Venyaminovich Moroz is already able to tell that this will not be a good day.

"Viktor Venyaminovich!" shouts Lydia Ivanovna as Viktor steps out of the Volga and looks up at the square of sky above the courtyard. "I wager you've never thought you'd be passing through these gates."

He has. Jackboots, leather, spit, and brains figure in many of the scenarios Viktor plays out on sleepless nights. A short, bubbly woman, in a glistening black karakul coat with a thin blue mink collar and a matching mink hat, doesn't.

Viktor is struck by the smallness of this courtyard. He notes the fire escapes and the smokestack—or is it a chute—at the front of one of the buildings. Reaching toward the still-dark sky, it tops off just above the roofline, unseen from the outside. Is it, perchance, connected to the crematorium? Is it operational?

A massive hulk of a car covered with a water-stained, iced-up canvas tarp and, upon it, a mound of fresh snow is hard to miss. The object under the tarp is very, very large, a shape from a different time. Any Russian who knows cars—even a fallen engineer—would recognize this shape as a ZIS, the acronym for Zavod Imeni Stalina, Stalin Auto Plant. It has to be a ZIS-110, a limousine that harkens to the era when cars and steam engines bore the Great Leader's name.

"Viktor Venyaminovich, it is exactly what you think," says Lydia Ivanovna, nodding at the car.

"How do you know what I am thinking? Was Virgil able to read Dante's thoughts?"

"I can't recall, but you are thinking that it's Lavrenty Pavlovich's ZIS."

"ZIS-110. Built in 1948, give or take a year."

"No, no. ZIS-110 wasn't armored. This is. It's ZIS-115. I know this car well. You may recall, I had the honor . . ."

"You've mentioned, Lydia Ivanovna."

"Some details have come out about the rapes, but not enough. Some of us were raped in this car. I, for example. This hulk has been sitting on its rims in this very spot for twenty-three years. They are afraid to lift the tarp and let out the demons that have made a home there."

"I feel demons all around."

"It's well known here that if anyone blows this thing up, it would be I. This is actually a very good exercise for me. It keeps me in control of my emotions. Now, follow me . . ."

"Are you taking me to be processed?"

"Like Solzhenitsyn? In Gulag? A worthy fantasy, but no. We'll enter here," says Lydia Ivanovna, pointing toward the door closest to the chute or smokestack.

"Perhaps you'll show me where they executed the Yiddish poets?"

"On August twelfth, 1952 . . ."

"The night of the murdered poets—yes. Do they teach you this organization's history in orientation?"

"No. But I know it—I have to. My specialty is *inakomysliye*, 'dissent,' as they call it on enemy radio stations."

"Where did they kill them?"

"In this complex. We are going to the morgue, which is contiguous to the execution cellar and the crematorium."

"Convenient . . ."

"What can I say?"

"You know, Viktor Venyaminovich, you and I wag our tongues entirely too much," she says in the elevator.

Is this some strange flirtation? She is a dozen years older and not his type—plus he is married, as she might be. A coquettish KGB curator is the last thing anyone needs.

"I would be wholly amenable to ceasing our so-called tongue-wagging."

Did this sound flirtatious? He hopes not.

"I am aware of that, Viktor Venyaminovich. As agreed, after this is done, we will stop."

Why is she talking about their interaction as though it's an affair? What if she decides to kiss him, here, in this cramped, crawling elevator, on the way down to the place where her colleagues famously murdered thirteen members of the Jewish intelligentsia not quite a quarter century ago, here, in a room conveniently contiguous to the morgue and the crematorium?

"We have no understanding, actually. We agree on nothing."

"You know the joke about this building? How it's the tallest in Moscow?"

"I am familiar."

"Siberia from the basement? Yes?"

He nods. He must be formal, correct. If there's an attack, he'll thwart it, swat it. And—this is even more important—why in the name of the Lord is this Lydia Ivanovna taking Viktor to the *morgue*, and not just any morgue, but the KGB morgue—here?

His back is pressed against the elevator's mesh wall.

"You know, Viktor Venyaminovich, I've been thinking about why I love my job so much," she says as the elevator bumps to a stop. "I love my job because it puts me in touch with cultured people, and I get official access to the same books that you—the genuine intelligentsia—read in this confused, confusing time."

As they walk down a long, harshly illuminated corridor, Viktor sees nothing that hints at names of departments, divisions, administrative units of any sort—only last names and initials next to the doors or on them: A. K. Ivanov, V. A. Petrov, Ye. I. Sidorov. No Georgians, no Jews, no Armenians, no Uzbeks, no Tatars. All the names are so Russian that, statistically, at least some of them have to be pseudonyms.

Lydia Ivanovna gives a swift kick to the steel door that reads "N. A. Baranova," turns the knob, and leads Viktor into a smallish room with a wall of oversized steel filing cabinets.

Viktor glances at the window to ascertain the room's position in relation to the chute or chimney he noticed while looking up in the courtyard.

"This would be the time and place to mention Peretz Markish, David Hofstein, Itzik Fefer, Leib Kvitko—that's just the poets."

"And David Bergelson," whispers Lydia Ivanovna. "He wrote

prose, of course, so not a poet. And Venyamin Zuskin, while you are listing names. An actor, I know, but still . . . Played Fool in *King Lear*, or *Nar* in *Kinig Lir*, since it was in Yiddish."

"The world became a poorer place that night."

"A bad, bad night—concurred. From what I hear, they were shot one by one next door to where we are right now. You saw the room. It has the name 'Ye. I. Sidorov' on the door."

"Is there such a person, this Ye. I. Sidorov?"

"I don't know," she whispers, then sings out, "Nadezhda Alexeyevna, we are he-ere!"

Nadezhda Alexeyevna Baranova is a woman of sixty or so, with hair dyed a solid shade of red, brick-like. She is shorter than Viktor, shorter even than Lydia Ivanovna. Her pallor speaks to a deficit of pigmentation and sunlight.

"I asked Nadezhda Alexeyevna to present the cases."

"So, well—fine. I can tell and I can show," Nadezhda Alexeyevna begins, pulling a sharp pencil out of a plastic pocket protector of her white coat.

Her speech is clipped. Viktor hears the exaggerated "o" sound of someone from the heart of Russia, probably the town of Vladimir and its environs.

"Please take this bag, just in case. People get nauseous here—and they don't give me a full-time cleaner. I have to either get out a mop and bucket and clean it up myself or step over it all day until someone from above sends me a woman with a mop."*

---

* "Возьмите пожалуйста пакетик на всякий пожарный. У нас многих, часто бывает, тошнит—а уборщицы мне на полную ставку никак не дают. Как кто, простите, наблюёт—мне либо самой брать ведро да швабру, либо переступать и ждать пока сверху прислать изволят."

Viktor didn't think another look at the corpses would make him vomit, but vomit he does, even now.

It may be something about the sharp pencil Nadezhda Alexeyevna uses as a pointer to demonstrate the separation of the ribs from Schwartz's spinal column, the wound that made the blood fill his chest cavity, the blow to Schwartz's head that freed that *kholodetz*-like substance from Schwartz's cranium, and the splintering of Schwartz's neck.

Foxman's head, which was still dangling at an unnatural angle when Viktor discovered the bodies, is now completely detached, resting on its side. The sight of Nadezhda Alexeyevna's rubber-gloved hand moving the head to demonstrate the view from beneath its base makes Viktor release another stream of vomit. These exsanguinated, frozen men are his friends. They are entitled to justice, both of them. What if this Lydia Ivanovna is truthful, in which case solving this heinous crime will be his ticket out, the price of freedom bought quietly, in darkness, the same darkness that on August 12, 1952, had claimed the lives of the poets?

Nadezhda Alexeyevna doesn't pause as Viktor bends over to emit another stream of vomit into the bag. She has a presentation to rush through, and if a listener is unable to keep up, well, it's not her problem, as long as the floor of her morgue stays clean. Viktor manages to hit the bag without much spillage as the details make his stomach twist. He continues to vomit even after Nadezhda Alexeyevna pushes closed the freezer doors and Schwartz and Foxman return to cold darkness, their home for the past four days.

"The weapon used was an ax?" he asks after Nadezhda Alexeyevna finishes her talk. "Could you describe it for me?"

"A simple midsized ax, with a twelve-centimeter blade, probably made here, in the USSR, as I said. The handle would be around fifty centimeters in length."

"What can you tell me about the murderer?"

"Nothing outstanding, really. A calm person, probably. I say this because he doesn't swing wildly. Sometimes, when the killer gets anxious, you see twenty, thirty whacks. Here, I see only one whack of questionable necessity, the cracking of the cranium of the active homosexual, the one on top, the Soviet citizen. He is already incapacitated, twitching as he bleeds into the chest. The killer can use the back of the ax, or even the blade, to clear access to the neck of the man below, the passive homosexual. Instead, he cracks the skull, which is unnecessary, really. But he is not swinging wildly."

"Economical movements, mostly?" asks Lydia Ivanovna. "Does the handling of the ax suggest expertise? Medical training, military training?"

"I am from Vladimir Oblast. We chop a lot of wood there. In my village, anyone would have the skills for this. Most of us know how to butcher a cow; a human isn't any harder. We keep saying 'he,' but I don't know, it could easily have been 'she.' My mother can still stick a pig, and she is eighty-seven. All I can tell you is it had to be a calm person, and women are calmer than men. But I don't know."

"What about the cleanup?" asks Lydia Ivanovna.

"What cleanup? You put on an overcoat, go outside, and wipe your face with snow. That's your cleanup."

"And carrying the ax in the street?"

"That's nonsense. Raskolnikov figured it out, in the book. And Raskolnikov had weak nerves and was a malaria-stricken, hallucinating coward. Normal, practical people can work up close. And all that nonsense about hiding the ax under the coat, the fool should have stolen a smaller ax. This one is fifty centimeters, maybe sixty-five. You put it in a bag and go."

"Go where?"

"Here, there, anywhere. That's all I have. Read my report."

AUTOPSY REPORT

Prepared by N. A. Baranova
Committee for State Security
Moscow, USSR

This report details the blunt traumatic deaths of two subjects. The subjects were linked because of antemortem activity. The bodies were discovered lying unclothed on top of each other. Both bodies were prone with the larger subject on top.

Time of death: Jan. 13, 1976. Early evening hours. (Estimated by liver temperature at the scene and muscle tone.)

THE VICTIMS:

Victim 1

Age: Midthirties.
Weight: 97 kg. (Because of exsanguination, collapse of the cranium and brain leakage, this needs to be estimated.)
Height: 184 cm.
Other data: Not circumcised. The subject has a tattoo on the left bicep: a six-corner Star of David, measuring 5 cm., blue ink.

Dental health: Poor. Evidence of advanced periodontal disease, where gums have receded beyond 5 mm, and a left upper abscessed molar.

General health: Poor. Diffuse atherosclerosis with significant plaque in the major vessels. Diffuse emphysematous lung disease and anthracosis. Heart enlarged, with diffuse myocardial hypertrophy, suggestive of untreated hypertension.

General hygiene: Poor. No recent bathing.

Injuries:

(1) Blunt blow by an ax to the mid posterior thorax. This laceration was a through-and-through injury leading to transection of the aorta, which caused the victim to rapidly exsanguinate into the chest.

(2) A blow with the flat of an ax to the back of the head, which accounts for loss of brains and their release onto the crime scene, i.e., the carpet.

(3) the back of the neck severed as the assailant seeks to get access to Victim 2 (see below), on the bottom.

Victim 2

Age: Midthirties.

Weight: 74kg estimated because of blood loss.

Height: 179 cm.

Other data: Circumcised.

Dental health: Excellent dental work,

suggesting access to dental care sys-
tem of an advanced capitalist country.
Partial gold crowns on three molars.
Excellent dental health.

General health: Lungs and musculature
suggest that the victim is a runner.

General hygiene: Meticulously groomed.

Perineal region: There was diffuse peri-
anal ecchymosis that was both recent
and old with surrounding blunt injury
with multiple fresh and healed lacera-
tions circumferential to the anus with
new tears that were recent and presumably immediately antemortem. Body flu-
ids were present in the area, while
not tested, suggesting very recent and
historical homosexual activity.

Injuries: Nearly complete decapitation.
Victim succumbed rapidly to injuries,
but only one side of the neck was at-
tacked, and death was associated with
the cervical multiple cardiovascular
injuries as well as the severed spinal cord that occurred with the most
penetrating blow. Decapitation was completed surgically by severing the still-
attached tissue.

DISCUSSION

The death of both subjects is further linked
by the mechanism of death and the instrument used. Both were victims of huge force
blunt trauma.

Victim 1 had fatal wounds to both chest
and head from a blunt object with a dull

cutting blade wielded repeatedly against first the posterior chest and then the skull. Either series of blows would have been fatal. However, it is likely that the chest strike was first, as the pattern of splatter suggests antemortem normal blood pressure. The details will be made clear in the individual report of Victim 1, whose body was found to be facing and directly on top of Victim 2 at the crime scene. The weight and size of Victim 1 would have made simply moving his body a challenge for the dependent Victim 2.

Victim 2 had a more limited injury pattern, largely due to the limited access to his body as he lay beneath Victim 1 (see above). Victim 2 had a similar massive exsanguination due to a single blunt force injury causing near decapitation.

The instrument used was capable of causing both blunt trauma and dull trauma, which is suggestive of a mid-to-large-size ax. Such an ax would appear to be a standard household item to many, and it is easy to speculate that it could have been secreted away inside an overcoat, backpack, or sack of any kind without arousing suspicion until it was covered in the brain, muscle, bone, and blood of the victims.

The weapon was not found on the scene.

Of note, the attacker demonstrated strength, skill, fitness, and determination in the fatal wounding of these two men. Unfortunately for the victims, the assailant was not very skilled in maintaining an edge to the murder weapon, as multiple blows were used, especially on Victim 1. The skull attack, which collapsed the skull, setting loose the brain tissue, also was forceful, but more of a statement than a fatal mechanism.

The cervical injury pattern observed in Victim 2 required great speed and force.

This completes the subject-specific autopsy report. As the mechanism of injury is plain, microscopic examination of all body organs was deferred and will not be conducted unless specifically requested by the investigating officers. Creating such unnecessary work would possibly delay the expedition of more urgent microscopic examination of others needing autopsy. It is with utmost confidence that conclusions about the causes of deaths for these individuals are hereby entered.

"Needless to say, they both had a very bad day," says Lydia Ivanovna after Nadezhda Alexeyevna concludes her presentation.

Back in the courtyard, Lydia Ivanovna motions to Viktor to get inside the mouse-gray Volga. The driver is at the wheel, awaiting her instructions to get going.

"Do you have any questions you didn't ask there?"

"Yes. Did you kill them?"

"I?"

"You, your organization—same thing..."

"If we did it, why would we be turning to you to help us?"

"To cover your tracks? Rewrite the story? Make it undecipherable? Was this organization of yours ever averse to complexity? Itzik Fefer was one of you, and he was shot that day in 1952—here. His smoke and ashes went up this chimney."

"That's history. This is now."

"Is there a difference? In our country? Please, Lydia Ivanovna..."

"I can provide assurances. Would that help?"

"Not very much."

"What about a private audience with my supervisor?"

"Andropov?"

"Yes. Yuri Vladimirovich is my direct supervisor on this case."

"What if your Yuri Vladimirovich was the one who ordered these murders?"

"He says he didn't."

"You asked directly?"

"I asked directly."

"How will he prove to me that he did not? Give me his word of a Communist?"

"He could. Would that settle the question for you?"

"Lydia Ivanovna, what do you think?"

"I think not."

"Maybe it wasn't you, maybe it wasn't your Andropov. Maybe it was one of the people who are staring at us from behind these windows or taping this conversation in this car? Maybe it was a renegade operation—theirs."

"We're going around in circles. Let me simplify it. You've surely done a calculation: facing an anti-Semitic trial versus becoming our secret collaborator. When you ran from us, maniacally crossing the Garden Ring at Sadovaya-Kudrinskaya, you made your thinking obvious. Historically, standing accused in an anti-Semitic trial does appear to give you a better chance. Unless your adversary understands your thought process. Which I do."

"If you arrest me now, there'd have to be some semblance of legal process, some glasnost."

"Are you certain about this?"

"In our country people don't just disappear—not anymore."

"You are analyzing a small, distorted sample. Dissidents usually don't disappear, at least now. But spies *do* disappear—believe me on this point. I know."

"Am I now a spy?"

"Not technically, not yet—no. But we can handle your case in a manner consistent with that track."

"So, then, my options are?"

"You can help us, accepting my word of honor and, through me, Yuri Vladimirovich's promise of a Communist. Or you don't have to leave this complex. There are people on my team who'd love to see you detained. Not everyone here is as flexible as I am."

"You are saying that there is room for me in one of Nadezhda Alexeyevna's freezers?"

"I am saying help us now, and you may get a way out."

"Why do you care so much about these murders, about Schwartz, about Foxman?"

"Because someone has killed a well-known Jew and what looks like his CIA handler right here, in the center of Moscow, before our nose, and the enemies of détente will use this, claiming, as you do, that we are the ones who did it. Which we did not, I'm assured. And because Henry Kissinger will be here in five days, and, very likely, questions will come up."

"If you know that Foxman was CIA, which I don't, what can I do for you that you can't accomplish without me?"

"You can make use of your name and your contacts to get at the answers quickly—and we do need them quickly. Some of my colleagues want to arrest you and present the incident as a fight between malcontents. Schwartz was involved in economic crimes, there was money involved—and he and Foxman were homosexual lovers, so jealous rage becomes a plausible theory."

"Do you think Kissinger will be fooled by this Reichstag-fire fabrication? The German refugee who fled from the Nazis? A Harvard professor of political science?"

"My colleagues argue that Kissinger will find it advantageous to accept any plausible explanation. Plus, we will not have to find out what Kissinger thinks, because you will help us and we will know exactly who did it. You may recall that I have described myself as your advocate. Well, a good curator is an advocate. I am defending you in an internal debate—here—with people who just want to hang this murder on you and not bother finding out who actually did it."

"What if I say yes, I will try to solve it—and fail? I've never solved any crime, not even some hypothetical case of a missing chicken, let alone a double ax murder that may or may not involve the CIA and most likely involves your organization."

"You mean if you say yes to me now, then try and fail?"

"If I try and fail, do I still get credit, a five for effort?"

"This hasn't been worked out, but it's not the most urgent question before us right now."

"Oh? What is the most urgent question?"

"The most urgent question? Do you, Viktor Venyaminovich Moroz, right now, wish to spend more time at home, with your Oksana? Or should I concede defeat and start making arrangements for you to get, as you say, processed?"

"I will let you know about my decision."

"When?"

"After I decide."

"Decide quickly—I can give you a day, maybe two. Do you still have questions for me?"

"I do. Did you kill Schwartz? And Foxman?"

"If I said no one more time, would you believe me?"

"No."

"So let's not waste time in idle conversation."

It's preferable not to be observed walking out of one of Lubyanka's side entrances, even if you didn't enter that complex voluntarily. The banged-up gray Volga driven by a glum operative in a neck brace drops Viktor off in a deserted courtyard in the close vicinity of the Lutheran cathedral just a few blocks away.

As Viktor emerges from the courtyard, puzzled operatives report that the subject is walking back—toward Lubyanka. Has the subject made up his mind? Will he cooperate? He stops short of trying to enter the building. Instead, he enters Gastronom No. 40, makes his way to the patisserie counter, and purchases a *tort Arakhis*; nothing else, not even the famed milk cocktail.

It's midmorning, and there is no other customer standing at the gray marble counters. Placing the cake on the marble, Viktor is suddenly observed breaking down and starting to sob. Ten minutes later, he regains control of his emotions and departs, leaving the entire *tort Arakhis* opened but uneaten, like an offering to the gods or flowers upon the grave of an unknown soldier.

17.

A few years ago, Oksana happened to reread *Evgeny Onegin* immediately after having reread *The Catcher in the Rye*. Thanks to this sequencing, for the first time, she recognized how well paired these novels can be.

Don't let the languages, centuries, and settings throw you off. Holden is set adrift by yet another prep school; Onegin is pondering the superfluous lives of his friends from his prep school, the Lyceum. Phonies abound. *Onegin* is verse, *The Catcher* prose, but what does it matter? The central question is the same, and it keeps you turning pages: What's a person to do in this cold, absurd, bloodthirsty time?

Whiteness of marble at the Pushkin Square Metro station sets the stage for blackness of the pedestal of the Pushkin monument. It makes Oksana think of Pushkin's blackness and of her own. Pushkin's great-grandfather was an African. Oksana's grandfather was an American Black man, a progressive worker, an autodidact, an almost-Communist. He passed through Moscow in 1936 and died in Spain a year later, a forgotten fighter in the Abraham Lincoln Brigade. His Blackness is the source of Oksana's otherness here, in this white city.

Pushkin Square is the former Passion Square, thus named

after the Passion of Christ Monastery that stood here, alongside Tverskaya, the thoroughfare rechristened Gorky Street.

Oksana takes a spot on her favorite side of the Pushkin pedestal, next to a stanza carved into black marble:

И долго буду тем любезен я народу,
Что чувства добрые я лирой пробуждал,
Что в мой жестокий век восславил я Свободу,
И милость к падшим призывал.*

Standing here, beside the stanza that encapsulates her patriotism, Oksana realizes that she has no idea what Olga Lenskaya looks like. Should she approach any woman who appears to look like she might be married to the Hóng Wèibīng Lensky and ask her whether her name is Olga Lenskaya and whether she happens to be carrying thirty copies of *The Laws of Jewish Life*?

There are fifty people here, give or take, milling around, waiting to meet other parties they may or may not have seen before for reasons that include everything under the sun. Oksana is presumably the only person here whose activities amount to flirtation with a three-year stay in a Mordovian prison camp.

Oksana focuses on women who look like they might be Jewish, an admittedly questionable and risky undertaking. You never know who is, of course, but sometimes you guess right. Consider Oksana, for example. After fifteen minutes without a hunch, she notices a chestnut-haired, broad-shouldered woman of about her

---

* And so, I'll serve my people, / By having placed my lyre in virtue's service, / Exalting Liberty in my bloodthirsty times, / And pleading for compassion toward the fallen.

age. She is carrying a black polyester bag with a floral design. It looks like it might have been purchased at Beryozka.

The woman has circled the monument four times, waiting for someone.

"Would you, perchance, be Olga?" Oksana asks.

"And who, may I ask, are you?"

This is a reasonable question, because Olga, if this is indeed her, would be expecting to hand thirty copies of *The Laws* to some-one else—Viktor. Viktor had no way to warn the Lenskys about this change of plans, because telephone service hasn't yet reached Novogireyevo. Cable hasn't been laid, switching stations haven't been built. People who live there, amid the cattails, rely on pay phones. Lines around those pay phones stretch as far as twenty people long. It takes two kopeks and an hour of waiting to place a two-minute outgoing call, and incoming calls are not an option.

Even if the Lenskys had a personal telephone, it would be monitored. Using it would be equivalent to communicating with the KGB.

Anything Oksana does now could be interpreted as a KGB provocation. A reminder: there is an article in the RSFSR Criminal Code—Article 190–1. Written with Oksana's ilk in mind, it applies to "systematic dissemination by word of mouth of deliberate fabrications that defame the Soviet political and social system, or the manufacture or dissemination in written, printed or other form of works of the same content." Such activities "shall be punished by deprivation of freedom for a term not exceeding three years, or by corrective labor for a term not exceeding one year, or by a fine not exceeding 100 rubles."

Having thirty copies of *The Laws* would get you the maximum under Article 190–1. You don't seek acquittal under this article. Any defense lawyer you hire would first need to admit guilt, have you express remorse, swear loyalty to the Soviet government and the Communist Party of the USSR if you can, and implore the court to show mercy. This Olga, if this is who she is, is indeed carrying a bag that looks like it might be large enough to contain thirty copies of *The Laws*. It's possible that the KGB knows about this shipment of *The Laws*, that they are watching the distribution chain, following its drift through the channels, exhibiting strategic restraint as they prepare cases under the more ominous Article 70—propaganda aimed at undermining the Soviet state—or Article 64—treason. Compared to that, Article 190–1—slander—is a petty crime, a trip to the camp for Young Pioneers.

It's possible that they are sitting in the bushes, ready to swoop in, or, more likely, that they are taking pictures, gathering intelligence, listening, watching.

Properly instructed, Olga would be wise to turn around and leave, no matter what Oksana says to her. Oksana has resigned to admitting an error, preparing to bid farewell to this Olga (or False Olga*), and leaving it up to Viktor and the Hóng Wèibīng to make alternative arrangements.

This is what would have happened, except this woman looks familiar to Oksana, perhaps a person she had met at another time. She dimly recalls Kratovo, the dachas, adolescence, a bit more than a decade ago, around 1963, before Daniel' and Sinyavsky were imprisoned, before *The Master and Margarita* was published, before the Six-Day War, before the emigration movement, before the Leningrad hijackers. What did people talk about in 1963?

And what was that Olga's name? That summer, Oksana was obsessively reading the Americans, mostly Hemingway, Steinbeck, Fitzgerald. Nothing clarifies the memory better than re-

---

* Лжеольга.

252 | PAUL GOLDBERG

constructing what you read and when you read it. What was that girl's name? It was something very long, garlicky-Jewish, as anti-Semites might say. Bobchinitzer! Olga Bobchinitzer! Olya!

It's coming back: Olya Bobchinitzer was less dull than most people. She cared passionately about boys. It was rumored at the time that Olya had her first abortion at age fifteen.

"Are you not, perchance, Olga Bobchinitzer?"

"Yes, this was my maiden name."

"You are not Lenskaya now, by any chance?"

"And why do you know me?"

Standing in Pushkin's shadow, Oksana gives Olga her name—Moskvina.

It evokes no recollection. She rattles off addresses of the dachas in Kratovo, names of people who lived there more than a decade ago, in the summer of 1963, even names of dogs: Slavik the Scottish terrier, Nayda the mostly German shepherd. Same history—confirmed, just no memory of Oksana.

Oksana works up to mentioning her husband, Viktor Moroz, whispers about the books from Montreal and the people from Indianapolis who brought them. This level of detail prompts Olga to consider handing the bag over to Oksana.

As Olga tentatively hands over her bag, something seems to have triggered her memory.

"There was someone named Oksana on my street in Kratovo, I think. But . . ."

"But?"

"But she was not Jewish."

As director of Moscow Special School No. 64 with Instruction in Multiple Subjects in Foreign Languages, Alla Markovna Shneerson, known as Ghryu, is required to outfit her office with an over-the-desk image of Lenin.

Lenin has to be positioned above her back. He can be pictured delivering an impassioned speech at Smolny, or standing in solitude, immersed in big thoughts at Gorki, or looking grandfatherly in the surrounding of little children—*Zayde* Lenin. It's up to you which Lenin you choose to hang above your desk, but he must be there.

Ghryu's predecessor, a drunk named Vassily Ivanovich Malakhov, counted a gold-framed oil portrait of Vladimir Ilyich among his cherished possessions. In his former career in the Red Army, the former director was given a military-issue portrait. His Lenin was big, resolute, parade-worthy, bravely facing the winds of history, possibly from atop an armored car. Malakhov's military Lenin was far more impressive than shabby, printed, plastic-framed black-and-white images issued by the Moscow City Department of People's Education, known under the complex acronym MosGorONO.

After Malakhov disappeared over unpleasantness that was rumored to involve two young teachers and multiple students, the oil Lenin vanished with him.

Now Malakhov's Lenin, which Ghryu used to find hilarious and referred to as "Vova," "Vovka," and "Vovochka," short, diminutive, and endearing forms of Vladimir, has returned to his place above her desk. Worse, Ghryu has had the same Vovka, whom she has privately referred to as "the chieftain of their gang of bandits,"* hung in an especially grotesque manner, at an angle, positioning Vovka to project his severe, determined karma over her head, over her desk, and into the lap of her visitor.

---

* "Их главный бандит."

Ghryu's demeanor has changed, too. As Oksana is ushered into her office, Ghryu, who in the past would have gone in for a hug, remains seated at her desk, as stiff as the first secretary of the regional committee.

"Oksana Yakovlevna," begins Ghryu, setting the tone. Oksana lets it sink in. She is no longer simply Oksana, no longer Oksanka. Being called Oksana Yakovlevna, her full, formal name, doesn't bode well.

Oksana nods, looking for a notepad on Ghryu's desk. Instead, an open file folder is centered on the green felt desktop, to the right of the ashtray. Oksana has never seen Ghryu's desk uncluttered: a personnel file, an ashtray, and a pen. She must have swept her desk junk, even her packs of Belomor, into a drawer. You don't get a surface this clean unless you are in a hurry.

Yes, it's always possible that the office is bugged, but can't she slip Oksana another note wishing her Godspeed?

"I was recently made aware of additional circumstances in your case."

This makes even less sense than the clean office, the formal salutation, and the resurrection of Malakhov's pervily hung Vovka. Please, Ghryu, a wink, a grimace, even crossed fingers would help.

Oksana joined a street protest in front of the synagogue, she did it on a lark, yes, but she did it, and she is proud of having done it. Now she is married—in a Jewish ceremony, sort of, but married—to a man she met in that group of refuseniks. All of this is true. What additional circumstances can there possibly be?

"Alla Markovna, I am not aware of any additional circumstances to which you may be referring. Things are exactly as they appear. I took part in a protest, and I am glad I did."

Oksana, too, can play the dead-faced game of formality.

Looking at the file on her desk, Ghryu chooses to roll over Oksana's objection.

"I have received an instruction . . ."

"What sort of instruction, Alla Markovna? From which authority?"

"I have received an instruction . . ."

"Alla Markovna, can you hear me? From whom did you receive this instruction? From MosGorONO?* From somewhere else?"

"I have received an instruction from appropriate authorities to extend to you an invitation to return to your job."

"You have received an instruction from an entity you are not at liberty to name to invite a dismissed-for-cause alleged Zionist into the classroom, where she will be enabled to poison the minds of Soviet children?"

Ghryu is barely making eye contact. Of course, it's the KGB, throwing crumbs, trying to make Oksana split away from her husband, betray him. There is room for nuanced analysis of such actions, but it's best to discard them entirely, in one big garbage pail.

How can Oksana tell Ghryu that she is still her friend, that their past conversations will remain private, that she has nothing to fear?

"Oksana Yakovlevna, what is your answer?"

"My answer is a categorical no. I cannot accept an offer from any organization that would not have the decency to speak its name, because organizations of this sort aren't interested in being just or doing decent deeds. They ask for something in return. Alla Markovna, I respect you today as much as I always have, but please relay this message to the people who have given you these

---

* МосГорОНО.

indecent instructions: I stand behind my actions, and I support my husband. I would a thousand times over rather be unemployed than get sucked into a Faustian swamp."

As she gets up to leave, Oksana reaches into her bag, pulls out a copy of *The Laws of Jewish Life*, and hands it to Ghryu.

Ghryu doesn't reach to accept it.

Oksana drops it on top of Ghryu's pristine desk, turns around on her heels, and leaves.

An airplane bearing the U.S. secretary of state will touch down in Moscow on Thursday January 22. Today is Saturday, January 17. Five days . . . Less, if you consider that this is the evening of January 17 and Kissinger will be arriving in the morning of January 22.

Kissinger's arrival, of course, is the entire reason for Viktor's cat-and-mouse games with the KGB.

Viktor is home for dinner, which consists of kreplach and chicken soup, followed by sweet-and-sour meatballs. This new diet of theirs doesn't rekindle cultural memories for either of them. Viktor's father banished the taste of the *shtetl* from his house. Oksana's mother is Russian, her father doesn't cook, and his parents—Oksana's Jewish grandparents—were gassed by the Nazis. This is food that people, for reasons of their own, wrap up for Viktor.

"Oksana, I promised that we wouldn't be thrown out of the country until we saw *The Cherry Orchard*."

"And I thank you for keeping your promise."

"I have another landmark date for you—January twenty-second."

"Next Thursday? What happens next Thursday?"

"Next Thursday, Kissinger arrives for nuclear talks."

"What does it have to do with you?"

"It just might—it's a feeling I have. Can you tell me about Kissinger? His moral character?"

"I don't know anything about Kissinger's moral character."

"Can't you pretend he is a character in a *samizdat* novella you are typing?"

"I can try. Give me some biographical details . . ."

"He escaped from Germany as an adolescent. Has a German accent, talks like a computer would, if a computer could talk. If he were a character in a book, what would you make of these details?"

"Just use my imagination?"

"Yes."

"I can see him as a boy, in short pants, playing a violin."

"Really?"

"You said turn my imagination loose. So here it is. Give me more details if you want a more nuanced interpretation."

"I heard on BBC that his mother worked in a pastry shop when they came to America, in the late 1930s. Do you ascribe any significance to that?"

"She knows about meringue."

"What does that say?"

"Meringue is a symbol of fragility. It's the pastry equivalent of cherry blossom."

"What about Henry? I think his real name would have been Heinz."

"Heinz would have learned from his mother how fragile civil society, democracy can be. If he left at an age when he was aware of the world around him, he would have been tormented as a Jew, seeing the meringue of civil society crumble. Do you know anything about his father?"

"No."

"Then let's develop his mother. She is working at a pastry shop twelve hours a day, comes home late, exhausted, makes sure Heinz practices his scales. She is tyrannical about that. This leads Heinz to develop compassion—to be nothing like her. Did anyone in his family die in the camps?"

"I assume yes."

"That would deepen his empathy and his belief in the redemptive power of hard work. I am starting to like this guy."

"Is Heinz guided by logic? By principles?"

"Logic. Definitely. And he seems to be of very high opinion of himself, as most logic-driven people are. As long as his sense of self-worth matches his achievements, that's excusable. Wasn't he behind the overthrow of Allende, in Chile?"

"I think so, Oksan. But with Chile, I don't know whom to believe, what to make of it."

"I like Pablo Neruda, quite a bit. A wonderful, courageous poet. I think he might have been killed in that coup."

"Not by Kissinger?"

"Not directly. He is a technocrat, despite his musical training. Violinists are often mathematicians also. He might not have known about Neruda, if that's indeed what happened. What did he do about us? The Jews? The dissident movement?"

"He opposed the Jackson-Vanik* Amendment in the American Congress."

---

* The Jackson-Vanik Amendment to the Trade Act of 1974 is a law that denies most-favored nation status to countries with "non-market economies" that restrict emigration and other human rights. That would be, first and foremost, the USSR. American Jews wanted the law, there was much breast-beating, legislation cleared Congress, and by the time it reached President Gerald Ford, all power was drained from the legislation. The president could invoke it—or not. The situation was classically American: the Jews got their Jackson-Vanik Amendment, and trade with the USSR went on unabated.

"Vit', I wouldn't read anything into that, based on what we see about his character, which is shaped by what he experienced as a child. Could he be opposed to it because Nixon opposes it? But personally, he wants Jackson-Vanik to pass, I think. Because it would look better if it passes in spite of his opposition."

"I see . . . This way he retains credibility with Brezhnev. He says, we opposed Jackson-Vanik, but it passed despite my efforts to kill it, so let's continue to focus on détente anyway, Mr. Brezhnev."

"Something like that. After Jackson-Vanik, human rights and emigration of Jews from the Soviet Union became an objective of American foreign policy. Failure to provide exit visas, to a man of his historical experience, is a moral equivalent of putting Jews into gas chambers. It's a humanitarian concern, and therefore an American concern."

"Sounds logical, Oksana. You seem to be saying that he believes all this while also trying to create an appearance of impartiality while clearly being on the side of the forces of good. Yes?"

"Yes."

"How would Kissinger react to, say, speaking strictly hypothetically, the KGB having killed a U.S. diplomat? Let's paraphrase that: How would he react to a sudden disappearance of a U.S. diplomat? Let's not say 'KGB' and 'murder.' Let's say we don't know that yet."

"He would be outraged. It would be a matter of principle. Something that's beyond appearance of impartiality! It would shake him to the marrow of his moral core!"

"And, Oksan, what if our troglodytes decide to hold a classic anti-Semitic trial—not something that is not clearly anti-Semitic, like the Leningrad hijacking case, but a real, classic anti-Semitic trial, like Dreyfus or Beilis?"

"With Kissinger as the U.S. secretary of state, they wouldn't dare."

"Are you sure about any of this, by the way?"

"No. You asked for character development, and I gave you that. It could be true, could be not true. It's all I have, a wide-ranging hypothesis rooted in a dearth of data."*

"Yet it's the most astute analysis I've seen so far."

---

* "Развесистая гипотеза, уходящая корнями в полное отсутствие данных."

18.

The woman's address is in Chertanovo, a part of Moscow Mad Dog hasn't yet had the pleasure to visit. The name of that neighborhood on the outskirts of Moscow has to come from the word "*chert*," a "devil."

Looking around as he drives, Mad Dog imagines that this had to have been a swamp; not just any swamp, but a "goat swamp,"* the sort of swamp where the devils live. He must have read about goat swamps in a Russian lit class; thanks again, Harvard.†

A swamp is the sort of thing you never put behind you. Behold this mud and these big concrete boxes! This country is either crumbling, like Mad Dog's part of Moscow, its center, or it's built out of concrete slabs glued together with tar. Give these buildings a shake and they will collapse, which, aesthetically, would be a good thing. Such are Mad Dog's thoughts as the Chihuahuamobile shakes and wheezes toward the woman's address: Kirovogradskaya 18, Building 2.

No cars in front; who the fuck can afford them here? Even Mad Dog's accursed jalopy is beyond the means. "Can a jalopy be small, like this one?" he asks himself. "Perhaps a *jalopino*. Ha . . .

---

* "Козье болото."

† Mad Dog doesn't know that Patriarch's Ponds, the setting of the first scene of *The Master and Margarita*, a novel he hasn't read, were once known as a goat swamp.

Funny . . . I am amusing myself with my own wit; a bad omen. Time to get the fuck out of the Big Potato. Maybe Melissa was right. Everyone has a breaking point. Maybe."

Two boys, each with a German shepherd on a leash, run out as Mad Dog opens the building's door. One of them pauses to look over Mad Dog, assessing his foreignness. It's the fucking Burberry he has to wear again, now that the old man has commandeered his dog-bitten, bloodstained Soviet coat. "You look smart, boy. I hope you are a mathematician or a chess player, or some such. Maybe you'll get out of this shithole someday," Mad Dog thinks in a moment of compassion.

The elevator is broken, the apartment he needs is on the fourth floor. It wouldn't matter if it were on the fourteenth, for Mad Dog, a nonsmoker, is in fine athletic shape.

The aroma on the staircase attests to the presence of human feces, a deposit of which is indeed located and not stepped upon between the first and second floors. In this country, everything has to be interpreted with proper detachment, everything is a symbol, and in this instance, here, between the first and second floors, a weathered turd might connote the uniquely Russian capacity to close the apartment door, delineating the inside from the outside, the private from the public. Mad Dog thinks these thoughts as he steps over the turd and continues to negotiate the staircase, which, a reader would agree, is far superior to thoughtlessly contributing vomit to the volume of unpleasant substances here in Chertanovo, the devil's swamp, where kilometer-long concrete buildings stick out of iced-up mud and piles of rubble and abandoned construction equipment.

Mad Dog knows that an astonishing story awaits him behind one of these vinyl-covered dystopian doors—the story of Yezhov, Stalin's Bloody Dwarf, perhaps in his own handwriting, with his own doodles! Imagine what a Yezhov doodle, especially a homo-erotic Yezhov doodle, would fetch in New York! Stalin's homosexual Marquis de Sade! Take out your wallets, folks! (He could give a cut to Amnesty International or whatever, to make the sale pass the smell test.) Mad Dog would purchase the original manuscript, draw up the papers on the spot. Surely the old man, who, fortuitously, is right here, in the Big Potato, "visiting," would spot him a few thou.

Someday, when Mad Dog trains his successor, he will instruct him on the importance of drinking tea with these people. Sometimes you must also eat sweets, even if you hate sweets, like Mad Dog does. It's a ritual, they demand it of you, you must force yourself. But don't go anyplace where they have a *banya*, where you get naked, get cooked with steam, whipped with birch brooms, and thrown out to roll in the snow. Tea, even when it's darker than crankcase oil and thick with sugar and berries, is as far as you should go.

The tea-drinking is a getting-to-know-you part of the meeting. He nods like an idiot, looking away from this woman's purple fuzzy slippers. She looks like one of those old little ladies at Rodef Shalom (Mad Dog prefers to call it St. Rodef). She looks like somebody's Aunt Frume, little, chubby, dressed like a tropical bird, complete with a beak and pictures of grandchildren in her shiny purple purse. Only this one is thirty or forty years younger than the archetypal Aunt Frume, and no charm bracelets. This makes her what . . . fifty? Fifty-five? Who knows, who cares? People are the same everywhere, and your instincts of whom-to-avoid-where protect you in exactly the same way.

The apartment looks like a family lives here. A heavy pram is in the entryway, a man's bicycle in the hallway. Long Live Soviet Prams, the Biggest and Heaviest Prams in the World! Long Live Soviet Bicycles, the Biggest and Heaviest Bicycles in the World! He should stop being snarky, he knows. But what else do you do when this victorious postrevolutionary world of theirs spins so much slower than his brain? At least he has the self-control to keep his thoughts to himself.

They are in the kitchen, tea-drinking. Mad Dog doesn't need to plop down on soft furniture to feel comfortable, but this kitchen chair is like a stick up your ass. What is Frume's name, by the way? Mad Dog realizes that the woman hasn't given him her name. So Frume it is, now and forever. Why the fuck not?

Come on, Aunt Frume, the shoebox with the papers, go get the shoebox!

Aunt Frume proceeds to tell him a joke about a Jew who is summoned to the visa office:

"'Abram Isaakovich, we here at the visa office would like to better understand your desire to emigrate. Is it about your career, a promotion that has been denied?'

"'No, my career is fine, thank you. I am a professor and a department chairman.'

"'What about an apartment? Do you have adequate living space?'

"'I have a very nice apartment, conveniently located.'

"'A dacha? Maybe you wish you had a dacha?'

"'I have a dacha. In Kratovo.'

"'A car?'

"'Just bought a new Moskvich.'

"'You have a job, an apartment and a dacha in Kratovo, a Moskvich . . . So why are you trying to leave the Motherland, you ungrateful, filthy Jewish swine?'"

Is this where Mad Dog should laugh?

By now, he has had three cups of this syrupy swill and eaten three crumbly cookies, one of which was quite stale. He is making do with his best Russian; it's not so bad, a wayward ending is a victimless crime, plus this woman is slow, so . . . fucking . . . slow. Perhaps he doesn't need Viktor, and this shit is too important to bring him in, assuming he even survived playing in traffic on the Garden Ring.

Besides, Mad Dog remembers suddenly that this Frume speaks passable English.

"What about your niece? Has she applied to leave for Israel since last time we spoke?"

"My daughter? Not yet. She should be home any minute now. Also, her husband."

"Do you live with them?" he asks, pretending to care.

"Yes. I had terrible, terrible divorce, and I take care of their children."

Terrible, terrible divorces cost terrible, terrible amounts of money. That's where Mad Dog can be of assistance! Isn't it time for the shoebox? Or does he have to keep gunking up his bladder with this, how you say, tea? He has had enough, enough, enough. He will need to ask about the shoebox—right now—or this tea-drinking will never end.

"Oh, so you want to see the Yezhov file?" she says finally.

He has just returned from what he privately dubbed a tea-expulsion ritual in the bathroom.

"I will not say no," he says, sitting back down on a rickety kitchen chair that has now been his home for forty-five excruciating minutes.

Mad Dog's hands shake a little as he unties the shoelaces that hold together the gray heavy-cardboard file. Soviet file folders have shoelace ties and are stamped with the words "Папка для бумаг," a "folder for papers." What else can it be, a shoe?

Inside the file, Mad Dog sees the plan for an execution chamber. Alas, it's a copy, a Xerox, same one he has seen before. There are Xerox machines in this country, but they are few in number, and you have to get your copying project cleared, i.e., censored. Or else the whole country will stand by their Xerox machines, making copies of Solzhenitsyn's *Gulag*, or Akhmatova's *Requiem*, apropos Yezhov. Should Mad Dog ask Aunt Frume about the Xerox, or would that spook her? It would, wrong timing, not worth it.

Next in the file is a stained transcript, which Mad Dog recognizes as a transcript of a document he has already been told about, audio monitoring of Mrs. Yezhov's tryst with Mikhail Sholokhov. At least this is not a Xerox. It's a carbon copy, stamped "Совершенно секретно," on every page, "Absolutely secret."

The paper is onionskin, a little too white and too new for a transcript of a four-decades-old tryst between a woman who would be murdered and a man who would win the Nobel Prize for literature.

The bright-red stamps seem new as well. Should he ask her about the stamps? What about the bright-red spot on page seven? He will ask Aunt Frume. He must, and he does. Is he asking her in Russian or English? Suddenly, he doesn't know, a first; maybe his Russian has improved.

"According to family lore, Yezhov confrontated her with transcript of sex with the Sholokhov, and after that he beat her cruelly. I told you this story when we met. Blood is hers."

Blood. Hers. From forty years ago almost, but still red. Wouldn't it turn brown, eat through the page? And xeroxed copies he saw on top of this file, and fresh-looking "Совершенно секретно" stamps on carbon copies? "Совершенно секретно" my foot. No.

None of it looks good. He should stand up; he better get out of here. He will try harder to get himself out of this stick-up-your-butt chair of Aunt Frume's, which isn't her real name, unless it is. What is her real name? He needs to know Aunt Frume's real name now, now that he has had all that tea: "What's your name?"

Why is he slurring, stuttering even, and what was the language he has just spoken?

"You can call me Galina Borisovna . . ."

Why is she smiling? Is she smiling at him? It's just a name like any other. Galina Borisovna. Is this a seduction?

"Would you like to look at next document?" she prods him.

Mad Dog stops perusing the transcript, ordering his suddenly thickened fingers to move to the next document in the file. The photo looks remarkably like him, the name, too. Galina Borisovna? Why? Why is his photo and his name beneath it being shown to him, Madison Dymshitz, here, in this apartment, in Chertanovo, where people think that the act of shitting on staircases represents an emanation of the soul? And this page from a reporter's notebook looks familiar. The handwriting seems to be Mad Dog's: "2 pm Tues = 3 pm Mon. Bureau: 297–8656."

It's Mad Dog's, but how did it get into this blurry dossier? He thought there were just the two of them in this kitchen, Mad Dog and Galina Borisovna, why is he having such extreme difficulty staying upright, even seated, in this chair, and who are all these people who've just shown up?

An hour later, at 6:49 p.m., an unusual convoy rolls into the courtyard of Sad Sam, off Yermolova Street, also known by its previous name, Bol'shoy Karetnyy.

Leading this convoy is a splendid blue Ural motorcycle, driven by a uniformed militiaman. In the sidecar of this splendid blue Ural motorcycle, covered with a thick vinyl tarp, rests Madison "Mad Dog" Dymshitz, the young Moscow bureau chief of a major American newspaper, a newsroom star and surely a future news executive. A black Volga with three senior officials of the Ministry of Foreign Affairs (MID for short), including the director of the press section, follows the splendid blue Ural motorcycle.

A flatbed truck carrying the blue Zhiguli belonging to the bureau of the major American newspaper closes the procession.

The militia motorcyclist and two most senior MIDniks involved in this operation carry Mad Dog upstairs, through the living room that also serves as the bureau's newsroom, past the telex that suddenly begins to spit out paper, and into the dark, cluttered bedroom, where, leaving Mad Dog in his street clothes, they tuck him in and do their best to answer his slurred questions that seek to uncover the identity of the woman who had served him that disgusting, syrupy hot tea.

"Galina Borisovna . . . Galina Borisovna," Mad Dog repeats.

"Is she really the niece of the nanny of Yezhov's daughter?" he wants to ask, and mostly does.

"Galina Borisovna . . . What would Galina Borisovna's initials be, little fool?"* one of the MIDniks asks his groggy, frostbitten charge in a mixture of English and Russian.

Did this MIDnik just call Mad Dog a little fool? A naif?

"Galina . . . G . . . Borisovna . . . B . . . ?"

"GB. Now you get it?"

"No."

"Galina Borisovna . . . GB . . . KGB . . . Understand? KGB! You've been warned now, idiot. Next time will be worse."

---

* Дурачок.

Under normal circumstances, Lydia Ivanovna is far too discreet to adopt a pseudonym as obvious as Galina Borisovna. That would be caricaturistic, disrespectful even. But then again, she is not Lydia Ivanovna, either.

As he drifts off to find inner calm, Mad Dog is starting to understand: he has, to quote the impertinent MIDnik, received a warning from *kagebe*, and isn't it always worse next time it happens? Maybe it will be worse, maybe it will not, we'll see about that, and that word he used to describe him is so undiplomatic, so inappropriate for someone who is tucking you into bed in an official capacity, as head of the MID press section. Mad Dog must remember to lodge a formal complaint, because a principle is involved; this is very important, maybe there is a notepad in the bedside table, to jot down a reminder for tomorrow. Also, there is suddenly a burning sensation on the tip of Mad Dog's nose, frostbite probably, probably from having been transported in that motorcycle sidecar at high speed on a cold Moscow night, and now probably his nose will fall off, like Lenin's, while he sleeps, except Lenin's, according to his Harvard TA, was falling off gradually, from syphilis, which is a chronic illness, while Mad Dog's nose, tonight, will fall off all at once, due to its owner having been driven preposterously, gratuitously, demonstratively through Moscow in a militia motorcycle's sidecar, which would be classified clinically as an acute event. He will lodge a formal complaint, maybe have Foxman help him do it, but not right away. Mad Dog is off duty now, not filing any formal complaints. It will need to wait, everything will need to wait.

19.

Norm's memory of the war lacks color.

Even today, three decades later, images of the war return to him in black-and-white, a newsreel, featuring him: Norm lying in wait, Norm throwing a grenade, Norm running, Norm's machine gun out, spraying from the gut. Even that craziest of days, the war's blood-drenched dramatic apex, its quintessence, the day of the raid, lives on in black, white, and shades in between. Not even a brown.

You wouldn't guess it if you know him from Pittsburgh, but Norm relives that raid every day of his life, even today, on January 17—today especially.

Under normal circumstances, Norm steers away from art galleries. Today, he makes an exception for the Tretyakov Gallery, in part because the place must be warm, and he has a day to kill.

Having devoted the morning to studying Moscow from above, he heads in the general direction of Red Square, noting with amazement that he is walking down the street named after Bogdan Khmelnitsky, one of history's champion Jew-killers.

Recognizing the name, Norm turns left on Arkhipov Street, walks downhill, noting the majestic balance of the curvature and the incline. He sees two old men scale the synagogue's icy steps. These aren't refuseniks, just people who pray. Norm turns right at the bottom of the hill and finds the Moskva River embankment. He doesn't pray; never has. But he is doing his part to accelerate an exodus, and this morning he almost died in the process. Sometimes missions don't go as planned. This morning, he may have killed somebody—possibly two men.

At Tretyakov Gallery, Norm rushes past the halls filled with portraits of various nobles, pausing for a moment in front of Pushkin, and after some meandering, finds himself in front of a colossus of a painting of Christ descending toward a body of water, presumably the Jordan.

The mountains behind the man Norm calls Yoshke look like they might be the Golan Heights, except they seem to be in the wrong place. No one knows this, especially not their son, but Miriam was once a novice nun, fully converted, a Catholic. This went on until the last of the Panzers was pushed out of Poland and her inner Jewess took charge of her outer Catholic and led her to the nearest DP camp, in freshly liberated Germany.

Now Norm tells people, "When in Rome do like the Romans" when asked about her improbable first name, suggesting that she changed it to fit in, in America. Bullshit! She changed her name in Poland, really changed it, actually became Mary. What happens if you let Christ into your heart to avoid being turned into a puff of smoke and a pile of ashes? Is that different from a real conversion? Maybe it is, maybe it isn't. Look at Miriam now. Even with this name, Mary, she is as Jewish as any other matron at Rodef Shalom's sisterhood, but did she unconvert? Debaptize? Unapostate? De-Christ? Not in any formal way. Do you go to a rabbi, or do you just perish the memory of that period in your life?

They went to Poland recently, to attend a memorial for the mother superior, the woman who risked her life to save her, and what did Miriam Dymshitz do? She took communion, ate the wafer, drank the wine, allowed the Savior to reconstitute in her *kishkes*. They didn't speak for three weeks after that, but when they did, she said that the wafer and wine she swallowed wasn't for her, it was out of respect, a debt of gratitude.

Show up is what you do out of respect! Norm did. Take part in their biggest ritual is what you do when you *are* them. What sense does this make? And now this, cancer, gone away for now, but these things come back, even after what Bernie Fisher had her worked over with, a drug Norm remembers only by the acronym—something to do with "fuck you." FU-2, or 3-FU, or 5-FU maybe. A quintuple fuck-you.

Norm didn't come here, to this gallery in godless Russia, to look at Christ revealing himself to the people. He came to this gallery to look at canvases from the war—soldiers, yes, but mostly partisans. These paintings are in the Socialist Realism exhibits, the rooms where no one goes.

Even on that day, the day of the raid with the Red Army paratroopers, the order was insane—go deep into a German encampment and blow up an ammunition dump.

At dawn, there were eight of them, four partisans, four paratroopers. They split into two groups, one of which had the misfortune to ski squarely into a German detachment. They were slaughtered one by one, of course, but during the firefight, the other four men found the ammo dump and carried out the order. The inferno must have been visible for twenty kilometers, but the only way out was through a minefield, which claimed two fighters.

By midafternoon, when there were two of them, one partisan and one paratrooper, they switched to Yiddish.

"*Kum mit mir in der royter armey. Mir darfn gite soldatn*,"* the

---

* "Come with me to the Red Army. We need good soldiers."

paratrooper, a lieutenant, said as he and Norm glided through the forest at the end of that day.

"*Ikh bin nisht kayn soldat. Ikh hob nisht genig distsiplin. Ikh bin a vald gazlen,*" Norm responded. "*Vi ahin vestu geyn nokh der milkhome?*"

"*Tsi mayn professor, in moskve.*"

"*Bistu shoyn a professor?*"

"*Nisht keyn professor—an aspirant. Nokh der milkhome, kim tsu moskve. Gedenk: Profesor Moskvin, in moskve, nokh der milkhome.*"

That was before they reached the railroad tracks, before the train, before the prisoners.

On January 17, 1976, in late afternoon, an older gentleman, pre-sumably a war veteran, is seen lingering in the exhibit of war paintings at the Tretyakov Gallery. This happens a lot, except this one is muttering in a language that, to an untrained ear, sounds a lot like German.

Norm has the address—obtained from Alex, in Pittsburgh, the same kid scientist who had lent him the wolf hat.

The Frunze Embankment—easy to find, just across the river and about three kilometers up from Tretyakovka. A yellow brick building, 14 Frunze Embankment.

Norm runs up the stairs.

As the door opens and Yakov Aronovich Moskvin attempts to adjust his sense of what can be real to that which actually is, Norm

---

"I am not a soldier. I don't have enough discipline. I am a forest brigand. Where will you go after the war?"

"To my institute, in Moscow."

"Are you already a professor?"

"Not a professor—a graduate student. After the war, come to Moscow, my friend. Remember: Professor Moskvin, in Moscow, after the war."

picks up the conversation the two young men had while skiing away from a bloody skirmish of more than three decades ago.

"*Ikh hob gedenkt: Profesor Moskvin, in moskve, nokh der milkhome*."*

"*Ikh ze, ikh ze*," says Yakov Aronovich as the two men embrace. I see this, I see this.

Updating a friend on the past thirty-three years of your life is something that might as well wait. Instead of seeking answers, you ponder the questions, separating those that can't be answered from those that shouldn't be asked. What if Norm had gone with Yakov Aronovich and joined the Red Army? Would he have survived the war? Would he have made his way to the DP camp, to America, to Pittsburgh? What would he have done in the USSR? Would he now be trying to leave? And what of Yakov Aronovich? Had he stayed with the partisans, would he have gone off to Palestine? Would he be the luminary he has become?

As questions swirl, you drink a shot, you share a meal.

Yakov Aronovich is once again divorced, once again reduced to cooking for himself, which means eating out of tins. Dinner tonight is something called "*Amerikanskaya tushenka*," which reminds him of cans of American stewed beef and pork that, thanks to the U.S. Lend-Lease program, fed and armed the USSR through the war. If you were a partisan, you remember *Amerikanskaya tushenka* being dropped off the supply planes; literally, food falling from the sky.

Norm and Yakov Aronovich sit silently, assessing the immensity of weight of everything that needs to be said.

---

* "I remembered: Professor Moskvin, in Moscow, after the war."

Yakov Aronovich has a tape he made of his favorite songs of the Moscow bards. There is some Galich, some Vysotsky, some Kim—and a lot of Okudzhava. He calls it "Избранное," "collected works." Oksana made it for him; she is good at that sort of thing.

The first song grabs Norm the way no poem ever has. Especially this part:

Нас ждет огонь смертельный,
И все ж бессилен он.
Сомненья прочь, уходит в ночь отдельный
Десятый наш десантный батальон.
Десятый наш десантный батальон.*

"He speaks to us, doesn't he, Nukhimchik?"

"Like no one ever has. In any language. Rewind the tape, *boychik*.

"Something happened that you should know about."

"Sounds ominous," says Yakov Aronovich, letting his index finger circle around, pointing at the ceiling—a universal sign for bugging.

After Norm acknowledges the gesture with a nod, Yakov Aronovich hands him a notepad.

"I brought money for the refuseniks—a lot," Norm scribbles in Russian.

Yakov Aronovich nods.

"Problem: My contact has vanished. Apartment cleaned out—with ammonia."

---

* As deadly fire awaits us, / We're off, we'll not be stopped. / Doubts aside, our Specialized / Tenth Paratroop Battalion / Is setting out into the night.

"Were they waiting for you?"

"Yes. But I got rid of them. Destroyed their cameras."

"Is anyone dead?"

"Could be. One, maybe both."

"Do you think you were followed after that? Now?"

"I don't think so, or I wouldn't have come."

"What was your contact's name?"

"Schwartz. Albert."

"I heard that name recently. He was expected at my daughter's wedding, and didn't show. Do you think he is dead?"

"I do."

On January 17, 1976, *The New York Times* publishes Professor Washington's account of her group's adventures in Moscow. It seems she wrote the piece on her flight back and knew the right editor at *The Times*.

The piece appears in the Travel section:

MOSCOW BECKONS WITH SITES OF . . . DEMOCRACY

By Monica Washington

I am reasonably sure that next time I ask for a visa to visit the USSR the answer will be a resounding *nyet*.

As someone who teaches Russian history at Columbia University, I should be worried about maintaining access to the land I study. Sadness, indeed, strikes every now and then, but I chase it away, repeating to myself that I am leaving on a high note.

Recently, a friend named Viktor Moroz led my students and me on a tour of Moscow. He called it the Democracy Tour, and it was indeed a tour unlike any other.

We saw the site where in August 1968 a handful of brave Muscovites unfurled banners to protest their country's invasion of Czechoslovakia, we walked around the KGB's ominous Lubyanka headquarters, watching little green trucks go in and come out, we visited Moscow's Great Choral Synagogue, we saw the yellowish column-adorned building where the Nobel laureate Andrei Sakharov lives, and we heard a dissident poet recite his own chef d'oeuvre titled "Communists Caught a Young Lad."

I laughed until I cried.

Make no mistake about it, what we saw was not Moscow of Intourist tours, but the other Moscow, the city where a spark of democracy has not been extinguished. I list some of these democracy sites below, so go, see, bring a bouquet, a box of candy, or a bottle of vodka for some of the most noble people you will ever meet.

The utmost highlight for me is probably also the reason I will not be allowed to set foot in the USSR until it finally crumbles: In an inspired maneuver masterfully choreographed by Viktor, my students and I entrapped and photographed a KGB operative whose task was to follow Viktor.

Not only that, but we pulled off this maneuver literally in the shadow of the Kremlin. As per plan, the film in my students' massive SLRs was exposed, but no one seemed to have noticed an insignificant little Minolta that I resourcefully stuffed inside my sweater.

So, ladies and gentlemen, I give you Viktor's goon. *Toptun* is the Russian word for that ignoble profession. Since we don't know his name, I suggest we call him

Alex. (All Russian men are named Alex until proven otherwise.)

If anyone here is worried about my using Viktor's full name, please rest assured that I do so with his blessing. Operating in accordance with the long-standing tradition of dissenters, Viktor insists that his activities are conducted entirely in the open.

There is more to the story, and it's wonderful, all of it.

Viktor has no idea that Monica's story has been published. He didn't know that she intended to write anything. It was never discussed, but it's fine that she did it. Having a photo in *The Times* probably wouldn't hurt Viktor's quest to make himself so obnoxious that he would be tossed out of the country. If you believe the logic of groups like Amnesty International, the more light shines upon Viktor, the lower the odds that one morning he will walk out and never return—and it may or may not save his life now, during this cat-and-mouse game with Lydia Ivanovna. Alas, *The Times* story features a large photo of Viktor's *toptun* and doesn't include any images of Viktor.*

Eventually, Monica will tell a mutual friend or hand a newspaper clipping and a letter to someone traveling to the USSR, or someone at the Union of Councils for Soviet Jews will tell someone in Moscow before the telephone conversation is cut off, or David Shipler, the *New York Times* Moscow bureau chief, whom Viktor knows, sort of, will think to bring the Travel section to the next press conference at Sakharov's.

---

* The editorial decision to omit Viktor's mug shot while publishing a large photo of his *toptun* shouldn't be overanalyzed. Usually, such decisions are made at the last minute, based on the availability of space, and it's easy to see how a mug shot of Viktor wouldn't be deemed especially compelling.

Mad Dog, too, might mention it to Viktor. He might even think to bring Viktor a copy. On second thought, their association has probably ended after the slam-on-the-brakes episode on the Garden Ring.

Mad Dog behaved honorably, true, but he isn't the sort you count on to behave honorably twice.

PART VI

20.

The Seminar on Jewish Culture is one of the three series of seminars organized by Moscow refuseniks.

The others are about science and engineering. If you've been locked out of your lab, barred from contact with colleagues and students, you need to find a new way to stay relevant. Real science is done. Sometimes sessions go on for four days. Luminaries, including a half dozen Nobel laureates from the West, come to Moscow to present to colleagues gathered in overcrowded apartments monitored by the KGB. Sakharov shows up often.

Golden's seminar isn't about natural sciences. It's about history, language, culture, literature, religion—themes that don't always coexist in peace.

On the evening of January 17, two men who don't appear to be in pursuit of any discernible academic goals stand in front of the building. These are flunkies in plainclothes, *toptuny*, the stompers, earning their ruble, looking into your face as you make your way up to the Goldens' apartment, to the Seminar on Jewish Culture. They stomp their feet, emitting a steaming mixture of stale breath and cigarette smoke.

Oksana runs up to the sixth floor. Ina Golden opens the door. Vitaly isn't here—not yet. The Goldens live at 18 Shukhov Street, a yellow-brick seven-story building that stands within a hundred meters of the Shukhov radio tower. Oksana would love to decline the tea-drinking and ask to go out onto the balcony and contemplate the view of the tower. The balcony is an airborne snowbank— it dumped a half meter last night, and no one has bothered to push off the snow.

The Shukhov Tower is a matter of obsession to Oksana. The Eiffel Tower stands twice as tall. With the strength of steel, it subjugates the Paris sky. The Shukhov Tower is a billowing net, as ethereal as radio itself. It doesn't cast an obelisk's shadow. It casts a web of short, dotted lines onto the city below.

Oksana's talk tonight is about *The Master and Margarita*. Golden suggested it in the midst of a debate that broke out after Viktor left the wedding to bring back Schwartz. *The Master and Margarita* is arguably the most passionate love letter any writer of significance has written to this big city. The year is unstated; circa 1930, Oksana guesses.*

At 6:17 p.m., Golden squeezes past two operatives and gets into the elevator. A third operative is positioned on the staircase. Photographic equipment is activated, but since no photographs are present in the dossiers, said equipment appears to have malfunctioned. Information that follows is based on audio monitoring and reports from human assets.

Viktor arrives at 6:38. By this time, forty-seven people have entered the apartment. Sakharov is not here tonight, but Elena Georgievna Bonner, his wife, is.

Olga and Vladimir Lensky are the last people in, arriving at 6:49, slightly after the seminar is scheduled to begin. Vladimir

---

* Bulgakovists venture a variety of guesses—1937, for example. Time marks, such as the existence of a trolleybus route to the Kiev Train Station, the date of demolition of the Cathedral of Christ the Savior, the date of an absurdly lavish ball at the residence of the U.S. ambassador, are inconsistent, but does it really matter? Bulgakov likely started work on the novel circa 1930 and, unequivocally, stopped at the time of his death in 1940.

Lensky continues to wear a hat inside the apartment. Olga Lenskaya removes her kerchief, under which she wears a wig. The Lenskys bring a carton of American cigarettes, Salem, which had been given to them by co-tribalists from the city of Indianapolis, state of Indiana, who had also brought exactly one hundred copies of *The Laws of Jewish Life*.

Packs of Salems are sent around to those in attendance.

Traditionally, Golden and the presenter at the seminar stand in front of the bookcase filled with books in Russian, English, Yiddish, and, increasingly, Hebrew. At some homes, people take precautions to hide their *samizdat* and *tamizdat*.* Golden has given up.

"Before we begin, we should say thank you to our American friends, who brought us these Salem cigarettes, which for many of us have become a taste of freedom. Freedom, I think, tastes like menthol. I am assured by my wife that they are the only cigarettes that don't aggravate conditions like asthma," says Golden, who has the emaciated look of a man suffering from ulcers and asthma that even Salems will not correct.

Today, the bookcase stands half-empty. The KGB has swept through, carting off two carloads of materials, mostly books.

"As you can see from the emptiness of the bookshelves here, we've had uninvited visitors. This time, our guests have helped themselves to English-language books they might classify as Zionist, but also my materials on Pushkin and the Decembrists. These people were dissidents, after all."

---

* *"Tamizdat"* is a term that combines the word *"tam,"* which means "there," with *"izdat,"* an abbreviation for "publishing house." So, there you have it: *samizdat* is self-published here, via typewriter, in Moscow, while *tamizdat* is published via printing presses in the outside world and smuggled in.

According to human assets, this comment engenders a laugh.

"In 1837, as our authorities found a way to rid themselves of Pushkin, they thought their headaches were over. In reality, their headaches had only begun. The study of Pushkin has become a national passion that unites academics and citizen scholars. Whatever else we are, we are all Pushkinists now. Only one other writer has shaped this country's spiritual essence as profoundly as Pushkin—and his name is Mikhail Bulgakov, a novelist and playwright, who died in 1940, a century and change after Pushkin.

"Someday, we will know more about Bulgakov the man. We do know that he was our neighbor. He lived on Bol'shaya Sadovaya. And we know the time he lived—the terror, the betrayals, absurd conspiracy theories of the Moscow Trials. His questions are the same questions Pushkin asks a century earlier: Do you hide from responsibility? Do you compromise with evil, even in the name of good, even a little bit?

"There are fewer Bulgakovists—*Bulgakovedy* is the term they prefer—than Pushkinists, for now, but one of them is with us today—Oksana Moskvina.

"If I were to give this talk a title, it would be 'Bulgakov and the Jews.'"

"That would be a fine title—thank you. 'Bulgakov and the Jews' it is. The Jew in the center of *The Master and Margarita* is a lot like a man commonly known as Jesus."

Teaching a roomful of children comes naturally to Oksana. With children, you work a clean piece of paper. With adults, you are up against ignorance posing as knowledge.

"Bulgakov plays with the name, but it's Jesus-like. Pontius Pilate and other actors appear under their own names."

A nervous drag on the cigarette doesn't help steady Oksana.

Usually not a smoker, she doesn't refuse cigarettes when they reach her. She can see the logic of Gitanes, Gauloises, Camels.

Salems are mint candies in disguise. They remind her of provincial confections sold in Odessa, Mogilev, or Berdichev.

"Everyone here remembers the day in late 1966—a decade ago—when the otherwise insignificant journal *Moskva* published the first installment of chapters from *The Master and Margarita*. It felt as though a missile had exploded in the center of Moscow."

She looks up at Viktor, who is standing near the door. He nods to her.

Viktor sees uncertainty in her eyes. He imagines the scene of Margarita shedding her clothes and, rendered invisible, flying her invisible broom above Arbat.

"What is there to be said about Bulgakov today, in January 1976? What can you know beyond the text on the page? You know what Bulgakov wrote—it's right here, put on the page—but if you want to find out what in his life prompted him to write these words, there are no documents, no memoirs of contemporaries, no accessible archives. Historical documents are either hidden in shoeboxes or kept out of the scholars' reach.

"Yet, a decade since this book's appearance, nothing is the same. In the past, we gleaned the Bible stories—New Testament and Old—from anti-religious tracts. Suddenly, because of Bulgakov, it became possible to think of Jerusalem as an actual, physical city, like Moscow—and to think of Christ as something other than a carnival charlatan.

"*The Master and Margarita* is a declaration of death of state-mandated atheism, the beginning of rebirth of spirituality, both Christian and Jewish. This novel challenges its people to ask themselves: Who am I? And to make appropriate declarations—publicly."

Oksana finds an ashtray and puts out her cigarette, alas, creating enough of a pause for someone to jump in.

"Are you suggesting that the Zionist movement—our movement—stems from a book by a Christian writer?"

It's Vladimir Lensky, the Hóng Wèibīng.

OKSANA: With this novel, Bulgakov has singlehandedly neutralized six decades of compulsory, ignorant, militant atheism. So—yes.

LENSKY: *The Master and Margarita* is a book about Jesus Christ, as you yourself admit. This is the Seminar on *Jewish* Culture. Are you perhaps addressing the wrong audience?

OKSANA: *The Master and Margarita* is in part the Gospel according to Bulgakov; his effort is to make a Christ he—an intellectual—is able to accept.

LENSKY: Are you propagandizing Christianity?

OKSANA: Not being a Christian, how can I? Bulgakov's Christ is a philosopher of sorts, he believes in goodness of man, speaks the truth. He is not an offspring of God any more than you and I.

LENSKY: You will never convince anyone that this book has anything to say about who we are. These tricks may work with Christians, but not here.

OKSANA: Actually, in our country, both Jewishness and Christianity are, by necessity, reinventions. What else can they be almost six decades since the revolution? That's longer than the lives of many of our parents. I don't know how to block out history, any part of it. You can't pretend that these decades didn't happen.

LENSKY: Why are we talking about Christian piety? We should talk about our historical Motherland, and the Leningrad case, and the Six-Day War—and Jewish observance!

OKSANA: Bulgakov has nothing to do with Christian piety. The book begins with Satan, speaking with a German accent at Patriarch's Ponds. The German consultant . . . I imagine him talking sort of like Henry Kissinger, now that I think of it.

LENSKY: She is propagandizing Satanism and slandering the American secretary of state before his visit!

OKSANA: Have you read *The Master and Margarita*?

LENSKY: No! Have you read *The Laws of Jewish Life*?

OKSANA: I glanced at it. It's full of prayers I can't understand in a language that's not ours, transliterated. You might as well be saying "shazam," "abracadabra," and so forth. I don't know about you, but I need to understand before I can believe.

LENSKY: Please be reminded about a rule we agreed on here at the seminar a long time ago: When a question of religion arises, we don't debate. We listen.

GOLDEN: The rule you cite, Volodya, doesn't apply in this situation. Oksana is presenting, and you should be listening. If you were to present something on the Montreal brochure, Oksana would be listening.

OLGA LENSKAYA: I have a bigger question: Who is she to tell us anything? I know who she is. Her grandfather was a Negro, and the rest of her family were Russians—except her stepfather.

OKSANA: Are you asking to see my passport, Olga? I promise you, on Item Five, it says "Jew." That was my choice.

OLGA LENSKAYA: Some people here may be missing a quarter or even a half. But she has no Jewish blood—not a single drop—none! I met you when we were children, so don't lie to me!

OKSANA: I have no hope that you would agree with this notion, but there may be more than one way to be a Jew. My stepfather—yes, he adopted me—is a person of honor. At sixteen, when I received my passport, I chose to be like him and took his nationality. And I haven't regretted it for an instant.

OLGA LENSKAYA: I don't care what her passport says. She has

no Jewish blood, and here she is, talking about Jesus Christ, here at the Seminar on *Jewish* Culture! The nerve!*

Elena Georgievna Bonner, who has just returned from Oslo, where she accepted the Nobel Peace Prize on behalf of Andrei Dmitrievich, snuffs out her cigarette (she has brought her own Marlboros) and clears her throat.

"I have some thoughts that need to be expressed. And I want everyone to hear this, especially you, young lady."

Her finger points at Olga Lenskaya, who stands within a meter of her.

"I came here because I wanted to hear a smart person talk about this very important novel. I didn't come here to listen to who is a Jew and who isn't a Jew and how you can tell the difference.

"That thing you said—about missing a quarter or missing a half—that made me cringe. My father was an Armenian by nationality. Am I missing a half? Do I get only one horn and a shorter tail?

"And my old friend Eduard Kuznetsov, in prison now, in the Leningrad case, the main *samolyotchik*, he is missing a half, too. Is he acceptable?

"Young lady, I want you to know that no one—no one—has ever benefited from fascism. In fact, I think that at this point one of us should leave.

"I have a question for Oksana Yakovlevna,† so I will stay. And you should take your swastika and go."

---

* "Наглость какая!"

† Bonner's use of Oksana's patronymic, which hasn't been mentioned before, indicates that she knows Prof. Yakov Aronovich Moskvin (not a surprise) and has connected him with his daughter.

Olga's response to this comment represents the nadir in the history of the seminar.

"And who, may I ask, are you?"*

Witnesses will never forget the ensuing silence.

On Elena Georgievna's face, a hedge of eyebrows is the facial feature that first expresses emotions. They are the place where her laughter begins. Also, the epicenter of moral indignation.

A Marlboro burning in her right hand, her gaze is frozen on the center of the top shelf of Golden's half-empty bookcase. Golden is silent. He stares at the paisley pattern on the carpet. Oksana pauses as well.

It is said that somewhere within this pregnant silence Vladimir Lensky grasps his wife above the elbow, Viktor helpfully grasps her other arm, and, snuffing out the brewing of another retort, the two men begin to drag Olga Lenskaya toward the door.

Some claim to have heard a deep hissing sound emanating from within Olga's inner depths, while others claim to have seen her neck extend menacingly toward Elena Georgievna in what looked like preparation for a ganderly beak-slam.

After the door closes, Elena Georgievna returns to her question.

BONNER: Oksana Yakovlevna, I can't say I fully appreciate the Jerusalem chapters of *The Master and Margarita*. I kind of understand them, and I kind of don't. To me, this has always been primarily a novel about Moscow. I'd love to hear your thoughts about the Jerusalem side of the book.

OKSANA: Thank you, Elena Georgievna. I've been asking

---

* Olga's question is surprisingly difficult to translate: "А что вы из себя представляете?" Exact translation might include tinges of "What is your essence?" or even "What is your worth?" "Who the hell are you?" also falls within the range of meaning.

people who understand Christianity better than I—and getting nowhere. A priest I know told me that Bulgakov's Christ is nonstandard and has nothing to do with the church. Nonstandard—hands washed!

Bulgakov's Christ isn't the son of God, he is the son of a prostitute, conceived by classic means. He doesn't walk on water, doesn't raise the dead, doesn't rise from the dead. When he dies, he dies, with finality.

How difficult is it to acknowledge Bulgakov's Christ, Christ the truth-teller, Christ stabbed in the back by someone he considers a friend? Think of Mandelstam Christ, someone who writes a poem—the truth—about Stalin and pays for it with his life. His Christ is an *intelligent* Christ, a *samizdatchik* Christ, a dissident Christ, a democrat Christ, a bard Christ, a Pushkin Christ, a Jew Christ, a refusenik Christ. It's a moral-ethical tradition we are all familiar with—particularly you, Elena Georgievna.

VIKTOR: How do you worship such a Christ, should you so choose?

OKSANA: Are you asking whether there is a church or a synagogue?

VIKTOR: How do you worship decency?

OKSANA: That's easy. You worship decency by being decent.*

"I need a kiss," says Oksana as they await a tramway at Shabolovka. "Not a grazing peck on the lips, but a deep, honest kiss."

The knife-sharpening hiss of the No. 26 tramway brings them back to the realization that they are standing in the center of the street.

---

* "Достойное поведение почитается достойным поведением."

Sometimes, rarely, you get one of the old streetcars—not the Hungarian Ikarus, which, of course, is a glorious machine—but an old Soviet tramway, the kind from the twenties or thirties, maybe older, with a driver czar-ing from an angled throne behind an angled partition, cutting a path through the tracks made freshly invisible by a coat of snow.

Red beneath the windows, taupe above, an old tramway is movable respite. The seats are birch, the bars brass. A trolleybus is about romance. A tramway trades in illumination, revelation even.

Until this cold, crisp night, Oksana hasn't thought through Bulgakov's decision to set *The Master and Margarita* in the spring. Doesn't our love of Moscow reach its apex in the winter? Is it possible that Bulgakov was playing it safe? Had this novel been set amid the snowdrifts, when Moscow's essence is inescapable, like it is on this cold, clear night, January 17, 1976, would Bulgakov not have been crushed, prostrated by the immensity of feelings, weeping onto the page, unable to write a single word?

Oksana and Viktor board the No. 26 and make their way to the bench in the back. A pair of lovers has carved their names onto this wooden bench—Masha+Petya=Love.* It's a deep carving, its edges worn, a reminder of a love that blossomed and wilted in the twenties or thirties. Thanks to jackknife calligraphy, Masha and Petya have joined fates with this tramway, become a part of this city, its legend, its poetry, its song. What happened to them? Petya died in the war, a tankist in the battle of Kursk; Oksana's guess is as good as any. Masha finished the pedagogical institute after the war. She is not the sort of schoolteacher you remember warmly for the rest of your life. She is the sort who terrorizes first graders till

---

* Маша+Петя=Любовь.

they shit their pants, pouncing on vestiges of individuality, playfulness, and creative thought, blowing out all candles, one by one.

Such are Oksana's thoughts as she sits next to Viktor, her head tilted upon his shoulder, her gloved hand caressing his arm.

"Oksan, listening to you there, I realized—to my bewilderment—that I am unable to pinpoint the spot in the novel where the Master makes a deal with Satan."

"He doesn't. Margarita does. He is in an insane asylum. Remember the scene?"

"I remember her deal—yes. It was on a bench, in Alexander's Garden. In the shadow of the Kremlin wall. She says that in exchange for seeing her lover she would give her soul to Satan."

"You remember correctly, Vitya. Weren't you just there recently, setting up a photo of your *toptun*, as part of your antics with those American students—on that very spot?"

"Yes. On that very spot."

Does Oksana know? Let's say for the sake of argument that she doesn't know; but does she feel it? Probably. Let's say she doesn't know yet. Can the depth of her understanding of deals with Satan be put to work in extracting me from this deal? Do I trust her enough to tell her?

I do.

21.

To get inside Barkin's studio, you must come up to a grate in the courtyard off Zemlyanoy Val (the entryway at 1/4 Chkalov Street, on the corner, works fine) and shout, "Erik!"

If Barkin is hammering, sawing, sanding, or carving, he will not hear you, but you must trust that inevitably he will stop hammering, sawing, sanding, or carving, at which time he will hear that you are outside, asking to be let in. You will know that Barkin has heard you because a window will open beneath the grate, in the cellar, and a broomstick with a spike on top will be lifted to you through the grate.

Upon the spike, you will find a key, which will allow you to open the lock on the heftily proportioned steel-clad door to your right. You will make a detailed visual inspection of the stairs that you will be descending in darkness after the door closes, which it must, in order to preserve heat. Note that one of the hinges on the steel-clad door has rusted out completely, which means that you will be applying upward pressure to make the door close. On descent, you should run your hand along the wall (there is no railing), remembering—first—to step lightly, because the stairs are slanted at randomly occurring angles, and remembering—second—that creaking, about which nothing can be done, is benign and is to be expected since these stairs and this cellar have been here for at least 100 years (probably more like 150), and, as far as it is known, no one of note has lost life or limb while descending them in pitch darkness, which is why the Residential Exploitation Office* sees no necessity in hanging a lightbulb capable of lighting these stairs and the dungeon to which they lead. It's an old building, electricity is tricky, drainage is tricky, heating is tricky. If you go through the door to the right, you will end up in the boiler room instead of Barkin's studio. You are not allowed to go there.

At 4:00 p.m., January 18, Yakov Aronovich Moskvin, a scientist, and another individual later determined to be an American citizen residing in the city of Pittsburgh, state of Pennsylvania, enter the studio of artist Elrad Rudol'fovich Barkin.

The American citizen is identified as Norman "Norm" Dymshitz, father of American correspondent Madison "Mad Dog" Dymshitz. Others, who appear within the ensuing fourteen minutes are, in order of arrival: Vitaly Aleksandrovich Golden, a historian seeking to exit the USSR and organizer of the Seminar on Jewish Culture; Oksana Yakovlevna Moskvina, a former teacher and daughter of Y. A. Moskvin; her purported husband, Viktor Venyaminovich Moroz, a former engineer; and Mikhail Saulovich Kiselenko, a priest known for consistently running afoul of the Patriarchate.

In the forest, you trust your instincts, or you die, and Norm's instincts tell him to pose an all-important question to Barkin, a man he has just met.

"Were you there?"†

---

* ЖЭК.

† "Там был?"

Of course, Barkin knows that "there" stands for the front, the war.*

Barkin nods.

NORM: Where?

BARKIN: Stalingrad, three months and a week. Wounded. You?

NORM: Sobibor, then partisan detachments, Belarus mostly. Not a scratch.

YAKOV ARONOVICH: I met Norm in the forest. I parachuted in, for a quick mission.

NORM: Quick, suicidal.

YAKOV ARONOVICH: It was. I landed. We went. We carried out the order. I left. He stayed.

NORM: Here we are. Suicide failed.

As they wait for others to arrive, Yakov Aronovich asks to see Barkin's works in progress, prompting the sculptor to shine a flashlight on an oval piece of alabaster, a meter-long inverted spheroid, spoonlike. Three pairs of eyes protrude from what looks like a face, with a gigantic seventh eye centered on the forehead. A round carve-out at the bottom represents the mouth. There is a rectangular lower lip and a square upper lip.

"It's *The Dissident*."†

Norm and Yakov Aronovich must have left the door unlocked.

This enables Golden to show up without the fanfare of passing the key through the grate.

---

* Had Norm sensed that his interlocutor had been in the camps (neither man has been), the word "there" would have had a different meaning, but the question would still have been answered with honesty and pride.

† There would be six works in this cycle. The sculpture Barkin shows his guests is the first. It can be seen in the permanent collection of the Tretyakov Gallery, the new building.

GOLDEN: A mask?

BARKIN: An identity.

GOLDEN: Why so many eyes?

BARKIN: Because otherwise-thinking is predicated upon otherwise-seeing.*

GOLDEN: Why aren't any of the eyes looking back?

BARKIN: You can look forward, or you can worry about the back. It's a choice.

Oksana and Viktor arrive next. Father Mikhail is the last to show up.

BARKIN: Since we are all here, I want to tell a story about what happened this morning. I walked out onto the street, Bol'shoy Karetnyy, and sniffed the air, cold Moscow air, taking it in, deep, like a wolf.

GOLDEN: What did you smell? A bus?

BARKIN: A new urgency. Urgency to declare who I am. Not just me—everyone around me feels it, I know. The time has come to put the cards on the table! Declare, publicly, for all to hear: I am a Christian, I am a democrat, I am a Jew, I believe in nothing at all, I am a pig and I want to remain a pig! I don't care what you are— just be honest! If you do not make your declaration, one will be made for you, and you may not like it. In my half century and change, I have never felt an urgency like this.

GOLDEN: Concurred on the urgency. This would have been a lot less confusing if our country had an actual history instead of an oscillating pendulum that swings from despotism to chaos, from chaos to despotism, tick-tock, ding-dong. We are at a point of withering despotism, and some of us don't want to be around

---

* "Ибо инакомыслие зиждется на инаковиденье."

for the next swing to chaos—and the swing to more despotism that will surely follow.

FR. MIKHAIL: Some of us don't have the luxury to escape, not to mention those of us to whom the word "Russia" isn't hollow—patriots. I agree that the state is a walking corpse. And that state-mandated atheism has withered. These are not sudden, seismic events. For some of us, the challenge to declare who we are is not daunting. And our Orthodox Christianity has ample room for visions that correlate the grandeur of creation with moral-ethical mandates placed on an individual.

GOLDEN: Elegantly put, but why should everything be about turning to God? Some of us simply want out, with God, without God, with cosmic implications, without—just out. Who is this God anyway?

BARKIN: But how do you explain the sense of urgency? Why now? Because—to answer my own question—it could be God, it could be a conspiracy of angels, it could be as ordinary as psychosis; not mass psychosis, but a small personal psychosis afflicting me alone.

OKSANA: What is it, then?

BARKIN: To a sculptor, what does it matter? I feel it, I sense it, I smell it, yes, everything short of being able to reach out and touch it—a new shape arising from the dark, amorphous vastness. Inert no more.

Change has occurred, maybe this instant; or maybe last year, or, incrementally, a decade ago, and I've just begun to fathom its significance. I say the urgency is new. It's a rebirth perhaps, or, perhaps, creation—a new whole.

Do you know how the world has the capacity to split suddenly into before and after?

. . .

This number of people can't possibly fit into Barkin's rubble-filled nine-square-meter studio. Oksana, Viktor, Father Mikhail, and Yakov Aronovich are relegated to standing in the anteroom not much larger than an average elevator. One steel-clad door—the open door—leads to Barkin's studio. The other steel-clad door, on the opposite side, is shut.

Barkin reaches across the anteroom and turns the handle of the second door.

"Wait here," he instructs the guests and, with a flashlight in hand, descends what appears to be a creaky ladder leaning against the door and leading at least a meter downward. A concerto of clanging and growling sounds is punctuated by what appears to be flames emanating into the darkness of a vast room.

"Careful on the ladder," Barkin shouts from below as two dim, yellowish lightbulbs come to life.

"You can write a history of the USSR around this place," says Barkin as guests one by one descend into the vast, cavernous space, looking in wonder at the growling, flame-throwing furnace at least thirty meters away and the tangles of clanging, asbestos-covered pipes on the ceiling.

"People don't know where the heat in their radiators comes from. It comes from this beautiful machine. This building was three stories high first. Then they added two floors and another larger building on the end. All that space had to be heated, so a new pit was dug here to make room for this beauty.

"Since it was the 1930s and Comrade Stalin was selling gold and art to pay for industrialization, this thing was brought in from America. State of Michigan. This machine is concordant with my artistic sensibilities, so I consider it an honor to help maintain it, and in exchange, they let me put this big table and some chairs here.

"The table once belonged to a woman who lived here from before. She was Czech, worked as a governess, didn't go back after the revolution. Olga Fyodorovna Zabranskaya. The Thonet chairs were hers, too. The pink silk shade belonged to a Red Cavalry commander, Levinson. Solomon Shimonovich Levinson. He became an actor at the State Jewish Theater.

"Everyone called him Komandir, because he always had that swagger. Lived in the same communal flat as Olga Fyodorovna; they were lovers at one point. A man named Rabinovich, the manager of Pharmacy No. 12, which is directly above us, lived in the same apartment. Some people say they had at one point conspired to kill Stalin. Maybe it's even true."

GOLDEN: This place looks like Schwartz's room—everything inherited, nothing newer than 1917. Speaking of which, why isn't Schwartz here?

BARKIN: Has anyone seen him since the wedding?

GOLDEN: You mean since before the wedding? He didn't show up at the wedding. That was, what, five days ago?

BARKIN: Missing out on the food. He doesn't drink much, poor guy, but he eats, he eats.

NORM: I came to see him day before yesterday. But . . .

YAKOV ARONOVICH: This is Norm, Nuchim, as he was known in the forest. He is my friend from the war. Now lives in America. His son is an American correspondent, Madison Dymshitz.

GOLDEN: Mad Dog Dymshitz? We will not hold it against you.

NORM: I am not him. He is not I. I went to Schwartz's apartment to drop off a suitcase. With money. And . . .

GOLDEN: And?

NORM: His room was completely cleaned out. Not a stick, not a thread—not even a curtain. Just the smell of ammonia.

YAKOV ARONOVICH: Plus, Nuchim walked into a trap.

GOLDEN: And?

NORM: Got away.

BARKIN: From them? How?

NORM: Like in the forest. It's the only way I know.

YAKOV ARONOVICH: Somebody may have died, I am afraid. They tell me the war ended thirty years ago, Norman.

NORM: What choice did I have? I had a suitcase full of money, for the movement, fifty thousand rubles.

BARKIN: You had fifty thousand rubles . . . Fuck your mother . . . You could get a really good sculpture for that. Who is dead? Is Schwartz dead?

VIKTOR: He is. He was dead long before Nuchim got there. He was killed on the day of the wedding. Remember when I took a taxi to get him and his *alterkakers*, the ones who knew how to have a wedding? I found the bodies.

FR. MIKHAIL: Bodies? Not just one body? Who else?

VIKTOR: Alan Foxman.

GOLDEN: The American embassy Alan Foxman?

VIKTOR: The American embassy Alan Foxman.

FR. MIKHAIL: What were they doing?

BARKIN: I think I can guess.

GOLDEN: I wouldn't have guessed.

VIKTOR: You guessed.

NORM: Did you walk into the same trap I walked into?

VIKTOR: It wasn't a trap—not at that time. I walked in not long after it happened, I think. There was blood everywhere. And brains . . . An ax was used. They showed me the autopsy report, and the bodies—but that was later.

YAKOV ARONOVICH: They? You later learned? You saw the autopsy report, and the bodies—later? You are a suspect?

VIKTOR: They say I am not a suspect, but that doesn't matter. If I fail to find and hand over the real murderer, I'll become the suspect of convenience.

GOLDEN: Suspect of convenience . . . That's why you wanted to talk about anti-Semitic trials. Blood libel. Beilis . . . Is that what's brewing?

YAKOV ARONOVICH: Sounds to me like all of it is the work of the GB. Fifth Directorate. They function outside established conventions.

VIKTOR: They swear it's not, and since an American diplomat is involved, they need to get this solved before Kissinger gets here—in less than four days. They need to have an explanation before the newspapers find out—and then the Democrats in Congress. These are people who swept out Nixon, you may recall.

GOLDEN: They see this détente as a sellout, which it is, I think.

BARKIN: Less than four days? When was the last time any of us cracked a murder case?

FR. MIKHAIL: Two men are dead. A prayer is called for. Does anyone know kaddish?

GOLDEN: No.

FR. MIKHAIL: Then I will take over:

Lord Jesus Christ, have mercy on thy servant Albert Schwartz and—what was the other man's name?

VIKTOR: Alan Foxman, if you must.

FR. MIKHAIL: And Alan Foxman . . . who have reposed in the faith and hope of life eternal, and in that thou art good and the lover of mankind, who remittest sins and blottest out iniquities, do thou loose, remit, and pardon all their sins, voluntary and involuntary.

GOLDEN: They would hate this, Schwartz and Foxman both.

FR. MIKHAIL: Deliver them from eternal torment and the fire of Gehenna . . .

VIKTOR: Oy . . .

FR. MIKHAIL: And grant unto them the communion and delight of thine eternal good things prepared for them that love thee.

BARKIN: Please, Father, stop here. The part coming up seems especially inapplicable . . .

FR. MIKHAIL: For though they hath sinned, yet hath not forsaken thee, and undoubtedly believed in the Father and the Son and the Holy Spirit . . .

NORM: Father, Son, the Holy Spirit?

FR. MIKHAIL: And even until last breath did confess thee in Orthodox fashion: God glorified in Trinity, Unity in Trinity and Trinity in Unity.

NORM: What does it matter? Dead is dead.

VIKTOR: Please, let's not argue over liturgy. We are here because I am being sucked into a deal with Satan, and if my friends don't help me, I am done for.

GOLDEN: How can we help?

VIKTOR: We need to approach this in a scientific fashion.

YAKOV ARONOVICH: This is not a scientific problem. It's not even an engineering problem.

VIKTOR: Help . . .

YAKOV ARONOVICH: What is the question, precisely, scientific or not?

VIKTOR: How do you dissolve a deal with Satan, should you make one?

OKSANA: This is not scientific, concurred, Father, but because of who we are, we have to treat it as a rational matter, legal even. The first question: Is there a deal?

VIKTOR: I have been plucked off the street, I have engaged in conversations, I have been threatened with a series of or-elses, but never, never have I said yes in exchange for a consideration.

FR. MIKHAIL: So your soul is still in your possession?

OKSANA: Let's go to the texts. In *Faust*, yes, a deal is done. In Marlowe, too. But not in our operative text, which is Bulgakov. The Master never says yes to Satan. He is not even asked. Margarita is the one who proposes the deal. She acts for him, not because she is weak, but because she is strong. The Master is informed that the deal has been done. Does this recap help?

GOLDEN: From the historical perspective, the Master's experience is more relevant to our situation.

FR. MIKHAIL: What are you suggesting?

GOLDEN: That history creates circumstances that drive free will into irrelevance.

FR. MIKHAIL: I disagree. Free will is always central.

BARKIN: I disagree as well, Father. Artistic impulse is what matters. That, plus technical ability to transform vision into shape. That's how we talk with God. Even if there is no God.

FR. MIKHAIL: You are asking wrong questions, all of you. You are overestimating Satan's craft.

NORM: I've seen Satan's work. While I disagree with his methodology, I would never accuse him of being *stupid*.

FR. MIKHAIL: Yet stupid he is. Very. Consistently. That's why we always win.

YAKOV ARONOVICH: Do we? I think we are losing, actually, slipping into a pit, deeper and deeper, century by century. I am not a historian, of course.

GOLDEN: I say the time we live in is what matters. You don't have to be a Stalinist to be sucked into Stalinism. You don't have to be a Nazi to be sucked into Nazism. What does it matter what your free will dictates when you are driven into a gas chamber?

NORM: Having narrowly escaped the fate to which you've just alluded, I wholeheartedly concur. My free will mattered to me—a lot. To history—not a bit. When I killed them in the forest, I killed for me, to free my soul from torment. Self-medication you might call it.

YAKOV ARONOVICH: I was right next to you for some of it, but I wasn't self-medicating. I was acting to rid history of disease, fighting a pathogen.

OKSANA: So, some of us say history matters, others wish to negate it, while the third group argues that our ability to look in the mirror without feeling disgust is all that matters. Is this a good summary?

YAKOV ARONOVICH: Yes, it's a good summary, Oksanka. Are you going to introduce it as a motion? Tally up the yeas, the nays?

OKSANA: Thank you for this bit of absurdity, as always, Father.

YAKOV ARONOVICH: Happy to oblige.

BARKIN: If a motion is indeed before us, I move we table it. The world is silly enough without further loosening the bowels of nonsense. I propose that we consider questions in order of their importance. I have a question that fits squarely on the pinnacle of our hierarchy of questions: Why does Satan need the Master?

OKSANA: And why did he need Faust before him?

GOLDEN: I have no answer.

YAKOV ARONOVICH: Nor I.

BARKIN: Nor I.

NORM: Don't look at me.

VIKTOR: I am an engineer; what can I possibly know?

FR. MIKHAIL: You really don't know? No clue? Satan needed Faust, and after him the Master, because Satan is a fallen angel, and angels are single-purpose creatures. They have no creativity, no capacity to engage in science, art. Man has all that. Hence, Satan has a need for souls. It's simple.

. . .

"I have been listening, and now it's my turn to speak," resounds a voice that drowns out the furnace. It's a woman's voice, weak on its own, but amplified by the room's stone walls and tangles of cast iron pipes.

Suddenly, the light gets turned on, revealing the silhouette of a petite woman in a black karakul coat with a blue mink collar and a matching hat. *Nomenklatura* wives wear such getups, except, as far as it is known, Lydia Ivanovna is nobody's wife, no one's handmaiden.

VIKTOR: Have you come to arrest me?

LYDIA IVANOVNA: No.

VIKTOR: Are you alone? Are you armed?

LYDIA IVANOVNA: Alone. Not armed. I have brought gifts, for you, Oksana Yakovlevna, and for you, Norman.

VIKTOR: This is my curator, Lydia Ivanovna No-Last-Name. The purchaser of souls.

BARKIN: How did you find us?

OKSANA: I am a careful organizer. Nothing was said on the phone.

NORM: Is there a traitor among us?

LYDIA IVANOVNA: Norm, I don't know—honestly. I don't curate all of you, and some of you aren't even curated. You, for example. Telephone communications were indeed not useful. You avoided that pitfall—well done, Oksana Yakovlevna.

Has everyone here heard that if you place a pencil in the telephone dial, our listening devices will be disabled? Well, it's not true. We can hear, pencil or no pencil. But the story about surveillance disbanding at midnight is true, alas.

Let me shed some light on this matter:

One: We didn't kill anyone. An ax does make it look like us

trying to make it appear that it's anyone but us, which would mean it's us. We've done similar things to cover our tracks here and there, true—but not this one. Accept it like an article of faith. It would be better for everyone.

Two: Viktor, you are quite right that you haven't said yes. It is also correct that you were pressured mightily. I like Norm's point. A Jew buried on the bottom of a pit is a player in a game waged by Hitler, just like I was a cog in the machine of Stalinism at the time of being raped by Lavrenty Pavlovich. You have to learn to be dispassionate and accept the world as it is.

Three: Father Mikhail, free will is overemphasized. It's not important to get Viktor's consent. He is our informant one way or another. We follow his every step to the best of our ability, and we learn. And this is for Oksana and several others—primarily for Oksana: How you feel when you look in the mirror is your own business. It doesn't touch upon us as an organization.*

Four: Correct—Satan needs the Master because creativity is a human capacity. Organizations, like Satan, lack it entirely. That's precisely why we need you, Viktor Venyaminovich. And now, in your effort to evade contractual entanglements, all of you have walked into our grasp. You might say that instead of one soul on one hook, we pulled out a netful.

Now, this is my favorite part—gifts. You don't have to dance for joy, but you will accept them.

First, for you, Oksana, I took a special trip to the archives and looked under "B" for Bulgakov. We have some interesting materials there. It made me wish briefly that you could have joined me. Maybe someday.

Many people in my organization wish we could have found

---

* "Нас, как организацию, это никак не волнует."

and burned *The Master and Margarita*. I can understand that line of thought. But I also saw meticulous preservation of materials obtained from searches of Bulgakov's flat, including one in 1925. That search netted a rather long poem titled "An Epistle to the Evangelist Demyan Bedny." The poem is anonymous. Some said it was Esenin, and maybe it was. But anyone can see that Bulgakov agreed with it. It shows you precisely what prompted him to write this novel. I copied this poem by hand—my handwriting is meticulous, so you will have no problem reading.

Now, you, Mr. Dymshitz, may have misplaced your suitcase, the one you had with you on the roof, when you got away from our operatives. We have recovered it for you. The money is still inside, nearly fifty thousand—you seem to have taken a wad. Put it to good use, just as you intended. You are probably indifferent to the fate of the operatives you worked over, but I will inform you anyway. One of them is technically back on duty, but we moved him to a desk job, to give him time to fully recover the use of his arm. Also, to make sure that he doesn't come across you during the rest of your stay in our country. It would end badly—for him. The second one, sadly, died on the operating table, but we have attributed that loss to a medical error. His injury was not trivial, but it shouldn't have been fatal. Anesthesia given badly has a way of causing cardiac arrest—not your fault.

That's it from me. You look so cozy there, around that table. I was hoping to be invited to tea, but it's a long schlep to Chertanovo. First, Metro, then bus—more than an hour.

And—this is really the point—Henry Kissinger's plane will land here, in Moscow, on January 22. So no time to waste. Get to work—solve it. You have less than four days.

NORM: Are you Jewish, by the way?

LYDIA IVANOVNA: Yes.

. . .

"I need to get to water," says Norm as he walks out into the courtyard.

"Will ice do?" responds Yakov Aronovich. "It's January, it's Moscow."

"Yes."

"Yauza is two trolleybus stops away, by the Sakharovs—theirs is the last building before Yauza."

They catch the B trolleybus.

"I don't think I could manage living here, in this city," says Norm as they get off the B and walk down to the Yauza embankment. "Would be afraid to."

"Afraid of what?"

"Afraid of not being able to recognize the edge of reality."

"The boundary between what is and what's imagined? Afraid of your own confusion?"

"How do you deal with it—with disorientation?"

"You can't. If it sets in, you don't know it has. No point worrying. What's it like in Pittsburgh?"

"In Pittsburgh? I don't understand my wife. My son is a stranger. Sometimes I think I am playing a role: a Florida-going, Cadillac-driving, gold-chain-wearing, cigar-chomping, forearm-flaunting millionaire Jew—a clown, *der payatz*."

"How do you keep from putting a bullet in your forehead?"

"In the mornings, before the staff arrives, I lock my office door, turn on music, any music, and draw scenes from memory, scenes from the war. Nothing from before the war, nothing from after."

"Does anyone see your drawings? Your wife? Your son? Your psychiatrist?"

"No. I burn them."

22.

n January 1976, Bulgakovists of the world get access to a poem, which had been confiscated at a search of Bulgakov's apartment half a century earlier.

Bulgakov was infuriated by a screed by an ignoramus poet named Demyan Bedny, enough so that Bedny would become the prototype for the ignoramus poet Ivan Bezdomny, who appears on the opening pages of *The Master and Margarita* and stays through the end.

Bedny's poem in question includes this stanza:

Точное суждение о Новом завете:
Иисуса Христа никогда не было на свете.
Так что некому было умирать и воскресать,
Не о ком было Евангелия писать.*

The Bedny-Bulgakov brawl is the genesis of *The Master and Margarita*.

After reading Bedny's idiocy in *Pravda*, an anonymous author angrily penned "An Epistle to the Evangelist Demyan Bedny," a poem that Bulgakov clearly agreed with.

---

* Here is the truth about the New Testament: / Never was there a Jesus Christ. / No one to die, no one to rise from the dead, / No one to write the gospels about.

The epistle was confiscated in an NKVD search of Bulgakov's apartment in 1925 and was kept in the NKVD archives, where it was found by Lydia Ivanovna, who copied it by hand and gave it as a goodwill gift to Oksana.

Recognizing its value, Oksana retypes it in multiple copies and sends it off into *samizdat*:

> Я часто думаю, за что Его казнили?
> За что Он жертвовал Своею головой?
> За то ль, что, враг суббот, Он против всякой гнили
> Отважно поднял голос Свой? . . .

> За то ли, что Себя на части разделя,
> Он к горю каждого был милосерд и чуток
> И всех благословлял, мучительно любя,
> И маленьких детей, и грязных проституток?*

Like the poem's anonymous author, Bulgakov doesn't have much love for the Russian Orthodox Church, either. His theology and his motivation for writing *The Master and Margarita* are spelled out in verse, preserved for all the wrong reasons, but preserved nonetheless:

> Я не люблю религию раба,
> Покорного от века и до века,
> И вера у меня в чудесные слова—
> Я верю в знание и силу Человека.

---

* I often ask: Why was He executed, / Why was He ready to sacrifice His head? / Was it because He, an enemy of the Sabbaths, had raised His voice / Against all forms of rot? // Was it because He tore Himself to bits, / Because He felt the pain of everyone around, / And blessed them, feeling love / For little children and filthy prostitutes alike?

Пусть миф Христос, как мифом был Сократ,
И может быть из вымысла всё взято—
Так что ж теперь со злобою подряд
Плевать на всё, что в человеке свято?*

A better goodwill gift could not be imagined. On January 18, at her apartment, Oksana stares at the telephone on the kitchen table. It's a modern apparatus, canary-yellow body, blue cords and trim, made in Hungary. There is, as always, a pencil in its dial.

"Call me if you can hear me. In ten seconds."

It's 11:31. Oksana counts silently. On what would have been the count of eleven, the phone rings. She listens to waves of silence on the other end. Then she pulls the pencil out of the dial, watching it wind back to the original position. It will never be inserted again.

On the ethical scale, what's lower than a KGB secret collaborator? A murderer might be several rungs beneath, a double murderer lower still.

Is nuance possible in matters of honor? Is every collaboration with the KGB a dishonorable collaboration with the KGB? If change is possible in our country, at some point people of honor will ultimately need to talk with—perhaps even negotiate with—people who lack it. Isn't that so?

Oksana has never spoken with Schwartz, she has never seen Foxman, but what difference does that make? Did their skulls merit being busted, their heads severed? What if she, Oksana,

---

* How I detest religion of a slave, / Obedient from century to century, / My faith is faith in wonder of the word— / Belief in knowledge and in might of Man. // Conceded, Christ is mythical, as much as Socrates was, / Quite possibly, there is invention present. / But why would we, today, so viciously, without thought, / Go forth and spit at everything that in man is sacred?

helps bring the killer to justice? Wouldn't that make the world a little less ugly? This Lydia Ivanovna seems like a person of intelligence. She may even have a tinge of honor.

"Lydia Ivanovna, are you there?" Oksana says to the phone. "Ring twice on the count of ten."

She counts to ten.

At exactly the right moment, the phone rings twice and the ringing stops.

"Do I have your word of honor that if I help you, you will leave us alone? Ring again on the count of ten."

On the count of ten, the phone rings three times.

"If you want me to help you, here are my conditions: I want every shred of paper you took from Schwartz's. Every single evidence bag must be delivered to my door by tomorrow morning. Don't ring the doorbell!

"And . . ."

Here, Oksana pauses.

"I want all surveillance to stop. If I see a *toptun*, if my husband— or anyone else—sees one of your Volgas . . . Or if you drag any one of us in for one of your interrogations, we will stop all activity . . . Completely. Forever.

"I will count to five—acknowledge, or we are done this instant. Make it five rings."

On the count of five, Oksana's telephone begins to ring. It stops after giving off five rings.

23.

Guards at Sad Sam are adept at spotting interlopers. Westerners don't get challenged to show identification on the way in; Soviet citizens do.

On January 18, a bit before midnight, a guard at Sad Sam asks Norm to present his documents. It could be his Soviet overcoat, except Mad Dog, his son, has never been asked to show ID while wearing it. Possibly, Norm's body language has returned to its mother tongue. Or, possibly, his American Tourister is now beat up enough to look Soviet. Surprised to see Norm's U.S. passport, the guard salutes. What else is there to do when you've misjudged someone?

Madison is presumably asleep, or at least the bedroom door is closed. Norm sits down at the boy's desk and, at 12:37 a.m., places a call to Pittsburgh, Pennsylvania. In Pittsburgh it's 4:00 p.m. Recording equipment malfunctions, alas, and only one side of the conversation is recorded and transcribed. It's possible that someday a full transcript, one that reflects Miriam "Mary" Dymshitz's part, will turn up in a filing cabinet time forgot, but the one-sided version, presumably captured by a listening device within the apartment, appears to be fully informative:

"Yes, yes, fine, fine, fine, everything is . . . Fine . . ."

"Long trip, but no longer than Japan, and we did that without a hiccup."

"To me, he seems happy. What do you expect? A big job, big responsibility."

"Pressure, aggravation."

"People here adore him, especially refuseniks—yes, not that I spoke with any."

"Was very happy to see me. Misses his mother. It's a special bond you two have."

"Has not mentioned her AT ALL. Like she never existed."

"I agree, probably a good thing."

"Definitely."

"Yes, you were right all along."

"It's a big, dirty, unhappy place. No wonder people want to leave."

"A big high-rise, with an armed guard in front."

"Very isolated, but very safe."

"Miserable . . . Everyone . . . Not that I've spoken to many people."

"Yes, I dropped off the jeans, as planned."

"Without a hitch."

"No, no, no! Of course, I was not followed. Why would I be?"

"You are right, of course, I wouldn't have known if I had been."

"How was your appointment? What did Bernie say?"

"Well, no news is good news."

"The sisterhood situation?"

"That place is becoming so political."

"At the latkes breakfast? Really?"

"I didn't know the sisterhood has taken over that . . ."

"Canasta?"

"Good, good, good . . ."

Norm never rifles through his son's desk. Didn't do it even before the boy turned eighteen. But, around the time the conversation with Miriam delved into geopolitics at St. Rodef—the backstabbing at the sisterhood, particularly the intrigue swirling around canasta and stewardship over the latkes breakfast—Norm starts to contemplate a pile of crumpled pieces of onionskin paper on the desk in front of him.

Every time Norm sits down at a desk, any desk, his gaze sweeps over its surface. It's a form of grazing; when it starts, it goes on and on, especially when one of Mary's stories is undergoing narration. Those stories star her as a maiden of pure heart and impeccable logic. Had Norm found any personal material, such as letters from his runaway daughter-in-law or, say, correspondence with her lawyer, if one has been engaged, he would have stopped—but why would that sort of material be left crumpled on the desk's surface?

The boy has always crumpled paper and left it in piles on top of his desks.

Why?

To throw crumpled papers across the room, trying to get them into a wastebasket.

This is not Norm's problem, but it infuriated Mary. It was as though the boy wanted her to complete his process of garbage-discarding, act as his final arbiter of paper refuse.

What if people come to visit?

Close the *farkakte* door to his room if people come to visit!

Complex psychoanalytical hypotheses were woven with the help of a certain Dr. Pferdekopf (not his real name), at great expense; Norm doesn't know how much. In the name of world peace, he gave the matter as much attention as he was able. If the boy wants to crumple papers to throw them into wastebaskets across the room, let him crumple papers to throw them into wastebaskets across the room, and if he wants to continue to crumple papers to throw them into wastebaskets across the room upon reaching adulthood, his mother should not feel ashamed. Garbage is garbage, and life is known for teeming with things that are bigger than garbage.

There is a piece of crumpled onionskin paper with typed text. A crumpled blue notepaper with a "From the Desk of Alan Foxman" on top is attached to it. The note is handwritten, and it's in English; the typed text on the onionskin paper is Russian.

It turns out there are four typed pages. The boy was preparing a large projectile, an ICBM, evidently. Norman smooths out the crumpled onionskin paper. The salutation on top is like no other: "To People of Goodwill:"* He smooths out three more pages, looking for signatures. Scanning through, he notes a few sentences:

> As Jewish activists in the USSR and their non-Jewish brethren, we say resolutely and authoritatively that the idea that the Jewish agenda, even if it is focused solely on emigration, can be separated from the democratic agenda is historically and morally bankrupt . . .
>
> Historical experience has demonstrated time and again that the democratic idea and the principles of human rights must be applied equitably and universally to all individuals.
>
> We urge you, people of goodwill across the world, to begin reporting on implementation of the Third Basket of the Final Act of the Conference on Security and Cooperation in Europe.

---

* "Людям доброй воли:"

Beneath that final, cryptic, unwieldy call to action, if that is
what it is, Norman finds five signatures. He recognizes two names:
Albert Schwartz is one. Fr. Mikhail Kiselenko, the priest he met at
the sculptor's studio earlier that evening, is another.

Norm hasn't heard much about the Helsinki agreements, other
than they were signed late last summer, in 1975. There was some
noise about them during the presidential campaign. Carter has
called them a "sellout" or some such—the Nixon-Ford administration had accepted Soviet domination of Eastern Europe in
exchange for the Sovs making some vague promises on human
rights.

Norm hasn't decided how he will vote in the election. Carter
is a guy who thinks he has a direct relationship with God. His
kind can bolt in any direction, an unguided missile. Ford is a stiff,
clueless goy, devoid of the neuroreceptors required for accepting
direct messages from deities. So Ford inhabits the world of real
things, which for a presidential candidate is a plus. Norm did vote
for Eisenhower, as an act of gratitude for Americans helping to
drive out the Nazis. But he hasn't voted Republican since. Besides,
Norm is uneasy about Ford's Court Jew Kissinger. Henry flaunts
his amorality, flashing it with his trench coat open wide—behold
my amorality, big, strong, juicy amorality, flaccid, but hey, that's
one of amorality's distinguishing characteristics . . . Perhaps Norm
will vote for Carter after all.

Next, Norm reads the blue note, the one "From the Desk of
Alan Foxman":

Dear Madison,
    I've just received this "appeal" from our mutual friend,
one of the signatories (see below). This is a significant
development—possibly, the beginning of conversation about

an international human rights agenda, to be <u>monitored by Soviet citizens themselves.</u>

And—this is the best aspect of it—it's not my idea. It seems to have sprung up independently, organically. (Perhaps there is hope of civil society developing here.) This idea of Helsinki monitoring seems to be something that, for whatever reason, is in the air here in the Big Potato.

I can tell you that it's going to piss off a lot of people here, as well as in Washington, especially a certain narcissistic prick, whom we are about to see here in person. Look at the signatures beneath the document. They include a Jewish activist with a human rights pedigree—and a Russian Orthodox priest I happen to know quite well, etc. This could go huge. Definitely merits coverage.

I know that Israelis in particular are averse to viewing the immigration movement through the lens of human rights.

This is happening for at least three reasons: (1) This would detract from specialness of the Jewish Question, (2) They don't want to provoke the Soviets any more than they have to, and (3) The Israelis could be cooking up some plots of their own (always a safe guess).

Yours,
Alan

P.S. I hope you deem this "appeal" (attached) worthy of coverage. But, <u>please,</u> please, please, burn this note. The fuckers will fry me if they learn I was anywhere near this.

Norm notes that the boy didn't burn this confidential missive from Foxman, per instructions. Now, that's bad. You can't assume that anything is safe here at Sad Sam. Cleaning people here are not cleaning people. At least some of them carry little cameras. Plus, the building is wired every which way. Why would you not burn documents so sensitive that they could destroy careers, perhaps even lead to deaths?

Why did the boy disregard explicit instructions? Is it because his paper basketball games require fresh fodder?

Norm gives the document another glance, folds it neatly, and places it in his pocket. Whatever it is, leaving it on this desk is clearly the wrong thing to do.

24.

f you want to talk about diplomacy in general and treaties specifically, it's better to start with someone other than Norm.

Norm didn't learn about the Geneva Conventions—specifically, the idea that it's treif to execute prisoners—until well after the war. The convention in the forest was simpler: finish them off.

At the end of their suicide mission and after deciding to derail that train, and carrying it through, and using up all machine-gun ammo in the process, he and Yakov—now Prof. Yakov Aronovich Moskvin—used their revolvers to execute the wounded Germans. If anyone was suspected of having writhed or twitched, they got a single round to the back of the head or under the chin, depending on how they lay.

When this was finished, Norm and Yakov opened the latches. Mostly, there was inanimate cargo, but there were people, too, about fifty, in the last freight car. Norm remembers their confusion as daylight hit them in the face. They were in street clothes—not stripes—freshly rounded up at some ghetto. Norm and Yakov helped them down, and some seemed to know exactly what to do—head into the forest, as deep as possible. How long would they survive there, without supplies?

Norm couldn't stay with them—he was carrying out orders,

which included an expectation of him coming back to the detachment. Yakov, too, had to return to his Red Army unit. Neither could do more for these people than they already had. These civilians—Jews all, it seemed—nodded to their liberators, thanking them silently, and then they ran toward the forest. All but an old man who needed a younger woman's help getting down.

"*Du bist a Yid!*" the old man declared to Norm. This wasn't a question. "*A greisse dank for unzer frayhayt. A lange leben auf dir—mit a sakh mazel.*"*

Norm will never lose the image of that old man as he and a middle-aged woman trudged off into the woods. Norm had nothing but a can of American stewed pork to give them. He asked them to wait as he checked whether he still had the can in his rucksack. He had some bread also. He should give it to them, too. He ended up giving them the rucksack.

A few years ago, Norm was found by one of the survivors, who told him that the old man had died within days in the forest, no surprise there, and that no one knows what became of the woman who remained by his side.

Has Norm received the allotment of *mazel* the old man had wished upon him? He is here, in Moscow, isn't he? He is trying to help, isn't he? Hasn't he just come closer to dying than at any point since the war? And by the look of it, he still has an American Tourister stuffed with stacks of rubles, jeans, and *Playboy*s. Didn't that Yiddena from the KGB just return it to him? He has been forgiven for what in the United States would be called murder. Long Live the Soviet System of Justice!

It's well after midnight here in the Big Potato, as the boy calls it. All the goons are probably tucked in, *shloffing*, dreaming of the

---

* "You are a Jew! Thank you for our freedom. May your life be long and happy."

bright future of mankind, snoring loudly, too. What's there to prevent Norm from going out into the street, circling the block to see whether he is being followed, and if he isn't, borrow the boy's car and take these lifesaving supplies to the second person on the list that Lou Rosenblum had given to him before he left.

The man's name is . . .

Norm reaches into his wallet and looks for the name and address scribbled on a piece of paper inserted into a small pocket in back of his driver's license. The name is . . .

Couldn't be . . .

Vladimir Lensky?

Like in *Onegin*?

He just saw that cursed opera again. Hated it again—a trite little melodrama. She loves him, he doesn't love her; he reconsiders, but it's too late—all that and bang-bang in the middle. God save him from the ballet of *Onegin*; he knows there is one, but no—please. Pushkin's novel in verse is another matter. Never has Norm loved a novel more, even with poetry not being his cup of tea.

Where does this Vladimir Lensky live? The address is Perovskaya 40, Building 4. Norm has a map. Norm always has a map.

Novogireyevo. It sounds far, but it's closer than you think.

At the boy's apartment, Norm puts on his American overcoat. Might as well not provoke suspicion from the guy in the booth by wearing the scratchy, dog-bitten, bloodstained Soviet number.

As he gets down from the seventh floor, Norm sees that he shouldn't have worried. Downstairs, in the booth, the guard is reclined in his chair, sleeping peacefully. Norm walks up the street, turns around sharply.

No one behind him. He meanders down the side streets off

Sadovaya-Samotechnaya, even steps into a courtyard and waits. No *toptun* in sight. The boy's Soviet Fiat is at the exact spot where Norm last saw it. The engine turns over with unexpected enthusiasm, Norm steps on the clutch, gives the thing some gas, making the wheels engage with a patch of crushed ice. The feel reminds Norm of the greenish Corvair convertible he had briefly, before the Cadillacs set in.

At 2:00 a.m., Sadovaya-Samotechnaya is deserted. As Norm gets away from the city's center, everything around him starts to look like the projects. A few dachas, one-story structures behind picket fences, are still left standing, but mostly it's built up with monstrously long five-story yellow brick buildings. The American Tourister sits in the trunk, with fifty thousand rubles inside it.

Norm sees no problem with showing up unannounced. Lou had given him the address, but no telephone number. Maybe this Lensky has no phone. Where is it written that he must? It's always safest to show up in the middle of the night unannounced. At least you know people are at home, unless, of course, this Lensky has been offed, too.

Norm has no problem finding the place. It's one of those yellow-brick buildings. You might be tempted to call it faceless, impersonal, but reality has a way of busting cliches. Some residents have personalized this façade, closing off their balconies with glass panels. On the first floor, where there are no balconies, residents have placed steel bars on the windows, prison style. These bars, too, come in different shapes, different colors. Some bend outward, to make room for window boxes that at this time of year contain dead plants that stick out of frozen dirt.

Lensky's apartment is on the first floor, presumably one of the places with bars on the windows. Norm rings the bell.

After a while, the light inside is turned on—he sees that

through the peephole and the crack beneath the vinyl-covered door. The peephole darkens as someone studies him. It's a good thing he is wearing his American overcoat.

"Oh, good, some American is here in the middle of the night— means money!"* a woman's voice whispers in Russian.

"Sh-sh, shut up, you fool," answers a man's voice.

This could be a setup. Momentarily, Norm wishes he had left the suitcase in the car, but it's too late.

"Excuse me for coming in the middle of the night . . ." he half whispers in English. "I am here from the Union of Councils . . ."

It comes out in English, Norm doesn't know why.

Strictly speaking, Norm is not from the Union of Councils for Soviet Jews. It's a good organization—so nothing against them.

They call themselves "grassroots." They got this battle going while Israel was against paying too much attention to Soviet Jews, and "establishment" Jewish groups in the United States took Israel's orders and did nothing. Some say they were formed by Israel with the express purpose to do nothing but counterbalance the grass-roots. Israelis and the establishment say they are working on it, but doing so behind the scenes, negotiating with the Sovs, through Kissinger perhaps. It's being handled, and you, America's rich Jews, should focus on generating money for Israel—by selling Israel Bonds.

These groups—"grassroots" and "establishment"—hate each other, as Jews often do.

Norm is not from the Union of Councils. Norm is from the forest. Norm is from Norm.

The door opens and Norm walks into the apartment. In front of him is a man in a striped, gold-and-black terry-cloth bathrobe

---

* "Ой хорошо, какой-то американашка посреди ночи пришел—значит бабки!"
  "Молчи, дура."

over paisley-patterned pajamas. The bathrobe looks vaguely Italian. (Norm can't tell you how he makes this determination.) Also, Norm is surprised to see a yarmulke and a thick gold chain with a big Star of David. The woman whose voice Norm heard earlier as he was being assessed through the peephole appears to have retreated into the depths of the apartment.

You don't just dump your fifty thousand rubles in public funds, unless absolutely necessary. You have to figure out who the recipients are, whether they are who they say they are. You might as well gather some intelligence. For the first time since landing in Moscow, Norm decides to play the role of an American.

He notices a black hat on the coat hanger. Is this man black-hat Orthodox? Is this woman? How do you become an Orthodox Jew in the Land of Victorious God-Knows-What? How do you even get your boys circumcised here in this forest? Actually, it's a reasonable question: Is this Orthodox Jew before Norm circumcised? This is none of Norm's business, but it's a valid question.

"Do you speak English?" Norm asks.

"Не дую . . ." responds the woman from what must be the kitchen—*ne duyu*. This strange echo sets Norm back for a moment: "Do you . . ." / "*Ne duyu*." The latter also means "I don't blow."*

Jesus . . . A sex joke? Certainly more than Norm wants to hear. Secular Zionist women make crude jokes routinely. Soviet women, too. Orthodox women may or may not. Norm doesn't know. Who are these people?

The man—Lensky—smiles at the joke and ushers Norm into the room.

---

* The joke, completely untranslatable, requires two languages, and is about oral sex:
Question: "Do you speak English?"
Answer: "Дую, дую, но хуёво." (Yes, I blow, but badly.)

Just then, the woman walks in, carrying a teapot, cups, and cookies on a tray. She, too, is wearing a massive bathrobe and—this is odd—she seems to have slapped on a wig. Her round face looks like an extension of her smile. It's a nice smile. How old is she? Maybe twenty-seven?

If these people are really Orthodox, why would this girl make jokes about oral sex, of all things, especially with a stranger in the room—even if the stranger doesn't appear to understand a word of Russian? Take away the black hats and wigs, the ultra-Orthodox are like the rest of us, maybe.

Norm knows of a halfway house some black hats have established in Pittsburgh. It's a full-service rehab. These aren't people who had too much wine at Passover and did too much rejoicing. It's not just alcoholism, but the whole range of stuff—heroin, coke, etc. Just because you believe HaShem is watching your every step doesn't mean you will not fuck yourself up. It's possible that the Lenskys are just learning to be Orthodox—quasi-Orthodox. Or maybe they are just Orthodox-style.

"I am Norman Dymshitz," Norm begins. He should have thought of another name, but never mind, what's done is done.

He looks around. The place is full of mahogany furniture, antiques, figurines, icons even. Too much of everything. And icons in an Orthodox Jewish home? Is it just about their monetary value? There is a stack of paintings in the corner. Norm would love to look at them, but, wisely, stops himself from expressing interest.

This looks like the kind of place lots of stuff moves through.

"*Yiddish?*"

"No . . ."

"Okay. I will . . . speak . . . slowly . . . I bring . . ."

"Bring, yes, bring . . ."

"*Playboy* . . . Levi's . . ."

"*Und* dollars?" asks the woman as she sets down the tray. Norm finds it interesting that she isn't completely clueless.

"*Da!*" says Norm. "I . . . come . . . here . . . with . . . group . . . Intourist . . ."

"Group . . . Intourist . . ." Lensky repeats. "Yes. *Fershtain.*"

Good, he is putting his German to use.

"*Farshtei*, we say," Norm corrects him. Might as well teach the kid some Yiddish in place of what sounds like a Soviet movie version of German. Yiddish is Germanic, yes, but it's not German.

"*Da* . . . It's in the . . . suitcase . . . I . . . know Russian . . . word. CHE-MU-DUN!"

"*Che-mO-dAn*," the woman corrects, for "*chemodan*" is indeed the word for "suitcase."

"Дядюшка слабоумный,"* she says to Vladimir.

Idiocy would be a reasonable inference, though it does hit a nerve; you can't help being offended. Norm opens the American Tourister and slowly pulls out the *Playboy*s. There are three. Also, one *Penthouse.*

With a nod, he apologizes to the lady of the house.

"*Dos is gelt*," she says in Yiddish, probably her only Yiddish. "It's money."

Porn is indeed money, in this city and others.

Norm pours himself a cup of tea, takes a cookie from a colorful plate, and takes a deep sip. This tastes quite good, actually. Maybe it's the black tea, maybe it's the way it was brewed. It seems the cover has been ripped off one of the *Playboy*s. Another one seems to be water-stained. Not a surprise. The magazines have been through a lot.

---

* "The old man is a moron."

"Что он, дрочил, этот твой слабоумный?"* asks Mrs. Lensky.

Less reasonable questions have been asked, though probably not by anyone claiming to be an ultra-Orthodox Jew, and not by ultra-Orthodox women in front of strangers.

They are looking at the Levi's now. Should I tell them about the fifty thousand rubles in the lining? What else would Norm do with this enormous sum? He couldn't possibly give it to the boy—he can't bring himself to say "Madison." That boy would immediately tell Miriam. Make that "Mary." Norm's goose would be cooked.

Yakov Aronovich would accept the money, sure, but only on condition that he would regift it to a public cause. That would be risky.

"I . . . need . . . a . . . knife . . ." Norm says slowly and loudly "Knife . . ."

"*Meser,*" Norm adds hopelessly in Yiddish.

He accompanies this pronouncement with a gesture evoking a saw cutting through wood. This doesn't work.

The Lenskys are without a clue. He sets down his teacup and heads to the kitchen, where in a pile of unwashed dishes he finds what looks like a thin, dull knife.

"A knife," he announces, holding up the object, and repeating: "A knife!"

Norm picks up the "knife," stabs the lining of the American Tourister, and continues to cut. The lining is pulled back, exposing stacks of one-hundred-ruble bills.

"Ёб твою . . . ,"† says Vladimir Lensky.

---

* "Has your moron been whacking off?"

† "Fuck your . . ." Norm resists the urge to complete the sentence with a "мать," "*mat*'"—mother.

"Может он не такой мудак, твой америкашка,"* says Mrs. Lensky.

Norm thanks the Lenskys in Yiddish and English and, puzzled, leaves that apartment. Could these people have been working for the KGB? He'd like to think the KGB would do better staging. And what would it matter if they are? The KGB has figured out his private Lend-Lease program. If they haven't nabbed Norm for it before, why would they nab him for it now?

Are these people actual observant Jews? Or are they playing dress-up? Hard to tell without opening their souls and looking for a divine spark. Perhaps they are only opportunists. Whatever the Lenskys are and whatever they believe, they seem to have some public role, which presumably means that they will distribute the money. And is it really so much? It's just $7,500.

Norm certainly can't take a chance on bringing this cash back through customs. One way or another, the money needs to be dumped, so Lenskys-shmenskis—what the hell?

---

* "Perhaps your American isn't such a fuckup."

25.

n the middle of the night, Oksana gets up and writes down the pronouncement Barkin had made in his studio yesterday.

It was about the new urgency he smells in the Moscow air.

"I sensed a new urgency, urgency to declare who I am. Not just me—everyone around me is feeling it, I know. The time has come to put cards on the table! Declare, publicly, for all to hear: I am a Christian, I am a democrat, I am a Jew, I believe in nothing at all, I am a pig and want to always remain a pig. If you do not make your declaration, one will be made for you, and you may not like it. In my half century and change, I have never felt an urgency like this one."

Has Oksana made her declaration, besides opting to declare herself a Jew in Item Five of the passport and taking that leap across Arkhipov Street? But the first action was an act of respect for her father, who despite being a genuine war hero and a hero of Soviet science could be treated badly by the idiots in the party organization in his institute. It's not Auschwitz-level mistreatment, to be sure, but is it not appalling that he is not allowed to attend meetings of the American Association for Cancer Research, for example?

Oksana was amused to see an American newspaper publish a photograph of her leap across Arkhipov Street. (Viktor brought back the paper from his Moscow meanderings.) She didn't stop to think before she took flight that evening; she didn't need to. Would it have been useful to consider potential consequences?

Not in the least.

That leap was fueled by affirmation of her feeling of defiance. It was engendered by *samizdat*, or perhaps by civic pride of seeing her countrymen in a genuine act of protest. If you were to ask Oksana at the time, she would have told you that religious devotion had nothing to do with it. Motivation for Oksana's flight was wholly terrestrial.

At 3:47 that morning, a sensitive, American-made device embedded in the apartment's wall captured the following discussion of religion and identity:

OKSANA: Vit', are you asleep?

VIKTOR: Not now. Was.

OKSANA: Have you read *The Laws*?

VIKTOR: Tried to, couldn't.

OKSANA: I did. Just now, probably because of all that nonsense with the Lenskys at the seminar. Couldn't sleep, so I got out of bed and read it. Underlined some passages.

VIKTOR: Was it enlightening?

OKSANA: No. Terrifying. I had to wake you up. Sure you don't mind?

VIKTOR: No . . . Not at all.

OKSANA: Can I read you the parts I underlined?* I'll turn on the light. You don't mind?

VIKTOR: No, no. I am awake now.

---

* You don't deface *samizdat* manuscripts, if only out of respect for the people who produced them. You might correct the typos, but that's a gesture of respect toward the person who will read the manuscript after you.

The same level of respect is extended to *tamizdat*.

Notably, the copy of *The Laws of Jewish Life* contained in Oksana's dossier is

OKSANA: My underlining starts immediately, on page one. Listen to this: "In the morning, a Jew is expected to get up rapidly and energetically, without falling prey to laziness. Laziness is a disgusting trait . . . The awakening and all activities of a Jew must be driven by modesty and decency. In order to reach exaltation of the soul, he must force himself to feel that G-d,* who fills the entire universe, stands next to him, observing his conduct. He must feel fear, supplication, and shame before G-d. He would thus be modest in all his actions, even in the most solitary of settings."

Vit', I don't want to feel fear, supplication, and shame. Do you?

VIKTOR: This was where I stopped reading—on page one.

OKSANA: Also, there is a presumption of masculinity here. What about she-Jews? Me, for example?

VIKTOR: Could be just grammar, or translation. But yes.

OKSANA: Let's go to page two: "One should not wear expensive clothes, because this engenders pride. But clothing should not be especially shabby or dirty, so as not to evoke disrespect on the part of others. Clothing must be modest and clean."

VIKTOR: I will try to remember this. Thank you, Jewish community of Montreal.

OKSANA: We skip over the sections that contain sundry blessings, until we get to page seventeen, where we encounter this pearl: "One must not talk during meals. It is harmful to health."

And if you think this is a singular fuckup,† stemming from arcane understanding of the physiological functioning of the human animal, turn to page twenty-one and find this: "It is healthful

---

underlined, commented upon, and otherwise marked up—in pen. This must be interpreted as an indication of disrespect toward the booklet.

* Б-г.

† Одноразовый заёб.

to lie down on the left side during the beginning of sleep, and at the end of sleep, to lie on the right side. You lie on the right side because a man's liver is on the right side and his stomach is on the left. Thus, when he lies on the left side, his liver is positioned above the stomach, thus promoting better digestion."

VIKTOR: What the fuck?*

OKSANA: It gets worse—on page fifty-five: "How great must our respect for our parents be? If a son is finely robed and sitting at the head of the table, and suddenly his father and mother enter the room and begin to tear his clothes, hit him over the head, and spit into his face, he must not contradict his parents, upset them, or be angered by them. He must remain silent before G-d, who willed that this be so."

VIKTOR: For me, this is familiar territory. If your parents don't let you leave for Israel, it's because G-d has willed that this be so.

As Viktor drifts back to sleep, his thoughts spiral:

Why didn't his father sign that document, that permission to leave? Why not let Viktor live his life? Is this punishment? Was he not a dutiful son? Did Viktor not try to earn his father's respect? Why else did he strive to become an engineer, subjecting himself to five years of mortification of the mind, only to end up playing in-out games with a slide rule?

Seeing Oksana and her father, he sees what might have been; why did Viktor get a cowardly Black Colonel (ret.), a keeper of discipline in all aspects of life? Discipline above all, Party discipline, discipline of everyday life. Why was it necessary to fold all clothes and line up all shoes? Are we in the barracks? Are we at war, Comrade Colonel? You and I—yes, Father, but not our country, not the real world.

---

* "Какого хуя?"

Why hasn't my mother stood up for me, protected me from your aggression? She was too busy at the construction bureau, designing heavy household goods, things with electric cords that pulverize vegetables, boil eggs (there really is such a thing as a яйцеварка, an egg boiler—her legacy upon this earth), etc. Emitting black smoke, like one of her creations, then finally toppling like a smokestack, making room for another woman for the Black Colonel to discipline, another set of rules to be drafted and adopted, another manual to be written. Absurdity of Kiev, absurdity of you, they are behind me now. Here in Moscow, I am one of the people you would deride in a manner worthy of Comrade Stalin: *intelligentiki*, little intellectuals.

Nature mismatched us, admit it, and let me go! Sign that moronic piece of paper, freeing me from your country, from your Iosif "Yid-face" Kobzon, from your Young Comrade Lenin, from your Comrade You! You! Old! Horseradish! You left me no choice but to execute a desperate plan, to try to make myself so obnoxious to them that they would eject me the fuck out of the country without your paternal blessing, without your release. The distance between Moscow and Kiev is 863 kilometers, obviously too far for you to have come to a wedding—mine. The distance between Moscow and Tel Aviv is 3,785 kilometers, as the bird flies. If I were that bird, I would slow down my flight to shit upon Kiev, upon your house, perhaps drop a payload upon your hairless head.

At dawn, Oksana hears footsteps outside her apartment door. Have they come to arrest her? Have they come to arrest Viktor? She puts her arm around her husband. Perhaps this will protect him. Perhaps this will protect both of them. No knock of the door, they are respecting her wishes—at least for now. She falls asleep.

When she wakes up, a bit after 7:00, Viktor is at the kitchen table, mixing instant powder into a coffee mug.

Four large, unmarked boxes are lined up on the kitchen floor.

"Good morning . . ." Her hands absorb the tension from his shoulders.

"They left a *toptun* sitting behind the elevator to make sure the wrong person didn't swipe the boxes. He got up and left as soon as I opened the door."

"This is it, I guess—the deal . . ."

"Yes—the deal . . ."

"What have I done . . ."

"What have we done . . ."

"This is not record-keeping. This is paper porridge," Oksana declares after opening the first cardboard box.

Whoever cleaned out the scene at Schwartz's must have been determined to get the hell out fast. Schwartz's papers are thrown haphazardly into pillow-sized canvas bags. The bags are held closed with jute drawstrings, sealed with brown wax seals, and thrown into boxes. There is no evidence of archiving—just four big cardboard boxes, each containing four bags.

Viktor and Oksana laugh when a copy of *The Laws* comes up on top of the first bag they open. There isn't much conversation after that.

After rifling through the bag, Viktor and Oksana are able to see clearly that these materials haven't been analyzed.

They find a fragment of an oddly addressed letter: to "People of Goodwill." A bloodstain indicates that it was on top of the piles of paper at the apartment. At least someone thought ahead and wiped off the brain fragment that landed on top of the onionskin paper. In triage, this page goes to the "important" pile.

For now, it gets merely a glance—careful reading will come later. There is no page two. It will turn up. Realizing that they are approaching the task in exactly the same way, Oksana and Viktor split up the work, each taking a canvas bag to triage.

Then, reaching into her second bag, Oksana finds a sealed yellow envelope.

Inside, she finds a notebook, a Soviet one. It's filled with writing. The envelope's addressed "To Irene, not for publication or dissemination." Why would a notebook be sitting in an envelope addressed in English? Also, "Irene" is not Irina. Clearly, intended for someone outside. America? England?

Perhaps the notebook was being picked up by Foxman, but one thing led to another. (This is, of course, just a hypothesis.)

"I better read this from cover to cover—now," she announces to Viktor, first leafing through the back pages.

"What did you find?"

"A diary, maybe? Looks like a diary. Schwartz's, of course."

"Give me the highlights, as you leaf through," says Viktor, continuing his triage. He doesn't mean this, not entirely. It's unsettling enough to chance upon a busted skull. Discovering what was in that skull is more unsettling still.

Oct. 9, 1975

Today brought a double celebration. The first and by far the most important is the announcement that Andrei Dmitrievich won the Nobel Peace Prize.

I got the word from Voinovich,* just as he and Kopelev†
went to Yura Tuvim's‡ apartment at Stoleshnikov, where A.
D. happened to be drinking tea. His mother-in-law, Ruf'
Grigorievna, was there, too. The tea-drinking was initially
a part of the Tuvims' going-away activities, but it grew into
a celebration as the news spread.

I was in the "second wave" of visitors—dissidents, reporters, flashing bulbs. Foxman was there, too. The bottle
of vodka on the table was for someone other than the laureate, who hasn't been known to touch alcohol. But the three
red roses that Voinovich and Kopelev must have brought
were more appropriate for the occasion.

Andrei Dmitrievich didn't seem surprised. He started
to speak: "I feel I share this honor with the prisoners of
conscience—they have sacrificed their most important
possession, their liberty, in defending others by open and
non-violent means."

These aren't just empty words. Andrei Dmitrievich really
is sharing this honor with political prisoners here, in our
country. Sometimes—not always, not often even—we win.

This moment—this Nobel Peace Prize!—gives momentum to all of us, momentum that we have no right
to lose. The world is watching. The fat-faced Masters of
our Fates are put on notice. If all of us unite behind one
agenda—the human rights agenda—victory will be ours. If
we remain splintered into a host of atomized movements,
we will suffocate in the camps.

---

* Vladimir Voinovich, a dissident writer.

† Lev Kopelev, a dissident writer.

‡ Yuri Tuvim, an engineer and Jewish activist.

The second celebration—which I mention only here, in the diary—is the fourth anniversary of my first refusal. What's there to celebrate in a refusal? It seems an entire lifetime has been lived in these four years. Accomplishments are too many to enumerate in one sitting.

But the biggest is the privilege to observe formation of a new culture: suddenly a group of people in a totalitarian state has set aside their fear and started to behave as free people.

What should Oksana do with this diary? Send it into *samizdat*? Locate this Irene* and find a way to send it to her for safekeeping (i.e., not publication), per Schwartz's wishes?

Certainly, the guardians of State Security will not miss it in their filing system. Oksana has no obligation toward those people—other than to help find the person who murdered the diarist.

Oksana keeps thumbing through the diary.

Nov. 30, 1975

The idea Andrei† discussed with me (and probably half of Moscow) sounds promising. It may even not be his. It may be Yura's.‡

This summer, the USSR signed the Helsinki agreements. They think it's a triumph of diplomacy—it's the closest thing to a peace treaty concluding World War II—and it recognizes postwar borders. Comrade Stalin has indeed tri-

---

* Irene Manekofsky, president of the Washington Committee for Soviet Jewry.

† Andrei Amalrik, a dissident writer.

‡ Yuri Orlov, Soviet physicist, ultimately founder of the Public Group of Assistance to Implementation of the Helsinki Agreements in the USSR.

umphed beyond his wildest dreams. But there is also stuff
on human rights—nothing earth-shattering, but it's there.

What if the public takes over monitoring the USSR's
delivery on promises they've made? Let's say it's not my
idea—but it's in the air, the logical next step for our
movement—by which I mean not just our Jewish, Zionist movement but the human rights movement—and all
public movements.

Dec. 3, 1975

I took the idea to Fr. Mikhail, our court evangelist, who
immediately saw promise. It's hard to imagine any group
more oppressed than believers.

Why not form a group to defend the rights of believers?
I introduced him to Foxman, who is displaying a surprising level of understanding of things Christian. This is not
easy for us, Jews.

Foxman said the idea will get a lot of "pushback" from
Kissinger and from Israel, not to mention the Masters of
Our Fates. He did agree to hand-deliver our letter to a reporter. I can do it myself, but I agree that it would get better
reception if it's "leaked" by a "U.S. Embassy source."

Dec. 31, 1975

Amalrik is right. We do what we do not out of foolishness
or an excess of courage but simply because we cannot behave otherwise.

Does any of us choose the way we express our thirst for freedom? Our thirst for love? Will any historian—by which I mean any historian of the future—ever appreciate the freedom that a small group of people has carved out here, in Moscow of 1976? Sometimes I ask myself, if it ends tragically for some or all of us, would it have been worth it? For me at least, the answer is an unequivocal yes.

26.

Yesterday, after returning from madness in Moscow—a Satanic play starring the KGB's Lydia Ivanovna—Father Mikhail was asked to sprinkle holy water on a piglet. He did it for a parishioner, a woman he barely knows. Father Mikhail didn't ask why, or even whether the piglet would ultimately end up on a dinner table.

Would a few drops of water that had washed past a silver cross make that poor piglet more succulent? Pigs are smart animals, the Jews of the barnyard, you might call them. Can anyone postulate a better reason not to eat them? Father Mikhail feels a powerful urge to return to writing.

He closes the gate of the Church of Peter and Paul and turns right onto Sovetskaya Street. He needs to get to Moscow—another evening of fishing for souls. It's a short walk to the train station—not quite a kilometer.

Wasn't it clever of the Bolsheviks to slap the name "Soviet" onto the street where his wooden church has stood since 1902? It looks so much like a dacha that some people have walked clear past it.

Had he turned left, Father Mikhail would have ended up on Lunacharsky Street, so named after Anatoly Lunacharsky, the commissar of enlightenment and a proponent of the concept of

"god-building," i.e., creation of the new religion of scientific so-
cialism. It's difficult for Father Mikhail to describe this teaching as
anything other than Satanism.

Privately, Father Mikhail refers to Lunacharsky Street as Satan
Street, because that's what it is. It should be noted that he doesn't
make special efforts to avoid Satan Street; isn't it all part of history,
a brick?

Here's one of the few axioms Father Mikhail has learned in
his life's not-quite-five-decade journey: no fear! Whenever Satan
makes himself felt, you summon your pride, your special kind of
pride, and you walk—you walk fearlessly down his street. Has he
had encounters with Satan? Have deals been done? In this country, you teach what you must teach and live as you must. Perhaps
others can stay cleaner. Perhaps Father Mikhail can teach them to
live better than he does.

Obviously, Father Mikhail doesn't avoid Soviet Street, either.
A few meters away, he will be turning on Griboyedov Street—at
least Griboyedov is one of us. Not a Jew one-of-us, of course, but
another sort of one-of-us, a humorist, a poet, a playwright, a com-
poser, a Muscovite—a lot like Father Mikhail's friends in today's
Moscow, people he is about to see, whose souls he will try to bring
into the light.

Earlier in the morning, the mailman brought over an interesting
telegram:

"The Lord's angels 7."*

It's from Oksana.

It's an obvious reference to an epic poem in prose, *Moskva-*

---

* "Ангелы Господни 7."

Petushki, a *samizdat* chef d'oeuvre, by Venedikt Yerofeyev, a hallucinating philosopher-*alkash*. Fighting off early morning DTs, the protagonist in Yerofeyev's odyssey finds himself at the Kursk Railroad Station desperately in need of a morning swig. Through the fog of nausea, he hears a choir of the Lord's angels. Softly, tenderly they sing:

"Here is what you do: Go to the railroad station restaurant. Surely, they have something. They had fortified red last night. No chance they sold out all the fortified red in one evening!"

"Yes, yes, yes. I will go. I will go right away. I will find out. Thank you, angels."

A blessedly long conversation ensues—the desperate protagonist speaks, the angels sing in response.

"The Lord's angels 7" means 7:00 p.m. at the Kursk Railroad Station restaurant.

It's unlikely in the extreme that people monitoring communications—the ladies of the Fifth Directorate—would be equipped to grasp the meaning of this message. They know how to listen, they know how to transcribe, but do they know how to read?

The rest of us know, and know well. It's easily the most crowded, foul-smelling spot in all of Moscow—the least expected and hence ideal venue for a discussion that must remain unheard.

Turning left on Malakhovka's Griboyedov Street, Father Mikhail suddenly recalls that Griboyedov's day job, as the czar's ambassador in Tehran, got him torn apart by a mob.

It is said that Ambassador Griboyedov's head was chopped off and displayed on a kabob skewer in an impromptu parade in the streets of Tehran. How is that not reminiscent of the fate of a Christian martyr? Surely, some martyrs (Christian and not) had

wicked senses of humor. Humor humanizes, despotism dehuman-
izes. It's an eternal battle. There had to be humor in the Holocaust,
for example, or else its wounds wouldn't be bleeding still.

After Griboyedov Street, Father Mikhail would be turning left
on Turgenev Street—also more than acceptable—then left on Theater Street, so named after Malakhovka's lovely summer theater.
Chagall used to come here, to teach art at a Jewish orphanage,
which stood around the corner from Father Mikhail's church. That
was before his escape to Paris. Chagall has walked along Sovetskaya
Street, and Griboyedov Street, and Turgenev Street—and, surely—
Lunacharsky "Satan" Street. If he hadn't, he wouldn't have become
as good as he was.

Father Mikhail hasn't completed the journey—not quite.

He is still on Griboyedov, contemplating Chagall. He thinks
of an illustrated book an American correspondent with a Russian
name—George Krimsky—gave him for Christmas before he left
for America. He is probably still skiing in the state of Vermont,
not far from Solzhenitsyn's house, right now. Father Mikhail un-
wrapped it on Christmas, Old Christmas, the Julian calendar
Christmas, January 7.

It's a glossy book filled with illustrations of Chagall's church
windows, a lot of them probably Catholic (Father Mikhail will
need to look it up at home), not even remotely reminiscent of
our icons, but so expressive, so blue, so reminiscent of Picasso's
paintings from the blue period, except more vibrant, because in a
church window the light lives.

On the corner of Griboyedov and Turgenev Streets, Father
Mikhail encounters a stranger, whose darkened figure blocks the
narrow path between the fence and the snowbank.

Maybe Father Mikhail keeps his mind on Chagall's stained-
glass windows. How can anything in life be more Picasso than

Picasso? Isn't the purpose of light to make images luminescent? He realizes that the second question is the answer to the first. Father Mikhail thinks of Chagall's white dove, Chagall's Virgin, Chagall's three Wise Men, Chagall's synagogue menorahs that hang from the sky.

Another figure is behind him.

With his back, Father Mikhail feels its appearance, its movement. He doesn't turn around. He feels the raising of an object. A sword? An ax? He feels it drop, crushing upon his skull, his neck, his shoulders, a gash, a chasm, a schism.

Crumpling facedown onto the snowbank, Father Mikhail thinks of Chagall's Christ: a man in pain.

27.

Barkin, who is the first to arrive, pushes together two circular high tables. You stand at such tables, leaning if you must. One, originally brown, has been discolored by a large spill of a green, glue-like substance. The other has a burn mark the size of a dinner plate.

The restaurant is on the second floor. The contours of the parking lot are seen through gigantic double-window panels dulled by filth. Automobile headlights and taillights flicker through that filth as though through fog.

It's a massive enclosure—two parallel glass walls hundreds of meters in length, maybe forty meters in height, and—this part is harrowing—one meter apart. Pigeons caught in the canyon between the glass panes fly frantically, looking for an opening, a break in the glass. None exists. Other pigeons have tired of struggle and given up. They sit on the cement floor, waiting for torment to end. In the winter, dead birds freeze and needn't be shoveled out with any regularity. In the summer, cleanings should be more regular, but aren't.

Here, people sit on the floor, waiting for the train to Serp i Molot, Karacharavo, Petushki, or, perhaps, more distant destinations: Anapa, Murmansk, Kislovodsk, Ordzhonikidze, Berdyansk, Voroshilovgrad, Zhdanov. As they sleep, their hands stretch defensively over their suitcases, boxes, sacks.

One of the waiting travelers, a man from the provinces, a laborer perhaps, or a farmer, sits down atop his suitcase by the glass pane, unpacks an accordion, and begins to play. By the time Norm and Yakov Aronovich arrive, the accordionist is playing "Varyag," a song about an imperial Russian Navy battleship, incompetently commanded and, in a spectacularly misguided maneuver misattributed to valor, scuttled by its captain.

Наверх, вы, товарищи, все по местам!
Последний парад наступает!
Врагу не сдаётся наш гордый Варяг,
Пощады никто не желает!*

Surprisingly, his isn't a raspy, squandered voice of a drunk. If you didn't know better, you might mistake him for a rigorously trained singer, a baritone. Norm places two ten-ruble bills in front of the accordionist, who nods and keeps playing. At this moment, Golden arrives.

Не скажет ни камень, ни крест, где легли
Во славу мы Русского флага,
Лишь волны морские прославят одни
Геройскую гибель Варяга!†

"What is it about our national obsession with death for the Motherland?" asks Golden as Oksana and Viktor arrive. "We sing about our defeats—and glorify senseless waste of lives. And this

* On deck, my dear comrades, the battle begins! / The final parade is upon us! / We will not surrender our proud Varyag, / And never will beg for their mercy!

† No headstone, no cross will mark the spot / Where we fell in honor of the Russian flag, / And only the waves will glorify / The heroic last stand of the Varyag!

is a prerevolutionary song! We can't blame Lenin and Stalin for this one. It's a national personality, possibly."

NORM: We are missing Father Mikhail.

OKSANA: I sent him the same telegram I sent everyone here.

NORM: I didn't understand it, but your father explained, so here I am. I should get that book.

OKSANA: Maybe the Malakhovka mailman slipped, fell, and broke his leg, maybe the electric trains are running late. It's seven o'clock exactly. We must begin without Father Mikhail.

The accordionist completes the final stanza of "The Sea Stretches Wide," another Russo-Japanese War classic:

Напрасно старушка ждет сына домой,

Ей скажут—она зарыдает,

А волны бегут от винта за кормой

И след их вдали пропадает . . . *

NORM: I missed this kind of music so much.

YAKOV ARONOVICH: I think our accordionist is moving through Russian history chronologically, starting with the Russo-Japanese War. Some gem from the Civil War will come next, I predict.

GOLDEN: I have six bottles of beer in my briefcase. A psychiatrist from New Jersey gave it to me this morning. Does anyone have an opener?

BARKIN: I can open on the edge of the table, like any normal person.

---

* The mother is waiting in vain for her son, / Oh, how she will cry when they tell her, / The waves disappear, away from the stern / Their traces are lost in the distance . . .

NORM: You don't have to. The caps twist off. Here . . .

BARKIN: They've thought of everything, those Americans.

GOLDEN: It's Dutch.

VIKTOR: You start, Oksana.

OKSANA: Today is January nineteenth, Kissinger arrives on January twenty-second. He arrives in the morning, probably, so two full days is all we have.

YAKOV ARONOVICH: Not enough time to solve the problem with classic methods of investigation. Our only hope is to provoke whoever it is to declare himself. Put out a lure and wait.

OKSANA: What kind of lure?

YAKOV ARONOVICH: We don't know yet.

OKSANA: The KGB is the most likely suspect, but it could also be a black-market connection of Schwartz's—or a jilted lover. We know nothing about those aspects of his life.

VIKTOR: We haven't even attempted to explore there—would need weeks to sift through those leads.

OKSANA: Let's work with what we know. All of us know something, some shreds of information—now we must share it. Put it on the table. Maybe a picture will emerge.

YAKOV ARONOVICH: First question, what was Schwartz working on—his public work?

NORM: I found a crumpled note on top of my son's desk. He was using it to play his favorite game. Trash-can basketball. He is a journalist. Foxman was pitching him a story.

BARKIN: Vitya, are we talking about the walrus prick you brought over? The one who wanted to buy *Uncle Grisha* for a hundred and fifty dollars?

VIKTOR: Hundred and eighty. Yes.

YAKOV ARONOVICH: Do you have it? The piece of paper you found?

NORM: Yes.

YAKOV ARONOVICH: Read out the relevant parts.

NORM: "I've just received this . . . from our mutual friend . . ." Blahblahblah . . . "This is a significant development—possibly, the beginning of conversation about an international human rights agenda, to be monitored by Soviet citizens themselves . . ." Underlined: "monitored by Soviet citizens themselves."

YAKOV ARONOVICH: That would have massive resonance. Both here and abroad, assuming someone in the press writes about it. And a lot of raised hackles . . . Is your son planning to write about it?

NORM: He throws crumpled paper into a wastebasket from across the room. He was using it for that endeavor. So—no.

The accordionist has hurried through "Through the mountains and the foothills / the division marched ahead," a splendid Civil War song. His tempo is getting faster. Perhaps his train is coming soon.

Luckily, instead of taking a bow, packing his accordion, and going off to wherever accordionists come from, he breaks into "Wide Is My Native Land," an interwar-era song about friendship of the people:

> Широка страна моя родная,
> Много в ней лесов, полей и рек.
> Я другой такой страны не знаю,
> Где так вольно дышит человек.*

---

* Wide is my native land, / Replete with forests, fields, and rivers, / I know of no other land / Where man can breathe so freely.

Surely, he will be playing "Katyusha" next.

OKSANA: When we got home last night, I sat down in front of my telephone and said: "Bring me all the documents taken from Schwartz's apartment."

YAKOV ARONOVICH: And?

OKSANA: Boxes filled with evidence bags were delivered this morning. We are going through them. I've brought Schwartz's diary, which I think is informative.

YAKOV ARONOVICH: Anything interesting?

OKSANA: The Helsinki monitoring idea—definitely. It sounds like the idea originates with Andrei Amalrik.

NORM: Who is he?

YAKOV ARONOVICH: A provocateur, in the best sense of the word. I've known him for a decade now. He wrote a pamphlet, *Will the Soviet Union Survive Until 1984?*

NORM: I remember that. It was published in *The New York Times*?

YAKOV ARONOVICH: How would I know? Andrei has many ideas. Sometimes he has two at the same time, which is unfortunate, because when that happens, one of them dies. He is strictly an idea man—he can't make anything happen.

OKSANA: Here's something I want you hear from Schwartz's diary: "The idea Andrei discussed with me (and probably half of Moscow) sounds promising. It may even not be his . . ." Blahblahblah . . . "This summer, the USSR signed the Helsinki agreements. They think it's a triumph of diplomacy—it's the closest thing to a peace treaty concluding World War II—and it recognizes postwar borders. Comrade Stalin has indeed triumphed beyond his wildest dreams. But there is also stuff on human rights—nothing earth-shattering, but it's there.

"What if the public takes over monitoring the USSR's delivery on promises they've made? Let's say it's not my idea—but it's in the air, the logical next step for us—by which I mean not just our Jewish, Zionist movement, but the human rights movement—and all public movements."

YAKOV ARONOVICH: So Schwartz takes Amalrik's idea and tries to make it happen?

OKSANA: Basically. But it's possible that Amalrik has forgotten he had this idea by now. He has a way of moving on. Also, he may have borrowed it from someone else—it's in the air, as I said.

Here, I have more, from a few days later. I thought it was important right away. Now I see a theme:

"I took the idea to Fr. Mikhail, our court evangelist, who immediately saw promise. It's hard to imagine any group more oppressed than believers.

"Why not form a group to defend the rights of believers? I introduced him to Foxman, who is displaying a surprising level of understanding of things Christian. This is not always easy for us, Jews.

"Foxman said the idea will get a lot of 'pushback' from Kissinger and from Israel, not to mention the Masters of Our Fates. He did agree to hand-deliver our letter to a reporter. I can do it myself, but it would get better reception if it's 'leaked' by a 'U.S. Embassy source.'"

Norm was hoping the accordionist would work his way up to "The Blue Shawl." It's one of the songs that makes him weep every time. He doesn't know why, and, as he would have predicted, he wipes away a tear as the accordionist belts out:

Строчит пулеметчик
За синий платочек,
Что был на плечах дорогих!*

Was there a beloved in Norm's life before the war? We don't know, and out of respect for this wise, valorous, tormented man, we will refrain from taking steps to find out. All of these people, his friends, are trying to get out of this country, and Norm can see why. But he, Norm, is feeling so at home here.

Why does every word he utters in this half-forgotten, fast-returning tongue awaken his soul? Norm loves this country, these people, this language so much that he could cry, and he does, he does, he does.

BARKIN: In Schwartz's diary, is there anything about their private situation, Schwartz's and Foxman's?

OKSANA: Not directly. Just a lot of *samizdat*. Poetry—light blue, some Lermontov, some contemporary. I like one by Zhenya Kharitonov. I know Zhenya. I've heard him read it.

YAKOV ARONOVICH: Give us a few lines.

OKSANA: Gladly. Here's one of the last things Schwartz jotted down, his last entry:

Во мне погиб боец.
Во мне погиб отец.
Во мне погиб певец!
Пиздец, пиздец, пиздец.†

---

* A machine gunner is blasting away / For the blue shawl, / Which once rested on the shoulders of his beloved!

† The fighter inside me has perished, / The father inside me has perished, / The singer inside me has perished! / The fucking end, the fucking end, the fucking end.

YAKOV ARONOVICH: You think it's premonition?

OKSANA: It's a poem. A good one.

Until this moment, the conversation flows in hushed tones, a near whisper drowned out by the accordionist and the din of the Kursk Railroad Station.

Norm, who stands with his back to the glass wall, is the first to notice Lydia Ivanovna as she approaches the table. Oksana, who stands to Norm's left, is the second person to see the rapid approach of Viktor's KGB curator, resplendent in karakul and *nomenklatura* blue mink.

OKSANA: Lydia Ivanovna! Why are you here?

LYDIA IVANOVNA: An unfortunate circumstance necessitates an exception from our agreement. Late this afternoon, Father Mikhail was killed on the way to the Malakhovka train station. You should know the circumstances of his death. He was hit from behind, probably with an ax. He died on the spot. By the time our operatives got there, he had expired, and the murderer had, of course, escaped.

VIKTOR: What do we do? What do we say? Father Mikhail was our guide in these situations. He would say a prayer, misplaced, inappropriate, but still a prayer.

NORM: We do what we did in the forest. We bow our heads and think about death. Ours, theirs. Death is death. A moment of silence, comrades?

OKSANA: How did you know where we would be meeting?

LYDIA IVANOVNA: Do you think we are fools?* Illiterates?

OKSANA: Yes, mostly.

---

* "Вы думаете у нас дураки сидят?"

LYDIA IVANOVNA: I read *samizdat*. For us, it's legal, required even. *Moskva-Petushki*. I love that book.

OKSANA: Your appearance here runs counter to our understanding.* You were obligated to stop surveillance.

LYDIA IVANOVNA: I like your use of the word "understanding." It lets you avoid using the word "deal."† A small detail, but important. Before I leave, I should also tell you that Father Mikhail, may earth be goose down to him, was working with us, just like you are, in a limited way. Why? Because we had vivid descriptions of his amorous adventures in the seminary, which proved to be sufficient leverage. Plus, the hierarchy of the Russian Orthodox Church is a KGB directorate in its own right—we need each other.

We set him up as a double, infiltrating the American diplomatic circles, mostly. He was about to receive another, shall we say, "honorarium" from Americans. Also, some instructions, and some tools of the trade in exchange for classified rubbish we gave him to photograph and pass on.

That's the problem with Americans: they get greedy. They used to be much smarter, even not so long ago. Now they are as dumb as goats.

NORM: As an American taxpayer, I'd like to hear what has changed.

LYDIA IVANOVNA: Recently, they started accepting walk-ins from our malcontents—it's much more prudent to use only people who just want money. At least with them you know where you stand.

Here's the problem with malcontents: you gather in your kitchens and you talk entirely too much. The Jews are the worst offenders, plus Jews fight among themselves, and it gets vicious.

---

* Взаимнопонимание.

† Сделка.

I wouldn't go as far as saying that this is a city of no secrets, but it's a city of few secrets.

I hope this detail about our late mutual friends helps you fill out the picture.

NORM: So, correct me if I am wrong: by taking Father Mikhail as a walk-in, our CIA has endangered a lot of people who are working for the good of the country, everyone he was in contact with, spreading the contagion?

This would be betrayal, a gift to the KGB.

LYDIA IVANOVNA: Not an unsolicited gift, but yes, a gift. It's moot now. Father Mikhail is gone, the operation is over, but not to worry, we have others.

OKSANA: I don't find your story convincing. I think Father Mikhail was an honorable man. It looks like another provocation—slandering Father Mikhail, speaking evil of the dead. His death—if he is indeed dead—strengthens my belief that all of this, from start to finish, is a KGB operation.

YAKOV ARONOVICH: That's an astute observation, Oksana. You can try to investigate one ax murder, and you may solve it, if it's a bone fide ax murder. But a string of ax murders muddles the picture. Ask yourself: Whose interests are served when the picture is muddled?

OKSANA: Is there anyone among us who believes the KGB is telling the truth? Raise your hand if you believe—on the count of three. One . . . Two . . . Three . . .

I don't see any hands, as I expected. You see, Lydia Ivanovna?

NORM: We have a lot of far-fetched hypotheses, but no idea who did it. And we have the same prime suspect we've had from the start—the KGB. Lydia Ivanovna, you shouldn't have come. You have damaged your case.

LYDIA IVANOVNA: Norm, you remind me of my late uncle

Hershel, actually. He was what we call an honest Communist. Usually, they are the first to end up in the camps. Amazingly, Uncle Hershel was never imprisoned, even in the thirties.

Here is your twenty rubles back—it's not enough. Fedya, who was regaling you with songs here, travels with the Bolshoi Opera, the Music Hall, the Alexandrov Ensemble. His specialty is defection management, but he is also a talented musician.

We are almost done, Fedya.

I leave you with a gentle reminder: you have two days before Kissinger. And if you feel that you have been doused from a vat of wastewater, you might have noticed that your resident historian, Vitaly Aleksandrovich Golden, has been uncharacteristically quiet. I am not his curator, but I've been made aware of one piquant detail. You look pale, Vitaly Aleksandrovich.

But I can see we aren't welcome.

Let's go, Fedya.

OKSANA: Piquant detail?

GOLDEN: I do have something I was hoping never to tell. Unfortunately, at least some of what she has said is true.

OKSANA: Which part?

GOLDEN: The part about Father Mikhail working with the CIA—I knew that. Who do you think introduced him to Foxman? But until this moment, I had no idea that he was planted by the KGB.

OKSANA: How did it happen?

GOLDEN: He told me he knew some guys, Russians, engineers at a helicopter factory, who said they wanted to help America. I believe they were offering some radar deflection or radar evasion technology. Some damned apparatus. I am a historian. They don't teach us about such things. So, at my house, with Foxman there, I introduced them.

OKSANA: Wait, so Foxman was with the CIA? How is that possible? I thought his job was to deal with public groups. These are two of the most incompatible functions imaginable.

GOLDEN: My guess was that Foxman was not with the CIA, because, as you said, Americans are too smart to combine these functions, but I thought that he would know how to find the right person.

I connect people every day. This was different. Big mistakes seem reasonable at first. Why would I object to Father Mikhail's meeting with Foxman? Isn't it obvious whose side I am on in this war?

I made the introduction and thought that would be the end of it, but Father Mikhail kept me apprised of the situation, though I expressly asked him to stop. He did stop at one point, but then I learned that he kept telling Ina, asking her not to tell me.

It turns out it wasn't some other CIA person who was running him. It was Foxman. At one point, unprompted, Father Mikhail told me that he was getting written instructions and receiving money for his efforts.

Could I have stopped their subsequent meetings? I told him several times that his meetings with the CIA were dangerous and unnecessary, but I was in no position to force him to stop. I knew the situation had created enormous danger for all of us, and there wasn't a thing I could do. I just kept hoping I would be let out of the country before this blew up. Or maybe it would not blow up.

OKSANA: Did Father Mikhail mention the method of communication?

GOLDEN: He described it to me in detail, yes, even though I asked him not to. Now I see that making me an accessory must have been a part of his assignment with the KGB. The place seems easy to find, based on that description: a green garage in the court-yard you can enter through Chernyshevsky or Chaplygin Street. There is a five-liter can labeled with something that has to do with herring.

Foxman waited at Schwartz's, then went there to drop off money or pick up materials.

VIKTOR: Did Schwartz know any of it?

GOLDEN: Probably not. I don't know. I was contemplating not letting him into the house and warning some key people at one point, but how do you do that without making the situation even worse?

OKSANA: When did they have their meetings?

GOLDEN: Father Mikhail told me that his communications with Foxman occurred every Tuesday morning, just after mid-night. The KGB would know this, of course, now I see.

OKSANA: Three hours from now?

YAKOV ARONOVICH: What are we trying to learn?

VIKTOR: If Father Mikhail hasn't alerted the Americans, which he wouldn't have had a chance to do, the Americans wouldn't know that Foxman is dead. They would just know that he hasn't been seen in a few days. That's it.

OKSANA: How does this change the situation? Does it mean it's more likely or less likely that the KGB did it?

VIKTOR: More likely, I think. Agents provocateurs get dis-carded routinely after they've served their purpose. Their purpose is to confuse the situation—and what's so difficult about commit-ting another ax murder?

OKSANA: If that's your logic, they would have no reason to stop. It could mean we are next, all of us, one by one or together. The more ax murders, the thicker the smoke screen.

BARKIN: It has the smell of a KGB operation—concurred. Then, as the poet said, it's the fucking end.

YAKOV ARONOVICH: We can rule out a crime of passion or something related to the black market. If that were the case, the killer would have stopped with Schwartz and Foxman, and Father Mikhail would be with us right now, writing his reports to his curator; Lydia Ivanovna perhaps.

NORM: It does look like the KGB. But what if it's not the KGB? They know about the meetings with Foxman, and yet they haven't acted. Why? I haven't got a clue. Maybe they want us to do their work. But speaking as an American citizen, I feel entitled to know whether this Lydia Ivanovna is right and the CIA has indeed betrayed my friends here, in this city, by taking a walk-in from a public group.

For starters, I'd love to see who at the CIA has stepped up to replace this Foxman gentleman, of blessed memory.

YAKOV ARONOVICH: What would you suggest we do with that information?

NORM: The usual: capture a "tongue," learn what's what.*

YAKOV ARONOVICH: God help us.

---

* "Обычное дело—языка возьмем, узнаем что к чему."

28.

n the forest, you had your white Lend-Lease skis, made in America, dropped from the sky. A machine gun dangled across your chest, there was no law, you killed to stay alive. There, you either refrained from thinking altogether or thought honest thoughts, knowing that the breath you just took was likely your last. Your every breath transformed your every step, all of which made you into a fundamentally different being than what you've become in your subsequent life, in Pittsburgh, a place where you were deluded into expectation that you will be respiring still at the end of the day, maybe not expanding your lungs to their capacity, but just deeply enough to enable a safe return from work, to the house where Miriam awaits, gruffly, because she suspects that at 5:00 a.m. every morning you meet a mistress, perhaps that Polish girl at the office, when in fact you lock the office door and, in solitude, execute charcoal drawings, returning images of what you saw, what you felt, there, then, but you don't want her, or anyone, to know what you do or why, because they couldn't possibly understand, not in Pittsburgh, not today, not so many years later, and so you burn what you draw, every sketch, immediately upon completion, making an offering of smoke and ashes, which is something Miriam doesn't even begin to suspect as she tells you about injustices that befell her at St. Rodef's sisterhood, her thoughts on suboptimal retail practices at the mall, where she often goes during the day, about excellent adventures of the Boy, who did get into Harvard and who, as a consequence, believes that he has overtaken you in the game of achievement he believes life to be, and, to make a timely escape, your mind conjures the image of the new bartender at the Green Oaks Country Club, and you puzzle about the depth of training he has received at the Bartenders Academy (or was it Brandeis, where the Boy might have gone had he not gotten into Harvard), and then your mind escapes deeper, into pondering whether at this exact moment Cadillacs are rolling off the assembly lines in Detroit, or is it Cleveland, or wherever it is that they roll off the Fisher Body assembly lines, and, finally, you think of piss-warm Florida waters that await you, an image you briefly pretend to regard as ointment for the soul as you shudder at the inevitability of going through with the purchase of a condo and devoting the balance of the healthy, lucid portion of your life to shooting crooked balls into alligator ponds during winters, when you would much rather be gliding through the Northwoods, trying desperately to recapture the pace you set on those wooden white Lend-Lease skis that were made in America and dropped from the sky, where a machine gun dangled across your chest, where there was no law, where you killed to stay alive, where you either refrained from thinking altogether or thought honest thoughts, where you knew that the breath you have taken could be presumed to be your last, where every breath transformed your every step.

God bless America, the country that closed its borders to Jews fleeing Hitler, then failed to bomb the Auschwitz crematoria. And now, here we are, our CIA is poaching refuseniks, trawling for desperate souls and introducing them to a life of espionage. Call it an open invitation to a KGB agent provocateur. This will be a catastrophe. Already is a catastrophe, and Americans are too dense to realize it. Goats.

Where is Israel in all this? Israel is threatening refuseniks to stay away from the dissidents. Why? Because their agenda is too broad? Because they don't recognize the specialness of the Jewish cause? Because they insist that all humans have rights? Shouldn't we—as Jews—agree with this concept?

This is so repugnant: in a country full of injustice, in a world full of pain, how is our Jewish pain different from the pain of others? If we want the world to learn a lesson from the Holocaust, shouldn't we be the first to demonstrate that we have learned the only possible lesson you can learn from any holocaust—to value human life and respect others?

And here he is, Norm, walking alongside a wartime friend on a mission to bust a CIA operation in Moscow. About fifteen minutes after setting out from the Kursk Railroad Station, Norm and Yakov Aronovich cross Khmelnitsky Street—which, of course, memorializes a perpetrator of a holocaust, but which never stopped being known as Pokrovka—and find themselves on Chaplygin Street, and turn into the courtyard that cuts across to Chernyshevsky Street.

At a subterranean gastronom on Chaplygin, they pick up a bottle of Ekstra and a couple of pieces of Volna processed cheese.

The courtyard is dotted with garages, and Norm and Yakov Aronovich have no difficulty finding the green one described by Golden.

"What are we looking for?" asks Norm.

"A five-liter can, behind the garage. Label should read, 'Сельдь атлантическая неразделанная, пряного посола.'"*

Indeed, a rusting can matching this description sits deep in the gap between two garages.

"Norm, where do you want to wait?"

"We could pull the garage gate open. I am learning that in this country the doors that appear to be locked aren't."

"Is it the same in America, or is it our cultural characteristic?"

"In America, it's the opposite."

The lock and the latch come out with a quick yank and the two men step into darkness.

The car inside the garage is covered with a canvas tarp. The shape strikes Norm as familiar.

"Is it an Opel?"

"Opel Kadett. I had the honor to shoot at more than a few of those, the ones with swastikas. You did, too. This one is likely in its Soviet incarnation. We took an entire assembly line from Germany and renamed the car Moskvich. Can't tell without lifting the tarp."

"The war. It's hard to get away from it in this country."

"And in America?"

"I got there by 1947, and by 1950, you might have thought that the war never happened. America was creating wealth. Maybe people in Brooklyn talked about the war, but not where I was. Mary's uncle, in Pittsburgh, advised me specifically not to talk about it."

"And?"

"I didn't. What was it like for you?"

"I spent 1945 and 1946 in hospitals—various complications, but I climbed out, and I went on to study physiology and mathe-

---

* "Atlantic herring, whole, in spiced brine."

matics. I just fine-tuned my course of study—nothing too drastic. They suspected me of being a geneticist, a cyberneticist, Virchowian. All of these were bourgeois pseudosciences, as per Comrade Stalin's teachings. That period, for me, was as dangerous as my war escapades. My mentors kept getting arrested. Some of them weren't even Jews. My turn would have come.

"I was there when computers were being built out of wooden parts, and I knew enough to make use of them. What I do is now called computational biology."

"I was too busy drawing dismembered figures and building a fortune."

"Do you think we should put some rubbish in that herring can outside?"

"There must be something here . . . Old newspapers? A plastic bag?"

"I see a technical manual for this Moskvich. They could be stupid enough to think it's for a missile system."

"Good. Here's a plastic bag."

A few minutes after midnight, Norm and Yakov Aronovich hear the sound of a car engine and, after the engine is cut off, the sound of tires crunching freshly fallen snow, the sound of a closing car door, and, finally, footsteps.

Norm grabs a large screwdriver, and as footsteps are heard behind the garage, the two men gently open the door and step outside, each cutting off an exit. The man, whoever he is, is trapped.

Of course, when no exculpatory explanation is feasible and the element of surprise is on your side, it's prudent to kill the bastard and then figure out whether he was armed. That was what Norm did at Makarenko Street a couple of days ago, when he was outnumbered two to one. A fighter less skilled than Norm would have stuck that screwdriver deep into the adversary's rib cage right now, as he rounds the corner, but this time it's two to one in Norm's and Yakov Aronovich's favor.

Capturing "tongues" was Norm's specialty in his youth. It takes steady nerves to do it: you go out deep into their territory, catch one of them—preferably an officer—work him over so he stays unconscious but still breathing, carry his Nazi carcass back to your waiting comrades, and finally torture him till his tongue loosens and he gives you what you need.

You kill him, of course, regardless of whether he talks.

Much of Norm's artistic work has to do with capturing tongues, torturing tongues, and liquidating tongues. Lately, the story lines of these drawings have broadened to include Norm's imagining of what these men's lives must have been before they donned the uniforms of the Reich—did they have living parents, wives, mistresses, children?

Even in the dark, Norm is able to see that the CIA goon is a younger man. When, taking full advantage of the element of surprise, Norm slams him against the garage door and places the screwdriver against the bastard's throat, he recognizes a lack of training, a fundamental inability to fight back.

"What the fuck . . . Dad . . ."

Recognizing Madison, Norm wishes he could muster the saliva to spit in the boy's treacherous face. Should he tell his weasel of a son that whatever respect, whatever pride he had in his achievements has vanished, now that he knows the depth of Mad Dog's betrayal, the betrayal of his profession, the betrayal of people who depend on his integrity?

"How could you . . ."

"Dad, get that fucking screwdriver away from my throat . . ."

"No."

"Are you going to kill me, you old fucker?"

"You will resign from the paper—effective right now. You will leave this country. Go to Langley. Go anywhere, just get out of this profession, which you have shamed! You have betrayed the people who trusted you, you have betrayed some of the finest people I know. They relied on you to tell the world about their struggles— this link with journalists, real journalists, not you, is a matter of life and death to them . . . and you . . . betrayed them. How can you be trusted? You are a fucking spy!"

This is how Mad Dog, who has never learned the system of Russian vulgarisms, interprets his father's words, and this is more or less accurate. Norm's actual language bespeaks full return of his forest Russian, a language he hasn't had an occasion to use since 1945 and thought he had lost. It is not for the meek.*

"Are you going to rat out your own son, you turd?"

"Watch me."

"Mother will tear off your balls."

"I am quaking in my boots."

Norm pulls back the screwdriver, releases his son, turns around, and starts to walk away.

At 12:39 a.m., January 20, Norm and Yakov Aronovich get out of a taxi at Oksana's apartment at 17 Bol'shaya Polyanka.

---

* "Сука, ты, блядь, уёбываешь, блядь, с работы по собственному, блядь, желанию, вот сейчас, сразу, блядь, и уёбываешь из этой, блядь, страны. Катись, блядь, в Лэнгли. Катись, блядь, куда, блядь, хошь. Какой ты в пизду журналист, ты, блядь, обосрался, продался, сука ты, блядь, и не просто блядь, а блядь, блядь *продажная*. Ты людей, блядь, обосрал. Таких, блядь, людей, что лучше хуй найдешь, блядь. Они тебе, блядь, доверились, думали ты, блядь, о них правду блядь—это им, блядь, жизнь или смерть—а ты их сука выебал. Хули тебе, бля, доверять? Ты-ж шпион, блядь!"

Transcripts of recordings made that night indicate that Oksana, Viktor, and the two guests, upon engaging in deep review of the documents, agree that they now have a better picture of the tangle of allegiances in the case, but that this deep new understanding doesn't help them one whit in determining who committed the murders of Albert Schwartz, Alan Foxman, and Father Mikhail.

The fact that the same instrument—an ax—was used indicates that the three deaths are probably connected. This, too, is a better than fifty-fifty probability, but not a certainty.

YAKOV ARONOVICH: We have a barrel of raw data, no organizing principle, no hypothesis. What do we do?

OKSANA: We tell a story.

YAKOV ARONOVICH: Do you need onionskin paper, some carbons?

OKSANA: I would, except this story will have to be told in English, so no need to type. Vitya, when you watch journalists submit articles, how do they do it?

VIKTOR: Often, they call a department called "Dictation," and someone there transcribes it.

OKSANA: Do you remember telephone numbers? Would you have a number for this Dictation?

VIKTOR: No.

NORM: What are you looking for? I could never remember Madison's phone number from before he was sent to Moscow, so I called the main switchboard. If you want Dictation, call the switchboard and ask for Dictation, and that should do the trick.

OKSANA: Thank you. Now, if you gentlemen would excuse me for an hour, I have a news story to write.

VIKTOR: It's usually very formulaic, almost like stenciling. Do you need help?

OKSANA: I can do it.

• • •

On the evening of January 19, in America, the easily amused, overcaffeinated natives of the Foreign Desk were informed that a young woman with a vaguely British accent had called in Mad Dog's story. It was too late to get it into the next morning's paper.

A few minutes of deft work with a machete turned the story into your basic Foreign Desk fodder, a three-and-a-half-incher suitable for burial on A19:

> MOSCOW, Jan. 20—A group of Soviet dissidents today announced formation of a unit to monitor Soviet compliance with the Helsinki Accords signed last year and to report human rights violations to other countries that signed that document.
>
> The rights unit, named the Committee for Fulfillment of Human Rights Obligations by the USSR, issued a statement that holds that it would focus on basic freedoms of conscience, religion and belief and those providing for greater human contacts and exchanges of information and culture.
>
> The group is led by Oksana Moskvina, a well-known activist of clandestine publishing, Fr. Mikhail Kiselenko, a Russian Orthodox priest, and Albert Schwartz, a leader of the Jewish emigration movement. The dissident group said it would accept written complaints by Soviet citizens about violation of the accords affecting them personally.
>
> It will also seek to collect information and in "special cases of inhumanity" will appeal to foreign governments to form international committees to try to verify information. It listed "special cases," such as removal of children from parents trying to give them religious education, enforced psychiatric treatment to change

people's beliefs, dramatic cases of dividing of families
and special inhumanity to "prisoners of conscience."

Next, Oksana places a telephone call to Natasha Bernshtein, her former colleague at Moscow Special School No. 64, who is now a resident of Alexandria, Virginia.

"Natashka, please don't ask any questions, just do as I say," she says to her friend.

Natashka's husband, Slavik Bernshtein, is employed by the Russian division of the Voice of America. Reached at the office by his wife, Slavik calls the Foreign Desk of Mad Dog's newspaper and, in broken English, asks whether a very important story from the newspaper's Moscow correspondent could be put on the AP wire as soon as possible.

With all due indifference, the Foreign Desk sends the piece of shit up the chain. Yeah, sure, whocareswhythefucknot.

As soon as the story comes off the telex, Slavik translates it into Russian and hands it to Ilya Suslov, who is getting ready to read the morning news. The story is similarly picked up by Radio Liberty, Radio Free Europe, Deutsche Welle, and the Voice of Israel.

The BBC Russian Service commentator Anatoly Maksimovich Goldberg pens a beautifully worded commentary about the nascent group. A silver-tongued orator, Goldberg is heartened by the fact that the group is headed by a heretofore unknown Soviet citizen.

Six hours after Oksana dictates the story about the human rights group, this transparent bit of disinformation has circled the globe and bounced back to the USSR from radio transmitters in Europe, America, and Israel, with no one even for a moment suspecting that the "rights unit," in fact, consists of a *samizdat* typist and two dead men.

Usually, shortwave radio transmissions to the USSR are jammed. On the afternoon of January 20, 1976, the jamming is suddenly and inexplicably paused.

Jamming resumes the morning of January 21.

29.

With a fleet of Golden Hands, columns of dump trucks, and dunes of sand and salt, Moscow barrels through almost any snowfall with no delay. Annushka continues to sail the curve tracing the banks of Clear Ponds, the B trolleybus doesn't fall behind schedule, and the Metro is always pristine.

Snow is a phenomenon that meteorologists cheapen, physicists vulgarize, psychologists are clueless about. On the morning of January 21, Oksana senses the magnitude of that night's snowfall. It's dark outside, but the room is mysteriously bright, crisp even.

"Today, my love, will be the day when we will do something normal people do."

Oksana bolts out of bed.

"Are you joining the Communist Party, Oksanochka?"

"Better! I am digging up the skis. Let's go while it's still dark—before they clear the streets!"

"Digging up" actually means "pulling down." The skis are in a storage loft beneath the ceiling in the apartment's hallway. Oksana has them down before the water for instant coffee begins to boil.

"Your shoe size better be forty-two! These are my father's boots."

"It's forty—close enough."

Oksana has pulled on woolen tights and an orange Norwegian

sweater, and a matching wool hat. Viktor is not as smartly dressed: his omnipresent Levi's and his alpaca sweater with opposing llamas. A spare hat Oksana has found smells like mothballs, but that goes away with the first blast of wind.

In the elevator, Viktor looks over the skis. They are slim, made of lacquered wood, probably cedar. The word "Madshus" is printed on the tips. The word "Holmenkollen" is stenciled in gold beneath the tips, and "Made in Norway" near the back.

"Holmenkollen—isn't that a ski area near Oslo?" Viktor notes into the air as the elevator jolts to a stop on the ground floor.

"Must be. It's a gift from Swedes who work with my father. Even with one pole, on skis he is a maniac."

It's a bit after 6:00 a.m., still pitch-dark. Snow has collected on the half-extended right arm of the Wanking Bulgarian. A full-blown snowbank clings to the negative space between his bronze legs, reaching under his open overcoat, rising to the mystery pocket of his trousers.

Oksana's leather boot clips onto the three prongs of the binding; she locks it with ease that verges on panache. Viktor struggles a bit, but figures it out. Even with two pairs of socks, the fit of the boot is a bit loose, but this will be just fine.

Oksana pushes off, skis across snowed-over Bol'shaya Polyanka, sprinting in ever-expanding circles around the Wanking Bulgarian while Viktor waddles across, aiming toward the river. If you care to be technical, too much of his weight gets transferred over to the heels. Viktor stomps where he should glide, looking like a penguin—yes—so what? Even with this technique, or absence thereof, he stays upright. Penguins manage quite well in snow and ice.

Without a word, they aim toward Gorky Park. Some people ski. Others fly. Oksana is at least one hundred meters ahead, slowing down every now and then to let Viktor catch up, and as he does, she bolts ahead again.

At 6:09, Oksana turns off into wide-open gates. Parks get deliveries; trucks must come in. Isn't it easier to just open the gates and keep them open? They pass by the garages and several crumbling structures, emerging at the heart of the park. Every winter, the alleys here are sprayed with hot water, to be converted into a gigantic outdoor skating area. If you easily tire of going around in the tight circles of a conventional skating rink, the paths of Gorky Park are for you! The ice is still present, albeit buckled and hidden under a coat of snow.

Viktor is familiar with only one movement, sliding the skis forward—classic. Oksana is doing something completely different. As she lunges into the park's alleys, she bends forward, her skis making wide outward movements, a technique borrowed from speed skaters.

As he tries to keep up, Viktor overdoes it a bit, leaning too far forward, and though he stumbles and goes flying into a snowbank, he recovers and gets the idea: you can ski like you skate. Not always, but sometimes, like here, on the snow-covered ice of Gorky Park. You get the theory, even the proof of concept, but it's hard to keep this going for a long time. Instead of emulating speed skaters, Viktor decides to continue to move forward in the classic motion, using his poles a little harder, a little faster.

They complete a couple of circles. He loses sight of Oksana, but sees her as she waits for him near the center of the park, at a white sculpture of a girl in a summer dress holding a machine gun. The girl's left hand is on the gun's trigger, her right on the barrel.

"What are your thoughts about this girl?" she asks.

"Standard Communist kitsch," he says, planting his poles like anchors in front of him.

"It is that, concurred. But that's just the genre, the style. Would you ever have guessed that this is one of my favorite sculptures in Moscow?"

"No, Oksana. I wouldn't have."

"Before you condemn, look at how her nipples are engorged."

"This could be because the sculptor is a pervert promulgating machine-gun pornography, further evidenced by her right hand sliding along the barrel?"

"Could be. But this doesn't diminish the artistic message: this girl has just discharged this gun. Into Nazis, perhaps surprising them. And it feels good. Very good. She could have just as easily been using a typewriter, sending art into *samizdat*."

Pushing off into a skating motion, Oksana completes the thought:

"I understand this girl, I admire this girl. On good days, I am this girl."

Not quite twenty minutes later, in the middle of Krymski Bridge, with the icebound river beneath them, Oksana slows down to give Viktor a chance to catch up.

In the moonlight, they see the Kremlin not quite a kilometer to the right, the Lenin Hills and the hulk of Moscow University to the left.

"I've heard you say it. Now I will. Do you get a feeling that we will always think of these days as the happiest in our lives?" he asks her.

Oksana speeds up, to think about this question; he keeps up with her.

"I do," she responds, waving back to the operator of Golden Hands that rattles past them. "Are we saying this because happiness this intense cannot last?"

"Maybe. Except I don't think it's that. I think it's the people we are with."

"People like Elena Georgievna, Andrei Dmitrievich, Lyuda Alexeyeva, Lara Bogoraz, Tolya Marchenko, Albert Schwartz—and Golden, despite his one big mistake."

"And Barkin. And your father. It can never happen again."

"You mean so much nobility assembled in one place?"

They glide in silence along the Frunze Embankment.

"You know what will happen tonight," she says as they near the river's bend at the start of the Lenin Hills. "Norm has a plan. And I will carry it through, Vitya. It's the only chance we have.

"In case there is a surprise, I want you to know that I am acting with full understanding of what can happen. And no matter what happens tonight, our lives will change irrevocably."

"Can you tell me?"

"Not even you. Not even my father knows. He is too protective of me. He would be prone to make mistakes."

"Oksanka, listen, it must be as risky as it gets. It should be me, not you."

"I made my plans, my deals. This is my path."

"Will we see each other again?"

"I believe we will, Vit', I just don't know when. You will take care of yourself, take care of us—until we meet again."

30.

At 1:09 p.m., January 21, the massive black phone at the bureau emitted its mighty ring. You can wake up a fire station or evacuate a medium-sized building with such a ring.

"Is this Mr. Mad Dog?" says a young man's voice.

A prankster; what else could it be? The night before, Mad Dog got so angry that he felt tempted to call his mother. What the fuck . . . Ensnared by the Old Geezer, nearly fucking murdered by him—in Moscow? Mad Dog is well over eighteen—why is it his father's responsibility to tell him whom to work for and whom not to work for, what to do and what not to do?

The old man didn't come home last night. Maybe he had a heart attack, the devil took him, that fucking fuck, they deserve each other. Still, Mad Dog is getting a late start. Couldn't get up with proper intensity.

"Friends call me Mad Dog. Who are you?"

"I want to join CIA."

"Is this some fucking prank?"

Stupid fucking question. What else can it fucking be?

"Do you have application?"

"What the fuck? Where did you get my number?"

"From *Vechorka* . . ." He is laughing now. It's a kid, pulling a prank, like calling unknown numbers and asking, "Is your refrigerator running? You better catch it . . ." Shit like that.

Except this is more specific. Like the giggling idiot knowing his nickname and connecting it with the phone number, and the thing about the CIA. Why would a Moscow adolescent know about any occasional water-carrying arrangements Mad Dog may or may not have made? Nobody knows that, except people at the agency—and the Old Geezer now. The High and Mighty Old Geezer, Mr. Morality Himself. Fuck him.

And that reference to *Vechorka* . . . *Vechorka* is short for *Vechernyaya Moskva, The Evening Moscow*. What the fuck?

Mad Dog descends to Sad Sam's lobby, if you can call it that. Sometimes there are Soviet newspapers here, but not today. He looks for *Vechorka* in the nearby kiosk on Sadovaya-Samotechnaya, but doesn't find it.

He is almost at Tsvetnoy Boulevard now—still no kiosk to buy the damned piece-of-shit rag. Finally, at the entrance to the boulevard, he spots a display of newspapers. They hang *Pravda* here, and *Izvestia*, and *Literaturnaya Gazeta, Sovetskaya Rossiya, Krasnaya Zvezda* even. Also—now he sees it—*Vechorka*.

Here it is—today's *Vechorka*, January 21.

He walks up to page one, scans it, walks up to the display with page two—nothing. On page three, he shudders at the sight of a *feuilleton*—a piece of satire—titled "'Mad Dog' and His Owners."*

Even before he slows down to read the headline, Mad Dog

---

* "Бешеный пёс и его хозяева."

notices the oversized cartoon, depicting a chained dog baring his fangs, spewing saliva.

The dog is held back by a thick chain. His wide collar is decorated with swastikas. He is straining to sink his teeth into large contours of the map of the USSR, adorned with hammers and sickles, bundles of wheat stalks, hydroelectric stations, and smokestacks.

The hand holding the chain of this rabid cur is identified as "CIA."

Mad Dog's thoughts here are difficult to reconcile with events of the previous night: he takes offense at the swastikas. He is Jewish, you see, and his parents, both of them, are survivors of the Holocaust. His father—don't forget—escaped from Sobibor and fought the Nazis, as a partisan, in the forests, where he killed human Nazis and their Nazi dogs. It's insensitive, offensive even, on their part to exploit that aspect of Mad Dog's personal history.

These thoughts may be a jumble, which thoughts often are, especially in situations when you are so damned scared that—to use a genuine Russian proverb Mad Dog learned at Harvard—your heart has dropped down into your heels.

The cartoon is done in the tradition that glorified the Red Terror and the Moscow Trials of the 1930s. The piece of satire it illustrates is even more ominous, especially to Soviet citizens who have come in contact with this Madison "Mad Dog" Dymshitz:

> For more than a year, American correspondent Madison Dymshitz has been living up to his nickname—Mad Dog—by spewing his poisonous saliva at everything we Soviet citizens hold dear.
>
> This Mad Dog is no ordinary street cur. His ambitions were lofty enough to earn him a place in im-

382 | PAUL GOLDBERG

perialism's most prestigious kennels—first Harvard University, then the Central Intelligence Agency.

To please his masters, this "mad dog" has made himself hoarse not only by barking but also by licking the hands of internal enemies, so-called dissidents, glorifying their treacherous "struggles" against the Motherland.

The editors of *Vechernyaya Moskva* have been informed that this vicious animal has howled out his last midnight aria as the USSR Ministry of Foreign Affairs is this afternoon informing Mr. Dymshitz that he will need to leave the boundaries of the USSR.

"Why is this mad dog being swatted with a rolled-up newspaper?" a reader might ask.

Well, Mr. Dymshitz's dogged determination has led him to attempt to obtain classified documents from the archives of . . . the KGB! It seems Mr. Dymshitz, in his eagerness, expected an "informant" to go inside the building and return with dossiers for his use!

Appropriate authorities have shared with us the instructions Mr. Mad Dog had given to his "informant," who—don't be surprised—turned out to be something other than what he thought.

Here are the instructions, photographically reproduced here: "2 pm Tues = 3 pm Mon. Bureau: 297–8656."

Do you recognize your handwriting, Mr. Dymshitz?

So that's how that juvenile delinquent got Mad Dog's name and number! That, of course, is an elegant explanation. Clearly, the KGB bastards—this fake-o-rama Galina Borisovna, the purveyor of the Yezhov file—had given *Vechorka* Mad Dog's dossier to work from. How could he have fallen for that Yezhov diary hoax? What, he, Mad Dog, stupid? No! It's them, they were damned good, conniving, duplicitous. What else do they know? Do they know about last night? About that ill-fated little pickup from Foxman's drop box?

Mad Dog keeps reading. Nothing on that. Would be hard to explain internally, especially with these Senate investigations of connections between the CIA and the press. Of course, we say it never happens, but we say many things. It's national security. Things aren't always as they seem. Favors are traded.

This sucks: according to *Vechorka*, Mad Dog will have to get out within forty-eight hours, not on his own terms.

The *feuilleton* concludes with a pithy little rhyme:

Оденем намордник на бешеных псов,
Обезопасим страну от врагов.*

Being targeted by the KGB in some bizarre, mysterious intrigue of theirs can be good for your career. It gets you to the next rung. Mad Dog knows this.

The story is silent on that other thing—that little favor he agreed to do for an old Harvard friend, who called at the last minute, when the embassy realized that Foxman is nowhere to be found. It should have been a small favor, and it went sideways in some spectacular ways, but at least he wasn't busted by the KGB.

Would the Mighty Geezer dare rat him out?

No. Not even he.

He would have Mother to answer to.

---

* We'll put our muzzle on their mad dogs, / And protect our country from enemies.

31.

Since Oksana Yakovlevna Moskvina is our primary concern, no effort will be made to explore the storms that rage within the soul of the man who climbs up the stairs of her apartment building, and, opting against ringing the bell to be let in, kneels down in front of the vinyl-tufted door, pulls a set of picks out of the pocket of his awkwardly fitting overcoat, and inserts one of the picks into the lock. This takes a while.

Slowly opening the door, he takes off his overcoat, hanging it carefully on the hook of a coatrack.

Inside the overcoat, below the shoulders and along the back, the man has been hiding the instrument both corporeally and metaphorically familiar to any person of Russian culture.

With said object now across the chest, with the right hand by the end of the oak handle and the left a few centimeters beneath the blade, the man moves carefully through the anteroom, then through the main room, to the spot where in a one-room apartment one might expect to encounter the bed.

This is always easier when you surprise your target. He did, after all, surprise the sodomites, now eternally locked in that which they do. The bloody boys, literally, a twist on Boris Godunov. He was looking for one man, but found two. A journey from love to death is an act of mercy, the enabling of a soul to ascend from corporeal heaven to heaven proper—beyond.

The apostate priest has been dispatched on that journey, too, rejoicing with the apostles. Here, on earth, in Moscow, he isn't missed one bit.

God willing, this again will be the case, except now it will be a bloody girl, and if need be, a bloody boy as well. He hasn't dispatched a girl, not yet, but how different can it be? A skull's a skull, a rib cage a rib cage. Orders have been received. Is it not up to him to interpret these orders and carry them out? What more can there be?

There is a bed in front of him, a human mass beneath a pile of blankets. Why think too much? He is told to make it stop, and he has made it stop—and no objections have been received.

The ax is raised—the ceiling is high enough to let it rise and drop, and let the power of earth embrace its plunge, the dive into the flesh. You feel it through the handle. On his first time, he didn't expect to find two men. The splattering of blood and brains was less surprising. But that was fine, the streets were dark, and no one is the wiser.

Above the shoulders, above the head, then down, unstoppably, above the torso, the lungs, the heart. Why would it matter how the target lies, faceup, facedown? If there are two of them again, that's not a problem.

The sound of flesh and bone stopping the impact of sharp, falling steel is whistle-like, it seems, yet this—right now—is not a whistle, not a thud. This, now, is a crunch, the sound of breaking glass. No gushing blood—just shards and feathers, and then there is sharp pain beneath the shoulder blade—his.

The voice he hears next seems so familiar, yet hard to place. A Russian, clearly, but, for some reason, with an accent, a tiny lilt.

"You may want to know that this burning sensation under your shoulder blade, on the right, is caused by a knife. It's peeking out into your chest, between the ribs, could be a couple of centimeters from the lung. If the tables were turned—if I were at the tip of your knife blade—I would refrain from moving very much. Just lower the handle of your ax, slowly, onto the bed.

"Be careful . . . Slow . . . Let it drop . . . That's right . . .

"Oksana Yakovlevna is like a daughter to me, and you are here to kill her. So I thank you for the pleasure of being able to stop you. We may well be collapsing your lung—or both lungs—before we are done, but no hurry, I have time."

"*Shema Israel* . . ."

"Spare me . . . I despise poseurs. You are a murderer, Comrade Lensky, not a victim. But then again, so am I—and, tell you what, I am better at it. More practiced. In the forest, my specialty was capturing tongues—torture."

"*Adonai Eloheinu* . . ."

"Poseurs pretending to be victims are a particular scourge . . ."

"*Adonai* . . ."

"You learned these words from a comic book, I bet. It doesn't feel like genuine religious commitment. But I could be wrong."

"*Ehod* . . ."

"Here's a question for you, Mr. Lensky: Why do we kill? I kill to even the score. I actually liked interrogations when I was in the forest. Let's call it torture, for convenience sake, but it's more than that. Speaking of which, my knifepoint should be about a centimeter from your lung, I drove it in a bit deeper now. We will not know with certainty until autopsy, if one is done. Did you kill Schwartz and Foxman?"

"Who?"

"This nonsense—now—has cost you a half centimeter more.

Who . . . Like you don't understand. You will not necessarily know this from the pain . . . I ask again, this time in all seriousness, did you kill Schwartz and Foxman?"

"The sodomites . . ."

"God, this is so ugly . . . Yes? You? Killed?"

"Yes."

"Why Schwartz?"

"To stop him from joining that group. The dissidents. That would be worse than hijacking airplanes."

"So, trying not to upset the Soviets. Why kill Foxman?"

"Wrong place, wrong time. He was there, with Schwartz. I couldn't kill one and not the other."

"And Father Mikhail? You killed him, too?"

"The apostate . . ."

"Yes, the apostate. I thought he was delightful when I met him. You did ax him?"

"No . . ."

"I hate liars. We should be getting quite close to the lung."

"Yes . . . I killed him."

"Why Father Kiselenko?"

"Same reason as Schwartz."

"Why did you kill them? What do you care about sodomites and apostates? For whom?"

"*Yitgadal . . . v'yitkadash . . .*"

"That's kaddish, you idiot. That's for others to say for you when you die. Wrong material, don't waste your precious breath.

"Why did you come to kill Oksana—now?"

"Same reason. She was picking up where Schwartz and the priest left off."

"Why an ax?"

"Because no one would think . . ."

"Think what?"

"Think that a Jew did it."

"I am with you on that. You'd think Jews would be reticent to hijack airplanes, too. But no . . . Four thousand years after Abraham, we can still surprise you."

"*Sh'me . . . raba . . . b'alma di-v'ra . . .*"

"You are still mouthing the wrong prayer, plus you don't know the rest. Repeat after me: *di v'ra chirute.* That's all you get. Is it the KGB you work for?"

"No."

"The CIA? This is not going anywhere . . . I am going in another half centimeter. Was it the CIA?"

"No."

"Not the CIA? I was rather hoping it would be, because I am a U.S. taxpayer, and I can do something about that, maybe. Your chest will start to hurt like hell a few moments from now, as your lung deflates. Your breath in the remaining lung will start getting shallow—and rapid. I'll need to know when the right lung deflates, so we can start on the left. It feels like it must have already happened. Oh my . . ."

"Fuck you . . ."*

"You don't sound so good, Mr. Lensky. One lung down, one to go. I'll yank out the knife and make a contralateral incision, as my good friend Bernie Fisher might say. He is a professional surgeon. I am an amateur. So, you can drag around without one lung for a bit. Without two, things get really problematic. There will be bleeding now. Was it Israel? Mossad?"

"Yes. Why . . . must . . . you . . . ask . . ."

---

* The word he uses is "сука," which translates as "bitch" and "traitor," but in this translator's determination, "Fuck you" is the message he intends to convey.

"Did you get explicit instructions to kill them?"

"Instructions . . . were . . . to . . . stop . . . them. Human rights . . . They don't want Jews in human rights. Stay away from dissidents."

"So, we are here because of what you heard on the shortwave radio stations—the human rights group? Yes?"

"Yes. No more Jewish blood on goyish altars."

"We don't have that problem here. Your blood is pouring out onto a properly Jewish altar, Khaver Lensky. And 'kill' was your interpretation of the word 'stop,' something you added in? Yes?"

"Yes . . . No other interpretation possible . . . Aren't you with them? Didn't you give me fifty thousand rubles?"

"I gave you fifty thousand rubles to help refuseniks, actually. For food, for application fees. You are an idiot, Lensky. And 'stop' doesn't have to mean 'kill.' Have you ever heard of convincing your opponent? Of disputation? Of the Talmud? When we Jews are idiots, we are complete idiots, and I so really want to kill you, in self-defense, lest someone think I am anything like you."

"If they were dissatisfied, they could have told us to stop."

"That's a good point. Sad but true. Did your lovely wife help you kill Schwartz and Foxman?"

"No."

"And Father Mikhail?"

"Yes."

"Where is she tonight?"

"With the children."

"A good mother . . . We are done . . . You can go now . . . And take your ax, if you are still able to lift it. If I were you, I'd flag down an ambulance, find a hospital—or feel free to die on the staircase; I don't care."

32.

SECRET

KISSINGER MOSCOW TRIP

Jan. 22–24, 1976

SENSITIVE EXCHANGES
<u>HAK/Brezhnev</u>
Thursday, Jan. 22
11:00–1:50
<u>Subjects</u>
SALT; Angola; Misc.

[*Brezhnev entered first, wearing a blue suit, blue shirt, red patterned tie, and four medals: Hero of Soviet Union; Hero of Socialist Labor; the Joliot-Curie Gold Medal. The speakers stood on one side of the long table on which stood, among other drinks, bottled Pepsi. Black-and-white portraits of Marx and Lenin were on the wall. Food included meat pies.*]

BREZHNEV: [*To gathered US and Soviet diplomats.*] This is a link-up of Soviet and American journalists, like Soyuz and Apollo.

KISSINGER: You look very well.

BREZHNEV: Thanks for the compliment.

KISSINGER: I'm fat.

BREZHNEV: No. You lost weight. That's why we have meat pies.

KISSINGER: My government will not believe that détente means being stuffed with meat pies.

[*The members of the Secretary's party and the American delegation are introduced. Photos are taken. Journalists are ushered out.*]

Here we must momentarily depart from the meeting's official transcript to convey other pertinent information.

As the last of the journalists, George Krimsky of the AP, is finally prevailed upon to stop schmoozing and is escorted out of the conference room, Brezhnev motions to an aide.

The aide, who has managed to go unnoticed despite being a ubiquitous presence in the photos of the general secretary, is somewhere in the early reaches of middle age. If you look back at the photos, you may recognize him by oversized, arguably unmanly Sophia Loren eyeglasses.

This gentleman is no ordinary flunky. He represents a very special variety of assistant, known as a "prompter,"* which requires being able to act as a translator as well as being an informational resource with deep understanding of policy matters and trivia.

The exchange between Brezhnev and this aide is captured by means of a targeted audio microphone deployed on the U.S. side

---

* The Russian word for a prompter, as in a person who sits in a booth on a theater stage to offer reminders to actors as they forget their lines, is "суфлёр," pronounced *suflyor*. Regrettably, the word "*suflyor*" rhymes with, and is uncomfortably close to, the word "вафлёр," pronounced *vaflyor*, which stands for an individual who, for lack of a better word, sucks the "waffle," i.e., a person of either sex who orally pleasures a male superior. Hence, in the unofficial lexicon of the USSR Ministry of Foreign Affairs, any individual serving as a prompter is known as a *vaflyor*, the waffler.

of the table. Though transcripts of the conversation do not identify the device used, it is most likely an XTRaKTR-2 model device of the sort concealed in a pen.*

By pointing the pen concealing the XTRaKTR-2 device toward the origin of the sound, a user is able to make a recording that, as the device's name suggests, "extracts" the sound of a whispered conversation. Capturing an exchange between Brezhnev and his prompter constitutes a classic use of the XTRaKTR-2.

These intercepts are so valuable that, per protocol, they are to be translated and interpreted fully, so no morsel, no drop, of intelligence is lost.†

BREZHNEV: [*To the prompter, who is kneeling next to him.*] Seryozha, tell me about that Bond Girl. Jill something? Is he still doing her?‡

PROMPTER: Would you like me to follow up with Comrade Andropov?

BREZHNEV: Yes, find out from him, definitely find out. Just for indulging my curiosity. He is a little Jew-boy, but what a stud! It's a healthy thing for us men.

PROMPTER: Very healthy.

BREZHNEV: What a specimen! I like English women.

---

* We can be reasonably confident that an XTRaKTR-2 device was deployed because the XTRaKTR-1 model, deployed extensively by the U.S. negotiators during SALT I talks, was able to produce no more than thirty seconds of recording per deployment.

† The appearance of the transcript and accompanying memoranda in the Gerald R. Ford Presidential Library is likely the consequence of a clerical error.

‡ This is clearly a reference to Jill St. John, an American actress who played a Bond girl, consorting with Sean Connery's James Bond in the 1971 film *Diamonds Are Forever*. On August 27, 1973, St. John was on Kissinger's arm during Brezhnev's visit to Richard Nixon's compound in San Clemente, California. Brezhnev's fascination with Ms. St. John's figure was captured on one of the most distinctive photographs from that visit. (For those who wish to see this image today, the following search words should be used: Brezhnev San Clemente St. John.]

PROMPTER: She is American, I think. At least she plays an American. They allowed us to see the film—*Diamonds Are Forever*.

BREZHNEV: Such a machine!* Sturdy, English. I love English women, to look at and wonder. What does she find in that little Jew? What the fuck does she need him for?

PROMPTER: I looked up her dossier two years ago, immediately after San Clemente, Leonid Ilych. St. John is a stage name. She's a 100 percent Jewess.

BREZHNEV: Have you gone insane? A Jewess, he says. Enough of this, they are starting. We'll make sense of it later.†

---

* Notably, Brezhnev uses the word "станок" in relation to Ms. St. John. Since every word in XTRaKTR-2 intercepts has to be not only translated but *interpreted*, i.e., understood, this word choice triggers a massive effort (and rift) at Foggy Bottom, Langley, and Fort Meade.

How is Ms. St. John reminiscent of a "machine"? What kind of machine? Could this be a veiled reference to the real-life inspiration for machines depicted in the film in which she stars with Sean Connery? (Notably, machines showcased in that film include a space laser designed to vaporize Washington.)

Memoranda of this sort are confined to a linguistic interpretation and do not substitute for technology assessment, which must be conducted independently. A matter this sensitive couldn't be entrusted to State Department–employed "natives," i.e., recent émigré native speakers of Russian.

Finally, the matter is presented in a blind fashion to a gentleman who is identified as "Alex," an émigré taxi driver chosen randomly at the State Department entrance on C Street NW.

After being asked to park his taxi in the limousine lane, he resolves this matter by demonstrating through a suggestive reenactment (that would ordinarily be considered highly inappropriate, especially al fresco, in the limousine lane) that standing at a machine, such as a lathe at a machine shop, can be reminiscent of a certain variety of sexual activity, thus confirming that members of the Politburo and Soviet prisoners use the same language and imagery of misogyny.

† A full, unedited, transcript of the exchange follows:

БРЕЖНЕВ: Серёг, скажи, этот Генри ту самую Бондовку Джил всё ещё трахает?

СУФЛЁР: Такое уж лучше у тов. Андропова узнавать.

БРЕЖНЕВ: Узнай, узнай. Просто так, интересно, так, даже по человечески. Кажется такой вроде бы жиденок, а на самом деле—кобель! Хорошо это дело для нашего мужицкого здоровья, что уж . . .

СУФЛЁР: Да что уж, Леонид Ильич. Хорошо.

БРЕЖНЕВ: Ну и бабец! До сих пор помню. Люблю Англичанок . . .

[After the above-cited consultation with his prompter, Brezhnev proceeds to consider important matters on the meeting's agreed-upon agenda. We now return to the official transcript.]

BREZHNEV: The primary subject is the achievement of a new SALT Agreement. There are also questions of the reduction of forces in Europe. And there is a matter of some sensitivity that we should remove distractions from our principal goals.

KISSINGER: As the General Secretary has observed on multiple occasions, the Ford Administration intends to minimize distractions from our core agenda.

BREZHNEV: In some matters it is best to think like a German. You are, of course, German.

KISSINGER: Yes, German it is, why not.

BREZHNEV: This matter of individuals of Jewish nationality wishing to leave the USSR must continue to be kept from the top of the agenda of Soviet-American relations.

KISSINGER: I have on occasion said to Mr. Nixon in no uncertain terms that even if, hypothetically, they put Jews into gas chambers in the Soviet Union, it is not an American concern. Maybe a humanitarian concern. But not a diplomatic concern.

BREZHNEV: Of course, we appreciate your candor—and,

СУФЛЁР: Американка она все-таки, кажется. Играет Американку по крайней мере. Нам фильм посмотреть разрешили. "Брильянты-это навечно."

БРЕЖНЕВ: Ну и станок! Забыть не могу. Добротный, английский! Люблю англичанок! Смотрю и наслаждаюсь. Чего она в этом еврейчике видит? На хера он ей?

СУФЛЁР: Да я ей в досье заглянул тогда еще, после Сан Клементе, Леонид Ильич. Сайнт Джон—псевдоним. Она стопроцентная еврейка.

БРЕЖНЕВ: Ты что, спятил? Еврейка, говоришь. Ну ладно, они там начинают. Потом разберемся.

of course, we are not doing anything of the sort. We arrest common criminals of all nationalities. Publicly conducted prosecution of individual criminals and traitors is a matter completely different from systematic extermination, which we could never support or attempt.

KISSINGER: And if you do, American diplomacy will continue to chart a course guided by pragmatism and national interest. However, there is a practical matter we need to discuss. One of our diplomats—a Mr. Foxberg, I believe—has vanished in Moscow. His family is being held back from seeing a certain Senator Frank Church, who is conducting an unfortunate series of investigations and hearings about our intelligence agencies and the tactics that they employ. This is purely vindictive.

BREZHNEV: There is a Mr. Foxman that I have been made aware of. Is that different from a Mr. Foxberg?

KISSINGER: No, it's the same person, I believe. I am not good with remembering the names of my subordinates.

BREZHNEV: I was informed by Comrade Andropov, the chairman of the Committee for State Security, that the matter has been resolved. Mr. Foxman and his homosexual lover, a Soviet citizen, who, like Mr. Foxman, is of Jewish nationality, have been found murdered here in Moscow.

KISSINGER: Have you identified the guilty party?

BREZHNEV: We have. It's an individual—one of ours— who claims to be acting on behalf of the Israeli intelligence services. We have no reasons to doubt that. The objective was to prevent Jewish groups here from acting alongside our human rights groups, which have given us much trouble.

KISSINGER: Does Mr. Andropov believe it was a Mossad operation?

BREZHNEV: We believe it may have been. Either directly controlled or a renegade operation—but definitely Mossad. Signals could have been crossed—or not.

KISSINGER: We are not historians. We don't need such details. Have you cremated the bodies?

BREZHNEV: Comrade Andropov has been awaiting your permission.

KISSINGER: He has my permission, and indeed my encouragement. You have, I presume, arrested the Mossad operative?

BREZHNEV: Comrade Andropov wanted us to make a bilateral decision on that matter. The individual—our citizen—is currently recuperating from a lung injury sustained as a consequence of his activities. His death was prevented.

KISSINGER: Thank you for your willingness to consider these matters in a linked fashion. If this person is trying to leave the country, my inclination would be to let him. Don't tell him you know anything at all. He has done us a favor. Does anyone else know?

BREZHNEV: Yes, several individuals, all our citizens.

KISSINGER: I suggest that you let all of them leave the country, but take one of them in custody and accuse him of something—very publicly. I understand you have three laws at your disposal. One article that you use for publishing books and circulating them. That's only three years—it's not enough. The other is treason—that's too much. Do the one in between—my staff has selected Article 70.

In a matter this sensitive, we will need a hostage.

EPILOGUE

C ells in prison trains have no windows, but you can stand by the bars and, across the narrow passageway, watch your beloved city recede into the past. In morning light, you watch newer buildings replace the old, then come the dachas, then snowy fields, then the forests.

If you are a *politzek*, it's reasonably clear that they are taking you to Kirov, and from there, chances are, to Perm—Camp 35.

For ten months now (with the exception of the trial), Viktor hasn't seen anyone but other politicals. For the first three months, he was in solitary, only going off to meetings with the prosecutors, or the investigators, whoever they are. Lydia Ivanovna, his curator, vanished after fulfilling her task of solving—or not solving—the string of murders.

A train to Kirov is the only place politicals meet common criminals. Viktor introduces himself. His companions are two guys named Sergei. They are both much younger than Viktor. One is eighteen, the other twenty-three. Now they are sitting up on two bunks in a cell, three of them. It's not so bad; other cells have eight inmates or more.

The elder Sergei is in for murder. His mother's lover, a collective farm chairman, got drunk and lunged at him with a knife. Sergei tried to defend himself with a shovel, but did it too well, apparently. Barely escaping the firing squad, the elder Sergei felt lucky to get ten years.

The younger Sergei, after graduating from school, joined up with friends who, on a lark, decided to break into a food store. They were going to get a few bottles of vodka and leave, but since it was cold outside, they decided to stay in, and after drinking, Sergei and a friend got into a fistfight over a girl, and the fistfight left the younger Sergei unconscious, passed out amid the glass shards on the floor, where he was found by the militia the next morning. The younger Sergei got seven years.

And what are you in for? one of the Sergeis asks Viktor. Which article?

Article 70, anti-Soviet agitation and propaganda with anti-Soviet intent; seven years in confinement, then five in internal exile. Article 70 is what you get when Article 190–1, dissemination of knowingly false fabrications that defame the Soviet state and social system, which will get you three years, isn't enough, and Article 64, treason, which can get you shot, seems excessive.

The Sergeis are peppering him with questions, and Viktor likes them enough to respond. They are snitches, possibly, but what does it matter? He has nothing to hide. A hundred kilometers into the journey, Viktor nods off, thinking about Oksana, her journey from Moscow to New York, then Pittsburgh just in time for Anya—Anna Viktorovna Moroz—to be born.

They are in Boston now. Yakov Aronovich has a dual appointment in mathematics and computational biology, and Oksana is applying to graduate school. In literature; what else? Russian literature.

Viktor tells the Sergeis; why not?

Viktor doesn't mention that Oksana is also carrying out a campaign for his release, with the help of his friend Monica Washington, the Columbia University professor, who is likely to get a job on the National Security Council after Jimmy Carter gets in, and Irene Manekofsky, of the Union of Councils for Soviet Jews. If anyone can get him out, these three women can.

Viktor doesn't mention that he is heading toward Camp 35 as a hostage, until further notice, at the behest of Henry Kissinger, to make certain that Oksana, her father, and Norm will never reveal the circumstances surrounding three murders that took place in Moscow in January 1976.

Viktor doesn't mention his surprise at his stepmother's response to his arrest. Displaying unexpected valor, she threw his father out of her apartment forever and, every day, attended the trial and reported on it to dissidents and foreign journalists who waited outside.

Viktor doesn't mention that Rabbi Fishman had testified for the prosecution at his trial and even wrote a letter to the Great Rabbinate of Israel, arguing that Oksana Yakovlevna Moskvina-Moroz is not authentically Jewish and that her marriage to Viktor Venyaminovich Moroz is invalid under Jewish law.

Viktor doesn't mention that Moscow's Jewish activists demonstrably shunned his stepmother, accusing her son of abandoning his co-religionists for the sake of Soviet dissidents. Of course, she was welcomed at the home of Elena Georgievna and Andrei Dmitrievich.

Viktor doesn't mention the series of deals with Satan that bring him to this prison train: the deals he made voluntarily, the deals he was forced to make, and the deals made on his behalf. At the trial, Viktor fired his lawyer and represented himself. What difference could this possibly make? He didn't mention the ax murders—that was the deal that got Oksana and her father out. He will not mention that his intent now is to atone for all his deals until such time when the slate is clean. He will not break, be damned the bone-chilling frosts, and knee-deep mud, and beatings by the guards, and weeks alone in a freezing shed they call "the isolator," the knocking out of his teeth, a stabbing by a band of snitches, and bouts of pneumonia, bleeding ulcers, dysentery, scurvy, and confiscation of his notebooks, drawings, letters unsent, letters received, until that day in April 1985 when a Gazik with GULAG license plates arrives at his Siberian peasant hut (by now he is in internal exile) and he is ordered into its windowless holding cell, believing that he is being rearrested and taken back, to pay for something that he said or didn't say, and he'll be loaded in a plane, believing he will be taken back to where he came from, to Moscow, to Lubyanka, to Lydia Ivanovna, his curator from days long gone, but, much to his surprise, the plane will land in an entirely unfamiliar place, and he'll be ushered into another Gazik, into another coffin of a cage, and taken to a place of many lights, where a short woman in a black karakul coat with a blue mink collar and a blue mink hat will raise her hand silently and smile at him, and uniformed guards will point him to a bridge, which he will cross alone, wondering whether death has come, and in the middle of that bridge, he'll see another man, whom he will greet with genuine goodwill, for that man, too, has made his deals for which he's paid the price, and on the other side he'll see Oksana, more beautiful than before, and their daughter, her name is Anna, and next to them, Yakov Aronovich and Norm, and the Hon. Monica Washington, and Lyuda Alexeyeva, and George Krimsky (Bob Toth would greet him later, in the United States), and Irene Manekofsky, of the Union of Councils—his tribe, the people who kept the memory alive and public pressure unrelenting, and after long embraces, Norm, Moses-like, will lead them to a restaurant he has commandeered for a Passover celebration—a real Seder, Viktor's first, on April 5—because sometimes you live to see the waters part, and as a festive meal is served, young Anna Viktorovna will climb into her father's lap, and he'll begin to tell her stories, and she'll ask questions and seek clarifications in clear, perfect Russian.

ACKNOWLEDGMENTS

A key moment that ignites this story occurred at Duke University, where, as an undergraduate, I met Michael Alexeev, a fellow Russian émigré, then a graduate student in economics. His mother, Ludmilla, one of the founders of the Public Group of Assistance to Implementation of the Helsinki Agreements in the USSR, also known as the Moscow Helsinki Watch Group, was by then living in exile. Michael and I formed the Duke Russian Boys Choir. This was not a sanctioned university activity, like, for example, Duke basketball. It involved drunken idiots—two drunken idiots—performing Stalin-era songs, presumably off-key, in Russian, at the Hideaway Bar, of blessed memory, on West Campus, usually right before closing. If you've heard us perform, we are sorry. At one point, Michael mentioned to his mother that he was hanging out with a Russian kid who wanted to become an American journalist, or a writer, or some such.

"А ну ка дай его мне," said Lyuda. "Why don't you give him to me."

Lyuda and I started our conversations before my 1981 graduation from Duke. Her suggestion boiled down to this: I have piles of documents—someone needs to make them into stories. Such stories should be told from the inside—which requires familiarity with our history, literature, and culture. In other words—language. To understand these piles of documents, you have to have walked Moscow streets and sat in Moscow kitchens. If you want to be a storyteller, here is a story.

After a couple of stints in journalism, I decided to take a dive into Lyuda's piles of papers. The material she stored in piles, boxes, and kitchen cabinets was, indeed, breathtaking—accounts of Kafkaesque trials, dispatches on conditions of political prisoners, letters, diaries, works of literature. Our collaboration produced two nonfiction books. Lyuda mentored me through *The Final Act*, and we cowrote *The Thaw Generation*. These books are alive in English and in Russian more than three decades later.

As I sifted through Lyuda's boxes of materials, my questions were fundamental: How did the Soviet human rights movement happen? Only human stories could answer these questions. In the process of reporting, I created an audio archive of oral histories. I didn't prospectively plan to create the archive—I just needed the stories, told directly by the participants. Then I labeled the tapes and preserved them.

My nonfiction books drilled deep into the story. Yet I always felt the urge to write a novel about *samizdat*, one of the most significant literary movements of the twentieth century, and to explore the twists and turns in the relationship between dissidents, refuseniks, journalists, diplomats, and spies.

Historical fiction can explore territories where historians cannot go. In Russia at least, distinguishing fact from literature is a fool's errand. You need *Onegin* to understand the Decembrists. For the Battle of Borodino you need *War and Peace*. Prerevolutionary intelligentsia is invisible without Chekhov's plays. The revolution and the Russian Civil War cannot be seen without *Doctor Zhivago*. You need *The Master and Margarita* and *One Day in the Life of*

Ivan Denisovich to grasp Stalinism. You need *Life and Fate* to understand the Battle of Stalingrad, and you need *The Thaw* to begin to understand Khrushchev's thaw.

As I dove into my piles of documents once again, the tapes made it possible to tap into the emotional center of this story—to hear voices of people now gone answering questions posed by a younger me. Whenever I felt stumped, I turned on my tape recorder to listen to these voices from the past—including Lyuda's. Recently, these audio tapes and my files were acquired by the Blavatnik Archive, where they are being digitized, transcribed, and translated. In a matter of months, they will be made available online.

Viktor and Oksana are fictional characters, but the city they love yet must leave is real. Their Moscow is Bulgakov's Moscow, and my Moscow.

The ax murder of two gay men, a Soviet refusenik and a U.S. diplomat, the pivotal scene in this novel, is my invention. However, the location, 17 Chistoprudnyy Boulevard and the room where it happened, is real. The place was once occupied by my uncle, Lev Finiasovich Goldberg. The time frame of the novel—the upcoming visit by U.S. secretary of state Henry A. Kissinger—is dictated by his actual arrival in Moscow.

The Jewish wedding scene is wholly a product of my imagination. Alas, Rabbi Yakov Leybovich Fishman, chief rabbi of the Moscow Choral Synagogue, is a historical character. Rabbi Fishman had on occasion called on Soviet authorities to restore order in front of his synagogue, which amounted to an invitation to rough up refuseniks who gathered there.

The Helsinki Watch movement is real, too. It started in Moscow in 1976. Much discussion preceded the founding of the

Public Group of Assistance to Implementation of the Helsinki Agreements in the USSR in 1976. The group was formed in May 1976 and initially led by Yuri Fyodorovich Orlov.

The struggle continues.

The relationship between the Soviet human rights movement and the Jewish emigration movement was complex. The emigration movement was mostly about leaving the country. The human rights movement pursues a much broader agenda, covering all rights of all people living in the USSR, and now in the newly imperial Russia.

The struggle to free Soviet Jewry defined a generation of Jews, primarily in the United States. I didn't make up the seething, global schism within the Soviet Jewry movement—I witnessed it after arriving in the United States and volunteering to help Irene Manekofsky of the Union of Councils for Soviet Jews and the Washington Committee for Soviet Jewry. Some documents of the time look like the work product of a fifteen-year-old with an Olivetti typewriter.

I didn't make up the interplay between dissidents, refuseniks, and the American press. This uneasy symbiosis was a central element in my nonfiction books and this novel.

Mad Dog Dymshitz is a wholly fictional character. The *Vechernyaya Moskva* story describing one of Mad Dog's misadventures is adapted from a piece of disinformation that same newspaper published about George Krimsky, an AP reporter. (I am not aware of any American reporter working in Moscow in the 1970s exchanging favors with the CIA.) Similarly, I wove fictional material into the dissident Yuri Tuvim's recollection of the evening Andrei Sakharov learned about having been awarded the Nobel Peace Prize.

I was delighted to find transcripts of banter that preceded

détente-era summits. The conversations between Kissinger, Gromyko, Brezhnev, et cetera, are drawn in part from these documents.

Kissinger's statement that securing freedom for Soviet Jews is not a U.S. foreign policy objective is taken out of context, but not invented. In a recording made in Nixon's Oval Office in 1973, Kissinger, then a national security advisor, is heard saying: "And if they put Jews into gas chambers in the Soviet Union, it is not an American concern. Maybe a humanitarian concern." Of course, it would be absurd to hold the historical HAK in any way responsible for the fate of Viktor Moroz, a character of my invention.

The roles of the KGB, the CIA, and Mossad are real, too. They were all present in the Moscow of the 1970s. The CIA's role, and its decision to start using at least one member of a Jewish group as a spy, was disastrous and real.

The Master and Margarita is in effect a character in *The Dissident*. The novel was completed—or arguably not completed—in 1940, when Bulgakov died, and for twenty-six years the manuscript evaded arrest. I was seven years old when the novel was published in an abbreviated form in the journal *Moskva*. Through my parents, I felt that a seismic event had occurred in their lives, and, by extension, mine. The beheading at Patriarch's Ponds, the absurdity of militant, state-mandated atheism, the elevation of the modes of Moscow's public transportation to a level of spirituality grew on me with every rereading.

I have never developed an appreciation for the Jerusalem chapters of the novel—the Gospel according to Bulgakov, even though I feel his presence when I walk on the ramparts of Jerusalem's Old City. Many formerly Soviet Jews and many of those who remained in Russia have embraced Christianity, and many apostates have gone into priesthood and monasteries. I am solidly Jewish, but I am able to stumble around amid the pillars of Christianity. To move forward with *The Dissident*, I needed to understand the Gospel according to Bulgakov and to distinguish it from the teachings of the Russian Orthodox Church.

In the summer of 2019, I returned to Russia, to see old friends and family members and correlate mental images with actual addresses and the routes of trolleybuses and tramways that appear in this novel.

Strange things happen when you ask questions about Bulgakov. On the first night in St. Petersburg, at an outdoor book stall on Nevsky Prospect, I found a little book titled *The Master and Margarita: With Christ or Against*, by Protodeacon Andrey Kurayev. That little book, written from the perspective of the Russian Orthodox Church, was exactly what I needed to get answers to my very narrow questions.

Later, I found myself at a vodka-drinking event at the apartment of Andrey Surotdinov, a violinist with the legendary group Aquarium, whose daughter, Katya, is my daughter Sarah's BFF in St. Petersburg. Andrey's apartment is literally around the corner—across the canal—from the site of the ax murder in *Crime and Punishment*. There, I ran into Surotdinov's new friend, Fr. Andrey Khordochkin, a Russian Orthodox priest from Madrid. Father Andrey was remarkably helpful in responding to my questions that night and in subsequent email exchanges.

In Moscow, we walked the streets of a city full of anti-Putin protesters and phalanxes of RoboCops. Lyuda, who had moved back to Moscow and took over her old job as head of the Moscow Helsinki Watch Group, had died the previous year. This was the last time I saw my cousin Yulik Dobrushin, who would die of COVID-19 in 2021, and my uncle Lev Goldberg, onetime inhabitant of the room I borrowed for an ax murder. Lev, or Lyova, would survive COVID, but die of pancreatic cancer.

In Moscow, I was able to ask friends to resolve problems that still stumped me in the plot for *The Dissident*. I presented the story to my cousin Yulik, who grudgingly agreed with the idea that the Jewish spiritual rebirth and rebirth of Christianity among the intelligentsia came from the same source—*The Master and Margarita*.

Later, at a Georgian restaurant not far from 17 Chistoprudnyy, between khachapuri and khinkali, Aleksandr (Sanya) Daniel' solved several plot problems that continued to mystify me. Thank you, Sanya.

Vassili Schedrin, a historian at Queen's University in Ontario, was helpful throughout the process, as was David Stephen, a friend from Duke, whom I consult on matters involving things Christian. My friend Patricia Lochmuller provided guidance and encouragement early in the project. Dudley Hudspeth, a cardiothoracic surgeon, helped me describe the ax murders and wrote the autopsy reports. Tatiana Yankelevich, the daughter of Elena Bonner and stepdaughter of Andrei Sakharov, answered key questions and helped arrange access to the Sakharov Archive on Zemlyanoy Val. Also, I am grateful to Bela Khasanovna Koval for spending a day with me at the Sakharov Archive and generously sharing copies of archival materials.

The character of Lydia Ivanovna, though fictional, is inspired by scenes from Lyuda's interrogations by the KGB. These scenes can be found in *The Thaw Generation*. The character of Norm is inspired by my many friends who survived the war and the prison camps, both Soviet and Nazi, ultimately reinventing their lives.

Most of them didn't know that there was such a thing as PTSD, though, God knows, the aftermath of the war was forever a part of their lives. Bob Toth and George Krimsky, reporters who covered the dissident story in the 1970s, were particularly generous with their time as I researched *The Final Act*. I thank them by giving them cameo appearances in *The Dissident*.

I am grateful to my childhood friend Alyoshka Pervov, his mother, Margarita, and Aleksandr Maltsev for hosting us in Moscow. As first graders, Alyoshka and I shared a desk at Moscow Special School No. 64, and we have been friends since. My thanks go to Peter Ericson, at the time the ambassador of Sweden in Moscow, and his wife, Stina Stohr, an outstanding Swedish writer, for hosting us in Moscow.

Michael Alexeev, Robert Peter Gale, Jackson Diehl, Otis Brawley, Cliff Hudis, Grisha and Anya Rolbin, Richard Liebeskind, Steve Lieberman, Peter Bach, Gardiner Harris, Ernie Ruskey and Laurie Wood, Richard and Lynda Goldberg, Cathy Cosman, Fred Hirsch, Wafik El-Deiry, Peter Garrett, Olga Voronina, Valerie Strauss, Anastasiia Aseeva, and Dmitri Makarov offered helpful suggestions. I am also grateful to my father, Boris Goldberg, his wife, Galina, and my mother-in-law, Marian Keselenko.

The staff members of *The Cancer Letter* have on occasion allowed me to play hooky from my day job as editor and publisher and were generous with critiques of the manuscript pages from *The Dissident*. Thank you, Katie Goldberg, Matt Ong, Alex Carolan, Alice Tracey, Jacquelyn Cobb, Mona Mirmortazavi, Jacqueline Ong, and David Koh.

My agent, Josh Getzler, has been a friend and an advocate through this process, which at this point has spanned three novels and one nonfiction book—and counting. Many thanks to Jonathan Cobb for his friendship and support.

My thanks go to my wise editor, Jackson Howard, and to his predecessor on this project, James Meader. The brilliant jacket design is the work of the FSG artist Cecilia Zhang. I am always in awe of what copy editors do, and Susan VanHecke is clearly among the best. My thanks go also to Gretchen Achilles for this book's interior design, Rima Weinberg and Kylie Byrd for their proofreading, and Janine Barlow, the production editor. Thanks also to the children of our big, blended family, organized here in ascending age order—Sarah Goldberg, Katie Goldberg, Max Coll, Emma Coll, and Ally Coll. And, of course, Charlie, the best partner in crime a *zeide* could ask for.

My wife, Susan Coll, a novelist, and a very funny one at that, helped me work through *The Dissident* from beginning to end, as she has with my preceding two novels. This time, on our trip to Russia, Susan soldiered through multiple late-night gatherings of the sort where vodka never runs out, English is not spoken, and the translator, yours truly, has been rendered unreliable.

A NOTE ABOUT THE AUTHOR

Paul Goldberg is the author of the novels *The Château* and *The Yid*, which was a finalist for the Sami Rohr Prize for Jewish Literature and the National Jewish Book Award's Goldberg Prize for Debut Fiction. As a reporter, Goldberg has written two books about the Soviet human rights movement, and coauthored (with Otis Brawley) *How We Do Harm*, an exposé of the U.S. health-care system. His writing has appeared in *The Washington Post*, *Slate*, and *The New York Times*, among other publications. He is also the editor and publisher of *The Cancer Letter*, a publication focused on the business and politics of cancer. He lives in Washington, D.C.

SAD SAM

Barkin's apartment ■

TSVETNOY BOULEVARD

MAYAKOVSKY ◇

GARDEN RING

■ Bulgakov's apartment

MOSCOW ZOO

PUSHKIN ◇

Old Territory

New Territory

GORKY STREET

■ PLANETARIUM

KGB HEADQUARTERS—Lubyanka ■

U.S. EMBASSY ■

THE KREMLIN

Moskva River

Viktor's apartment ■

TRETYAKOV GALLERY ■

Oksana's apartment ■

GEORGI DIMITROV ◇

Moskva River

Prof. Yakov Moskvin's apartment ■

GORKY PARK

GORKY ◇

to Golden's apartment
to Shukhov tower

to Chertanovo

© 2023 Jeffrey L. Ward